"Would you like

Caroline's eyes l                                         n.
"No, thank you."

"Why?"

Though she tried to snip at him, she couldn't quite keep her voice from quivering. "What would *you* do, Philip? Watch my every move?"

"Better yet, I think I'll bathe you."

Caroline rose to her feet, her trembling lower lip belying the defiant thrust of her chin. "You will not."

"Aye, Caroline. I will." He grinned and took two steps toward her. "Take off your clothes."

"No!"

"Then I'll remove them for you."

"You will not!" Caroline took a step back and removed the boots he'd brought for her. Licking her lips, she fought the tight frisson of excitement rushing up her spine. "Please. Turn around."

"No." Arms folded across his chest, feet splayed, his grin grew wider. "I think I'll watch this time."

"Oh!" She averted her eyes, seeing his arousal press full against his taut breeches.

"What is it, Caroline? Are you afraid?"

"I'm never afraid." With that, she tore the shift over her head and stood, hands clenched at her sides. Her chin lifted. "So. Is this what you want to see, Philip?"

"Yes, he replied thickly. "Now come here."

Without another word, Caroline did as he requested.

# SALLY STONE

# SILVER FIRE

**ZEBRA BOOKS**
**KENSINGTON PUBLISHING CORP.**

*To Carl.*
*The first one's for you.*

ZEBRA BOOKS are published by

Kensington Publishing Corp.
475 Park Avenue South
New York, NY 10016

First Printing: December, 1993

Printed in the United States of America

# *Prologue*

Three-year-old Caroline Swanson's brow furrowed. "Is the babe not coming back, Mama?"

Emmaline made the sign of the cross, then forced a smile. "No, child. But perhaps we'll have another."

"When, Mama?"

"Not ever, if I have a say in it," William Swanson said, striding into the small log cabin.

"William, please, you mustn't upset her."

"Why mustn't I? You coddle the child. Caroline, go outside. Your brother's chopping wood; see if you can find some pieces to use for kindling."

"But, Papa, I don't want to—"

*"Now!* When will you learn to be less willful? Your mother needs to sleep; your ceaseless questions are tiring her."

Outside, Caroline took tiny steps toward the tree trunk where her older brother, Austin, was splitting wood with ferocious intensity.

"Can I help?" she asked tentatively.

Austin barely heard her above the cracking sound of the ax splitting wood. Nine years her senior, he glanced at her with blue eyes a shade lighter than her own.

"You're so little you could hardly lift a twig, let alone this ax."

"But I could try," she insisted.

"And what if I let you and you hurt yourself? Then it would only give Mother and Father something else to worry about."

After a few minutes of watching her brother, Caroline felt the earth tremble beneath her feet. "Horsies are coming," she said, looking at Austin with big blue eyes.

"Horses? Yes, I feel it, too. Maybe it's deer."

"No." Caroline shook her head, sending silvery curls shimmering around her face. "Horsies."

Austin's eyes narrowed. "Are you certain?"

She nodded stubbornly.

He hesitated before dropping the ax to the ground. "I can't believe I'm listening to a three-year-old," he muttered. "Still, if you're right, I guess I'd better tell Father."

Worry lines creased William's forehead at Austin's announcement.

"What do you mean, horses?"

"I could feel hoofbeats against the ground. Caroline felt them, too."

"Indians," Emmaline murmured.

William rose to his feet and strode to the doorway. "Let me check outside. They could be passing some distance away, it doesn't mean—" He swore softly. "They're Indians, all right. I can't tell if they're peaceful or not, but I think we'd better go out back, just in case."

6

Emmaline quickly sat up, then clutched the sides of the bed as a wave of dizziness swept over her.

"No, my dear. I'll carry you." He darted a meaningful glance at Austin. "You take Caroline out back; hide to the east by the brook. We'll meet you there."

"But Father—"

*"Now*, Austin. Why won't either of my children listen to—"

Caroline heard her father's voice fade, her feet scampering to keep up with Austin as he half dragged, half pushed her along.

"Hurry," he commanded.

"Mama, Papa," she whimpered.

*"Hush*, Caroline. For once in your life, follow me and *be quiet!"*

Minutes later, well-hidden in a grove of pine trees, Austin pried Caroline's hand loose and shoved her down low.

"Where's Mother and Father?" he said, half-aloud. "Oh, thank God, they've gotten out. I don't think the Indians have spotted them, no . . . " He wrung his hands together.

Caroline stared at her brother in amazement. He'd told her to be quiet, but he was talking. Austin, unlike her, always did everything right, so it must be all right to talk if she did so quietly.

"Mama? Papa?" she asked.

"They're coming, Caroline," he whispered. "Just be quiet."

She listened and could hear leaves rustle. Then her father, carrying her mother, nearly collapsed on the ground next to them.

"Are they friendly?" Austin asked.

"I—I don't know," William gasped, still holding Emmaline tightly in his arms, trying to stop her shivering. He paused to catch his breath. "Quiet, now. Watch. We'll know in a moment."

Over twenty Indians rode up to the small clearing around the cabin. The leader held up his arm, and at his signal about half of them dismounted. One Indian walked to the tree stump, lifted half of the small log Austin had just split, and smelled it.

"They're trying to find out how long it's been since we left." William spoke as calmly as possible, trying to ease his family's fears.

"Are they bad, Papa?"

"I don't know, Caroline. We'll wait and see. We'll just wait and see."

Another Indian, the apparent leader, glided inside the building and came out almost instantly. The others gathered around him as he spoke to them. Two of them nodded and reached behind their backs to the long, tubular packs they carried.

"This isn't good," William said in a hushed voice. "Everyone keep quiet."

Caroline peeked curiously through the leaves, but could see nothing. Her knees ached from stooping, and she didn't like the expression on her mother's face. Her wrist throbbed from where Austin held it. She was about to try to wrest herself free, when she wrinkled her nose at the acrid odor that wafted toward them. Then her father spoke to Austin.

"We have a chance to get away," he said. "I'll carry your mother, you take Caroline."

"William, no." Resignation filled Emmaline's voice. "You'd never be able to outrun them. You've just now caught your breath from carrying me this short distance. The chil—"

Caroline's eyes widened. She could see a bright, wicked flame lick through the trees. "Home . . . " she whispered.

"We'll stay here as long as we're able," William said to Austin. "Mayhap they won't look for us; I don't see them searching the ground for any sign of our leave-taking. Now, no more talk. Everyone hush."

Caroline watched in horror as the fire ate away at her home, her place of safety, the place where they all slept at night and took their meals during the day. Where would they live, if their home burned?

She darted a glance at her mama, who now looked the same color as the babe that had died, and—and her eyes were closed. Oh, what would she do if her mama died, too? What would she do with no home to shelter her and no mama to care for—

Caroline howled, a fear-laden, mournful cry.

"They heard her," William said hoarsely. "Quick, Austin, take her and run."

"But, Father, I can't leave—"

*"Don't argue!* I'll follow, but if we become separated, we'll return here as soon as it's safe. Now go, and take care of Caroline."

Emmaline's eyes fluttered open. "Please, Austin," she echoed weakly. "Take care of Caroline."

Caroline felt herself being picked up in Austin's thin arms. She fastened her arms around him. He ran, tearing through the woods, heedless of the branches stinging her legs and arms, whipping at her face. She heard him breathe faster, faster, until he inhaled in great, wrenching gulps. When he could run no longer, he staggered under

9

the weight of her until they finally stopped. Caroline slid from his arms as he collapsed against a towering oak.

"Are we lost?"

Austin shook his head, taking deep, hearty draughts of air until he could speak. "I—think not. We've been running alongside a stream. If we follow it back, we should find home."

Tears rolled down Caroline's cheeks. "I want Mama and Papa!"

"Stop being such a baby. We'll find them tomorrow. Now be quiet and go to sleep."

"I'm hungry."

Austin's eyes narrowed and he spoke through clenched teeth. "I don't give a damn if you're hungry or not. You can starve to death for all I care. This was all your fault, you know. If it weren't for you, we'd have already left this wretched place and been living like kings in Philadelphia. But no, Mother was too weak after you were born to travel. In fact, I heard Father tell her you weakened her so much, that's why the next babe died. And now we have no home at all . . . " His voice trailed off.

Caroline watched him. "Are Mama and Papa all right?" she asked at last.

Austin looked at her as if he'd forgotten she was there. "They're all right. We'll go back tomorrow and meet them. Everything will be fine tomorrow. Everything will be fine." He curled up on the ground, his back to her.

After a few minutes, Caroline curled up next to him and wrapped her arms around his neck. "I love you, Austin," she said tremulously.

But Austin had already gone to sleep.

\* \* \*

10

Early the next morning, Austin shook her. "Wake up, Caroline. It's time to go back. I want to be ho—*back* by sunset, and I don't intend to run the whole way. Come on, let's get going."

Caroline rubbed her fists against her eyes and stood up, yawning. "I'm hungry."

"Mayhap we'll find some berries along the way. Now come."

She thought they'd never get home. Most of the time she walked, but when her legs got so tired she plopped down on the ground and refused to budge, Austin picked her up and carried her. He saw some red berries on a bush and tugged one free.

"No!" Caroline said.

"No?"

"No. Bad fruit."

Austin eyed her quizzically. "How do you know?"

"Chipmunks won't eat it."

Austin grunted and threw the berry on the ground, then shifted her on his back. "I forgot about your stupid pets. Well, we'll just have to go hungry, until we find Mother and Father."


When they were about twenty yards from home, Austin said, "I see no sign of Indians; I'm certain they're gone. Tell Mother and Father we're back."

Caroline ran into the clearing and stopped. The charred framework smoldered, sending smoke in lazy wisps up to the sky. She shuffled forward past a blackened mound of rubble, then another, until she stood just feet away from what had been her home. A chipmunk ran over her foot; she giggled.

Austin uttered a strangled cry. "No!"

She turned and walked over to him.

"Don't kick that," she said sternly, watching him push the rubble around with his feet. "It's hot."

He looked at her, his face contorted with pain, his voice the voice of an old man. "It's Mother and Father, Caroline. See what you did? You cried, and the Indians killed them. Then they burned them."

She looked down at horror at the charred remains of two twisted bodies. "Not Mama and Papa," she whispered.

"Yes!" Austin laughed hysterically. "Yes, it's Mama and Papa. Your crying led the Indians to them. It's all your fault, it's all your fault . . . "

# Chapter One

Michigan Territory
*JUNE 18, 1812*

From her seat atop the horse-drawn cart, Caroline Swanson pulled on the reins and stared down at the man on the path in front of her. A man with a pistol glinting silver in the sun.

Despite her surprise, she sat transfixed, watching piercing eyes change from green to gray to blue, while full lips compressed together into a grimace. His pale face grew whiter, contrasting sharply with the dark thatch of hair falling over his brow.

The man wavered, loosening his grip on his weapon. It fell with a soft thud. Caroline dropped her gaze and inhaled sharply.

An angry red rash flared on the lower half of his leg, where he'd torn his stocking free. None of her injured animals had ever appeared so grievously hurt.

"Snake . . . " the man mumbled, before he crumpled face down to the ground.

Caroline dismounted and crouched next to the stranger. His eyes opened, then shut. Thank God it wasn't one of the British, who wore their vivid scarlet uniforms like a banner. This man, attired in brown kerseymere breeches and a dingy white cotton shirt, was obviously one of their own militia men. She wondered if she should hurry back home to ask her brother for help, then realized the foolishness of that notion.

Even if Austin had not already headed for the fort in Detroit, she'd have to convince him his efforts would benefit him in some fashion. There was no time for that now.

As for Titus—why, her suitor hadn't the stomach for helping injured animals, let alone men.

That left only Maeve, and Caroline knew that by the time she traveled the two miles to fetch her maid, the man could wander off into the hands of the Indians. Blast the British! The Potawatomi tribes in the area had posed no threat, until the redcoats had begun bribing them with rum and brandy.

No, if the man were to be helped, she would have to do it.

By his pasty face, Caroline could tell he would not awaken long enough to climb into her high cart. In preparation for the quarter-mile's journey to the animal shelter, she took a length of rope from her small cache of supplies. She trussed and bound the stranger like a turkey for roasting, so her gelding, Derby, could pull him on the ground. As slowly as the horse usually moved, she had no fear he would injure the man in a sudden spurt of energy.

When she finished, she tucked the pistol into the deerskin pouch around her waist, and unhitched Derby from the cart. She could have sworn she heard the old roan sigh.

14

"Come," she coaxed. "Come, Derby, show me what a mighty, strong beast you are."

Tying the end of the rope to the horse's halter, she took the reins and led Derby, dragging the man, his head and shoulders padded by the blanket. The stranger groaned, then lapsed back into unconsciousness, each time they stopped and started up again.

For once grateful for Derby's leisurely gait, Caroline followed the narrow path Titus had cleared in case the British attacked and she needed to escape. Austin had laughed derisively, saying the British would not waste their shot and powder on his grotesque sister. The British were accustomed to ladies with hair artfully arranged, dressed in silk and satin, not scrawny, silver-haired women in deerhide clothing.

Directing Derby off the trail, Caroline wished her brother would volunteer his precious self to fight. Then she crossed herself for her uncharitable thoughts, in an automatic gesture dating back to her childhood. Sometimes Caroline's right arm ached from crossing herself.

By the time the abandoned log shelter came into view, Caroline wondered what had compelled her to act so rashly. With trembling fingers she untied her patient's bonds, ignoring the robin pecking at her moccasin-shod toes.

As the breeze picked up her scent and carried it into the woods, the animals came to her from behind the trees. Fawn, the baby deer with the broken leg, the squirrel with the injured tail, and Willie, the blind raccoon cub, comforted and strengthened her. She had saved them, and with their every breath, they reminded her she wasn't completely worthless. Not completely.

From her pouch she withdrew a scrap of mutton and

15

threw it to Willie, wincing as he devoured another animal's flesh. The other hungry creatures would have to wait.

Her human patient, not her animals, concerned her now.

His bonds loosened, Caroline knelt over him and looked down at his wound. One glance told her that he needed a physician, but a physician would cut off his leg.

She moved her hands down to his shoulders and rubbed them, fearful she had tied the man's ropes too tight. Studying the doorway to the cabin, she ruefully noted it had not grown any wider. Derby would never be able to fit through it.

The stranger would have to walk. She could help him, but he would have to awaken long enough to brace himself against her. He *had* to.

His shoulders were broad and hard, and Caroline's eyes widened in surprise at the hard muscles beneath her hands. Rubbing his body continually to restore his circulation, she worked down past her patient's nondescript, grime-covered shirt. The Americans had not yet seen fit to outfit their militia men in uniforms, at least not here in Michigan Territory. It was as if this part of the country did not exist, much to Caroline's pleasure and her brother's chagrin.

Her patient's broad chest rose and fell with reassuring regularity. Caroline checked for further injury, hoping that when the man had collapsed, he did not break any bones. Her fingers fumbled downward, skipping along the sides of his body toward his hips. Narrow hips leading to well-muscled thighs. She stopped, swallowed, and resumed her cursory inspection. Convinced nothing else was awry, she removed the blanket from behind his head, then proceeded to the knot around his ankles, reluctant to use her knife to cut it, in case he woke, mistook her intentions, and grabbed it from her. The honed blade could harm either one of them.

Untying the knot at his feet, looking up at him, Caroline saw him fully: a solid man of muscle and sinew, his perfection marred only by his injured leg. Purplish splotches mingled with gray shadows from the sun filtering through the dense growth of pine and maple trees. She knew for a certainty that the man would be crippled at the very least. Though snakebites were rarely lethal in this part of the country, the ensuing fever killed victims more often than not. Of those who lived, none came away unblemished.

She wondered what kind of mettle this man had, if he would rant and rave and blame her for the incapacity that would surely result. *If* he survived. She shook her head to dispel that thought. He would survive; she would see to it. Then she wondered if she would do him more harm than good by saving him, and her heart welled with sorrow. It would be difficult enough for someone like Titus—with his watery, dull brown eyes and slight physique—to become a cripple. She could not imagine how this man would cope with having his strength diminished. She wished he would open his eyes so she could look into them, to temper his sorrow with her sympathy. Did he have a wife? Would she accept her husband when he returned less than perfect?

"Please," she pleaded. "Wake up. I have to help you. Someone must be worried about you. You must tell me your name, so we can send word."

The man's eyes remained closed; he moaned.

17

"Stay awake," Caroline commanded. "You must open your eyes and stay awake."

He only grunted in response.

"Water, then. Water will wake you."

A small creek flowed about thirty yards away. Knowing she had no time to waste, Caroline fetched a scrap of muslin she'd painstakingly washed after using it to tie a pigeon's broken wing. She ran to the creek and dipped the cloth into the clear, icy water. Her fingers growing numb from holding the dripping fabric, she hurried back to the stranger and reached over him. She meant to place the cloth gently on his forehead, but her frozen fingers would not comply. The fabric plopped from her hands over the man's eyes and nose, covering his face to his upper lip.

He yelled and flailed.

"That's good." Caroline shoved one arm under his shoulders, as he tore the cloth from his face. "Get up now, get up."

His eyes started to roll, and she slapped his cheek.

"No, you don't," she commanded. "You are going to get up *now*, so I can take care of you. *Now.*"

The man gasped and nodded, groaning as she helped him to his feet. His right leg bore his full weight, and he swayed. Caroline positioned herself against his side to support him, pulling his arm across her shoulders. Grabbing his right hand with her left and reaching around his waist with her other, she jabbered a steady stream of instructions. "That's it, keep going. Just a few more steps. We'll make it."

They proceeded unsteadily, making fair progress until they came to the slight incline of the doorless threshold. The man held his breath as he tried to hop up on his good leg, then crashed sideways against the jamb. His face remained impassive, despite the beads of sweat dotting his forehead.

Caroline chewed her lip. "We're almost there."

"Liar," the man sputtered.

"Pardon me?"

"Liar. You said we were almost there an hour ago."

Caroline shifted under his intense scrutiny. "I certainly hope you're nicer than you're acting. Why, you're such an ungrateful lout, I have a mind to let you fall right here."

"Liar," the man muttered again. He lowered his head and shrugged her off, limping to the plank that would serve as his bed. "Here?"

Caroline stood stock-still, momentarily afraid. He wasn't so very large, not really, but no one had ever shared this cabin with her except for her animals. The very breadth of him seemed to fill up her space. Though Austin was taller, she sensed in this man a contained strength that could unleash as soon as his leg healed, the fever abated. She nodded.

The man gritted his teeth and turned, lowering himself to the plank. "Fine. This—" He fell with a thud on the bench.

Rushing forward, Caroline pushed his shoulders and chest up onto the plank, so he would not fall off. His feet still rested on the floor. She took his sound right leg and lifted it onto the bench. Then, pushing him gently at the hips, she managed to straighten him. The angry scarlet path winding around his left calf, glared up at her from where he'd torn his stocking in an attempt to cool his wound. A ball of wadded cambric, another store left from the animals, served as a batting, and onto this she gently lifted and rested his injured limb.

Now that her patient was prone and still, the import of

her predicament stunned her. This was no animal, no pigeon with a broken wing, no deer with a flesh wound! This was a man, a living, breathing man. For the moment at least, his fate rested fully in her hands. What if she failed him? How many times had Austin warned her to think before acting? How many times had he told her, and rightly, her impulsiveness was at the root of the latest calamity to befall them? When a pot broke free of its crane over the fire, wasn't it due to her laxity, her sloth, and lack of attention? And when they had no water in the rain barrel and had to haul it from the creek, wasn't it because she'd lapsed in her duties and forgotten to upend it? Austin's words pounded in her brain. *It's all your fault, it's all your fault.*

This time when Caroline crossed herself, it wasn't for repentance. She cried for help from the merciful God in Heaven.

The first few moments her patient slept, Caroline paced the cabin, vacillating between leaving to fetch help, or staying and doing what she could. Half of her—the more logical half—told her that her medical knowledge, of the simplest sort and confined to animals, would do no good. Some men, she knew, died of snakebite, despite the best medical physicians.

The instinctive part of her argued that by the time she fetched someone with a greater knowledge than her own, the man would be dead for a certainty. *If* he had any chance of living at all.

Caroline frantically tried to remember all she'd heard of treating snakebites. When she was a child, the Indians had not minded when she'd observed their rituals from a distance. Once, when she was very young, an Indian woman had been bitten by a snake and had sucked the venom out. Though she racked her brain, Caroline could not recall if the woman had lived or died—and the type of snake had always been a mystery.

For that matter, she didn't know what kind of snake had poisoned this man, either. There was only one thing to do.

Before she could change her mind, she struggled to uncork the bottle of spirits she'd pilfered from her brother's supply. When she'd taken it, she had no idea when it might come in useful, but virtually every discard from her home eventually found its way to her animal shed.

Now the man battled to open his eyes and watch her, in the same manner as her wary animals watched when she first tried to treat them. He seemed intent on keeping her at arm's length, though a corner of his mouth turned up slightly.

"Shall I help, *chérie?*" he mumbled.

Caroline stopped at the heavily accented words. French. The man must be one of their soldiers from the settlement known as Frenchtown, some thirty miles from Detroit. Though she knew the French settlers had been in Michigan longer than most other American citizens, Austin kept her so close to home, she'd never come in contact with one before. Ignoring his gaze, she thrust the cork between her teeth.

The man watched her as she closed her lips around the stopper and pulled and tugged. His groan just as she popped the cork brought Caroline rushing to his side. "Here," she said, pushing the bottle at him. "Drink it. It will make what follows much easier."

Forcing her arm under his shoulders, she brought the bottle to his mouth. His arms circled her neck, bringing

21

her closer, but she poured the contents down his throat so quickly, he had to swallow to keep from choking. His body already weakened by the snake's poison, the liquor seeped into his bloodstream like lightning. By the time Caroline was satisfied he'd drunk enough, the man's heavily lidded eyes closed in a deep, drugged sleep.

She worked quickly, having no idea how long her patient would remain under the spirits' numbing power. She took the knife, the same tool she'd used to sever the rope, and ran her thumb lightly across the edge. Frowning when her tool did not draw blood, she removed a wisp of clinging twine from the tip. As an afterthought, she splashed a generous gurgle of spirits over the blade to clean it. Finally, the last of her reasons to procrastinate exhausted, she knew she had to proceed—now, before her courage failed her.

Gritting her teeth, she plunged the knife's tip alongside the tiny fang marks.

The man's agonized yell sent chills down her spine. She paused a moment to make certain he would not spring up from his bed and wrestle her to the ground. But he remained still, eyes closed.

She exhaled, bent over, put her lips to his leg, and sucked. The minute she felt the warm blood touch her tongue, she turned and spat. Slurred moans escaped the man's lips from time to time, but he offered no resistance to her ministrations. Minutes seemed like hours as she sucked and spat, sucked and spat. After she was certain she had emptied his leg of every last drop of blood, she rinsed her mouth with a few drops of the spirits and leaned against the wall, wondering if her shaking legs would ever permit her to walk again. To test them, she stumbled to the door opening and took several deep, steadying gulps of fresh air.

At one time she'd dragged the old mounting block inside that had stood beyond the shelter's door. She returned to the makeshift stool and sat, chin in her hands, studying the stranger across from her.

"What am I going to do with you?" she whispered. "Austin's always saying I should think before acting. Even Titus says I'm too impulsive at times. But I couldn't have left you to die. It must have been fate that brought you to the path just as I was taking it." Her chin rose a notch. "Yes, that's it. It's as if the fates knew only I could help you. Anyone else would have fled in fear, or left you to die."

Her conscience eased, she walked to the barrel in the corner, reached deep inside, and took out some ears of dried corn and a handful of seed for her animals. After tossing the food outdoors and watching her pets descend on their meal, she returned to the stranger and laid her palm on his forehead. His skin felt warm to her touch.

Frowning, she strode outside to the small herbal garden and gathered an assortment of roots and herbs for a tisane, efficiently grinding them into a powder with a stick, and mixing the compound with the clear creek water. Certain the stranger was too lethargic to drink from the mug, she coated her fingers with the thick mixture. He licked them gratefully, like the orphaned chipmunks Caroline had rescued. But his tongue, unlike theirs, was warm and eager, accepting her ministrations with little coaxing. Though his eyes remained closed, soon he raised his head, and Caroline brought the mug to his lips, pleased to see him drink reflexively at intervals.

As daylight waned, the stranger tossed and turned.

Caroline wished she had a pine-needle-stuffed mattress to offer him. She'd have to talk to Maeve. Maybe between the two of them, they could come up with something.

Her eyes narrowed. The stranger's chest rose and fell, the outlines of his muscles readily visible beneath his light shirt. "What kind of man are you? And what was your purpose here?" she murmured. "And why were you alone? We're several miles from the fort, and even farther from Frenchtown."

The stranger remained silent, no different in this way from the only two men she really knew. They never answered her questions either.

But he was different in other respects. "A fine specimen of a man," she knew Maeve would call him if she saw him. *When* she saw him, Caroline corrected herself, shifting uncomfortably at the thought of another woman seeing her—rather, *this* man.

Her fingers traced the stranger's cheek. More than his face affected her. She drew a shaky breath. The tight outline of his breeches gave blatant testimony to his maleness. Indeed, his entire body had a most bewildering effect on her. She wondered if he had some malady beyond his injured leg, some contagious illness.

His eyes fluttered open, as if sensing her perusal of him. "Who—who are you, *madame?*"

His heavily accented words verified her suspicions. "You are of French descent?"

The man licked his dried lips and nodded affirmatively.

"That would make you American, as I supposed. You must be from Frenchtown. It's thirty miles or so from here, is it not? Is it your intent to fight there? I hear it's a likely spot for a battle."

His eyes now hooded, the stranger nodded. *"Oui, madame.* What are you called?"

"Caroline. Caroline Swanson. And you?"

He licked his lips. "Philippe."

"Will Philip work as well?" In his eyes she saw a twinge of fear. "Well, then, Philippe it is, if Philip is distasteful to you. And your surname?"

After a moment's hesitation he answered. "Desjardin."

"Well, Philippe Desjardin, I know your leg pains you sorely, but have you the strength to ride back to my home with me?"

He laughed in relief. "I thought this was your home."

Caroline watched him scan the dwelling with an interest that belied his condition. She wondered what the handsome Philippe would think if he knew that animals lived here, but from his horizontal position, he could see no hint of them unless he turned his head. And for the moment, he seemed to have no inclination to move at all. Hazel eyes stared into hers; she wondered if the man were as changeable as the color of his eyes.

Barely suppressing an odd but not unpleasant shiver, Caroline said, "Well?"

"Well, *madame?"*

"I would like to know if you can get yourself up into my cart. Or if you can manage, you could ride on my seat, and I could take a place in the back of the cart."

"Ride on your seat? An interesting proposal to be sure, Caroline Swanson."

Caroline felt her cheeks grow hot, and she crossed herself without thinking. The timbre of his words combined with his accent sounded wicked. She'd always thought she'd delight in some wickedness, but she'd never ventured beyond mere mischievousness. She wondered what wickedness with this stranger might be like.

"You, sir, are avoiding my question," she said, hoping she sounded brisk. After all, the man was in no condition to hurt her.

The stranger closed his eyes.

He stalled for time, hoping the woman who studied him believed he was once more unconscious. None of his past circumstances had ever brought him as close to danger as this. His options had never been so few.

He didn't know how long it had been since the snakebite. Was it today or yester morn? He'd been searching through the woods, gleaning as much information about the area as he could to take back to his men. He'd seen little, really—just endless trees and clear sky. And he'd felt an unaccustomed sensation of spaciousness and freedom. Then the snake, from out of nowhere, struck.

The venom worked much faster than he'd anticipated. He'd begun to make his way back to his men, but dizziness clouded his instincts, and he'd lost his bearing. That no one came to look for him came as a small surprise; they must have thought he was still out studying the area. Apparently they'd thought he was joking, just as he intended them to, when he'd said he hoped to part their illustrious company as soon as he could find better men to fight with. But he'd never intended to fall into the hands of an enemy, even if she were a woman. This spying had been naught more than a game before, but suddenly it had turned serious. Deadly serious.

When he'd heard the horse's hooves in the distance, he'd stepped into the path, assuming an Indian was its master. He hadn't expected a white man to live in such a dense part of the forest, but these Americans were a strange lot.

He hoped his feigned accent would allay any suspicions the woman might have, but he was uncertain if he'd actually spoken like a Frenchman, or only thought he had. And *Philippe*. Why had he chosen a name so near his own?

He groaned inwardly. He'd never made such an error. The venom must have fogged his brain . . .

But not as much as this woman did. In another time, in another place, he'd ask the lovely Caroline to a dance, to a fete, or a presentation, later to join her in a pleasant romp in bed.

Her eyes sparkled a delightful gold-flecked sapphire, her hair the color of spun silver. And her voice! For the briefest moment when she'd first spoken, he'd thought he'd died and angels sang. He briefly relished the cover his feigned unconsciousness gave him, enjoying the few private moments in which he could imagine her full mouth pressed against his lips, her slender legs entwined with his.

This time his moan rose from the pit of his stomach. His eyes fluttered open, and he concentrated on the searing pain in his leg, rather than the warmer heat in his groin. It would not do to show any physical threat to the Lady Caroline. He'd have to get her to trust him, as no one had ever trusted him before. Manipulation. He was a master at it.

*Control, Philip. Remember, you must remain in control.*

Looking at her through half-closed lids, he fought the fog tugging at his brain. He smiled as if at an errant child, imbuing his grin with as much sensuality as he could muster. Which wasn't difficult at the moment, when he shifted his attention from his throbbing leg to the woman in front of him. "Do I frighten you, *chérie?* There's no need to be frightened. I cannot harm you, nor would I."

"I'm not frightened. I'm never frightened. Though I didn't expect another white man so near, and with your dark hair, at first I thought you belonged to one of the Indian tribes who live near here, and . . . " She knew she rambled, but she couldn't help herself. "If I'd known you were one of our soldiers from the beginning, well, it would have helped."

Again Philip smiled, hoping he didn't look as ghastly as he felt. Flirting had always worked before. He took one of Caroline's white-knuckled hands from where she gripped the bed's edge, and caressed it softly within his own, careful to make the light, tickling circles he drew on the inside of her palm seem absentminded. "Are there many Indians about, *chérie?*"

Caroline wondered where her tongue had gone, as she bobbed her head up and down. She'd think the cat had gotten it, except she had no cats. Birds and deer maybe, but no cats. She looked at his hands, idly wondering how a man from these parts managed to have palms so uncallused. Could the settlement called Frenchtown really be that different from the rest of the area?

His voice flowed like honey. "Then it was my good fortune you found me, *oui?* You are obviously an accomplished healer. How were you able to tend the blind raccoon, eh? I hear they're quite vicious."

Caroline gasped. "How did you know he was blind? How did you know he was here at all? He only came in for a moment."

"And then he left, hissing and spitting. He has no love of strangers, does he, *ma belle?*"

28

"No," she said, echoing his tender, soothing tone. "But enough of my pet. Tell me, have you the strength to get yourself into my cart?"

"No," Philip whispered. "You will have to care for me here. Just for a short time. I have not slept in a few days. Once I've rested, I will borrow your horse, if you will permit me, and head back to my regiment."

"But that isn't necessary," Caroline protested. "Austin and Titus can help you. As soon as they come back, I'll tell them, and they'll be hap—"

He forced his eyes to widen in horror, though they felt like narrow slits. "No, *madame*. This you must not do."

"But why?" She leaned forward, her hair falling over her shoulders, tickling his cheek.

"Because." He thought fast, compelling himself to focus on his situation though he felt sleepy. So very sleepy. "Much confusion. There was much confusion. One of my fellow soldiers, he shot one of our generals. He made it look as if I, Philippe Desjardin, fired the weapon. I need time to clear my name. If you betray me, at the very least I will be court-martialed. At the most, hanged."

Caroline's protective instincts rushed to the fore. "I'll not let them find you, Philippe Desjardin. I'll help you all I can." This time when Caroline crossed herself, she did so with a purpose. Maybe the saints in heaven would take pity on her, and help her aid this man. Surely they would not jeopardize the life of one so faithful, so noble.

She had promised him she would tell no one. She'd never broken a promise, regardless of the consequences, and now was no time to start. If she broke her word, he could end up at the gallows on a platform with spectators cheering, eager to see his neck snap.

29

Philip's eyes fluttered open, then closed. His last thoughts were of the sweet yet sensual woman bending over him. He hoped he read trust in her eyes. He could stay awake no longer.

## Chapter Two

As the moon climbed into the night sky, Caroline stole into her house, expecting Austin to confront her, demanding to know why she'd taken so long to return. She'd always been certain to be home in time to help Maeve prepare the evening meal. Instead, the little log cabin was startlingly quiet. One candle flickered to light the darkness.

"Maeve?" she whispered. "Maeve, are you there?"

The dark-haired maid descended the ladder from the loft. "Why, an' of course I'm here. Where else would ye be expectin' me?"

Caroline smiled. Regardless of how dreadful things were, Maeve managed to cheer her, ever since she'd come into their employ two years before. "It's just odd that Austin isn't back yet. Or did he return home from the fort and then go elsewhere?"

"Nay. It wouldn't be enough time for him to be returnin' now, would it? If he had anything important to say, that is." The maid shook her head. "To be certain, I've been frettin' about ye, what with it bein' so late and all. But I could hardly blame ye if ye'd run off. Ye deserve a better life than ye get at the hands of her brother. And he keepin' ye hidden away in the depths of the forest, like some kind of addled person! He's the one what's addled, if ye don't mind me sayin' so."

Caroline's eyes widened. "I *want* to live here. To be truthful, Austin wishes to reside in a city, but not me. He'd leave in a minute, if he didn't have my welfare to contend with. That's why he's so eager for me to wed Titus."

"Ye never told me that, lass. No wonder he treats ye so poorly. Yer his ball and chain, as it were."

Caroline crossed herself. The moonless night cast a pall over the cabin, reminding her again of the late hour. "You don't think Austin could have come to harm, do you?" The ensuing guilt she felt after indulging in the fantasy of some mishap befalling her brother always brought an automatic crossing, followed by mental images far worse than any reality that could possibly occur. "Do you think he's safe, then? Truly?"

Maeve shrugged. "He could come to no good. But then, what's the worst that could happen? Yer wedding would just come a mite sooner. There's no way ye could put off Mr. Duffy any longer. He's too fine a gentleman to allow ye to live by yerself here, and what with the two of ye betrothed, he'd right likely do the honorable thing and wed ye right away. But these supposin's are most likely all for naught. Do ye really think the Indians would be wantin' yer brother's scalp?"

Caroline laughed despite her anxiety. Although he was only twenty-seven years of age, Austin's locks had started to thin drastically some years before. Now he combed the few remaining waxen strands from his left ear over to his right, and his right ear over to his left. Sometimes a hair or two met in the middle and gave rise to a little cockscomb, which Caroline never commented on, only word-lessly offering him a hat as she walked past.

Composing herself, though an occasional giggle still escaped her lips, Caroline said, "We really must be serious for a moment, Maeve. I need your help."

The maid rolled her eyes. "Of course, ye do, lass. For what little household good should I now lay down me life?"

A cloud passed over Caroline's eyes and her demeanor turned markedly serious. "It's not a household good, Maeve. I have a problem. A considerable problem, I fear." Clasping her hands together, she leaned forward and told Maeve what had happened since she'd left that morning.

"But surely ye don't intend on keepin' this man as one of yer pets?"

"Of course not. But I couldn't just leave him to die, now, could I?"

"Yer so certain ye can save him?" Maeve asked.

Caroline shook her head slowly. "No. I know my skills are sufficient for animals, but for men?" She straightened her shoulders. "But I was the only one there. No one else ever takes that path, except maybe an Indian once in a while. At one time they would have helped him, but now they're so sympathetic to the British, who knows what they would have done had they found him? Anyway, it might have been too late."

"How do ye know he's not likin' to harm ye?"

"I don't," Caroline answered impatiently. "But he's in no condition to hurt me now. I'll worry about that later. Think on it, Maeve. He trusted me enough to take care of him, when Titus and Austin think my skills are child's

33

play. And he confided in me. He's wrongly accused, and I'm his only hope at the moment."

"How injured is the man?"

Shaking her head as if to dispel cobwebs, Caroline replied, "Very. That is, I think he'll live, but I don't know what to do! If only I could get a doctor to him, but he refuses, says his identity has to be kept secret or he'll hang, and I just can't allow that to happen. As for Austin, you know that if I ask him for help, he'd head right to some bloodthirsty general to tell him I have a traitor in my care. Austin would probably earn a medal for his troubles, and Philippe would die."

Maeve nodded.

"I removed as much of the venom as I was able, but it's been coursing through his body a long time. I hope I'm wrong, but I do believe he has an infection. He was still fevered when I left. The fever will—" She stopped, choking on her words.

"Tell me, lass. How exactly did ye remove the poison? Did ye do as my dear mother taught me, and give him the garlic and treacle to drink?"

Wincing, Caroline said, "I did not know of that remedy."

"Then what did ye do? Did ye cup him?"

"No. I've never cupped any of my animals, ever since I tried with a baby fox and he bit me."

"Did ye put leeches on him?"

"No."

"Then what exactly did ye do?"

Exasperated, Caroline put her hands on her hips and gave her head a toss. "I did as I used to see the Indians do, and sucked the poison out. Or at least I tried, but I fear I was too late."

"Ye sucked it out? The poison? From his leg?"

"No, his eyeball! Of course, his leg. That's where he was injured, after all."

"Ye sucked on a man?"

"Yes."

"How was it?"

Blushing furiously, Caroline saw the twinkle in her maid's eyes and laughed in embarrassment. "Oh, you try me sorely, you do. I did nothing more than if he were an animal. But my God, Maeve—" Caroline crossed herself at taking the Lord's name—"My God, he's no animal. He's a *man*. What if the poison's through him, as I fear? What do I do? And look," she said, pulling the gun from her deerskin pouch, "I have his pistol. I don't know why I took it, but I was afraid if they came upon him and found it, they'd find him guilty. Perhaps 'twas a pistol that killed the other soldier, and not one of our flintlocks."

"Why, 'tis a fine weapon, it is."

"Yes. I suppose. We must hide it from Austin, or he'll want it for his own."

"Then you're going to give it back to the man?"

"Maybe someday."

Later, with a candle to light her way, Caroline dug a shallow hole behind the shed. She gingerly dropped the pistol in it, then filled the cavity with dirt. She didn't want to run the risk of Austin finding the weapon. It could be dangerous in his hands—especially if he learned where she'd gotten it. He'd never understand about Philippe.

That night, sleep eluded Caroline for a long time. She could scarcely wait to be up again, and out of her home before her brother returned.

\* \* \*

In the morning, she hurried about the cabin so as to complete her household chores as early as possible. She and Maeve were busily peeling carrots for the evening stew, when an insistent knocking at the door startled them. While Caroline fetched the flintlock hanging on the wall, Maeve peered out the peephole to make sure no Indians knocked politely before bludgeoning them to death.

"Hello, Master Titus," Maeve said, opening the door.

Removing his hat, the sandy-haired man bowed and strode over to Caroline and took her hand, ignoring her squirm when he kissed it.

"Hello, Caroline. Is your brother at home?"

"No, he went to the fort in Detroit. I thought perhaps you'd gone with him."

"No. I didn't know he was going."

At the disappointment in his response, Caroline felt a stab of sympathy. She could endure her brother's cruelty, but it wasn't fair of him to alternate between ignoring and condescending to Titus. Titus was far more sensitive than she.

Titus coughed. "Well, then, I suppose I had better leave. It's not seemly I should visit my intended without her brother present."

"Oh, stay just a moment, won't you please? I have a favor to ask you. And Maeve, you can chaperone, can't you?" Maeve nodded her head obligingly. "See Titus, she will. If you stay only a short time, it will be all right."

Reluctantly, Titus sat in one of the four sturdy wooden chairs around the planked table.

Caroline drew up a chair and clasped and unclasped her hands. "Titus," she began.

"Yes?"

"Would you, could you possibly get me a physician's manual? Something that deals with—oh, fevers and the pus and snakebites and the like."

Titus's shoulders relaxed. "It's not such a big thing to ask for, Caroline. Not nearly as dangerous as some of those . . . " He darted a nervous look at Maeve, but Caroline interrupted.

"It's all right, Titus. Maeve knows all about the pamphlets you give me. Why, I've even taught her to read a bit."

His eyebrows rose, but Caroline was at a loss to discern whether he approved or nay. She thought Titus probably didn't have an opinion on the subject of women reading. He hardly had an opinion on anything, unless influenced by someone else.

He replied, "I don't think we have any such papers. My father prints political essays, as you know."

"There's no physicians' manuals at all? Nothing?"

Her face fell so forlornly, Titus reached out a hand to comfort her, then jerked it back as if mindful of the impropriety of their situation.

"I'll see what I can find," he said. "Why do you need it? Have you another injured animal? Is it something I can help with? Why don't you let me go over to the shelter? Tell me where it is, and I'll see if—"

"No!" Caroline almost leaped out of her chair. She looked to Maeve for help.

"The mistress, she's right," Maeve broke in. "The animal, he's a vicious one, he is."

"Oh? Well then, I don't think it's worth saving. If it threatens your safety in any way—"

"Oh, pshaw!" Caroline exclaimed, rushing to the door to open it. "It's not harmful, really. He doesn't like strangers, that's all. He trusts only me."

37

Titus rubbed his fingers against his chin as he walked to the door. Taking his hat in his hands, he tipped it to her before leaving. "I'll do my best, Caroline. There may be something I can find."

He strode out the door. From his squared shoulders, Caroline knew he would search the entire country if need be, to find her pamphlet. And knowing Titus, if he couldn't find a physician's treatise, why, he'd write one just for her. He would think it was his responsibility.

Once Titus left, Caroline and Maeve "borrowed" as many medicinals and supplies as they could safely take from the family cellar.

"Are ye sure ye don't want me to come with ye?" Maeve asked in concern.

"No. When Austin returns, I'll need you to make excuses for me. You will do that, won't you?"

"I cannot believe ye would even ask me such a thing. Of course, I will. If not for ye, for the kind man who will fight our battles, if there's any to be fought."

Caroline bit her lip. "I don't know how to thank you for this, Maeve. If there's anything I can do for you—ever—remind me of this. I owe you sorely."

"The only thing that's going to be sore in these parts is the leg of yer young man, if ye don't hurry."

Smiling, Caroline answered, "Aye. I'll be gone, then. And Maeve?"

"Aye?"

"Pray for him, will you? For both of us, to grant me safe journey. Though the way is short, this last week I've felt more in danger going to my animals than ever before. It's as if something evil lurks in the forest."

"Back home, I would swear the druids are haunting ye, lass."

38

Caroline attempted a smile. "It's no druid. Indians, perhaps. They've ignored us before, but now—it doesn't matter. If I let some peculiar fancies stop me, surely my animals will be slaughtered."

*Not to mention yer soldier boy,* Maeve thought, but she said nothing as her mistress drove away.

When Caroline arrived at her animal shelter, she heaved a sigh of relief. So far, her hiding place had been undisturbed by Indians. Unlike her brother, Caroline firmly believed the Shawnee and Potawatomi in the area would leave the white man alone, as long as they were allowed to hunt the land and fish the waters as they had for centuries. And the moss-covered cabin, long since abandoned, had been reclaimed by the forest. It was of no consequence to anyone but herself. The Indians couldn't begrudge her this.

She tied Derby to the old hitching post, a task done more to discourage an Indian from stealing him than to keep him from running away. Caroline doubted Derby would run anywhere. She took some grain and seed from the pouch around her waist, and threw it on the ground. While her animals came from the forest and swooped down on their feed, she strode past them inside.

Her smile vanished. Face flushed scarlet, the militia man's chest rose and fell alarmingly fast. The light woolen blanket had been pushed to the floor, and his muscle-rippled body glistened with a soft sheen of sweat. He turned his head in her direction, opened his eyes a fraction, then closed them.

"Philippe! Philippe, wake up. You must talk to me."

Again he opened his eyes, glazed with fever. "My—my leg," he groaned.

Inhaling deeply, Caroline looked down. He had pulled his breeches off during the night. His nakedness made the heat rise in her cheeks; she felt them flame almost as brightly as the scarlet path winding around his leg. She wanted to cry in frustration at the sight of his infection—*and* at his strapping physique, which was distracting her from the more serious matter at hand.

Her hands flew to his forehead, where an errant lock was plastered to his brow. Suddenly, he grabbed her wrists and held them with an iron grip.

"Stop," he commanded thickly. "You torture me, *chérie.* I cannot bear any more torture."

"I will help you all I can. I've asked Titus for a pamphlet that will tell me what to do. He thinks you're an animal; I dare not tell him you're a man. But oh, Philippe, other than my brother and Titus, there's no one for miles around but Indians. There's a physician at the fort, and I daresay he could help you more than I, if you would only let me fetch him."

He tightened his grip on her wrists. *"No,"* he said fiercely. "They will hang me." Then he dropped her hands, as if he were too weak to hold them. "Pardon, *chérie.* But if you will only help me to my feet and lend me a horse, I will be on my way."

"Are you mad? You haven't even the strength to hold me, let alone stand on your own two feet and leave here." She winced at the unwitting cruelty of her words.

He struggled to ward off the fevered fingers that clutched at the edges of his mind. *Control.* "Oh, no?" he whispered.

Before Caroline could anticipate his action, he reached

up and grabbed her wrists once again, and pulled her down to him. He'd meant only to show his strength, for if this woman betrayed him, his life would indeed be in jeopardy. As further proof of his fitness, he pressed his lips hard against her mouth, delighting in the soft sweetness of her.

Caroline was too shocked to protest. Shocked that he had strength enough to grab her, shocked that he would kiss her, shocked that she enjoyed this kiss, this deep, delicious kiss . . .

Philip relaxed his grip and pulled away, his mouth turned up at the corner in a lopsided grin that Caroline found absolutely endearing. She knew she should be furious, but her jellied knees and shaking limbs would not allow her to summon enough energy to be properly angry.

"You—you shouldn't have done that," she protested.

"Do you doubt my strength?"

"No. But, Philippe, you can't go."

"Why?"

"Because whether you want to admit it or not, your leg is faring terribly. You're in the beginnings of a fever, and it will get worse."

"I thought *you* made me warm, Lady Caroline." He grinned wickedly.

"And besides," she continued, her hands fluttering as she pulled the bedcover from the floor and covered him, refusing to look below his neck, "no physician will treat you for miles around, at least not without taking you to the fort and having you hanged. You said as much yourself. Do you know how they treat legs such as yours? They cut them off. Is that what you want?"

Philip struggled to stand. When he realized he would

not be able to do so by himself, he looked at Caroline for help, but she crossed her arms in front of her and tapped a foot, humming as she looked out the door.

The tune she hummed, a medley of vaguely remembered lullabies and Maeve's Irish folk songs, wafted through the air. Caroline paid no heed to the haunting melody she created. She only thought this man was certain to crumple to the floor as soon as he stood up, and it wouldn't be ladylike to tell him "I told you so."

But Philip heard every note, every enchanting tone. The woman's voice rose like silver clarion bells. A voice like that could lead men to ecstasy, if it moaned in rapture. Or to their deaths, if it betrayed their secrets.

Gritting his teeth, he summoned his waning strength and forced himself to his feet.

Though Caroline anticipated his fall, she did not reach him in time to check his swayed collapse to the floor, barely managing to conceal her concern. "Now. Will you please let me care for you?"

Philip shook his head, but his knees buckled as he tried to stand. "I suppose I must," he muttered.

Caroline wondered why he had kissed her, when it was obvious he couldn't wait to get away, despite the threat to his life. Feeling guilty that she had liked his kiss so much, she pushed it out of her mind, convinced it was nothing more than a display of male pride on Philippe's part, and a rare moment of weakness for her. She concentrated on helping her patient to the makeshift bed.

Once situated, he looked up at her. "Now, *chérie*. What would you have me do?"

Caroline gulped down the words that rose in her throat. She didn't dare say what she *really* wanted him to do. "I am going to apply a bread and milk poultice."

"As you will, Lady Caroline. But when you are finished, you will let me go, no?"

*No,* Caroline thought, but pretended she didn't hear his question and made her way to the stock of supplies she'd brought. From a deerskin parcel she withdrew a roll of linen for bandages, a pitcher and basin, a bone knitting needle, and some silver needles and pins. The Swansons owned only two pitcher and basin sets. Caroline knew Austin would be furious when she told him that Maeve had broken hers and serving wench and family alike would have to share the same—but sometimes, punishment was worth the crime.

The needles and pins, even harder to come by, Caroline guarded with her life. She took the broom back and forth from her home to the cabin, until she could find time to craft one of her own. She'd also brought some vegetable seeds, hoping it was not too late to grow some quick sprouting carrots and beans. The trick would be to keep the animals from eating them.

At no time did Caroline question why she thought her patient's recuperation would last as long as it would take these vegetables to grow. She only focused on meeting his every need. Well, not *every* one.

She mixed the crust of bread and a few precious drops of the milk she'd managed to sneak from home. When she was satisfied the poultice was firm enough to adhere to his flesh, but soft enough so the milk would seep into the wound, she hesitated, biting her lip.

Philip crossed his arms behind his head, struggling to keep his head clear, and grinned at her. "Well, *madame?* Is it time for me to suffer your ministrations?"

Her cheeks felt like they were aflame. She looked at the

walls, the ceiling, everywhere but at his face. Or his long, muscular torso. Or his bare legs. Or . . .

"The fever has addled my brain to be sure, but is it my bed that needs the poultice?"

Caroline looked down at the plank on which she'd just earnestly applied her concoction. "I—I'm sorry."

Reaching over, Philip grabbed her arm gently, mouth twitching at her stiffening resistance. "No need to fear," he whispered. "I am simply showing you where to put your hands."

Suddenly, Titus's voice rang out dangerously near. "Get back! Get back I say! Caro-*linne!*"

Alarmed, Caroline pulled away, her discomfort forgotten. She ran to the doorway, peered out, and gasped. Titus had never come here before. She'd heard neither horse nor cart, how had he found . . .

"Caro-linne! Call off your animals before they gnaw me to pieces!"

Caroline strode toward Titus who stood stock-still, the glance he darted in her direction his only sign of life. Bringing her hand to her mouth, she barely managed to suppress the giggle threatening to erupt. Fawn nipped at Titus's toes, Robin perched on the brim of his hat, and Willie bared his teeth at the stranger's odd scent. Titus looked like an impaled scarecrow.

For a moment, Caroline forgot her predicament and burst out laughing. "Why, Titus! I never knew you could speak without moving your lips. What a singular talent!"

At his scowl Caroline bit back another bubble of laughter. "I'm sorry," she gasped. "But you look like a talking statue."

"It isn't funny, Caroline. Call off your animals, will you?"

After distracting her pets with bits of the molasses-sweetened treats she carried in her pouch, Caroline concentrated on getting her visitor as far from the cabin as possible. "What brings you here? And how came you?"

Humiliated, Titus stepped forward, hoping to redeem himself. "I brought you the pamphlet you asked for."

Caroline took the well-worn medical papers from his outstretched hands. "Why, thank you. I certainly never expected you to find any so fast."

"What's happened to you?"

"What do you mean?"

"Your hands. What's on them?"

Caroline looked at the incriminating bits of milk-soaked bread clinging to her fingers. She had a mind to wipe them furiously against her dress, to erase all traces of her deed from Titus's accusing stare. Instead she clenched them tightly at her sides and affected an air of calm.

"I have another animal that needs tending. In fact, I should not dally here. Good day, Titus."

He reached out and touched her on the shoulder, then jumped back. It had been perfectly acceptable to touch Caroline in such a manner when they were just friends, but now . . . "Forgive me. I just thought I could help you. With your animal, I mean. What manner of beast is it? What ails it? It's important for me to know these things. Once we're wed—"

"Oh, no, I couldn't ask you to help, not with this animal. He's hurt sorely, a bit of bird shot, a lot of bird shot, actually."

Just then a muffled groan came from the cabin.

Titus's brow furrowed. "What on earth?"

"A—a bear, Titus."

His demeanor changed instantly from puzzlement to

45

alarm. "Caroline, it's foolhardy to endanger your life for a—"

"A bear *cub,* I should have said. Just a little cub, that's all. Scarcely larger than a hound. A very small hound."

"Then I must insist you allow me to help you with it. In your brother's absence, I must take responsibility for your welfare."

"My brother! Yes, I meant to ask you about him. Have you seen Austin?"

"No, but he sent a message from the fort. Said he should be back late today or early tomorrow. I don't know why he's gone so long, do you?"

"No. He said nothing to me, but that's to be expected."

"Well," Titus said, "I expect to see him at the volunteers' muster this afternoon. Do you want me to give him a message, if he hasn't returned before then?"

"Yes, do tell him I asked after him. And, Titus, you won't tell him about the cub, will you? I don't know what he'd do to me, if he found out I was harboring such an animal."

"No, Caroline. You know I don't want any harm to come to you, but maybe your brother wouldn't be so—"

"Oh, do you hear that? My bear awakes. You'd better make haste, in case he decides to come out here; he'd eat you alive. Look, even the horses are getting skittish."

Caroline knew her rapid movement and fluttering of hands in the direction of Titus's horse caused it to prance in place and toss his head. Derby lifted his head a fraction of an inch, then resumed his catatonic stance.

Reluctantly Titus agreed. "Yes, Myron does seem to want to get away. Perhaps he senses something awry."

"Then you had better trust his instinct. I daresay he

46

knows Cub isn't fond of strangers, unless as part of a meal. Now quick, be off with you!"

In seconds Titus mounted his horse, tipped his hat, and rode off.

Caroline sighed and almost crossed herself, before thinking better of it. She couldn't help it if Titus thought she was petrified at the prospect of Austin locking her in the shed behind their house overnight, as he was wont to do when angered with her. She hated being locked up, but she wasn't afraid of it. Neither was it her fault that Titus thought she feared being beaten. Austin's beatings were for her own good.

She gave her head a defiant toss. Austin wouldn't dare lock her in the shed now, with the increasing threat of war and Indians lurking about. He wouldn't dare.

"So, how goes your soldier?" Maeve asked that evening.

Caroline ran a weary hand across her brow and sighed. "I don't know for certain. His body's weak, but his will is strong. Shortly before I left I made him drink the rest of the spirits. He should sleep soundly during the night, I'd think."

"Is there anything else ye'll be wantin', then?"

"He needs to eat."

"Why, and ye have enough critters there to make a fine repast."

"I'm not in the mood for jesting, Maeve. In fact, that very thought troubles me. I have no idea how long it will take him to heal"—*if he heals*—"and if he should awaken with a hungry stomach when I'm not there, he's likely to make a meal of my pets. Fawn's so tame she'd never run

47

away. I think he's too deep in his cups to know the difference now, but when the spirits wear off . . . But we're wasting time. Before Austin returns, I need to borrow as much food and supplies as I can."

"Borrow? You're intendin' on bringin' the food back, then?"

Wringing her hands, Caroline entreated, "Please, Maeve, don't jest. Will you help?"

"Why, and of course I will."

General Hull extended his hand to Austin. "I understand you seek a position. Let's not mince words. I need an advisor, a guide of sorts, one who's familiar with the terrain in the area. You are a native here, I understand, and come highly commended."

"Aye, sir." Austin didn't think it necessary to tell the general he'd paid dearly for such commendations, or that he intended on earning that money back as quickly as possible. By any means possible.

Hull harrumphed loudly. "Well. The land here is so scarcely populated with English-speaking people, I doubt I'd find anyone better. I have a task for you to start with. A simple one. I believe war will be declared any day now, and I'd like to have my personal possessions shipped ahead, so they don't burden us in travel. Can you take care of that?"

"Certainly, sir."

"Here, then." Hull led Austin into his tent, where several trunks were piled on the ground in the corner. "All of these can go, except . . . " He shook his head.

"What is it, sir?"

"That one, on top."

Austin looked to where the general pointed to a brass-bound trunk. "Is there a problem with that one, sir?"

"No. It's just that I'd prefer not to take it with us when we're ordered to leave. Takes up the horses, slows me down. But I don't want to send it ahead."

"Why not, sir?"

"It holds our battle maps. Our strategic locations, number of troops, things of that nature."

Austin puffed up importantly. "As your advisor and guide, I'd consider it an honor, sir, if you'd entrust your trunk to my care."

Hull's eyebrows rose. "Are you certain?"

"Aye, sir. An honor."

Smiling broadly, Hull clapped Austin on the back. "You're a good man. I'm pleased to have you here. Yes, definitely pleased."


The next morning, as the women loaded the cart with pots of deer-bone broth (which Maeve assured her protesting mistress was made from an old withered stag that just happened to drop dead on their doorstep), Caroline paused and made a mental inventory of the items she would take with her. Dried herbs, crocks of preserves and fresh fruits and vegetables, a loaf of bread, stoneware jars of sauces, jugs of cider, ripened applejack, and pots of soup crammed the small conveyance. The supply of meat Caroline had been forced to lay in last fall was more than enough to supply Austin, Maeve, and herself. Especially since Maeve didn't relish animal flesh as much as she had before she'd come to know Caroline. So Caroline, against her own heartfelt objections, finally submitted to Maeve's insistence that injured men needed meat to heal, and reluctantly allowed some slabs of dried pork to be added to her larder. She wasn't terribly fond of hogs.

Two plates and cups, along with Austin's chamber pot, took up the remaining space in the cart.

"Do you think my brother will notice?"

Packing her treasures snugly into the corners, Maeve answered over her shoulder. "That he hasn't a pot to piss in? Well, he ought to notice. Can't be much of a man if he doesn't."

When her retort did not bring the expected laugh, Maeve hopped down from the cart and put a hand on her mistress's shoulder. "I was only jestin' with ye, lass. He's not likely to pay any heed. Ye've always been the one in charge of the food and libations, and as long as he's well fed . . . " She narrowed her eyes. "We did put up plenty last fall, didn't we?"

"Yes."

"And ye haven't given any of it away, have ye? Or seen it gone spoiled?"

"No. There's no one to give it to even if I wanted. Titus's family has plenty."

"And how long has it been since yer brother's checked on our supply? Not in the two years since I've been with ye, as far as I know."

Caroline smiled, trying to look unconcerned. "You're right, of course. Now, I do think I'd better make haste and be off, before Titus comes to check on me."

"Pshaw, lass," Maeve scolded. "He's only seein' to yer welfare, what with yer brother gone and a war in the offin' and Indians lurkin' about and all."

"I know. You're right again. He's a good man." By this time Caroline had climbed into the seat and taken the reins in her hands. A minute or so after she flicked them against Derby's back, the horse started off in a slow-motion walk. "Come on, you beast," Caroline commanded. "Trot!"

As they drew near the shelter, she jerked the reins sharply and Derby came to a halt. Caroline sat frozen, not daring to breathe. There was no way to tell for sure if her imagination was playing tricks on her, but she thought that out of the corner of her eye, she saw an Indian scurrying out of the shelter and off into the woods.

Had he slaughtered a weak and defenseless Philippe?

Moistening her suddenly parched lips, she calculated which risk to take.

She could turn and go back.

But that would not likely work. She couldn't hide a horse on the narrow path home. If there *were* Indians close by, they'd follow her and she'd lead them straight to Maeve, and after the Indians had killed and scalped the two of them, they'd lie in wait for her brother and Titus. Caroline sighed. That would just give Austin another excuse to berate her. If by some remote chance she managed to get to Heaven, it would be her luck that he'd slip in the Pearly Gates just to make a Hell of it for her.

But if she unhitched the cart and left it, the savages would return and help themselves to the food. There would be nothing left for Philippe. She'd never manage to purloin such an abundance a second time without being discovered. No, that would never do.

Caroline urged Derby nearer the shelter. After she dismounted from the cart, she hurried around to the rear, unfastened the wagon's back gate, and pulled out the closest object, a jug of hard cider. For a fleeting moment she contemplated uncorking the vessel and taking a swig of the contents, but she pressed her lips together and strode forward. In the past, even the slightest sip of spirits had made her light-headed. She needed all the wit she could muster.

Peering anxiously into the doorway, she breathed a sigh of relief. Nothing seemed disturbed. The animals clustered around her, nibbling at the grain she tossed them. And Philippe—Philippe!

Setting the jug on the earthen floor, she paced swiftly toward him, and pressed a cool hand against his forehead.

At her touch, the formerly still body jumped and thrashed, fists flailing wildly.

"Philippe, shush, it's only me, Caroline Swanson. I mean you no harm."

For a moment, from the deep recesses of his consciousness, Philip relaxed. The calming peal of clarion bells far in the distance soothed his ears, working their hypnotic timbres down his body, pouring liquid, healing balm over his wounds, like a Siren's poultice.

A Siren! That must be it, it must be a trick by the enemy! They were always trying to trick him, to capture him. No earthly sound could ring as sweet. Women's voices were brassy and bossy, like Daphne's. No, it was a trick, as sure as his name was Philip Masterson.

His blow glanced off her before she could avoid it. Caroline fell in a heap to the floor and rubbed her aching jaw. She watched in bewilderment while he tossed and turned, fighting unseen demons in the air.

"Philippe, please. I'm only trying to help."

She glanced at his leg and clutched her stomach. His makeshift bandage was half-torn away, revealing a bright, fiery red path surrounded by blackened splotches.

Her patient went deathly still, eyes closed. Hesitating just an instant, Caroline bit her lower lip and began to remove the stained wrapping. He jerked; she backed away. "It can't hurt you that much," she murmured.

He quieted.

"You like to hear me speak to you, is that it?" Carefully, she murmured to him in soft, soothing tones. His eyes opened, and his gaze fastened on hers. Caroline blinked and instinctively stepped back, the intensity of his gaze sending currents of fear down her spine. But then his eyes closed and she continued her task, carefully unwinding the bandage, until it lay in a coil on the ground.

She studied the wound, keeping up a soothing chatter all the while, keenly aware that the moment she stopped, her patient tensed.

Caroline decided exactly what she needed to do. Although Titus's book, as she'd expected, didn't mention it, she couldn't imagine applying another poultice until the wound had been thoroughly cleansed. Frowning, she tried to think of something she could use. Water was the first possibility—she had never completely subscribed to the theory that it was as unhealthy when applied externally as when drunk. Instead, she secretly agreed with former President Adams, who made no apologies for his daily swim. But after spying the Indian that morning, she thought that leaving the relative safety of the shelter for the creek *could* prove unhealthy. Loath to leave her patient, she tried to remember if she'd brought anything satisfactory in the cart. Then her gaze fell to the jug of cider on the floor.

Uncorking the vessel, she raised it with both hands just above Philip's leg, and tipped it. The liquid splashed over the wound.

"Ow!" Philip sat bolt upright, glaring at her through

glazed eyes. "What do you mean to do, woman? Kill me?"

Caroline paused, apprehensive. She remembered Austin had come down with a fever once, and had fought her like a demon. Would Philippe fight her, while she tried to help? The fever was apparent in the glitter of his deep-set eyes, and the color on his high cheekbones. A slight tremor ran up and down his injured leg, visible testimony to his pain. For all that, she expected no clarity of mind, but . . .

"You speak the most excellent English," she said.

"I, I, uh . . . "

While he struggled for words, Caroline swiftly pulled his head back and poured the hard cider down his throat.

Philip allowed himself a healthy swallow of the cold, biting brew. By the second gulp, his entire body tensed.

He sputtered, jerked his head to the side, and spit the contents to the floor. "What—who . . . ?" he gasped.

Caroline moved just quickly enough to catch the heavy jug, struggling to keep it from dropping. A scant second later Philip grabbed it from her. With the might of a crazed man he pulled her down, threw himself atop her, and pinned her with his free arm and good leg.

He gritted his teeth to ward off the pain, concentrating on keeping his head clear. "Is this poison? I dreamed I was being poisoned, but it was no dream, was it?"

Paralyzed with fear, Caroline tried to answer, but could only shake her head.

"How do I know, *chérie?*"

Mouth suddenly dry, she tried to reply, but found she couldn't even shrug her shoulders.

"I think there is only one answer that will reassure me."

Still holding her down with his left arm, he took the jug

and poured it down her throat. "There, there, not to worry, *ma petite,*" he said to the struggling form beneath him. "If it was good enough for me, it should be good enough for you, no?"

By now the pain in his leg had grown so intense, Philip could barely keep his attention on the girl beneath him. Indeed, he didn't realize she'd quit fighting him, until a few moments after she stopped and stared up at him drowsily.

Struggling to keep his eyes open, he sighed and held the bottle aloft. "Well, one more swallow can't kill me, even if it is poison." He took a long pull, set the jug down on the ground next to him, and closed his eyes.


When Caroline woke, it was dusk.

Squinting, she tried to bring the room into focus, but only the ceiling came into view. The logs weaved and undulated in a most perplexing pattern. She swallowed and closed her eyes once again.

A few hours later, remembering the reeling of her head the last time she woke, Caroline moved very, very slowly. Her limbs felt like lead. Heavy, weighted lead.

She became dimly aware of the sound of breathing near her. Fawn?

But no, this breath, now that it wafted over her, lacked the slightly sweet scent of the deer. Instead, it smelled somewhat like—cider. Suddenly remembering, Caroline tried to push herself away from the body that weighted her down.

The movement made her head spin, and she instantly laid back down on the strong, muscled arm stretched out under her neck. She shifted, and Philip pulled her tightly

55

against him. Sighing, she tried to find a way out of her predicament.

Her patient obviously held her captive. If she moved even a little, she was bound to push him off the bed.

*The bed.* Caroline gulped. Here she lay, in the middle of the night, with a man in a bed. Well, not exactly a bed. More to the point, a plank. And—she wrinkled her brow, wondering why her thoughts were so muddled.

"Mmmm, be still, *chérie,*" Philip whispered into her ear.

The warm tickle of his breath almost made her want to giggle, but a giggle didn't seem quite appropriate. Her heavy lids started to close. Her last thought was of the sheer futility of trying to steal away in the middle of the night, through a land rife with angry Indians. And of a fevered man next to her, and a thankfulness that it was only the warmth from his body that made her so hot.

With the first streaks of pink dawn, Philip woke. He turned onto his stomach, his elbows on either side of the woman sleeping beneath him.

He smiled and ran the tip of his index finger lightly under her full bottom lip. So she hadn't tried to poison him after all. In fact, the intense pain in his leg had lessened to a bearable throb. Perhaps she truly did mean to help him. Or had she found out the truth about him? Had he told her in a fevered delirium? Women had told him that he talked in his sleep, but he'd always doubted them. What if they'd been right? Was yesterday a precursor of worse things to come? Had the woman intended to ply him with liquor, so he'd reveal his secrets? And if so, who had told her to do such a thing? Surely it had not been her doing alone. Or had it?

His head unmuddled by pain, fever, or spirits for the first time in days, he tried to concentrate on what had happened to him since the snakebite.

Bits and pieces of his dreams came back. No wonder he'd dreamed of mythical beings who lured men to their graves. This woman must be as close to a Siren as any mortal.

Philip thought once again of silver.

Her long, unbound hair splayed over the wooden plank. He ached to see it arrayed against a length of satin, for surely the shimmery fabric would dull in comparison. He picked up a wavy ringlet and ran it through his fingers, admiring the combination of silver strands intertwined with faint glints of gold. The maiden must tie it back with a ribbon in her waking hours, or he knew he'd remember it flowing loosely over her shoulders, as it did now. No fever could befuddle his brain to that extent. He was equally certain she didn't torture it up in an elaborate hairstyle like Daphne's. Daphne could hide a strapping man for years in the locks of her coiffures. *If* the sorry individual didn't leap from his hiding place in a desperate bid to save his eardrums.

Shrugging off that chilling thought, once more he turned his attention to the woman beneath him.

He tried to remember the color of her eyes, and decided he must have been in worse shape than he'd thought. No one's eyes were the particular hue he remembered, like blue diamonds.

Her lashes, the color reminiscent of highly polished pewter, fanned thickly from her closed lids. The tips appeared burnished with gold, but that fancy he attributed to the lingering effects of his fever. Her nose tipped upwards, above a lush set of lips that looked as if they could sing celestial arias. And she had a most determined-looking chin.

*Careful, careful. You're in enough trouble already. Besides, you usually prefer meatier women.*

He turned his head slightly to the shelter's opening, wishing it had a door. The whisper of approaching footsteps would not normally have escaped his ears, and he berated himself for his mental lapse. Covering the sleeping form beneath him with his body, he gripped the side of the plank, silently cursed the loss of his pistol, and looked up.

An Indian in full war paint blocked the doorway.

## Chapter Three

"What are you doing here, Mad Bird?" Philip asked.

"Your pain gone." The Indian spoke in his own tongue and grinned, looking with obvious relish at what little he could see of Caroline.

Philip pressed his lips together. "Pain gone," he stated in the same guttural tongue.

He stared, waiting for the Indian to make a move. As the minutes dragged on, Philip, continuing to shield Caroline from Mad Bird's greedy stare, grew uncomfortably aware of the disadvantages of his prone position.

Finally, the Indian broke the silence. "Woman's hair make good scalp."

"No. This one is not for you."

The savage scowled. "White man has no power to command Indian customs. Potawatomi good friends of redcoats. Now Mad Bird wants white woman's scalp. Would make good trophy."

A muscle in Philip's cheek twitched. "Mad Bird, we understand each other, yes. But *friends?* Your people are our friends as long as we supply you with gifts. You would turn on me in an instant if I fail to meet your demands,

59

or if I don't understand your ways and somehow breach your code of honor. I'm not stupid."

Mad Bird appeared to weigh this for a moment, then folded his arms across his chest. "Mad Bird asks one more gift for his loyalty. White woman's scalp."

Crossing his fingers, Philip said, "I would give her to you if I could, but she is not mine to give. This woman is the Great One's." He made a motion at the side of his head signifying insanity.

Curiosity aroused, the Indian drew closer, while Philip forced himself not to tighten his arms protectively around Caroline.

"See?" he continued, gambling that holding up a strand of the unusually colored hair would not tempt the Indian too much. "The moon color. It is one of the Great One's signs."

The awestruck Indian backed away. Those rare people the Great One talked to in his own tongue, whether Potawatomi or white man, often had a sign of their special favor. Sometimes the eyes slanted, other times the nose flattened, but always the Special Ones had the extraordinary happiness that came from the Great One talking in their heads. Mad Bird had never seen or heard of the silver hair before. The man from across the waters knew of it, and he was very wise, with magic sticks that shot fire and smoke, and water that warmed a man's belly. This woman must hold a very special place at the Great One's side. She had saved the white man from a certain death with her special gifts; the tribe's medicine man could do no better. She was to be revered. Bowing low, he left the cabin.

In the beginning Caroline slept, the fearsome tongue penetrating the fingers of her brain, stirring up dreams. In her half-wakeful state, she dreamed she was being chased by Indians, until a handsome Frenchman came to her rescue, fighting them off single-handedly. Then he picked her up and carried her to a secluded glen, covering her face and neck with kisses, while his hands explored her body . . .

After the Potawatomi left, Philip looked once again at the woman beneath him, wondering if he'd sent her into a permanent stupor with too much drink. No, the way his luck had been going the past couple of years, he wouldn't be so fortunate as to have a living, breathing, warm-blooded *silent* woman beside him. He seemed to have a knack for attracting verbal women. Loud, nasal-voiced women. Women who spoke like clanging cymbals, their demands ringing in his ears.

He took a deep breath, wiped a hand across his brow, and thought of as many reasons as he could to keep from ravishing the female pressed against him.

For one thing, he'd never taken advantage of a woman in his life. He'd never had to. More often than not they invited him to their chambers. Of course, he never knew for certain whether they wanted him for himself, or so they could boast to their friends they'd bedded the wealthy Philip Masterson.

Second, he could not get involved with a woman right now, especially an American. He had too much work to do, and a woman would only complicate matters. Women could never keep quiet about their affairs. They always promised to be discreet, but the truth always came out in a moment of weakness. Who knew who'd she'd tell, compromising his situation? Things could get messy . . .

He remembered hearing her talk to a man she'd called Titus—either that or the conversation had been the figment of his fevered imagination. He seemed to remember her telling the man that she was keeping an animal inside. Philip chuckled softly at the irony, wondering what type of creature Caroline had said he was. A fox or a wolf? Or a ferret?

Sharp stabs of pain pierced his calf, drawing his attention to his predicament. Now more than ever he needed to exercise extreme caution, regardless of the temptation of the woman beneath him. She was not to be trusted, anymore than any other American. Or any other woman.

But then Caroline opened her eyes. As he gazed into their startling depths, she murmured one word.

"Philippe."

He was utterly, irrevocably lost.

Groaning, Philip looked down at her. Once more he thought of silver and white, of diamonds and pearls, the translucent blue of her eyes sending white hot fire flashing through him.

Caroline gasped as he plunged his tongue between her lips. Accustomed to obeying male commands and befuddled by sleep and drink, she offered no resistance to this man, surrendering instantly to the strange sensations coursing through her, the pleasant tingling that began in her groin and traveled to the nape of her neck. His mouth tasted of spirits—or was it hers?—and she drank deeply, savoring the cidery taste and smooth, slick feel of his parrying tongue. Her bones turned liquid, she accepted his surprising intrusion, sucking lightly on his tongue's tip.

She thought she must be dreaming from fever, so hot felt her brow, so rapid the beating of her heart. She remembered the leaden feeling in her limbs when last she woke, and instantly concluded her arms and legs must have separated themselves from her body and moved of their own accord around Philip's broad, strong back and hard, taut hips. *She* would never act so wantonly. Her deerskin frock creeping higher, she arched her body closer, mewling softly and wriggling as his hands traveled down her throat, stopping just short of the round crest of her breasts.

Then came the unmistakable sound of a horse pawing, and the clink and clatter of pottery and tin.

Derby *pawing?*

An alarm sounded in Caroline's head. She pulled back as Philip sat upright and stood up. He, too, had heard the sounds outside the door.

"Someone, someone's out there," she said, sitting up on the plank. Her head spun, and a wave of nausea climbed up her throat. She must have an ague. Why else would her words sound so far away, and her tongue thicken and her stomach churn and her head wobble so? She brought both hands up to hold it on, then to her stomach to stop the turmoil in her gut, then back again. Then she looked at Philip's back, as he hobbled to the door. Recalling his violation of her mouth and her shameless response, she crossed herself.

Philip smothered an oath as walking sent pain careening through him. Looking back over his shoulder, he saw the woman's arms flail the air. Odd. He'd seen few flies that morning.

Turning his attention back to the growing din, he struggled to step into his breeches, pulled his shirt over his head, placed his weight on his good leg, and limped outdoors.

Caroline listened to Philip and another man, an Indian, waiting for their argument to escalate into a full-blown fight. The harsh, clipped sounds left no mistake that they disagreed, even if she couldn't understand the language. Crossing herself over and over, Caroline trembled with foreboding. What a most unfortunate time to die! Why couldn't a savage have murdered her any other day, any day prior to this one, when she had just spent a *full night* lying side by side with a man! Even if she hadn't been fully aware of how she had come to that—that *position,* she should have fought off his strange attack, or—what had it been, exactly? She was condemned to burn in the fires of the hereafter, for certain! It couldn't have been a kiss, she'd never heard tell of such a manner of kissing.

Unless it was the way the French kissed. Yes, she thought, taking small comfort in the feeble excuse that she'd only reciprocated an innocent greeting. Why, she'd heard that even men of some of those odd European countries exchanged kisses upon meeting each other. Though Frenchtown was in Michigan Territory, it was likely its inhabitants clung to the ways of their mother country.

Yes, a simple greeting, nothing more.

That deduction made her feel a little better, though not much. There was still no ignoring the fact that she'd lain with a man and fully enjoyed his kisses, peculiar though they were.

She rose to her feet on wobbly legs. After the room slowed from a fast whirl to a slow spin, she made her way carefully to Philip, who had come back inside and now stood, staring out the door.

When she came close enough to touch him, he spun around as if startled. The quick action unbalanced Caroline. She fixed unblinking eyes on him, and felt her knees give way.

In an instant he reached out to her, stretching toward

her without thinking. When she slumped against him, the bulk of his weight shifted to his weakened leg. A moment later they both collapsed to the earth, Philip taking the brunt of the fall.

Caroline's lids half-opened. "Mmmm," she said, grasping his powerful neck. "I'm not very good to my patient, am I?"

"No," he answered thickly. "Not at all."

"What happened to the Indian?"

"He tried to steal some things from your cart. I chased him away."

"Is that all you talked about? I saw you point at me, as if you argued about me."

*"Oui,* we did. He came for your scalp for the second time today."

A frisson of fear scurried up Caroline's spine.

"The second time?"

"Not to worry, *chérie.* I saved you. I told him you were mad. In the head."

Caroline backed away, helped by a snuffling Fawn pushing between their arms. Philip looked at the deer in amazement.

*"Mon Dieu!* Fresh venison, and young besides! If only I had my pistol!"

Thinking quickly, Caroline responded, "A gun? But, sir, you had no such armament when I first came upon you." Then, placing a hand on his brow, she frowned. "Perhaps the fever is worse than I thought. You should—"

Shoving her hand away, Philip snapped, "I may be fevered, but I haven't lost my mind. Not where my pistol's concerned at least. What have you done with it?"

"Nothing, I saw no pist—"

"Spare me your lies, *madame!*"

Caroline crossed herself. "You're right. I'm a liar. I hid your pistol."

"Hid it?" Philip looked at her, appalled. "Where?"

She spoke to him like a little boy. "I'll give it to you, when I'm certain it's safe for you to have it."

The corner of his mouth twitched; then his eyes narrowed dangerously. "Who have you shown it to? Doesn't the *madame* have a husband?"

"A husband?" Caroline's brows knitted together as she tried to clear the cobwebs from her brain. "No, I have no husband, but I do have a brother—oh, no! Austin, Titus! Oh, good heavens, what time is it? What *day* is it? I must get back, they'll be looking for me surely. They can't find me here, they can't, *they can't!*"

Philip answered brusquely, helping her to her feet. *"Oui,* you must be off."

He steadied her with a strong arm and helped her outside. "Are you certain you are well enough to make the trip back?"

"Yes," she answered, right before she grabbed the cart's side, just managing to keep from falling in head first. Then she saw all the goods she'd brought the day before. "Oh, no."

"What is it?"

"I can't take all this back. I'll surely be questioned as to why I've put so much of our larder into the cart. Besides, you'll be needing it. You're not planning on going anywhere, are you?"

He grimaced. "Not quite. I can barely walk from the cabin to here." At her sharp intake of breath and the pity in her eyes, he wished he hadn't spoken so honestly. But the morning's activities had caused the pain to flare up again, and a dampness on his brow told him the fever had only momentarily abated. "If you are certain you can ride, I will unhitch the cart. You can leave it here and come back for it later."

"Yes. That's the best we can do for the moment." The words were hardly out of her mouth before the task was done.

"There is a cellar under the shed," she continued. "The entrance is in the far corner behind the barrel." She looked doubtfully at his leg, blushing hotly at his half-dressed state. His breeches, pulled high over his good leg and ripped from his bad one, left nothing to the imagination. And his shirt, open at the neck, framed curly, dark hair that grew thicker at the lower point of the collar's vee.

She swallowed. "I don't know if there's a ladder; I've never gone down. But perhaps you can fashion a means to lower the goods into it."

"Not to worry, Lady Caroline. I will devise a way."

Once he'd unhitched the wagon he looked at her expectantly, but the absence of a sidesaddle didn't faze Caroline in the least. Austin had never seen fit to purchase such a device, and the young woman had learned to ride bareback. It was just another of her quiet rebellions against a brother who would keep her subject to his will.

Without giving Philip's impression of her a thought, Caroline backed up, licked her lips, rubbed her hands together, and raced to the horse, jumping astride with one easy vault. Her hair streaming behind her, she tugged lightly on the reins, turning Derby toward home.

Philip's mouth dropped open. He didn't know whether to retreat in disgust, or fall to the ground and give thanks for this creature who now sat guilelessly astride the dull-coated roan horse, her frock hiked above her knees. Caroline did not see the mixed expression of horror and joy on his face. With nary a backward glance, she kicked Derby in the side.

Philip stepped back, fully expecting the horse to tear away in a blinding flash of speed, befitting the animal of such a wild, untamed woman.

Instead the horse plodded off, groaning and wheezing.

The day was still young when Caroline drew near her home. The sun seemed unnaturally bright, forcing her to squint. She wondered if she were afflicted by some sort of plague, the kind that caused blindness.

Her back ramrod-straight, she urged Derby on, hoping that Austin hadn't returned yet. Maybe he'd been delayed, or had decided to spend another night at the fort. Or perhaps Titus had persuaded him to go to the Duffys' after the muster. If luck was with her . . .

Her shoulders slumped. Austin's sorrel gelding was tied up outside.

Sighing, she dismounted and led Derby around back, keeping her eyes studiously averted from the hated shed. She gave the horse a handful of oats, and set about combing and brushing him, prolonging the moment when she'd either have to suffer the immediate consequences of telling the truth, or face eternal hellfire later. Unless she could redeem herself with charitable acts in the meantime.

Derby whickered; Caroline dropped his comb and whirled around.

"Faith an' begorrah, have ye seen a ghost? Yer white as one, an' that's for sure. And where have ye been all night?"

"Maeve, thank heavens! I didn't think it was you."

"No, and I don't expect ye did." The maid wrinkled her nose. "And now that I can smell yer breath, I think ye ought to be chewin' some mint leaves at the very least. Yer brother'll be certain to question ye as to yer doings these past several hours, when he smells hard cider on ye."

"Do you mean he doesn't know I've been gone?"

"Nay. He came back in the middle of the night, he did. I shoved a bundle of hay under yer blanket, when ye weren't home by dark. Don't know how I would've explained it, if ye had turned up dead. He'd be havin' me hide for lyin', sure enough." Arms crossed in front of her, Maeve tapped her foot.

For a moment Caroline wondered if maids were *supposed* to act this way? But then, Maeve had helped her, after all. Now if only she could stand up straight, think clearly. She rubbed her temples.

"I—I think I'll go lie down for a little while."

"Oh, no, ye won't, lass. Master Austin will be here any minute, and ye'll be havin' to make like ye've had a good night's sleep."

Caroline leaned against Derby to steady herself, and tried to look threatening. "You can tell him I've taken ill."

"It won't work."

"Why not?"

"The bale of hay's still up there. I can't think of any way of throwin' it down without him noticin', can ye?"

Sighing loudly, Caroline admitted defeat. Her sleeping loft, accessible only by ladder, was in full view of the living quarters. A bale of hay hurtling from the loft to the floor would certainly not go unnoticed.

"Look busy, lass. He's comin'."

Caroline grabbed the curry comb and vigorously applied it to Derby's haunches, while Maeve headed toward the garden.

"Oh, you startled me!" Caroline had no need to feign surprise. She couldn't recall the last time her brother had cast a smile in her direction.

For a fleeting, precious moment, she tentatively smiled back.

But Austin's features slowly changed, the corners of his mouth turned downward, the light in his eyes dulled.

*What have I done?* Caroline wanted to cry. Then she realized his dissatisfaction most assuredly stemmed from her disheveled appearance. No wonder he was ashamed of her. After all his lessons . . .

She patted the stained deerskin dress, trying to brush away the dirt and grime, willing away the spots of Philip's blood that stubbornly remained. When that didn't work, she put her hands to her hair, combing it back with her fingers, praying it would turn gold like her mother's. Well, why couldn't it? Miracles did happen, and she hadn't asked for much lately. Just the lives of a few animals. And one man.

Austin glared at her. "Have you been awake long?"

"Yes." So far, so good. After all, she hadn't told a falsehood.

Just then Maeve sauntered in their midst, carrying a basket of young dewy carrots. "Here, lass, I brought the carrots ye requested for the—oh, beg yer pardon, Mr. Swanson. I didn't know ye was here. Why, but it's no wonder, the mistress has had me at it since shortly after ye came home; and what with all the cookin' and scrubbin' she's been havin' me do, my brain's so tired, I wouldn't have heard lightnin' strike."

Austin ignored her and addressed Caroline with his customary curtness. "We have a maid who works from dawn to dusk—well, on occasion—yet she appears more rested than you."

Caroline wanted to reply that they had a maid because Austin won her at a game of chance, but her brother spoke before she could answer.

"You've so thoroughly ruined her, I suppose there's not much I can do about *her*. But you're a different matter. Take to your bed. You are to retire for the remainder of the day."

Caroline's mouth dropped open. Retire? In the daytime? Austin wanted her to rest? *Her?*

"It wouldn't behoove us for you to come down with some sort of ailment."

Now Caroline thought her chin would hit the ground.

"Tonight we have a celebration to attend," Austin announced.

"A celebration?"

"Yes. At the Duffys.'" With that, he turned on his heel and walked away.

Dumbfounded, Caroline stared at his back. *I need sleep,* she thought numbly. *After I've rested, I'll be able to think more clearly.*

But her sleep was beset by dreams, dreams of an American soldier with eyes conveying kindness, even as he lay dying from the wound she had so poorly treated. And of Titus, shooting her animals one by one, and offering their carcasses to her as wedding gifts.

Usually when Caroline woke from dreams, she woke happy.

This time she woke in a cold sweat.

She wedged back against the blanket-covered bale and

71

turned toward the chinked log wall. A piece of hay tickled her nose. She sneezed, and unwittingly arched her bottom against the prickly bale. "Ouch!"

She sneezed again, louder, and coughed for good measure. Perhaps if Austin thought she ailed, she could stay home. She'd never felt comfortable around large groups of people. Maeve was her only confidante, the only person with whom she felt at ease. Until Philippe. If Austin thought she had some sort of affliction, perhaps she could steal away to check on Philippe. To make sure he was all right, of course. Nothing more.

Caroline worried a piece of hay between her hands and paced. Her brother would hear none of her protests of ill health. Even when she'd hinted she had something terribly catching, he'd insisted she'd get over it and attend the celebration. She slumped in a chair to wait Maeve's ministrations.

"Settle down now, lass, and let me plait yer hair," Maeve ordered, pulling her mistress's locks back so tightly that her blue eyes slanted up at the corners. Caroline thought her ears must have been relocated at the back of her head, square in the middle of the knotted braids Maeve pinned on each side.

"Ye do look fine, all dressed up in Mrs. Duffy's frock. Ye have nothing to be nervous about."

Maeve's remark pulled Caroline's attention to her attire. Her brother had borrowed one of the two evening dresses that Genevieve Duffy had brought with her when she and her husband had settled in Michigan Territory years before. Though Caroline found no fault with the ivory dress, it felt hot and cloying in the humid weather.

She wished she had a mirror, then changed her mind. Her reflection was bound to make her feel worse. If she looked half as disgusting as she felt, with her plaited hair and Genevieve's gown, how truly horrid she must have looked yesterday, when she'd worn her old, much too short deerskin tunic while tending to Philippe. And she must have been pale. She still didn't feel quite right.

"Maeve, by any miracle do you have any face powders I could borrow? The kind you told me the fine ladies use to color their cheeks? For tomorrow, of course, not to-night."

"Where would ye be thinkin' I'd be gettin' such a thing as powders? Besides, whatever would ye be needin' powder for tomorrow? Ye can't be any whiter than ye are today, and if Master Titus doesn't mind yer ghastliness tonight, why would ye be—ah, but it isn't Master Titus ye be thinkin' about, is it?"

Groping for words, Caroline said, "It's my pets. I'm just a little worried about my pets. I know they'll fare well without me for just a day, they've done so before, but now, well, I'm certain I saw an Indian, and what if he kills one of them?"

"I thought ye believed in a Divine Plan."

"Oh, yes," Caroline replied quickly. "Yes, of course, I do."

"Then, if any of them do not survive, is it not according to the Plan?"

Caroline's eyes blazed. "I think the Plan does not allow for a person to save somebody only to have him killed." She averted her eyes at Maeve's smug expression. "Well, I *am* worried about the animals, too, you know. I just wish—I just wish," she whispered, "I'd had time to visit him today. To check on him. To make certain he's all right."

Her toilette finished, she trudged outdoors to Austin, who waited in the secondhand carriage the Duffys had lent them for the occasion. Upon climbing the pair of steps into the black, moldy conveyance, Caroline stifled the nausea that always besieged her in close quarters. She wished they were going on horseback instead. Of course, if she had to depend on Derby's arthritic legs to take her, she wouldn't arrive at the party at all. On the other hand, better never than late.

When she entered the carriage, Austin said sharply, "You will behave with the propriety befitting a lady, won't you?"

Caroline chafed at the words. Then, knowing Austin would not want her to appear in public bruised, her frown vanished and she smiled.

"Of course. Even we backwoods women know how to act like ladies when we have to." Taking the piece of hay she'd been fiddling with, she sucked it between her teeth, crossed her eyes, and chewed.

Austin clenched his jaw and sat rigidly on the bouncing seat, crossing his arms in front of him.


He was dreaming again.

Philip woke, trying to separate reality from hallucination. He struggled to focus his blurred vision.

The animals. A motley assortment scurried in and out, sniffing at his arm or pawing at the open barrel of grain in the corner. Frowning, he decided that some of them, at least, must be real. His days spent reconnoitering had taught him an abundance of creatures thrived in these

74

woods, and it was not unlikely that they would seek refuge in an enclosed area. But not this variety, not all together. And none so fearless of men they would sniff at his arm, unless they were hungry vultures waiting for him to die.

*But he would not die.*

After a few moments, the stillness inside the shelter told him the animals had departed. He closed his eyes and tried to concentrate on other sounds coming from outside.

He heard brushing, a soft brushing against the building's roof. Bats? No, not bats. It was too light outside for bats. Trees, probably. Yes, trees. What kind surrounded this building? What kind had he seen when he was outside with the woman?

Or had she, too, been a figment of his imagination?

She'd certainly seemed like a creature of the forest.

Or a witch, perhaps.

A forest witch?

Chuckling, Philip licked his lips and allowed himself the luxury of succumbing to his crazed fancies for just a moment.

To assure himself he hadn't imagined her completely, he reached down, touched his leg and flinched.

His leg was still intact, and he knew he hadn't attended to it. That much he would remember.

It must have been the witch.

Or was she a spy? A beautiful, bewitching spy that haunted men's dreams. Why would such a one embark on such a dangerous mission? Of course, she could always be intensely loyal to her country, but that was a remote possibility. His experience told him that when men undertook this type of assignment, they did so for adventure or escape from miserable lives.

This Caroline was skilled. She tortured him, filling his

every thought, until he did not know where reality ended and dreams began.

He thought of the worried look on her deceptively sweet face, of the care and concern she feigned as she caressed his cheek, of the convincing way she pretended submitting so easily to the effects of the drink, her long, lithe legs twining around his as she lay next to him on the plank. He thought of her voice, surely trained by the best European song masters, and wondered if she danced with the same grace and beauty as she sang. She must. No expense would have been spared on developing her attributes. Her beauty and skills were too valuable to leave anything to chance.

He puzzled over incongruities still unclear to him.

From the little he'd seen, no opportunities existed for men of such talents—dancing masters and the like—to make a living in these parts. Perhaps Michigan Territory had a token aristocracy, but he doubted it. All he'd seen were uncultured men who looked as if they were kin with the craggy forests and turbulent lakes.

Could she be British?

Not likely. Why would they send one of his own after him? Unless they were trying to verify that he was, indeed, the Ferret before they rescued him. But no, she couldn't be British. Such a one would have some semblance of propriety. The proper way to ride a horse, for one. And tight-lacing, for another. Though the slip of supple animal hide she wore hardly called for tight-lacing.

His heavy lids half-closed as he savored the memory of the slim, coltish body pressed against him. The woman was skilled indeed. He had to admire the way she appeared to not care a whit for her appearance, knowing full well the effect her moonlit-kissed hair and transparent eyes would have on men. That is, on men much weaker than he, of course.

Dying was not so bad, if it had to be done at the velvet hands of such a creature, as much wild nymph as woman. If she was to be his undoing, what was she waiting for?

And why didn't she come back?


Titus's parents, Howard and Genevieve Duffy, made certain the evening's affair would long be remembered.

"You really shouldn't have," Caroline protested, as Mrs. Duffy proudly showed her the feast-laden table in the front parlor.

The Duffy log house was almost four times the size of the Swansons'. The printing business hadn't been profitable enough for the family to build a frame structure, but Genevieve saw to it that it was furnished as genteelly as possible.

"But my dear, of course, we should have. Mr. Duffy will include our modest little celebration in the week's handbill. It will offer a needed respite from all the talk of a war brewing, you know."

"As if I had any doubt," Caroline muttered under her breath.

"What's that?"

"I'm sorry. I simply said if I ate all this, I should grow quite stout."

"Oh, dear, I forgot. You don't eat meat, do you? But ours is absolutely delectable. You really should try some of these ducklings. They're very young, and look, isn't it darling how the cook managed to stuff their little beaks with cherries?"

Caroline tried to think of something to say. Titus

walked up to her and with unaccustomed authority took her by the elbow.

"You look nice tonight. With your hair plaited back and dressed properly, you look quite as decent as the other ladies."

"Thank you. What an extravagant compliment, indeed."

Many couples had accepted the rare invitation. So few diversions existed in the sparsely populated area, that the ladies would not be deterred by the harrowing ride to the Duffys' cabin, situated just far enough from the most dense part of the forest to be considered civilized. The Swansons' cabin lay another seven miles into the woods, accessible only via a nerve-wracking ride over bumpy, rutted paths—where there were paths—and hoof- and wheel-sucking mud where there were not.

In the dining room a linen-clothed table was laden with food, displaying the best of Genevieve's wedding gifts. A three-tiered silver dish held fresh berries and nuts, while other equally sparkling plates flaunted syllabubs, sweetmeats, and confections. The mahogany sideboard held the overflow of turkey, geese, and baby ducklings, which Genevieve had so proudly pointed out to her guest of honor.

After a maid, borrowed for the evening—the Duffys had adamantly refused Caroline's gracious offer of Maeve's services—rang the dinner bell, the guests seated themselves. Introductions were made, and for the first time Caroline noted the guests' attire.

Most of the men's simple deerskin breeches and best muslin shirts were similar to what Austin and Titus wore.

And the women . . . their fragile lawn and sheer gauze frocks, saved for rare special occasions, seemed woefully out of place in this tough, rugged land. But then, Caroline thought, looking closely at her own gown, she looked the most out of place. Perhaps her brother had stumbled on the better idea. The voluminous gown totally disguised her body. Austin always mocked her skeleton shape. Perhaps he only wanted to protect her from the scorn of other men. Or more than likely, of Titus. If he compared her to the other women, he'd cease courting her for certain. Maybe she should strip clear down to her chemise, climb up on the middle of the table, and imitate a scarecrow.

"Umm, Caroline." Titus coughed. "Are you feeling quite well?"

Turning to face him, Caroline momentarily had a vision of a green-eyed man grinning wickedly back at her, before Titus's watery stare brought her back to reality. "Yes. I'm fine."

"Then may I make a toast?"

Caroline shrugged. Whether or not Titus proposed a toast to this dignified assemblage was of no concern to her.

Titus signaled the maid to circulate and offer his father's finest rum to his guests. That done, he coughed, held his glass high until he had everyone's attention, then cleared his throat. "As some of the gentlemen present are already aware, first, Master Austin Swanson, and later, myself, have these past few days visited the fort."

Low murmurs and knowing smiles from the men verified his pronouncement. Caroline stifled a yawn.

"Master Swanson wished to learn the full scope of what will occur if war is finally declared. Some of you already know the . . . er, situation here—and for those who don't, the ladies, mostly, I'll leave it to your gentlemen to explain later."

Caroline thought this wasn't Titus's most inspired statement. If the men wanted their wives to know whatever he so gloatingly withheld, they'd have already been told. She imagined heated arguments would erupt after the gala.

Several pointed glances by the women in attendance verified her assumption. Envisioning a score of brandished rolling pins, Caroline smothered a giggle and listened absently to Titus amble on.

"I am pleased to announce Master Austin Swanson has enlisted in the army as General Hull's personal aide. At their persuasion, so, I am equally pleased to announce, have I. At this point I'm a foot soldier, but perhaps in time I'll attain a higher position. As you know, I asked for Miss Caroline Swanson's hand some months ago, and—"

Gulping down her sip of cider, Caroline barely managed to keep from spewing the contents across the room. Bookish Titus in the army? And cockscomb Austin? He'd threatened before, but she'd never taken him seriously. She opened her mouth to protest, but the penetrating glares of Austin and Titus effectively stilled her. Then she became aware of a deathly quiet. Everyone was staring at her, wondering why she didn't join in their applause. She crossed herself, then repeated the gesture with more sincerity, accompanying it with a prayer of forgiveness for her omission.

"I'm sorry," she murmured. "I—I always—"

"Ladies and gentlemen, please excuse my bride-to-be," Titus interrupted smoothly. "The excitement of the day's news is almost too much for her to bear. You know how frail women's constitutions are."

Caroline stared at him. *What are you talking about?* she wanted to scream. *Frail? You pompous oaf! I'd like to see you suck snake venom from a man's leg and get a little into your cups and ride home with your head bursting and*—bride to be? *We may have been betrothed for months, but I haven't given you permission to address me thus publicly, you, you . . .*

Titus, not a little warmed by the rum he'd been steadily imbibing all evening, said, "Some of us, because of our proximity to the fort, will be allowed to take occasional leaves to come home. Depending, of course, on the war status at the time. I will visit home as often as I'm able, as Austin Swanson has given his approval for Miss Caroline and I to wed in three months' time."

The blood drained from Caroline's face. *Three months?*

Polite clapping almost drowned out the rushing in her ears. Dazed and numb, she accepted the congratulations of the well-wishers, cowed by the threatening look on Austin's face.

The meal passed in a blur. Her wit failed her. She could not think of a way out, not here, not in front of everyone. If she even tried to reason with Titus in public, her brother, who watched her like a hawk, would surely punish her. Just how, she couldn't imagine.

After they dined, the women retired to one room, the men to another, where the latter indulged in games of whist and dice.

For as long as she could bear it, Caroline exchanged tidbits of gossip with the older women, feeling painfully out of place. Their disapproval of her earlier behavior was apparent in their sly glances, though none would insult the guest of honor in front of their hostess. Genevieve, keeping Caroline firmly in tow, made excuses for her future daughter-in-law's behavior, so that some of the women relented and endeavored to draw Caroline into their conversations. After all, marriage almost always transformed the most irrepressible young lady into the very image of respectability.

"Have you heard of the man they call the Ferret, my dear?" one of the women, Lydia Griswold, asked.

Frowning, Caroline poured the tea from her cup into her saucer to cool it. "The Ferret? No, I don't believe I have."

"That's to be expected," Harriet Meyers interjected. "You don't expect Titus would have told her, do you? After all, our men may call him the Ferret, but I've heard other *ladies* call him the Cock."

Shocked titters followed. Harriet leaned over and whispered loud enough so that all the women could hear, "I've heard it said the Ferret is a rake and a scoundrel, but also quite the ladies' man. Apparently he's some sort of important spy for the British, and he's missing.

"What has he done?" Caroline asked.

"No one knows for certain," Genevieve answered. "There are all sorts of rumors, but—"

"He's probably cavorting in the hay with some little strumpet," Lydia interrupted, rolling her eyes.

"You wouldn't be wanting to help with his *pitchfork*, would you?" Harriet retorted.

For several minutes the women bantered and teased, their scratching voices reminding Caroline of spitting cats. How was it, she thought irritably, that these women all knew details of their standing with Britain that she did not? Why did Austin and supposedly devoted Titus tell her nothing? Maybe if they knew about this Ferret, they also knew something of the hunt for Philippe.

Careful to keep her voice as nonchalant as possible, she asked, "What about the man who shot one of our generals? Has he been hanged yet?"

"A shooting before war has been declared? My, my," Harriet said, waving a handkerchief in front of her face. "I haven't heard of such a thing, have any of you?"

The other women shook their heads and studied Caroline, their curiosity piqued.

"What's the man's name?" Lydia asked.

"The general's or the soldier's?" Caroline responded.

"The general's, of course. I'm certain the soldier who carried out such a wretched act has been dealt with by now. More than likely our men sought to spare us the sorry details."

"Yes. My, you're all so fortunate. As to the general's name, it just this minute slipped my mind. If you'll excuse me . . . "

The women watched Caroline walk off in the direction of the men. She knew they likely believed she wished to be near her betrothed. And she had no intention of correcting them.

Her temples throbbed. What if the Ferret was looking for Philippe? Maybe the British spy hoped to bribe the wrongly accused American soldier by offering him an appointment on the British side. What an asset an American familiar with the territory and conversant in the Indian tongue would be to them. She *had* heard him speak in some Indian language. What a most knowledgeable man, fluent in not only French and English, but Potawatomi as well! He'd be such an asset to the British. She had to protect him.

It took her only minutes to locate Austin, engaged, as she'd expected, in the middle of a game of whist. Oblivious to his sister's presence, he inhaled deeply from his pipe and addressed his opponent, Jasper Brockton. "If I could just find the Ferret, I'd turn him in and collect the reward. I understand there's quite a bounty on his head."

Jasper rocked back in his chair and hooted. "If that's a ploy to distract my attention and turn the tide of this game in your favor, Swanson, it's most clever. There's not a man among us who wouldn't shoot the Ferret on the spot. Though you will need the reward money more than most, especially once I'm done with you."

"I've got plenty of money, Brockton."

Caroline gasped as Austin slid a pile of gold coins onto the table.

Jasper let out a low whistle. "You've been pulling the wool over our eyes, Swanson. I never would have guessed you were so well heeled. Are you certain you haven't already turned the Ferret in and collected the reward?"

"Someone as despicable as that shouldn't be allowed to live, as far as I'm concerned. If I ever lay eyes on him, you can be sure he'll be wearing one of my bullets."

"Only one, Swanson? You're as good a shot as all that, are you?"

"But why would you shoot him?" Caroline blurted.

Silence descended as the men realized a lady hovered nearby. Austin pressed his lips together and answered evenly. "Because if the spy is turned over to the British, they'll have all the information they want. There are signs all over Detroit offering a reward for his return. We're not safe until the man's dead." His look clearly told her to hold her tongue, but Caroline, her head splitting and her temper fanned by the men's condescending stares, ignored her common sense and threw caution to the winds.

"Then isn't that rather stupid? To advertise a reward for the man? Wouldn't the British be better off keeping his loss quiet, and looking for him secretly?"

Eyebrows rose at the novel idea, especially coming from a woman. Jasper guffawed.

"She's right, you know. Maybe you need to ask your sister's assistance in this game, Swanson. She seems to have inherited the brains in the family."

Scowling, Austin threw his cards on the table and grabbed Caroline's arm. "It's time we leave," he barked. Moments later, after a perfunctory farewell to Titus, Caroline found herself compacted between the side of the carriage and the unyielding body of her brother.

For the first mile they rode in tense silence. Then Austin, his temper rising, threw his hat on the carriage's floor and spewed out his outrage. "Your behavior was despicable. Despicable! First you humiliate us by failing to congratulate us on our military commission, then you look like you're going to faint dead away when Titus announces your nuptial date, then you dare to come to my table and interrupt the game, causing me to lose when I was close to winning, then you offer your exalted opinions of military strategy—"

Caroline wavered between being petrified of Austin's wrath, and amused by the way he worked himself into a frenzy. But his reference to her nuptials dampened her humor like a dash of cold water.

"How *dare* you chastise me! And where did you get so much gold?"

"From gambling, of course. I've been saving to give you a respectable dowry, so Titus would consent to marry you."

"You're *buying* him? What are you trying to do, Austin, manipulate us both into whatever warped little plans you have for our futures? Titus and I have always been friends, but—"

"But you voiced no objection last December, when he asked for your hand."

"After or before you offered him gold for me, you—you Judas!"

"Enough!" Austin trembled with anger. "I cannot wait to be rid of you. Haven't you destroyed my life already? *If* Titus agrees to accept you after tonight, he needs a wife who knows how to behave, and I daresay you need a lesson or two in that regard. All my life I've done everything for you—*everything*. Have you forgotten Beatrice?" When she didn't respond, he continued. "You refuse to be grateful. Yes, punishment is fitting. I owe it to a fellow soldier to give him a bride who won't disgrace him."

Caroline glowered at him, her chin jutting out in defiance.

He nodded and rubbed his palms together. "You said you knew how to behave like a lady, but you act like a doxy instead. Your word is for naught. Further lecturing is useless. You'd probably use a beating to your advantage and look at Titus with your pathetic cow eyes, so he'd have sympathy for your bruises. I'll not lay a hand on you, Caroline. It must be the shed. A night in the shed will do you good."

## Chapter Four

When the latch fell outside the door, Caroline closed her eyes and talked to herself. "Stay calm, Caroline, stay calm."

She squinted to adjust her vision to the blackness, hugging her shoulders. It had been six months since Austin had last locked her in the shed.

Now, in the darkness, she could barely make out any distinguishing shapes. Trying to quell her growing terror, she paced first the room's length, then its width, a practice that took less than a minute. The building that Austin had hastily erected as a storage shed measured little more than twelve feet square. The few farm implements consisted of a treasured shovel, hoe, and ax. Feed bags, some full, others empty, were stacked high in the corners, while among other necessities were those every frontier family kept in case of fire: a ladder to aid in reaching burning roofs, a forty-gallon, wood-staved barrel filled with water, and two leather buckets, one on each side of a wooden crosspiece, to carry the barrel's contents to the flames.

Cautiously Caroline touched her fingertips to the log wall. Something scurried across her hand. Startled, she jumped back. If only she hadn't chinked tufts of moss between the logs a few winters past—to offer some protection from the elements when she'd been imprisoned on a cold December eve—the room would be slightly illuminated. Surely some light from the moon would penetrate the thick growth of trees and seep between the logs. But she had done her job too well.

Breathing faster, heart pounding, she felt as though someone were pulling a scarf across her mouth to cut off air to her straining lungs. The walls encircled her, ready to crush her between them, and the coffinlike enclosure seemed to march closer, shrinking.

Her heart thumped like drumming fingers on a hardwood tabletop, providing a militant staccato to her inner battle. She had to get out, and quickly.

Now she swiftly traced the various implements leaning against the walls, ignoring the whispery feel of minute claws slipping over her bare feet, and bats' wings fluttering overhead. She focused instead on the task at hand, and away from the energy-sapping anger that pulled at the edges of her mind. Anger at Austin for so calmly bolting the door behind her. Anger at Titus for not consulting her about their nuptial date. Anger at the wretchedly hot weather. The deerskin frock she'd changed into was unmercifully hot and sticky. Why else would sweat stream down her brow?

At last she found the shovel. She'd tried various means of escape on other occasions, but the ladder wasn't long enough to reach the roof, nor were the feed bags, even if stacked on top of each other. The shovel was her last recourse.

The ground beneath the shed was a mixture of sand and dirt. The warped sides had pulled away from the bottom, creating an opening large enough to admit the thickness of a man's hand. This compacted earth Caroline dug with a vengeance, digging to make a hole just deep enough and long enough so she could slip under the shed's side and out into the forest. Her arms, used to hefting buckets of water from the creek and pulling a stubborn Derby in the right direction, did not start to protest until she was half-done, and by then she was so overcome with anger and determination, she paid her aches and pains little heed. She had to get out.

Finally the hole formed a long, shallow tunnel suitable for escape, if she crouched and crept underneath. Kneeling into it, she slowly thrust her head through, then her shoulders, ignoring the wood scraping her back. *I should have dug just a few moments longer.*

Her head and upper body out, she turned her face to the side, drawing in deep draughts of cool night air. An ominous clap of thunder from off in the distance seemed to applaud her progress. Heartened, she grunted, pulled, and pushed, feeling the rough log ends abrade her back and the dirt beneath her scratch her thighs, her frock having crept up to her hips. For a fleeting moment she wondered if she would ever get out, or if she would be found here, stuck in the middle, in the morning.

It began to rain. At first the drops came down like a wet caress, but then lightning cracked. The clouds unleashed a waterfall from the sky.

Thick branches of maples, elms, and pines creaked in the wind. The dirt turned slick. Choking back sobs, Caroline tasted mud, but the sodden ground aided her struggle. Slipping and sliding, she propelled herself forward. Something furry squealed beneath her and ran between her fingers, but at last she was free. Trees groaned and snapped, and like the rabbits scampering to their burrows, Caroline thought, *safety*. On trembling legs she ran through the night, arms extended outward like a blind animal feeling for obstacles, dodging trees, to the shed that housed the only creatures who loved her unconditionally.

By the time she reached her shelter, bruised and shaken, the soles of her feet bleeding and sore, the storm's fury had lessened to a controlled anger. Exhausted, drained, Caroline crept onto the bench next to Philip. From the depths of his slumber, he extended his arms and pulled her, trembling and shaking, to him.

"Where is she?" Austin demanded, the vein in his forehead pulsating. "Why did you let her out?"

Maeve's eyes darted away from Austin's thin, murderous glare to Titus, who stood meekly nearby. She'd waited for this with apprehension since the first light of dawn, when she'd gone to the outbuilding to check on her mistress. The hole in the ground could have been dug by an animal, but Maeve, knowing Caroline's terror of enclosed spaces, guessed what had happened. She'd filled the tunnel and tamped mud into it with her feet, trusting the trees would screen out enough light that Austin would not notice it. Apparently, that much of her deception had worked. But where had Caroline gone? And why wasn't she back?

"I—um, that is, the mistress, she—um, she had to use the chamber pot, and I heard her callin', and it were past dawn, it were, and I figured she'd been punished enough."

"Then where is she now?" Austin asked.

"Sir?"

He stepped forward, hands on hips, standing almost nose to nose with her. "You heard me. I want to know what's become of my sister."

"And I of my intended," Titus said, aping Austin's stance.

"I think she went down to the creek to wash."

"You *think?* You're not certain?" Austin bellowed. "Though that would be just the sort of hare-brained notion Caroline's likely to indulge in. What do you think, being as you're so fond of thinking? Could my sister be in any kind of trouble? Could the Indians have gotten her?"

Maeve's eyes narrowed. "It's possible. There's many an Indian prowlin' these parts."

Austin turned to Titus. "My sister could be in trouble."

"Then I think we'd better go look for her at once."

"No, Titus. I insist. You go ahead to the fort. If I find Caroline and nothing's dreadfully amiss, I'll ride all night if I have to, to get back in time. If I'm not there in the morning, tell General Hull I'll arrive directly."

"And what of Caroline?"

"What *of* her?"

"What if—what if something's happened to her?"

Exasperation passed over Austin's face. "Nothing has happened to Caroline! She's too contrary to allow anything to happen to her. The Indians would have her all of ten minutes before they realized their mistake. Now, have a care to the promises we made when we enlisted. We were very fortunate that General Hull agreed to let me serve as his personal assistant. He likes you. I think he means to give you a higher rank in the future. Go ahead to the fort. I'll be there directly. And you," he said, turning to Maeve, "you ring the bell if Caroline returns without me. Do you understand?"

"Aye."

After Titus left, Austin turned to Maeve. "In the event my sister's not near the creek, do you know where this animal house is she keeps?"

"Nay."

"You're lying. But it doesn't matter. I see she left Derby here. That old nag will probably lead me right to her."

Austin stomped out and Maeve leaned against the door, shaking her head. How could he live less than two miles from the abandoned building, and not know where it was? Especially after Caroline had told him a thousand times, more or less. She hoped her young mistress had been crossing herself a lot lately. If she were still alive, she was going to need all the help she could get.

Caroline woke in the crook of Philip's arm to see him looking at her.

"Hello," she said shyly, acutely conscious of her shift, now drying to a stiff scratchiness. Her hair, which the rain had plastered around her face, hung loosely about her shoulders. She moved slightly and flinched, scratches and scrapes reminding her of how she'd come to this awkward position.

Philip stared at her. Until she'd spoken, he'd had every intention of questioning her despite the bruises on her arms and legs that seemed to indicate a beating. Yes, he'd fully intended to interrogate her, even though she aroused his every protective instinct, even though he couldn't shake the certainty that she'd come to him for safety.

It had taken him several moments after she'd crawled

into his arms for him to realize that he wasn't dreaming. It had taken him a few moments more to realize, despite her suggestive appearance, that she'd come to him not for carnal pleasures or to entrap him. Instead she'd crawled next to him like a wounded and frightened animal. If she were an actress, trained in deceptive ploys, she was a master indeed. He could not force himself to believe that she was sent to betray him.

Still, his training told him to be wary, and he intended to question her.

And then she spoke.

"Hello again," she repeated.

How did she manage to speak and sing at the same time?

Her forehead creased. "Philippe, are you all right? Can you hear me? Has the fever deafened your ears?"

Groaning, he pulled her to him. He might as well surrender right now. "Caroline," he whispered, wondering why he did so when no one else was present.

"Why, you remember my name," she responded, eyes wide. "I didn't think you'd remember my name. You've been in such a sorry state the last few days, I wasn't certain you'd remember. But you look—well." She blushed, eyes downcast, and he did not know whether he'd been ensnared by her voice or her eyes or the lashes fanning her cheeks.

"Actually, you're a bit pale, but then again, so am I."

Her giggle reminded Philip more of a bubbling brook than a human sound.

"I do think you have more cause than me to look ill, what with your sore leg, though that cider you forced on me a couple nights past was enough to—Why did you make me drink it?"

93

Philip closed his eyes. Maybe when he opened them again, she'd be gone, and he'd know he'd snatched a glimpse of heaven.

"You don't remember?" she continued in her lyrical voice. "But that's understandable. You were most unwell. Why, Fawn, good morning."

The deer had pushed beneath Caroline's arm, and Philip blinked as the silver-voiced, silver-haired woman affectionately patted the animal's head.

"What are you?" he asked hoarsely.

Not quite knowing how to respond, Caroline looked at him in confusion.

He tried again, licking his lips. "Where are you from?" *Bother,* he thought wryly. *What do you expect her to say? I'm a spy, come to have you hanged and quartered?*

Bewildered, Caroline did not know what to make of this man. When she'd found him and he'd first spoken to her, she knew he was French, born and raised. That came as no surprise, as Frenchtown was so near. But then he'd spoken English better than her own, and at another point she could have sworn he'd spoken Potawatomi. Or *some* Indian language.

Then there were his eyes. They varied from palest green to dark emerald, from piercing blue the color of the creek in spring, to green flecked with blue. How could one man's eyes change so?

More puzzling was his manner. He seemed alternately attracted to and repulsed by her, though even when he seemed most wary, she did not feel threatened by him. Even when, as now, the muscle in his cheek twitched in irritation, the curiosity never left his eyes. No man had ever looked at her so.

Her lack of a response threw Philip into a turmoil. If

94

she were a skilled informant, wouldn't she answer his question? Make up a falsehood of some sort? But to simply fix that innocent stare on him, those round, saucer-shaped eyes . . .

"I'm from two miles away," she answered at last.

Philip cleared his throat and croaked, "Is that your home?"

"Why, yes." What a peculiar man! She smiled. "You didn't think I lived here, did you?"

Following her outstretched hand, Philip's mouth twisted. "Forgive me, *madame*. I have never seen such a—a place. Are all these wild animals yours?"

"No, of course not. They belong to the forest." Her words trailed off.

She swung her legs over the side, wondering why the man gaped at her so. Most women in these parts wore similar apparel for doing their chores, having quickly learned that lighter feminine garb didn't hold up well in the frontier. Perhaps the women in Frenchtown were different. Perhaps they wore more ladylike attire. Heavens! Perhaps their ankles didn't even show, let alone their lower limbs. And she had once again spent the night with this man. She knew she should be ashamed, but no memories of indecent acts haunted her. Only a rare security.

Caroline sat up completely.

Philip did the same, and looked at her closely. "When you said the animals belonged to the forest, you sounded almost—how do you say it—envious?"

"It must be your fever makes you imagine such things." She rose, but as soon as she put both feet on the floor, she winced and sat back down.

Philip knelt and took her feet in his hands, tenderly

rubbing his fingers over the tops, then her long, slender toes, then her soles.

"Have you no slippers, *chérie?*"

Caroline laughed softly. "Please, do not feel sorry for me. I have slippers. A fine pair of moccasins, at any rate. I just—I just forgot them, that's all."

For a few moments he mulled over her response, trying to shake off the spell of her laughter. "And why did you come here in the middle of the night? Surely it was not to see your animals. What were you running from?"

When again she did not respond, he looked into her eyes. *What the hell, Philip. This is no time to turn stupid. If she's going to betray you, get a taste of her first. You have time. If someone followed her here, you'd already be dead. And if this is what dead feels like, you might as well enjoy it, because it's not half-bad.*

Lifting her lightly in his arms, he picked her up and limped outside.

"No, you shouldn't," she protested.

He stopped mid-stride. "Why not?"

"Your leg," she said, struggling. "You surely risk further injury, your leg cannot be healed. You grimace even as you walk."

"What a pair we must make then, eh? Neither of us can walk, you with your sore feet, me with my wounded leg. Perhaps we will just have to stay here indefinitely." He flashed a wicked grin, and Caroline's limbs turned to jelly.

*If he smiles at me once more like that, he's absolutely right. I'll never be able to walk again. I'll simply melt on the ground like an opened crock of honey, and he'll have to lick me up . . .*

Her face felt like it was afire. "I think—I think you had better put me down."

"As you please." Philip didn't know why he just plopped her on the ground, other than his leg hurt and he was annoyed she didn't turn to butter in his arms, and she used that damned hypnotic voice every time she opened her pretty little mouth. His *savoir faire* had definitely suffered a mortal blow. She'd spent the night with him, for heaven's sakes. Twice. And hadn't even hinted she wanted him to make love to her. She couldn't possibly be as naive as she acted.

Caroline looked with concern at Philip's irritated expression. Was it her lot in life she should make all men angry? Maybe she should join the sisterhood, become cloistered somewhere. But then she thought of the sequestered life of the sisters, living in tiny cells, and changed her mind. She crossed herself for her uncharitableness.

Out of the corner of his eye, Philip saw the religious gesture, and his mouth pursed. Thinking the fever must have addled his brain and it would all sort itself out eventually, he said, "I ask you one more time. Tell me why you sounded envious of the animals."

Caroline sighed. "Because the forest . . . it's like a cathedral. But a most beautiful cathedral, with the green of the trees and the yellow of the sun and the blue of the sky for stained glass. And the birds, like angels, flying in the middle, singing notes no person could ever hope to imitate."

"Try, Caroline."

"I beg your pardon?"

"Try to imitate the bird song." To encourage her, he took her hand and enclosed it in his own, stroking it with his thumb.

She knew this was most ill-advised, sitting in the middle of the forest hand in hand with a man. A most kind-looking, generous-seeming man. Better-looking men had crossed her path; indeed, some of the guests at the Duffys' gala would take a woman's breath away. But all of them looked at her in ways that sent loathsome chills up and down her spine. Some of them licked their lips when she passed them, or peered at her lecherously over the rims of their drinking glasses. Others looked upon her with disgust, much as her brother did.

She looked into Philip's eyes and saw in their green blue depths only understanding, and this most unnatural of situations seemed the most natural in the world. She began to sing.

Philip stared at her in amazement. Arias pouring forth from the silver-haired girl's mouth, from her soul, encircled him. In the past he'd felt like he was caught up in a world criss-crossed by incoherent, demanding voices and shrill commands that wove a web of disorder and confusion around him, enslaving him like painful, chafing chains. Then, without forewarning, out of the midst of the chaos, one voice, sweet and pure, interpreted for him and him alone his true meaning, his purpose in life.

He was brought here to be with her.

*God help me if I am wrong.* He ran his hand across his brow. While he stared at her, he allowed her song to pour into him, believing in the deepest recesses of his heart that the tunes, unadorned by maestros or stringed instruments or brass horns—he grimaced as Daphne's image flashed across his mind—were the key to his life. When he'd started out on his journey, he hadn't known why he'd come here, not really. It had been a symbolic gesture, a secret thumbing of his nose at his dead father, who would rise from the dead if he could, to prevent his son from taking on such a base mission. It was also a show of defiance against Daphne and the other women he'd known.

It had been no secret in the small town of Clothclyde that Philip Masterson would one day inherit his father's enormous estate. Though a bastard child, Philip was the last male of a long line of Mastersons, dating back to the days of William the Conqueror, when an ancestor, Norman the Loyal, was given the vast lands of Strathmore. Norman's home, Strathmore Castle, was not finished in his lifetime, due to its palatial size and intricate stonework.

The castle and its lands eventually fell to Philip's father, Henry Masterson.

Philip would inherit Strathmore, as he always knew he would, but Daphne—he hadn't counted on Daphne. She had never been in his plans, though Strathmore Castle most assuredly was. The castle was his calling card, his automatic acceptance into the best taverns and inns and gentlemen's clubs, the home he never had when his father all but refused to acknowledge him. It was also his invitation into the beds of women from Wales to Scotland, and everywhere in between.

Philip was no fool. He knew he wasn't as handsome as most of the men women flocked to. He cared little for society's affectations, though he could fool anyone in that regard. Philip knew his gifts: his ability to deceive his friends and acquaintances into believing he was something he was not, his incredible memory that allowed him to retain the most minute details of whatever he saw—an attribute that came in handy when he aped the manners of the foppish gentlemen the ladies loved—his ability to not take any part of his life too seriously, and, of course, Strathmore Castle.

"There," Caroline said, blushing. "I hope that was enough song for you, and took your mind off your pains.

Really, I must go. Austin will be looking for me. And I must feed the animals before I go."

By now Robin had lighted on her shoulder, Fawn nibbled at her sleeve, and Willie had curled up on her foot, waiting patiently.

Philip blinked. "How do they stay with you?"

"They trust me. When someone saves your life, you trust them, don't you?" She fixed wide, unblinking eyes on him.

Philip felt what little control he had over his life slip out of his hands. If this sorceress were to bring him down, then so be it. He had no will to fight her. *"Oui."*

"It is so with them. Though why Fawn should trust me when I'm wearing the skin of one of her kind, I do not know. I prefer to think she knows I wear it, because I have no choice."

"Why do you have no choice, Caroline?"

She looked at him, wondering why he could not see the obvious. It was totally at odds with that analytical part of him she'd seen. She answered his question with one of her own. "What is Frenchtown like, Philippe?"

"It's . . . more settled than this." He pulled details from his memory. "Several families live there together. And there's a fur warehouse, a few buildings of business—it was settled, you know, many years ago, so it's much more of a town than this."

"And the women, what do they wear?"

Ah, she was clever. "Furs in winter, some deerskin in summer. But also some imported clothing. It's shipped to them from the Continent."

She shrugged. "Ah, then, you see, they have more money than my brother and me. We must live off the land. Though Titus's mother has some fabric clothes. She brought them with her when she and Mr. Duffy settled here, some six years ago."

He weighed this new information. "Who is Titus?"

"He's my—my betrothed."

"And have you told him about me?"

"No."

"Why not?"

"Because you told me not to. And I never break a promise." She tore her gaze away. "Philippe, I must go back, but I have to bandage my feet first. I don't think I can walk the distance as I am."

"Then do it," Philip said gruffly. "I'll feed your animals."

Caroline looked at him in surprise, then tended her aching soles.

When her feet were bound, she gingerly tested her handiwork. Satisfied the wadded cloth would serve her on her way home, she resolutely pushed out of her mind what would happen if Austin discovered she'd escaped. Hopefully, he would do as he had the last time, and leave the door to the shed locked until well after noon. Dismissing thoughts of Austin, she took the broom, swept the floor's earthen surface, and sprinkled over the old, a fresh supply of dirt taken from the barrel.

Her tasks done, she walked back outside where Philip sat on the ground, his back against the cabin, legs outstretched, sifting dirt through his fingers.

"Don't you want to get back?" Caroline asked.

"To where?" He hadn't told her about Britain in his fever, had he?

"To your regiment. Or your family, at least."

"My regiment will hang me," he snapped.

Caroline hesitated. "Is there no one to aid your cause?

101

No one to speak up for you, to declare your innocence?"

"No. No one."

"Then I shall."

"No," he growled.

"Do you always order people around this way?"

"Yes."

Despite herself, she smiled. "Don't you ever say please?"

"No. Never."

"Oh, for heaven's sake! It will be quite all right if I work to clear your name. And I'll ask Titus for help. He'll find out who shot your general. It's peculiar, though, isn't it?"

He looked at her out of the corner of his eye. "What's peculiar?"

"There's no war yet. There's talk of it, but how did you manage to get involved in a skirmish, when war hasn't been declared?"

Philip ran his fingers through his hair. So this part of the country still hadn't discovered they were at war. How could that be, when they were the ones who declared it? They were mere babes as far as strategy was concerned.

When he didn't answer, Caroline said, "Oh, well. I suppose it doesn't matter. I'm certain you must have good reason, and it's really none of my business. Austin is always saying that. That things are none of my business."

His head jerked up. What an insolent pup Austin must be! Was Austin her brother? Whatever he was to her, he was insolent and—brutal? Philip knew he saw fear flicker in her eyes at Austin's name.

"You'd better lie down," Caroline called over her shoulder, as she took tentative steps in the distance. "You don't look at all well. I'll be back to check on you as soon as I talk to Titus."

Philip meant to tell her not to bother coming back, that he wasn't going to stay. But he was afraid he'd start laughing. The woman's small mincing steps and unsteady walk as she avoided stones on the ground looked like a drunken dance, and he didn't want her to misinterpret his humor. Even if he had no intention of being anywhere nearby when she returned, she had nursed him back to health, and deserved more than his amusement for gratitude.

## Chapter Five

Derby ignored Austin's kicks and yanked out another tuft of grass.

"You blasted animal. *Move.*"

It had been a good two hours since Austin had started looking for Caroline. By now he'd expected to have given her the tongue-lashing of her life. Not that it would do any good.

The corner of his lip curled, and he gave Derby another hearty kick. "You worthless piece of horseflesh."

The horse turned his head just enough to bite Austin's booted toes.

"That does it. We're going back. I've had quite enough of your stubbornness. You're as bad as your mistress. I could have walked two miles and back by now." But as he looked down at his new boots, Austin knew he didn't want to scuff them. He had no intention of getting his new clothes dirty. If President Madison continued procrastinating, and war wasn't declared, he ought to be able to sell them for a pretty penny—or use them to up his ante in his next game of whist with that miserable Jasper Brockton.

Hearing Austin curse, Caroline flattened herself against a tree trunk, glad she'd stayed off her normal path. He sounded in worse humor than usual. If she took extra care, she could evade him. Silently she stole her way home.

The horse came much too near the animal shelter for comfort.

At the sound of thudding hooves, Philip stole out of the cabin as quickly as his limping leg allowed and hid behind the building's far corner, peering around the edge at the rider, a gaunt, tall man whose face was contorted in rage. Drat! He'd hoped this was one of his own, one of his soldiers come to search for him, but the man's weapon clearly indicated that he was an American.

Not daring to breathe, his hands curled in tight fists at his sides, Philip tried to judge how long it would take him to reach the lake. He squinted and looked at the sun to get his bearings, and estimated he was southwest of the small rowboat he'd beached along the shore several days ago. He sniffed; the sharp tang of pine trees mingled with pungent mustiness from the humid earth overpowered any scent of fresh water. He knew he'd deviated from his chosen course to begin with. Then the snake had bitten him, and he'd lost all sense of time and direction. How far had he come? Where was he?

He clenched and unclenched his fists several times, seeking the comforting feel of his pistol handle, but grasped only air. Whiskers rasped against his tongue, as he licked the bead of perspiration on his upper lip. A beard would help disguise him. It wasn't likely anyone knew what he looked like; so far he'd had no interaction with Americans. Except for Caroline . . .

His brain must have been addled to allow himself to become entangled with her. Besides the fact that she was the enemy, the woman had problems. No lady, married or otherwise, would come to spend the night with a man unless she were far less than a lady—or unless she were in serious trouble. Why had he entertained the possibility of becoming involved with her? He had enough troubles without another woman complicating matters.

Every nerve taut, he waited for the stranger to come nearer. The animals scurried about, then hid—all except Willie, who crept to Philip's leg and crouched against him. Unconsciously, Philip stood and petted the shivering animal, then jerked his hand back, appalled. Raccoons were known to be dangerous. This was no pet, no trusty bloodhound from home.

Willie squatted on Philip's foot, did his duty, then crept away as Philip kept his eyes glued to the stranger.

Austin turned his horse toward home, when a smothered oath came from the trees. Pulling on the reins, he headed toward the sound. Still on horseback, he almost entered the structure before he realized the overgrown tangle of logs had once been a building.

His lip curled up at the corner. This couldn't be Caroline's animal shelter. Not even animals could live in this ramshackle—*thing;* he couldn't bring himself to call it a structure.

Some sort of vine twining around the exterior held the building together. Suckers firmly fastened the logs, filling otherwise gaping holes. The roof, such as it was, appeared to be little more than compacted earth thick with moss. If it hadn't been for the doorless opening, he'd have been totally convinced that no human being could have stepped foot inside.

But knowing Caroline's fear of enclosed spaces, combined with the hovel's forestry look, forced him to admit she probably did indeed run to this, this *shack*, at every opportunity. His disgust mounted. No one would ever find out that his sister came here like some wild, uncivilized creature. He dismounted to take a look inside. The sound he'd heard came from somewhere in this vicinity. And though Caroline had a way with animals, he doubted she could make them talk.

When the stranger dismounted, Philip gulped. He had to make a run for it, had to get away in spite of his legs, one lame, one foot soaked with Willie's urine. But first he had to listen attentively, so he'd know which direction to take. The last thing he needed was to run straight into the arms of his pursuer.

The moment he heard Austin step inside the cabin, Philip broke away.

Austin, gun in hand, whirled and raced outside. His long legs easily overcame the crippled man, and within seconds he grabbed Philip by the shoulder and spun him around.

When Austin turned him, Philip's blank expression gave no clue as to his thoughts. As soon as he felt the rifle shoved against his ribs, he stalled for time by fixing his eyes on the ground—and on two pairs of feet, his and his adversary's. He was not encouraged by what he saw.

Opposite him, army-issue boots with a spit shine reflected his face, barely recognizable under a scrubby, unkempt beard and streaked with dirt. Glancing back to his own feet, Philip quickly took in the appalling reality of his situation.

Besides being weaponless and barefooted, his wounded leg displayed an angry red line spiraling up, fading at the edges to a bright pink. The wound itself was surrounded by graying skin. His other leg, with his yellow-stained foot, simply reeked.

Under the circumstances, he could see no way to overpower the American. He had only one option open to him.

Austin's expression changed from bloodthirsty to irritated. "Who are you, man?" he demanded.

Philip's chin sagged. A trace of spittle ran down his lip; he wiped his mouth with his sleeve and stared blankly at the stranger.

"I said, who are you? Where do you come from?" Austin repeated.

"Bu—Da—" Philip blubbered, waving aimlessly in the direction of the cabin.

Austin sighed in relief. "Thank God. For a horrible moment, I thought someone I knew used that—that *pigsty!* Instead, it's your home. But you don't understand, do you? You're a mindless idiot."

Philip's eyes grew teary. He shuffled his feet, his lower lip trembling.

Wrinkling his nose, Austin backed away. "Pew! Don't you know how to use a chamber pot? No, obviously not."
He took another step backward. "Um, say," he said, his

words muffled by the kerchief he'd pulled from his pocket to cover his nose. "I know you can talk. Cuss words, at any rate. Have you seen a woman come by these parts?"

Philip shrugged, secretly wondering if this pinch-faced excuse for a man was Caroline's brother. "Like attracts like," his father always said, thus the reasoning behind the engagement to Daphne. Somewhere down the long genealogical line, their ancestors had been related. This gaunt man's blue eyes were much the same color as Caroline's, and they both had spare frames. There the resemblance ended.

"Anybody? Indians?"

Hesitating, Philip wondered if he should speak. Too much silence might only arouse the man's suspicions.

Then Austin had an idea. A superb idea, if he thought so himself. If the man had enough reason to enable him to convey written messages, no one would ever be able to put any blame on *him*. The idiot could never put enough words together to tell anyone the source of the information. What a stroke of luck!

"You haven't seen any British, have you?"

Philip's eyes rounded in fear. He crossed his arms protectively in front of him, and stumbled backwards. Stifling his natural instinct to stay erect, he fell on his behind in a pile of leaves.

Austin eyes narrowed. "Hmm. You do understand, don't you? I wasn't certain you'd know what a British soldier was. Have you seen any?"

Trusting that his years of manipulating people made him an accurate judge of human character, Philip nodded affirmatively. The satisfied look on the stranger's face told him he'd given the right answer.

"Did they hurt you?"

*Now why on earth would anyone harm a poor, simple mute?* But Philip only again mimed a negative response.

"Do you like liquor, my good man?"

Philip nodded harder, his tongue lolling outside his mouth like a hound's. He smothered the urge to kneel and adopt a begging stance.

Holding his breath, Austin said, "I'd be glad to give you some. A whole jug, just your own. Would you like that?"

*Good God. What does he want me to do, pant?* He shook his head so hard he became dizzy, telling himself a certain unsteadiness lent credibility to his character.

"Well, then," Austin adopted a patronizing tone, though he still kept his distance. "I'll give you a whole big jug, if you know where they went. Do you?"

A slug of whiskey sounded good right now, though Philip had no intention of telling the stranger where his comrades were. Besides, he was so disoriented, he didn't think even he could find them. As a test of the stranger's purpose, he shrank back in horror.

"That's right, my good man." Austin reached out a hand in reassurance, but caught himself in time. The stranger must be crawling with vermin. "I have no intention of hurting them. Or going near them; I don't want to get shot. In fact, I have something I think they want. Can you deliver something to them?"

For what seemed like the hundredth time, Philip nodded.

"Good. You—you stay here. I'll be right back. You won't go anywhere now, will you?"

"D—drink."

"Well. You do know the important words. No need to worry. I'll bring a small bit of liquor with me. I don't want you in your cups at the outset. But if you do what I ask,

110

you'll get more when you're done. Understood? Good. Now stay right here, I'll be back directly."

"Oh, lass, he's gonna kill ye, he is. Look at his face. He's been ridin' like a banshee."

Caroline, home for barely ten minutes, peered out the small opening that passed for a window. Austin looked red-faced, yet Derby was barely panting, as if he'd only been ridden a short distance. Maeve said they'd been gone for hours. It was most puzzling.

"Oh, Maeve, he's not going to kill me. Since I'm betrothed to Titus, he knows he has another man to answer to."

"Aye, indeed. And what kind of a threat do ye think one as meek as Master Titus would be to yer brother?"

Feeling trapped, Caroline seated herself in the chair at the table, and tucked her bandaged feet under her just in time to hide them.

"Where," Austin gasped, practically falling in the doorway, "where's your paper?"

"What?"

"Your paper, something I can write on! And with."

Taken aback, Caroline responded, "Paper? What makes you think I would have such a luxury?"

Gripping the table's edge, Austin glared at her with colorless eyes. "Get me one of those trivial little pamphlets Titus bestows on you, and get it *now*. Otherwise, a night in the shed will look like a romp compared to what I'll do to you."

She believed him. Quickly rising from the chair, she bit her lip and kept her face impassive as she hobbled toward the ladder.

Eyes darting from the testy Austin to her hurting mistress, Maeve said, "I'll get it for ye, lass." Within moments she scampered up the ladder to Caroline's bed, reached underneath the pine-needle-stuffed ticking that served as a mattress, and came back down, clutching a pamphlet and quill pen.

Snatching them, Austin snarled, "Bolt the door, when I'm gone. I don't wish to be called back from the fort to be told there are bodies to be buried. I don't have the time." He stalked to the door, slamming it behind him.

"Whew, lass. It seems ye got away with that one."

"Yes," Caroline agreed. "But I wonder why Austin needs a piece of paper? I've never known him to write so much as a word."

"Ye mean he can't read nor write?"

"He can read. I've just never seen him want to. I hope nothing's wrong."

"Well, if ye don't mind me saying so, where yer brother's concerned, not much goes right."

After Austin left, Philip had ample time to weigh all the advantages and disadvantages of his predicament. He also had time to get up out of the pile of leaves and limp to the creek, though once there, he thought better of washing. He could give the stranger no room for doubt. *What I must go through for the sake of my country.* By the time Austin came back, Philip had resumed his previous position, slumped cross-legged in a pile of leaves.

"Here, my man," Austin said, his arm outstretched. The very tips of his fingers held out the piece of paper.

*I suppose I must get up*, Philip thought. With a show of great effort he struggled to his feet, falling back a couple of times in the process. After snatching the paper, which Austin released as soon as he touched it, Philip turned it this way and that, brow furrowed. Finally he stared at it upside down, looking at Austin with an expression of pure bewilderment.

"You're not supposed to read it, fool," Austin snarled. "Just take it to the British, and return as soon as possible with a reply. Can you find your way back?"

Nodding vigorously, Philip waved his arm at the sun and the sky, indicating that the stars and the heavens would be his markers.

Austin sighed. "I suppose you're the best I can do. If nothing else, you certainly aren't about to tell anyone else what I've done. You've barely said three words since I first encountered you." He studied Philip from head to toe, taking in the blank stare, the slack jaw, the trace of spittle running down his chin, the soiled leg. "No, I've nothing to worry about," he muttered. "The worst that can happen is you become lost. You won't show anybody but the British this paper now, will you?"

Philip shook his head and crunched the paper tightly in his fist.

"Good. Well—I'll check back here for you daily. Oh, and one more thing."

Philip arched his eyebrows.

"My sister has peculiar fancies. I doubt she comes this way, but if she does, you stay away from her, or you're dead. I'll not have her betrothal to a certain gentleman jeopardized because she decides to take you under her wing, like some dumb animal. I won't have her disgrace the Swanson name any more than she already has. Understand?"

Philip stood, refusing to budge. He'd read the paper,

and the words burned through his palm. His dislike for the stranger rose by the minute. And now the American was turning, walking away from a promise to a brainless fool. If only he had his pistol to issue a warning shot . . .

"Wait!" he yelled.

Austin turned slowly. "Another word." Eyes narrowing, he said, "How many words exactly do you speak, fool?"

Tossing his head back and bringing a cupped hand to his mouth, Philip mimed taking a drink.

"You'll get your rum, when you've fulfilled your duty," Austin snarled. "Now off with you."

Exaggerating his limp ever so slightly, Philip stumbled away. If nothing else, the American made him feel better about himself. He may have used people in the past, but never for anything as base as money. And he'd never mistreated those less fortunate.

"You don't think he suspects, do you?" The British general, Brock, asked.

Philip grinned. A second later the bright-eyed man transformed into a mindless, staggering idiot.

Brock laughed. "Good. The sum he asks is paltry enough for such valuable information. We've worked with him once before on a lesser matter for a few gold coins. You have enough in your pouch, don't you? And it's quite safe? Good, then. We'll take the risk." He wrinkled his nose. "Now, bathe that leg and see the physician. And afterwards, get some food and rest. You look like hell."

*Thank you very much,* Philip wanted to respond. But he really wasn't in the mood for repartee.

It had taken him two days to find the boat he'd left beached in the heavy underbrush, row across the endless lake, and work his way back to the British-held Canadian fort. Two rainless days with the sun beating down on his head, and the letter searing a hole in his heart. The letter signed, "Austin Swanson."

Never had he been so sorry to learn his instincts had proven him right. Austin Swanson, American traitor, was Caroline's brother. Philip knew the strength of blood ties. Blood was the reason he was inheriting the castle; blood the reason he was to marry Daphne. Blood meant Caroline was probably helping her brother.

The letter should have eased his fears slightly in one respect. Apparently the couple didn't suspect he was the Ferret. If Caroline had had any indication, she would have told her brother about the stranger in the shelter, and Austin would not have been so easily fooled by the idiot act. Swanson was scum and stupid, to be sure, but not that stupid.

Though early July, the lake was cold. Philip plunged in, welcoming the icy bite to his skin, the renewed ache in his leg caused by the chill water. Grabbing a clam shell from the sandy bottom, he brought it to his arms and scraped them clean, then his shoulders and stomach and upper back. He held his breath, chin touching the water, and rubbed the shell against his sound leg, then, much more gently, the sore one.

The feel of his calf, bumpy and uneven, forced him to face facts. There was little use seeing the physician. He had been doctored by the best, by the most tender of healers . . . He shoved the memory out of his mind.

Daphne would be appalled at his scarred limb, at his limp. His lips twisted. Perhaps she would be so appalled, she wouldn't want him touching her.

In that case, the snakebite would be a blessing. In the thick forest, his limp hardly seemed to matter. After the first few days, with Caroline, he'd scarcely been aware he'd been hurt. Indeed. He'd felt more whole than he'd felt in his entire life. She hadn't seemed the least bit repulsed by his injury. In fact, she had confronted and accepted it. But then, in light of her brother's character, she probably had a penchant for men aberrant in one form or another.

He ducked and swam underwater before coming up, gasping. Frigid water and throbbing leg brought the strangest sensation, a most peculiar stinging behind his eyes. The general was right. He needed to see the physician.

Caroline sat on a stool in the Swanson's cabin, holding yarn on her outstretched arms, while Maeve wound it into a ball.

"I—I don't know what's become of him, Maeve. If only I knew he were safe, but there's no sign of a struggle in the shelter. He must have wandered off. Perhaps his fever came back and he got lost, but I've searched all the way to the shore and found nothing. It's almost as if I imagined him."

Maeve's lips pursed. "Ye have been under a bit of a strain lately." She looked at her mistress out of the corner of her eye. "Ye haven't been imaginin' anythin' else, have ye? Thoughts that folks in these here parts wouldn't think fittin' fer a young lady? Though by my stars, any of them with a drop of blood runnin' in their veins have thought the same kind of thing."

Exhaling a long, exasperated sigh, Caroline said, "Why must you talk in riddles? Why can't you just come out and say what you mean?"

"All right, then. What I mean is—well, when ye came home that one night, the heavy smell of spirits was on yer breath. And yer not givin' to drinkin'. Now don't get me wrong, but no one's seen yer young man except ye. Or so ye say. And ye might be foolin' everyone else, but there's no light in yer eyes when Master Titus comes to call. He doesn't, as my dear mum used to say, get the sap runnin' in yer veins. And no one's likely talked to ye of the comin' together of men and women, though ye know how it's done."

Caroline tensed, and had a mind to slip her yarn around Maeve's neck.

"What are you talking about?" she practically screamed.

"I'm sayin'," Maeve said a bit louder than necessary, "that maybe ye dreamed up this young man. Now, now, shush until I'm finished. No one would blame ye. It's quite normal to make up stories, have dream men as it were."

"He isn't a dream man! The way he held me, the way he—" She stopped, blushing. "Never mind."

Maeve stood up, carefully putting the ball of partially wound yarn on the chair beside her, and wiped her palms on her skirt. "If ye've made a cuckold of Master Titus, I think ye owe it to him to call off yer weddin'."

"For your information," Caroline replied, smarting, "I have never made a cuckold of Master Titus." *Though I almost wish I had.*

Huffing, Maeve walked out of the cabin, leaving Caroline to wonder why they'd had their first argument.

Two days later, Titus paid his first visit to Caroline since the night he'd announced their engagement. He knocked, then called, "Caroline, are you there?"

"Yes, Titus." She walked hesitantly to the open door.

"Is Austin here?"

"No. Why, should he be?"

Twisting his hat in his hands he said, "I saw him yesterday. He said he had some surveying to do that would take him away from the fort, and he'd try to stop in to check on you. If he's not here, I suppose I'd better leave."

"No, Titus. Stay. We need to talk."

"But it isn't prop—"

"We'll go outside. Maeve will wander about, won't you, Maeve?"

"Aye, lass."

Before Titus could protest, Caroline stepped outside and led him to a tree stump. She sat, pulling her shift past her knees.

"Titus, why did you set our nuptial date without consulting me?"

Titus's brow furrowed. "I didn't think there was any need. I thought you'd be pleased."

"When did you begin doing my thinking for me?" At the hurt look on his face, she said, "I'm sorry, truly I am. But it's all wrong, don't you see?"

"I don't understand what you're talking about."

She licked her lips and tried again. "Titus, I know how dearly you and your father want a new printing press. It's all you've talked about since I first met you. But—is it enough to base a marriage on?"

His confusion gave way to understanding. "You think I'm only wedding you for your dowry."

She stared at him without blinking. "Yes."

"Caroline, that's not true. We've been good friends a long time, and—"

"Friends, yes, but nothing more," she interrupted. "And since our betrothal, even our friendship has changed. For the worse. We used to talk easily; now you're always concerned about the propriety of the situation. No, Titus, don't argue, it's true. Tell me honestly. Can you think of me as a—as a—" She swallowed, unable to go on.

"Caroline!" Reddening, Titus said, "I can't believe you would speak so, so—"

"Honestly?" When he didn't respond, she continued, "Titus, let's not rush into things."

"We've been betrothed these six months past! I—I don't understand your change of heart."

"Titus." She rose, walked over to him, and kissed him lightly on the forehead. "You are very dear to me. If I think of some way for you to get your printing press, will you agree to call off the wedding?"

"But—but what will people think?"

Caroline laughed. "They'll probably think you're a very smart man. No matter how hard I try, people around here would rather see you wed a scullery maid than someone who grew up like I have."

"But, Caroline, I'm no longer of an age where I should be unwed. And neither are you."

"But to each other?" She sighed and shook her head.

119

"I'd rather have you as my very dear friend, than as my dissatisfied husband."

"But—"

"Please, Titus. Consider what I've said. And remember, I'll come up with some way for you to get your printing press."

"How?"

"I don't know. But I will. I won't let you down."

Five days after he'd reached Canada, Philip once again landed on American soil.

A couple days' rest and good food before setting off again made him feel like a new man. Those two days had given him time to think.

The possibility that Caroline was a spy, like him, would have been humorous if it weren't so pathetic. On the journey from Britain to Canada, he'd clung to the hope that his uncle had been wrong, that people of uncompromised honesty lived somewhere. Once he'd met Caroline, he'd clung to the hope that here was someone who offered help with no thought of reward. For a brief time the fortress he'd built around himself had softened. Now it was back, harder and more impervious than before.

The discovery that Caroline had used him reinforced what he'd learned from his uncle. He would never again question that people used each other for personal gain, nothing more. Now he knew. The lines were clearly drawn, and from them Philip took a strange measure of comfort. His brief dalliance with Caroline had been unsettling, the ensuing pain in his gut, in his heart, far more severe than the constant ache in his leg. He was almost eager to go back to Britain, where rules for acquaintances in his social circle never varied: Loyalty to self at all costs, everyone else be damned. What was the Roman creed? Ah, yes. *Eat, drink, and be merry.*

He'd brought nothing back with him from Canada. Brock had informed him that no extra firearms existed. They could spare some gunpowder, but nothing more. At this news, Philip scolded himself unmercifully. How had he forgotten so soon? *Loyalty to self.* He'd find his own weapon, the pistol he'd so carelessly lost. It had to be somewhere.

Caroline and Maeve made peace, though a slight tension lingered between them.

"Ye know, we'd better be makin' the plans for yer weddin'. How many notes has Master Titus sent to ye now?"

"Two," Caroline answered. "And in the last he says Austin will be coming back tomorrow. For someone who's supposed to be so invaluable to General Hull, my brother is certainly able to leave the fort often." She tossed the latest missive on the table. "I'm going to the animal shelter. I'll be back shortly."

"Wait," Maeve said.

Caroline turned slowly, eyebrows arched.

"Look, lass, I know I'm just a servant and oughtn't to be orderin' ye around. It's just that ye are my only friend here, and I'm worried about ye."

"I'm sorry too, Maeve. I guess I'm not used to having people worry about me."

Stepping back, Maeve appraised her. "Well, someone should. Now. Can I say what I feel?"

"Of course."

Waiting a split second before replying, Maeve said, "I don't feel safe here without protection. Remember the pistol ye showed me?"

"Oh, yes. My 'dream' man's. Must be a dream pistol, then."

Maeve looked her straight in the eye. "I've searched high and low, but I cannot find it. I think ye ought to be bringin' it out from where ivver ye hid it. The flintlock is good for one of us, but with the pistol, we'd each have a weapon."

Caroline shuddered.

"Look, I know ye don't like killin' pieces, but what do ye think the Indians are likely to attack us with, if they're sympathizin' with the British as much as everyone seems to believe? A loaf o' bread?" When Caroline didn't answer, Maeve continued. "Well, I guess we'll just have to fight back with a crock o' butter. What a messy fight that'll be."

In spite of herself, Caroline laughed. "Oh, all right, then. I'll give the pistol to you. I certainly have no intention of using it."

"I want ye to take it with ye, when ye go to the shelter."

Caroline recognized it as an order, not a question. Flicking her hand in surrender, she replied, "Yes. I'll take it with me."

A short time later, using the shovel she'd loaded in the cart, Caroline dug up the pistol. After brushing away the last remnants of dirt, she held the gun gingerly, admiring the fine scrollwork etched in the slightly tarnished silver decoration. When she'd first found it, she'd been too distracted to look at it closely, but now the detailed design seemed to form some sort of a pattern. Curious, she traced her finger over the surface, trying to determine what the swirling curves and lines indicated. Letters. They seemed to form letters. Bringing the pistol closer, Caroline's eyes narrowed. "PM?" Or was the last letter a "D"? Turning it over a few more times, she decided she'd been mistaken. The elaborate linework, running above and below the letters, confused the eye. Philippe must have had a relative in Europe, who'd sent him this beautiful piece. She'd heard many of the men had such family heirlooms; Austin often complained he didn't have one. She hoped Philippe would come back, so she could give it to him. It would make him so happy. She refused to think he could be dead.

From the relative coolness of a grove of trees, Philip saw her coming.

He blinked. God, it was hard to believe she could be a traitor.

The feelings he'd thought he'd erased, the warm, trusting feelings, rushed through him. *You're a spy,* he said to himself. *You're not supposed to trust anybody.*

Caroline dismounted from the cart, cradling a baby woodchuck in her hands, and headed to the shelter. A few paces from the entrance she stopped and looked around, as if sensing an intruder, then quickly stepped inside. Philip watched and listened, wondering if fate ordained he would have to deal with her, instead of her brother, about the trunk. Had Austin told her about him? Had she figured out the idiot and the soldier were one and the same?

After several moments she came back outside, surrounded by animals. He thought she looked like a princess from some fairy tale, the sun filtering down through the trees, sprinkling gold dust in her hair. Birds flitted around her, the doe nuzzled her side.

He stepped from behind a huge maple tree. The doe stopped and sniffed, sensing danger, then sprinted in the opposite direction. Birds flitted nervously, snatching bits of seed before flying away again, chirping from the trees. Willie huddled closer to her, shivering, and she looked around, puzzled, before her eyes lit.

"Philippe!"

Hurrying to him, arms outstretched, she looked the very picture of joy and innocence.

The lump in his throat refused to go away.

"Hello, Caroline."

Two paces from him she stopped. Something was different, something other than the clothing, the breeches that fitted snugly over his hips. While not new, they were not the same he'd worn before, though they were the same brown color.

His loose-fitting green shirt was also different, and his changeable eyes reflected its color. She didn't like the murkiness in them. Something else she disliked even more, a hardness, like flint-edged steel. Then his eyes turned gray.

She shoved aside her unsettled feeling. Often her newly healed animals acted strangely, just before becoming docile and tame.

"Philippe?"

This time it was a question, a soft, barely whispered question.

Stifling a sigh, he stepped forward and took her hands in his own.

She shivered. His hands were cold, like his eyes. At least his fever had vanished.

"Where have you been?" she asked. "I've been so worried. I thought the Indians had gotten you, or your men had found you and turned you in. Or perhaps they'd found you innocent, and you'd gone back to the fort. I was waiting for Austin to return, so I could ask him about you, but—" She stopped. The way he looked at her sent a shiver up her spine.

"I have been fine. My name is not yet cleared, but one of our men found me."

"Here?" she asked, horrified.

"No, *chérie*, not here." He brought her fingers slowly to his lips and kissed them, never taking his eyes off her. Why was she so fearful of having her ramshackle shelter discovered? One would think it a palace. "I wandered away, hoping to find some evidence that would prove my innocence." *And I was looking for my gun. I know I had it when I first encountered you on the path. What have you done with my gun?* "I happened upon one of our men, the only one who believes I didn't kill the general. He brought me a fresh change of clothes. I worked alongside him looking for evidence, but . . . " He shrugged, indicating the search was futile.

A warm, mellow sensation began where he stroked her hands. Caroline knew she should withdraw them, but couldn't.

"But you never showed him the animal shelter?" she asked.

"We must have our secrets, *oui?*" He looked deep into her eyes, waiting for her to look away, for then he would know she'd told Austin.

Her gaze never wavered.

"Yes," she replied. "Oh—oh, Philippe, I have something for you!" Pulling away from his grasp, she ran to the

125

cart and reached down into the corner, where she'd tucked the gun. "Look."

"My pistol!" He seized it from her, checked it for signs of firing, then pulled her tightly to him.

"Why does it mean so much to you? It's only a gun."

"No, it's more than that." Philip turned it over and over in his hands, stroking it. "It was my father's. It was the only thing he ever gave me." Then he stopped, as if he'd said too much. "To whom have you shown this, *chérie?*"

A chill coursed through her at the suspicion in his voice, but she derided herself for feeling uneasy. Of course, he should be suspicious! He was a hunted man! Still, with herself a virtual prisoner in his arms and a gun at her back—well, not aimed at her back, but clutched tightly in his hand—she thought this was not a good time to tease him. "I didn't show it to anybody."

"No one?"

"No one. Philippe, I saved your life. Don't you trust me?"

He sighed, circled his arm around her shoulder, and propelled her toward the cabin. "Yes, *chérie,* I trust you." And the sad part was, he almost did.

# Chapter Six

Philip rested his back against a towering maple's rough bark, taking advantage of the shady spot which provided a small measure of relief from the heat.

Legs outstretched and crossed at the ankles, Caroline sat next to him, battling conflicting sensations. The soft mossy earth cooled her bare legs from her knees to her moccasin-clad feet, while higher up the deerskin shift rubbed against her body. Flashes of heat seared through her where it touched. She felt Philip's eyes upon her, and had a sudden urge to cover herself, despite the stifling warmth.

She knew she should go home, but the heat sapped her energy. Even the animals lolled, panting, lifting an eyelid whenever Philip moved. Then they peered at him, before closing their eyes again. Caroline had the eerie feeling they were watching them, watching *him*, ready to spring at a moment's notice, their apparent lethargy an agreed-upon deception. She saw Willie tremble whenever Philip's thigh brushed against him.

Tilting her head slightly, she studied Philip. She knew he sensed her watching him, yet he gazed off to the right, away from her. She could not see the color of his eyes, but imagined they had turned emerald. A green ribbon held his hair back in a queue, and an errant lock fell over his forehead. His deep green shirt fitted loosely over his broad shoulders, the sleeves rolled up to his elbow. Tan breeches, stretched taut over narrow hips, tucked into knee-high boots fringed at the top, similar to those Indians wore.

She felt a kinship with this man who, in his tree-and-earth-colored clothing, blended so well with the forest. He reminded her of her animals, and she felt a passing longing for the closeness she'd shared with him while he was ill. After her creatures recovered from their injuries, they demonstrated their love for her in little ways: by cautiously taking a few seeds of grain from her hand, or like Willie, allowing themselves to be petted. But this man, though he sat not four feet away, had erected a barrier between them she could not break through.

When he spoke, he did not look at her, but continued staring straight ahead. "Tell me about yourself, Caroline."

His tone unsettled her, a command cloaked by kindness. He'd spoken to her the way enemies spoke at a social occasion, trying to hide their animosity from the other guests. What had changed him in the few days he'd been away? Had something happened between him and the friend who'd believed in his innocence? Had they had a disagreement? Was that why he acted so distrustful, so wary?

"What do you wish to know?" she asked, in the same soft way she spoke to her animals when she did not wish to startle them.

Now, turning his head, his eyes pierced her. Instead of

green, as she'd imagined, they'd turned an impenetrable gray. "Whatever you wish to tell me, *chérie*."

She shivered at the term, which now sounded more like a thinly veiled threat than an endearment. Willie growled softly, but did not move.

"I—I'm not used to confiding in people. Especially men."

"What of your beloved Titus?"

She looked at him, perplexed. "I told you before. Titus is a *friend* to me, not my beloved. And yes, I've confided in him somewhat, but—not the way you want."

"How do you know what I want?"

The air hung between them, heavy and tense. "I don't. Why don't you tell me, Philippe?"

"Start at the beginning. With your name."

Now she felt more bewildered than ever. "You know my name. Caroline Swanson."

She wondered why his face paled so quickly, as if she'd put a knife through his heart. If he was going to respond so to something he already knew, what would his reaction be to other things? *I must be very careful with him. Something has happened, I must tread gently.*

Philip sensed her withdrawal, expecting it, yet sorry, oh, so sorry, to see her stop before she'd begun. *It is as I thought. She does help her brother.* For some inexplicable reason, he'd hoped he'd dreamed her name in his fever, hoped she'd say Caroline Smaston or Caroline Swanhill, anything but Caroline Swanson. By telling him her given name, she'd admitted guilt by association. He wanted to jump up, tell her he knew her for what she was, not what she pretended to be. Yet if he did so, his work here would be done almost before it had started. He clung to the knowledge that his country needed him. No one else did. Not Daphne. Or Caroline.

"Go on," he muttered.

Caroline hesitated. If she bared her soul to this man, would he think ill of her? And what should it matter if he did? She was intended for another. But still, though his body was beginning to mend, Philippe's soul needed to learn how to trust. It was a risk she had to take. She would tell him everything, so that whatever it was that now stood between them, drifted away. And if it did not, she could take comfort in knowing she'd done all she could.

"I—I grew up in the forest, you see. I'm more comfortable with my animals than people. When my parents—died, we were just children, Austin and me. No one else lived in this area but Indians, and they killed my parents, so we could not trust them. Austin says I became like a wild animal. I suppose he was right."

"How did you live with no money?"

"Money isn't important. We had plenty of fruits and berries, though the winters were hard. Austin killed animals for their meat, and to keep us warm. We lived in abandoned animals' dens, at times."

She interpreted his silence as shock, and bit her lip. "Anyway, after several years, the Duffys moved here and then—well, Austin only wanted to live like normal people. *Better* than normal people, actually. So Mr. Duffy helped him build our little house, and . . . " She shrugged. "There really isn't much more to say. Except that Austin would have had a much easier time of it, if it weren't for me. To be only twelve years of age and have to care for a three-year-old—why, I owe Austin my life."

The pain in his gut seared anew. So that was why she

was a spy like her brother. Out of a misguided sense of guilt.

Or perhaps Austin forced her to help him, perhaps she had no choice in the matter. An overriding empathy welled up in Philip, and a hope that perhaps Caroline was a little bit of the woman he'd first glimpsed, her natural honesty cloaked under her brother's harshness.

Her words broke into his thoughts, as she tried to make him understand.

"I like it here, in the forest. Most people would think our home too modest, but it suits my needs fine. In fact, sometimes I like the animal shelter, as poor as it is, even more than my home." She didn't say "because Austin isn't there," but the unspoken words drifted in the air.

"In addition, I eat no meat. I cannot bear to eat the flesh of animals. Everyone in these parts, as you well know, feasts on turkey or geese or rabbit or—"

"Or what?"

"Or deer. I could never bring myself to eat a deer."

"So what do you eat, *dear* Caroline?"

She ignored his sarcasm. "We have plenty. There are fruits and vegetables, and I make the best cheese." She crossed herself.

"Why do you do that?"

Puzzled, she waited until he crossed himself by way of explanation.

"I—I boasted, and boasting is sinful."

"So you cross yourself every time you think you've done something wrong."

"Not *think*, Philippe. It's quite automatic, you see, as I'm always doing things wrong. And lest I forget, there's always—"

"There's always what, Caroline?"

131

"Austin to remind me. Without Austin, I'd be way-ward, indeed."

"Is he cruel to you?"

"He punishes me, but it isn't cruelty. He simply points out the error of my ways. And if sometimes he seems a little severe, it's only that he'd have a much better life if it weren't for me. I—basically ruined his life."

"Was Austin always cruel to you?"

She shifted, and took her hand off a now sleeping Willie. "No, not always. He was supposed to wed a fine young lady once, a friend of the Duffys. But she refused him, because I was too young to live on my own and I was too . . . uncivilized to take into their home. She lived in Boston, you see, and said I'd never fit in. So you see, it's not fair of you to call Austin cruel. I've cost him his happiness."

"You? Uncivilized? You're different, yes. Not as re-fined as many of the young ladies I know. But refinement isn't eve—"

"You don't understand," Caroline cut in impatiently. "Though I still have much to learn, I'm nothing like the child I was before."

"Explain."

She looked at him through her lashes. "No."

"Then if you'll tell me no more about yourself, tell me what Austin is like." Perhaps if he pretended he'd never met her brother, she would give him some clues to the man's character.

"He's not bad, not really. He tries to do his best by me. It's just that he'd do anything for money, I think. And that clouds his judgment sometimes."

Well, that told him nothing he didn't already know. Anyone willing to sell his country's secrets had to be either

132

desperate or greedy. And Austin's note to the British had made it clear he was the latter. His price had been high. "And you don't desire wealth?"

She laughed bitterly. "No. Everything, everybody I've ever heard of who comes in contact with it, seems to become tainted somehow. I detest it. If Austin had money, he'd control more people than just me. Servants and the like, for example. People with money—their values are distorted. I didn't know that when Austin was supposed to wed Beatrice, but I know it now. Titus's parents have some money, a little, and do you know what his mother's most recent accomplishment was? Killing poor baby ducklings—" She stopped, unable to speak any further.

Her words strangled him. Did she know more about him than he'd thought? That he was heir to a fortune? Had Austin somehow learned his true identity and told Caroline? It was possible. The American could be using him until he'd exhausted all possibilities of earning money from the British. Then Mr. Swanson would simply turn Philip in to the Americans. In doing so he'd earn a higher rank. Hell, they'd probably make him a national hero.

And even if Caroline didn't know he was the Ferret, if she learned he'd been Philip Masterson long before he'd become the infamous spy, she'd never want him. Even if he could surmount the obstacles in the form of her brother, and the fact that she worked along with him as a traitor to her own country, Philip knew he was—what had she said? Ah, yes, *tainted*. Even though he'd been called much worse, nothing had cut him as deeply.

He shook his head and asked, "How do the rich become tainted?"

"Well, for one, my grandfather valued money more

than his own daughter. And what it does to cities . . . Austin wants to move somewhere like Philadelphia. He's always talking about the brick paved streets and the elegant landscaping and the tall buildings with their velvet draperies and polished wood.

"But tell me, Philippe. Can any of that be more beautiful than this?" She gestured to the sky and trees. "I don't deny anyone their right to appreciate things that are different from what I like, you understand. It's just that I would rather feel the warm, moist earth in spring, and the crisp crack of leaves and snapping twigs in autumn than hard, heavy bricks. And who would rather touch a woven silk than this?"

She tore a tuft of moss from the ground next to her and rubbed it lightly against his cheek, above his beard.

Her words surrounded him like a lulling chant, relaxing him. He leaned back, savoring the velvety texture gliding across his face. She reached across him and traced it over his other cheekbone, his forehead, and then the moss was gone, and he felt her fingertips outline first one brow, then the other, working their way toward his temples ever so softly, like a summer's breeze wafting through his hair.

He grabbed her wrists and pulled her to him, pleased that she offered no resistance, that her lips parted at his invitation. He plunged in, ravenous for the taste of her, for the feel of her. Their tongues danced and parried; his demanding, coaxing, wheedling; hers hesitating before accepting his intrusion, before surrendering to his demands. Her breathing came faster, and his mouth seared with the warmth of her. She was molten, as warm as the hot summer's day, and her fluid body melted into his.

He pulled his lips from hers and kissed her brows, her lids, her long lashes so much lusher than the moss. His mouth trailed kisses to her ear, and he felt her tense and tingle, and heard her little cry of surprise and pleasure as her arms clasped tightly around his neck. Quicker, faster, he moved to her throat, to her long, velvety throat, and lightly suckled the hollow at the base, while she twisted beneath him. His hands moved to her shoulders, feeling the smooth buttery dress, then stroked her bare arm lightly before moving down to her hips.

"Philippe, stop. Please stop."

He heard her words from far away, the melody an allegro played to a backdrop of leaves rustling gently in an intermittent breeze, but he was the conductor urging her on.

"No. We mustn't do this. No!"

She pushed against him harder. Dazed, he pulled away, looking down at her.

Breathing heavily, Caroline went limp, feeling as if her limbs had turned to jelly. She tried to cross herself, but her arm wouldn't cooperate and fell to her side. His kiss had caught her off guard. She had meant only to get him to trust her, to break down the barriers between them. Instead, she'd done, without thinking, what she had done in the past to her animals. She had reached out to him as she had reached out to them, but . . .

*No, Caroline. Be honest with yourself. You wanted him. He is so beautiful, and you wanted him.*

She crossed herself, jumped up, and ran to Derby.

"No, wait! Come back." By the time Philip struggled to his feet, the throbbing in his groin threatening to turn into a full-fledged explosion, she was astride Derby, heading toward home.

For a moment, Philip thought of running after her. Even with a bad leg he could catch up to the grunting, protesting horse trudging away from him. But then he thought better of it. Caroline must be the better agent; her instincts were right, while his, obviously, were secondary to his male desires. They should never have gotten so intimate.

The devil take it, he wanted her so much. Just to *pretend* his dream was real would be enough to last him a lifetime.

Maeve's brow creased as she watched from the doorway.

Caroline slid off Derby, slapping him on the haunches. The horse sighed and made his way to the water bucket.

"Lass, what is it? What's wrong? I' faith, I thought the Indians got ye, I did."

Avoiding her maid's eyes, Caroline went into the house and practically fell into the chair pulled up to the table. Her trembling legs would carry her no farther. "Nay, no Indians."

"What? Speak up, lass, I can barely hear ye."

Caroline's voice rose a measure louder, but Maeve still had to strain to hear.

"I said, no Indians."

When it became obvious she would say no more, Maeve huffed. "Well, then, I hope ye got the gun."

Pushing a strand of sweat-slicked hair behind her ear, Caroline looked at Maeve. "The gun? Oh, I forgot. I mean, I couldn't find it. It's lost, Maeve. I thought I'd remember what tree I buried it under, but—I just couldn't."

Maeve's eyes narrowed. "I'm not used to ye lyin' to me, but yer the mistress and I'm the servant, so I guess there's little use in me arguin' the point. Whatever yer reason for keepin' the gun, though, I'd be wonderin' if ye'd change yer mind if ye knew they were back."

"The Indians? They didn't harm you, did they? No, never mind, I can see they didn't."

Sighing loudly, Maeve answered, "Nay, they didn't hardly harm me. In fact, they left somethin' for ye again."

"Again? What this time?"

"Go out to the tree trunk. Ye practically rode right by it."

Cautiously, with Maeve at her side, Caroline walked out of the house, her gaze darting back and forth into the woods. On the fallen tree trunk about ten yards from the house, rested a leather-covered parcel.

"This is most peculiar." Caroline dipped her hand inside and pulled out some crystals of maple sugar. "How do you know it's for me?"

"Look closer. Yer slippin'. Ye used to notice everythin' about ye. It's a sad state, it is, when I can heed more than ye."

For once Caroline had no retort. She studied the leather bag for some minutes before spying the sign: a strand of her hair, a long silver wisp, twined around the rawhide string that pulled the bag tight.

She shuddered. "I don't like this. Wherever did they find a strand of my hair? Is it a warning of some sort, that they'll come to scalp me? I had a dream once . . . " She frowned and shook her head. It was no dream, it was real. Philippe had told her the Indians wanted her scalp.

"Ha! See, yer dreamin' again."

"Oh, Maeve, do be quiet."

The maid straightened and turned on her heel.

"Maeve, wait! I'm sorry, I have so much to talk to you about."

Caroline ran to apologize. For the remainder of the day, she tried to explain her feelings about Philippe, but finally gave up in frutration. How could she explain what she herself couldn't understand?

Mad Bird stole into the shelter, startling Philip.

"I didn't hear you come in," Philip explained in the Potawatomi language.

"The Silver Hair is gone."

"Yes."

Mad Bird laughed. "It looks, brother, like you would be one with her."

Philip was nonplussed, until he realized the savage referred to his appearance. Expecting Austin to arrive at any time, he'd pulled his shirt half out of his breeches so as to look disarrayed.

"Aye," he answered, laughing in agreement.

"The Potawatomi say the Special Ones are good bedders. Say the Great One gives them special happiness. When they bed with others, happiness comes to their partners as well."

His face impassive, Philip said, careful to keep his words even, "I wouldn't know. Tell me, Mad Bird, why did you come?"

He hoped it wasn't for food. The supply Caroline had brought had long been stored below in the root cellar. Philip was quite certain the Indian had not discovered it. The opening, hidden behind the animals' feed barrel, was not visible from where the Indian stood.

"Firewater." Mad Bird tipped his head back, mimicked drinking, then rubbed his belly, and smiled.

"I have no firewater now." At the Indian's angry scowl,

Philip said, thinking quickly, "But I should have some soon. If not when the sun rises tomorrow, then the day after. But you must do something for me first, Mad Bird."

Philip thought it good that from the first, all "gifts" to the savages had been tied to conditions. The Indians had been too happy to provide information regarding the Americans—at the moment, Philip had a hard time thinking of all the colonists as the enemy—in exchange for articles of clothing, hard liquor, and simple curiosities such as halfpennies and buttons.

He explained to the savage his latest stipulation: delivery of a certain trunk to the Canadian fort. After bringing back a message from the British general that the trunk was in good hands, the Indian would be rewarded with a jug containing firewater. Mad Bird agreed and left.

The burden of delivering Austin's parcel now lifted from his shoulders, Philip was surprised to feel a tremendous relief. He just hoped Austin came through with the liquor, as well as the trunk, or Mad Bird would turn on him. He hadn't realized how reluctant he'd been to become involved in a mission with blood money attached.

And for better or ill, he didn't want to go away from Caroline. He knew it was foolishness, this perception that as long as he remained in Michigan Territory, she'd be safe. She had a brother, after all.

A brother willing to sell military secrets.

When no one came to the cabin by dusk, Philip lay down on the plank, crossed his arms under his head, and willed the emptiness inside him to leave.

But like a clinging leech it remained locked inside, sucking his heart's blood away.

\* \* \*

It rained during the night, a light sprinkling rain that by morning turned into a steady downpour.

"Good," Caroline said, as she and Maeve tidied up the cabin. "It should cool things down. It's been unbearably hot lately."

"No warmer than other summers," Maeve replied. Then she looked at her mistress busily dusting the table. A slight flush stained Caroline's cheeks a rosy hue, although the air inside had chilled, and a refreshing breeze drifted through cracks between the logs. Once again Caroline sang to herself.

"I never heard ye sing that tune before. About a lover and a lass, is it? Did ye make it up?"

Caroline shrugged, embarrassed. "I guess so. I'm sorry, I didn't realize I was making so much noise."

"Nothing to be sorry about. But ye know, we should be plannin' yer weddin' today. Mrs. Duffy, if ye don't mind me sayin so, probably doesn't think ye can make the arrangements by yerself. And if ye don't be tellin' her yer plans soon, she'll be here, fixin' it all for ye."

When Caroline didn't respond, Maeve added, "She'll be seein' to it that hundreds of animals will be gettin' slaughtered to feed yer guests."

Her pronouncement brought the expected response.

"Oh! Oh, no, that will never do." Wrapping a tattered shawl around her, Caroline called over her shoulder as she went out the door, "Maeve, can you start the plans, please? I've taught you enough reading and writing for you to make a list, and we'll go over it when I get back."

Maeve ran to the door and called after her. "But where are ye goin'? Ye'll catch an ague. It's pourin' out there!"

Caroline worked at untying Derby's reins from the hitching post. The soaked leather squeaked and squished, while she undid first one knot, then the other. "There's a baby woodchuck I found, and I'm afraid it will catch a chill. I'll be back soon, don't worry."

"What if yer brother comes back?"

Her hair dripping water onto her eyelashes, Caroline looked up and smiled broadly. "He won't come today. Austin, go out in the rain?"

Chuckling, Maeve waved goodbye. A woodchuck indeed.

*Chapter Seven*

In her eagerness to reach the animal shelter, Caroline had forgotten how the wet weather bothered Derby's knees. She guessed that was why he hated mud. Even more than mud, he hated water, gingerly circumventing puddles as if they were raging whirlpools ready to swallow him instantly. By the time they arrived at the shelter, Caroline estimated that they'd covered four miles, instead of slightly over two. Her deerskin shift repelled the rain at first, but now it had absorbed twice its weight in water, and clung to her in heavy folds. Her bare legs and arms showed tiny goose bumps, and water sloshed in her loose-fitting moccasins.

But as she dismounted, glimpsing Philip's green shirt inside the doorway, warmth surged inside her.

"Philippe." The rain's patter drowned out her soft call. "Philippe," she tried again. "It's me, Caroline."

Exhaling in relief, Philip tucked his pistol back inside his breeches. Then he thought of the coin-laden pouch, ripped it from his waist, and tossed it behind the barrel in the corner. Grabbing the squirrel he'd set down moments before, he cradled it in his arms just as Caroline stepped inside.

"Oh." Her features softened. "You've been taking care of my squirrel for me."

Reddening, Philip suddenly thought of how ridiculous he looked, a brave British spy clutching a baby squirrel close to his chest, just as he'd held it since dawn to keep it warm. Then he took in Caroline's drenched appearance. "You'll freeze." Mentally slapping himself on the forehead, he thought, *French, Philip. You're supposed to be French.* "Come, *chérie*, dry off."

For the first time that morning, Caroline shivered. "I'm all right, really." She scanned the dark interior. Fawn huddled against a wall, Willie in a corner, a piece of meat under one paw. "You fed them."

Philip swallowed, wondering how a beam of sunlight filled the room in the middle of a steady rain. "They were hungry. I didn't know if you would come today."

She blushed, eyes downcast, and shivered again.

Placing the squirrel in her arms, he stepped behind her, removing the sodden shawl. He lifted her hair, kissing the base of her neck. White-hot spots of fire coursed through her where his lips scorched her skin, made all the hotter by the cold drops of water dripping from her hair down her arms. Then his tongue caressed her where his lips had branded her just moments before, and she felt a strange warmth between her legs, the heat radiating to the inner parts of her cold thighs.

He kissed her again.

"Philippe, no." She was amazed at the strength in her voice, when her limbs felt so weak, when her knees threatened to give way.

Still at her back, he breathed in her ear, a husky whis-

143

per with an undercurrent of teasing obedience. "Yes, *chérie*. I'll stop."

She waited, eyes half-closed, lips half-parted, breathing rapidly.

As he had been trained, Philip took a step back so stealthily no one would know he had moved by listening alone. And Caroline, with her eyes half-closed and ears filled with the sound of her quick, shallow gasps of breath, did not know he looked at her face in profile.

God, she was beautiful, in an unpolished sort of way. And practiced, to know how to respond so willingly to him. He'd deduced little love in Caroline's talk of Titus. Just references to pleasing Austin.

Shaking his head, Philip wondered if Titus had taught Caroline her skills. As hot-blooded as the woman was, it would be almost presumptuous to assume she only responded so eagerly to him. He gave a short, bitter laugh.

Caroline, still poised for the expectant kiss, heard him. Her eyes fluttered open.

"Oh!" Her cheeks turned hot. "Oh! I'm sorry, I'm such a fool, oh, oh . . . " Tears pricked behind her lids. Philip grabbed her wrist and stopped her just as she reached the door.

"Caroline, you can't go back out in that rain." Instantly remorseful, he guessed he'd hurt her somehow.

"No. I have to leave."

"But you just got here. Surely you didn't come just to leave again so quickly."

She refused to look at him, refused to see ridicule reflected in those eyes. For once she thought she should have listened to Austin. He'd always told her her spindly body and unsightly appearance warranted only aversion. How could she ever have thought Philippe would want

144

her, would love her for herself? His laughter confirmed what Austin always told her.

"I came to see my animals, and now that I know they're all right, I can go home."

"Nonsense. You will get yourself out of those soaked clothes right now."

He put his hands on either side of her to lift the garment over her head, but she crossed her arms and clamped her hands tightly over her shoulders. "No!"

*"Oui, chérie.* Not to worry. I'll turn my back to you. I won't see a thing."

She eyed him suspiciously. "And how do I know you won't turn around?" *I can't bear to have you laugh at me again.*

Sighing, he answered, ruing the irony in his question, "Don't you trust me?" The last person in the world she should trust was a British spy. He wanted to laugh again, but stopped himself.

"And—and what shall I change into?"

"Ah, you are just like most women, eh?" He clucked his tongue. "Always wondering what to wear. Well, Miss Caroline, I just happen to have here, in my possession, the most beautiful cape." With a flourish he yanked the blanket from the plank bed. At a loss for something to do after she'd left the day before, he'd washed it in the creek and hung it over some tree branches, where it had dried to a crackly stiffness.

He waited, wondering what she would do. Daphne would rather perish than clothe herself in a moth-eaten blanket, no matter how warm.

"Fine." She snatched it from him and waved him away. "Now, turn around."

When she pulled the shift up over her head, she shivered. The thought of Philippe standing near her, in the same room, caused little prickles to travel the length of her spine, and she rubbed her hands over her shoulders, warming herself. Then, with a heightened awareness of her nudity, she felt her chemise touch every part of her body, her breasts, the slight swell of her hips, the mound between her legs. She yanked the blanket from the bench and wrapped it around her, feeling vulnerable beneath her wrap. She knew she should cross herself, but then she'd have to let go of her blanket, and it would fall to the ground, exposing her. Oh, if only she had a form such as Maeve's, with her plump bosom and ample hips, he would have no cause to laugh at her!

*Caroline, you're going to be damned to hell if you keep thinking such things.*

*Well,* she argued with her conscience. *Perhaps I've just discovered I rather like heat.*

"May I turn around now?" Philip thought if he had to listen to the rustle of her clothing or the crackle of the blanket one moment longer, he'd burst. For a minute she had been nearly naked in the same room with him. He'd clenched his fists and counted, trying to quell his mounting desire. *Count, Philip, count. Think of something else. One, two, three* . . . A minute had never lasted so long.

"I—I'm finished now."

He turned.

Her eyes shone luminous and bright, while trembling hands clutched the ends of the blanket around her. Her hair still glistened with the water's sheen, a few defiant wisps about her face drying, forming soft curls.

Philip thought she had never looked more beautiful.

*"Madame."* He coughed. "Surely you will never warm up wearing those."

Caroline looked at her sodden moccasins, now caked

146

with mud. "Oh." She kicked them off and curled her toes. Her calves flexed with the motion.

For one brief moment Philip wished he could start over and abandon everything he'd ever known: his country, his estate and wealth, his own identity, and Daphne.

Much as the thought tempted him, his training forced him to consider both sides of every issue. Abandoning Britain would not instantly pave the way for a future with Caroline. From what he'd learned of Austin Swanson, the man would have no compunction in seeing Caroline's reputation ruined, especially if she married an enemy. And where would they go to live? To London or Clothclyde? She would be as unhappy in either place as a wild violet in a hothouse, and would likely wilt and die as fast.

And then, if he were truly honest with himself, he had no proof at all that she loved him. Women had responded to him physically before, had even professed their love for him, but it had been lies. All lies. Even Jane, when he'd told her he would only come into his inheritance if he'd wed Daphne, had suddenly had second thoughts. And third, and fourth. He'd assumed she loved him enough to marry him without his fortune, but he'd learned his lesson. He was a spy, and spies could not operate on conjecture. If he forced himself to face facts, he had to admit that Caroline could easily have something in common with the women back home. She may not be using him for his money, but she was using him for something else.

"Sit down," he ordered.

Caroline, never taking her eyes from him, scooted to the far end of the plank, her body flattened against the wall next to her.

Philip's lips twitched. Maintaining his distance was

going to be easier than he thought, if she continued hugging the wall.

"I—I've got to get my clothes dry," she squeaked.

"I know, *madame*. I'm going to build a small fire."

"Won't it get hot in here? It's just now started to cool off."

"I had no intention of building it in here, *madame*."

She flinched. The *madame* sounded sarcastic to her ears. Still, it was better than that, that *chérie!* His back now turned to her, he stooped over, gathering leaves the animals had dragged inside. His breeches stretched taut across his buttocks. Caroline swallowed and watched him saunter outside, his hands fisted shut.

The rain had stopped. Caroline tried to look through the cracks in the walls, but climbing ivy had grown so thick over the structure, she couldn't see anything but darkness. Hesitating an instant, she pulled the blanket tightly around her, then rose, and peeked around the corner of the doorway.

Philip had taken some sticks and arranged them in a tepee shape as high as her knee. Somehow he'd managed to start a fire on the ground beneath it, and the damp wood smoked.

When he came back inside, she stepped back out of his way. "Those sticks will never spark a fire. They're too wet."

"I know, *chérie*."

Caroline felt her cheeks grow hot. Why did he have to say *chérie?*

He coughed slightly. "The fire beneath it will dry the sticks. If they dry soon enough we should be able to make a fire of them as well, and dry your frock so it's fit to wear."

"Oh. How did you get it to start?"

"I used the dried leaves I picked up inside."

"Oh. But how will you keep it hot?"

*I can keep anything hot,* he wanted to say, but didn't. "How do you manage to live in these parts, Lady Caroline? Surely Austin can make a fire."

Chuckling, she replied, "If there's any fire to be had, Philippe, I start it."

He stared at her, nodding slowly. A hot flush crept up her cheeks and she turned away, feeling like a cornered animal seeking escape.

"Sit down where you were before, Lady Caroline. I will get you something to eat."

Before she could protest, he lifted the barrel top that covered the entrance to the root cellar and dropped himself down. Caroline smiled when she heard him smother an oath. He must have landed on his sore leg. Just as she thought, he was the type of man who would conveniently forget he had ever been injured or sick.

The cellar extended beyond the shelter, so as not to weaken the floor, supported by a few rotted tree branches Philip had found. While he sorted through the crocks and jars she had brought, Caroline breathed easier. When he was in the same room with her, she felt like he took all the air.

Scanning the shelter, now devoid of animals, she noted a few droppings in a corner. Apparently Willie hadn't wanted to leave the shelter during the rain. Always fastidious, it suddenly became extremely important to her that the shelter sparkled—as much as it could sparkle, considering its dank interior. Quickly, before Philip returned, she let the blanket fall from her shoulders to the plank and hurried over to the broom, sweeping the droppings out-

149

side and around the door into the high growth of weeds. Water dripped from the uneven overhang to the nape of her neck. Squealing in shock at the coldness, she ran inside, grabbed her blanket, and flung it back around her, then went to the corner to replace the broom. She set it behind the barrel, but the bottom did not touch the ground. Puzzled, she pushed a little harder. The broom pushed down, then popped back slightly. Afraid a small animal had died behind the barrel, she bent down on her hands and knees and forced her hand between the staves and the wall. Her fingers touched something coarse. Not an animal's fur, surely. Tugging, she yanked, baffled at its heavy weight despite its small size. Finally she freed the pouch, looked at it in bewilderment, released the tie—and her mouth dropped open.

Coins. Gold coins.

Philip's fingertips showed over the cellar's opening.

"If I hand you something, will you take it from me?" he asked.

"Umm, yes. Just one minute." Looking around, she hesitated, then tied the pouch, and shoved it back in the corner, hidden behind the barrel.

Imagining Caroline fumbling with her blanket, Philip was tempted to pull himself up and peek over the side. Really, her modesty was tiresome. He could, he supposed, push the crocks she'd selected up and out of the cellar, but he feared they would break and leak their contents all over the earthen floor. The grit of dirt mixed with food never did much for his appetite.

Caroline tied the blanket in a knot at her throat, then knelt, keeping the ends tucked under her knees. As much as she deplored wearing clothing fashioned of animal skins, at the moment her shift seemed much less cumbersome and more appealing than the blanket, which covered every inch of her skin except her hands and neck.

One by one she took from him three crocks and two small wooden boxes, careful to avoid letting their fingertips touch.

After pulling himself up and over the side, Philip made a low, swooping bow. "Join me in my repast, Lady Caroline."

The precious butter and strawberry jam, spread thickly on some hard, dry crackers, melted on Caroline's tongue. Curious, how the same food she ate at home tasted so much better here.

Then she thought of the coins, and the food congealed in her throat.

"What is it?" Philip asked.

She wanted to throttle him. Did he have to notice everything? "I was—I was just wondering if the sticks were dry enough yet to start a fire. I need to get back, or Austin will come looking for me."

"Come looking for you? But how is he to do that? I thought you said he served in the army."

Shrugging, she bit once more into the cracker, chewed and swallowed it before answering.

"Yes, but at least until a war's declared, the men who live nearby are allowed to visit home. It saves the government money." As soon as the words were out of her mouth, she wanted to grab them and stuff them back inside. She hadn't meant to mention the word "money." Would he suspect? Did he know?

But Philip munched away on his slice of smoked pork, as if he hadn't a care in the world.

She watched him, and blanched.

"All right, *madame*. I'll start a fire and hang your dress."

*You think you know everything.* "That's not why I—" she fumbled for the word.

"Turned whiter than a summer cloud, *chérie?*"

"Don't call me *chérie!*"

"Why, *ma petite?*" he asked innocently.

"Or *ma* whatever-it-is, either. Oh! You're insufferable! No wonder you're not married!"

His lips turning up at the corner, Philip rose, dusted the dirt clinging to his knees, and taking an inordinate amount of time, brushed it from his bottom. Then he grabbed her shift, flung it over his shoulder, and winked at her as he walked outside.

"That—that *man!*" Caroline wished she had something to throw, but all she had was her blanket, and that wouldn't do at all.


Titus saw Caroline walking in the Swansons' garden. His horse drooped from being ridden hard. It plodded slowly toward the house, giving him ample time to study her from afar.

As she bent over to pick up some vegetables, a basket flung over her arm and a large-brimmed hat shading her face, he marked how well she looked. Her ample bosom spilled over her neckline while her plump thighs, their outline visible beneath the snug dress, instilled in him a surge of desire. Thank God. For a few weeks there, as the soldiers had filled his ears with tales of their amorous adventures, he'd wondered if something was wrong with him. He'd always thought of Caroline as a friend, but as she'd reminded him, he'd never thought of her *that* way. Apparently, being away from her brother had improved her. She'd filled out in all the places he'd found lacking.

As he neared, imagining nestling his face between those plump pillows of breasts, she looked up at him . . .

*The maid.*

Gulping, he doffed his hat and dismounted, leading his horse the rest of the way.

"Why, Master Titus!" Maeve beamed with pleasure.

He stared at the enchanting sprinkling of freckles on her nose, wondering how he'd never noticed them before.

"Um—" drat! Oh, yes. "Maeve, is your mistress home?" He finally remembered her name.

A shadow fell over her face. "No, I'm sorry, sir. She went ridin' this mornin'."

"This morning? But didn't it rain here?"

"Aye, sir. But ye know how Miss Caroline is about her animals."

*Oh, yes. Those blasted animals.* "How long ago did she leave?"

Looking up at the sky, then back at him, Maeve replied, "I wouldn't be knowin' exactly, sir." She hesitated. "I reckon its been a few hours, though."

Titus's brows shot up. "A few hours? The Indians—"

"Nay," Maeve interrupted. "I don't think we have anythin' to be fearin' from the Indians, sir. For some reason, they seem to like the lass."

Frowning, Titus examined the polished pebbles that Maeve took from her apron and poured into his hand. Some caught the sun, glittering and winking back at him, specks of silver captured in an almost translucent pink rock. "What's the meaning behind these?"

Maeve shrugged. "I don't know, sir. Except the Indians have been leavin' all sorts of pretties for her. They always put them on that tree stump." She pointed across the yard.

"How do you know they're for Caroline?"

"Well, sir, whatever they bring always has somethin' of that color in it." She pointed to the flecks in the rocks, and he looked at her, perplexed.

"Ye know, silver, like her hair."

He grunted, saying half-aloud, "It always seemed more like gray to me. Well, we'll figure this out later. So more than likely, it isn't the Indians who've delayed her. Say, does she still have that bear cub?"

It was Maeve's turn to be confused. "Bear cub?"

"Yes. I'd better go there and see if something's wrong." He led Myron away to save the horse from exhausting itself. If Caroline were sick or injured, Myron might have to carry her back. "If our paths cross and she comes back, would you give her a message for me?"

"Aye, sir."

"Tell her my mother's invited all the guests for the wedding. Since you and Caroline are making the plans for the food, Mother says you should count on fifty."

"Fifty," Maeve echoed hollowly. "Aye, sir."


By the time Philip had hung her shift to dry and reentered the shelter, Caroline decided she'd have to make the best of her situation and use the time to good purpose. "Sit down," she commanded.

This time he couldn't resist. Philip sat cross-legged on the ground, his arms curved in a begging position, tongue hanging out while he panted. Philip prided himself on his ability to assume disguises without so much as changing his hat, but he'd never imagined imitating a dog.

Caroline laughed despite herself.

"Ah, that is good, *chérie*. One who can laugh at himself

154

is a rare person indeed." He rose, dusting his pants off, and bowed. "I presume my performance entitles me to a seat?"

Nodding, she tried to maintain a serious demeanor, but the twinkle in her eyes gave her away.

"Now, what would the *madame* wish me to do?"

"Tell me about yourself."

His eyes became unreadable. "About me? But there is so little to tell."

*The devil take it, Philippe. Trust me.* The involuntary oath surprised her. She thought of crossing herself, but if she let go of the blanket, the loosely tied knot could come undone, and her scant covering would fall to the floor. A time and a place for everything. "As there was little for me to tell you," she said patiently. "But I confided in you."

Sighing, he replied, "Very well, then. What do you wish to know about?"

"Oh, about your home. What is Frenchtown like? I know it's not far, but I've never been there."

"Frenchtown." He paused. "Frenchtown is not much different than this, really. Many trees, small creeks. Not the big lake you have here."

"And is everyone of French descent?"

He looked away, wondering how much she really knew about Frenchtown, wondering if this was a test. He would have to be careful to keep his answers vague. "Most people are French, yes." That seemed a reasonable deduction.

"And the homes?"

"Not like this."

She giggled. "Well, our homes aren't like this, either. This is more of a cave, almost. Thank heavens, it has no door, otherwise, I don't think I'd be able to bear it."

*"Oui,* it is dark, is it not?"

"Yes. But you're avoiding my question."

"Which is . . . "

"Your home. How many rooms has it?

The urge to say oh, thirty-seven, unless you count the servant's quarters, sprang to mind, but instead Philip answered, "Four." Her response would tell him whether he'd given the right answer.

"Well, four is a nice size, I should think. Titus's parents have six rooms, counting the two up, and it's much too large for me."

He arched a brow. Too large? Really.

"Your family?" she prodded gently.

It certainly sounded like a test. "I have no family." But that was too close to the truth, so he felt compelled to add, "I have a brother, but he doesn't live in Frenchtown."

"Oh? Where does he live?"

"Philadelphia."

She wrinkled her nose. "No wonder you like it here better. That is, you do, don't you?"

"Yes." He was surprised to find that he meant it. Whatever Philadelphia was like, it sounded far too much like London. He'd always enjoyed London, but now . . .

"Have you—have you ever been married?"

He thought a minute, trying to figure out how to answer this question, when inspiration struck. Sighing loudly, he clasped a hand over his heart. *"Oui, chérie,* long ago. She died." He forced a tear down his cheek. His right cheek, the one nearest Caroline. "Both my, my son and she—they were slaughtered by Indians." He buried his face in his hands so he could keep a straight face. This was too much fun!

"Oh, Philippe, I'm sorry. Was your wife Daphne?"

A flicker of surprise crossed his face. "Yes. How did you know?"

"You spoke about her when you were fevered. What was she like, Philippe?"

"She was pretty and charming. Everyone loved her. She was so . . . "

He brought his hands to his face. Imagining the look on Daphne's face if she found out he'd gone and buried her, brought tears to his eyes. His shoulders shook from muffled laughter.

Caroline crossed herself; that pang of jealousy was a most uncharitable feeling.

"Oh, you poor man! I never should have asked you, it was none of my business." Her heart almost broke for him, as she patted his shaking shoulders over and over. How sad! No wonder he didn't trust anybody. First his wife and child slaughtered by Indians, then falsely accused of a crime he didn't commit, then bitten by a snake that left him with a bad leg . . . her own troubles seemed mild in comparison. This must be an example of Divine Providence. God must have brought him here for her to heal him, his soul as well as his body. She'd have to do the best she could. First, though, she needed to find out if he was in any danger, because if he was, she'd have to tell Titus. Titus would help him.

As gently as possible, she asked, "Are the Indians after you?"

Instantly his shoulders stopped shaking. "Pardon, *madame?*" he asked, his words muffled by his hands.

"I wondered if the Indians were after you. Because, you see, I remember you arguing, I think, with one of them. I wondered if they were trying to murder you as well. You know, to make it—to make their deed complete."

Philip looked at her, his eyes soulful. "No. They—they are fearful I will summon all my friends and attack them, even though I keep assuring them I will not. It's the wrong band, you see. It's the Potawatomi who killed my—my wife and child, not the Shawnee."

"Oh. Oh dear, it's true then. I always thought the Potawatomi to be peaceful, but—"

"Oh, no, *madame*. None of them are peaceful. Stay as far from them as you can."

"Oh. Yes, of course." Twisting a long strand of her hair around her fingers, another thought struck her. "Philippe, may I ask you just one more question?" She looked at him uneasily. "I promise, I'll never ask you another about your—about your wife."

Swallowing, he gestured in supplication.

He looked so beaten, Caroline spoke hurriedly before she lost her nerve. "The Indians. Did they give your wife any sort of—presents—before they—you know."

"Presents?"

"Yes, presents. Gifts."

"No, *madame*. Why do you ask?"

Keeping her response as nonchalant as possible, for she didn't wish to trouble him anymore, Caroline said, "Oh, nothing. I just wondered."

After a few minutes of Caroline gently stroking his hand, she said, "Philippe, it's getting late. I hate to leave you, but if I don't, I fear someone will come looking for you." She chuckled wryly. "Maeve's afeared of leaving our home, but I believe she's more fearful of staying there by herself."

His brows shot up. "Maeve?"

"My maid. More my friend, really. Philippe, you—you need a friend."

Bringing her hand to his lips, he said, *"Oui, madame.* But who would befriend a poor soul like me?"

*I have,* she wanted to reply. But somehow, she couldn't. He would have to see that himself. She withdrew her hand. "Would you please check to see if my shift is dry?"

*"Oui, madame."* Then he whispered so low she thought she imagined it. "For you I would do anything."


Titus peered around the tree.

Derby was asleep on his feet outside the shelter. Myron whinnied a soft greeting, which Derby acknowledged by opening one eye.

Smoke rose beyond the far side of the building. Titus was impressed but not surprised by Caroline's skill at setting the cone-shaped sticks afire. She hardly needed a man for anything.

Her frock hung from a tree over the fire. Again he begrudgingly admired her for having the good sense to dry what had obviously become wet before returning home.

Tying Myron to a tree, he took a few steps, then stopped.

If her dress was hanging from a tree, what was she wearing?

It wouldn't do, not at all, to walk in on his intended to discover her . . .

He shivered.

Then another, more fearsome thought struck him.

He could see most of her animals tugging at weeds, or in the case of the birds, pulling worms from the moist, pungent ground. The deer was curled up near the fire, though he couldn't see the raccoon.

But what of the cub? The bear cub?

Had it—had it devoured Caroline? If she'd been—oh, heaven help her, if she'd been in an—an *unnatural* state, without clothing to protect her, one well-placed bite could mortally wound her.

He straightened his shoulders. Regardless of her dishabille, he had to make the sacrifice. He had to make certain she was safe.

He took three steps and ducked behind a tree. A scuffling came from inside the shelter; he wondered if the bear had torn loose. Gulping, Titus watched and waited. Then he heard something else. Whistling. Strange. He'd heard Caroline hum before, even sing on occasion, and her voice was undoubtedly the most pleasant thing about her, but whistling? He shook his head. He couldn't ever remember hearing her whistle, and if she did, she certainly wouldn't sound like that. Unless she had an ague. Yes, that must be it; she must have taken an ague during her ride through the rain and . . .

His mouth dropped. Out of the shelter strode a man. A man not much taller than himself, but certainly broader, at least across the shoulders. If he hadn't heard the whistling, he might not have seen the man leave the shelter, so well did the green and tan clothing and high brown boots blend into the trees. And—did he have a limp? Titus squinted, but couldn't tell for certain.

The man's back was to him as he headed to the fire. No, to the tree. He was going to the tree, and he was taking down—he was taking down Caroline's dress! And now he was heading, with a smile on his face to—oh, the shame of it all! He has heading back inside!

"Ho! You there, halt!"

But the man had already gone inside. Racing to the shelter, Titus wondered if he'd save Caroline in time.

Caroline took the shift from Philip. "Thank you. I really must be getting home."

"Well, I should say *so!*" Titus sputtered from the doorway.

Caroline looked at him in surprise.

"Why, Titus! I never expected you here!"

"Obviously!"

Philip watched the exchange. This was Caroline's lover? This little dumpling of a man? Well, if she wanted someone the exact opposite of her brother, she'd found him, someone short and squat where Austin was gaunt and tall, that was for certain.

"You!" Titus's face turned purple as he squared off in front of Philip.

"Oh, put your fists down, *monsieur*. I am hardly in the mood for a fight."

"If you don't want to fight with your hands, then perhaps *this* will change your mind." Too late, Titus realized he'd left his pistol in the holster strapped to Myron's back. All he could point at the stranger was a finger.

Philip cocked an eyebrow. "Oh, you want to finger wrestle, do you? *Mon Dieu*, I don't know if I am up to it."

Caroline bit her nails. She didn't dare burst into laughter, especially when she saw the look of humiliation pass across Titus's face—a feeling with which she was too well acquainted. "Titus," she began gently.

"Don't! Oh, Caroline, just don't!" He shook her arm off his shoulder before stalking to the wall, arms crossed in front of him.

"Titus, it's not what it seems."

"Oh, it's not, is it? Tell me, Caroline," he said, mimicking Austin's best sarcastic tone. "What is it? Is it your *bear cub?*"

Caroline winced. Titus didn't deserve this. "He's a soldier, Titus."

"So, that makes it all right? Is this how you show your fealty to God and your country?"

"Titus, listen to me, please."

Her intended stared at her and sighed. He could not look at the man with the dark hair tied elegantly back in a queue, leaning against the doorjamb. "Go ahead, Caroline. Explain."

Philip coughed. "If you'll pardon me, I'll excuse myself."

Neither Caroline nor Titus looked at him as he went outside, though Caroline knew he listened just out of sight.

"All right, Caroline," Titus said wearily. "Let's get it over with."

"Titus, it's not how it looks. He's an American soldier. I found him injured; he had a snakebite."

"So you brought him here like one of your pets," he said flatly.

She averted her gaze. "Yes."

The bite of sarcasm once more crept into Titus's voice. "Did you not think to tell someone, Caroline? A physician, perhaps? Ah, now I remember. *That's* why you wanted a physician's manual! I remember distinctly, you said you wanted something to do with snakebites. And all along I thought it was—" His voice broke.

"Titus, please. I did think of taking him to a physician, I did, you must believe me. But he would get in trouble. He's been accused of taking someone's life, another soldier's, but it wasn't him, it was someone else, and——and they'll hang him!"

He rued her gullibility, but knew she wasn't intentionally lying to him. He'd never known Caroline to lie, even when it would behoove her to do so. "And you believed him, of course. You believed that someone who would take advantage of a woman would be so honorable as to be innocent of a crime which he's been accused of committing."

"But he hasn't taken advantage of me, Titus," she said softly.

"*Oui,* my good man." Philip walked back in and put a hand on Titus's shoulder, noticing the younger man stiffen. "I did not take advantage of your Caroline. Why, she's spoken so fondly of you, I would be a rake indeed to take advantage of one so loyal."

Titus missed the look of gratitude Caroline flashed Philip. "She did?" he asked doubtfully. "She spoke fondly of me?"

"Yes, of course, I did, Titus. Now, listen to the rest. Perhaps you can help."

"Me?" His chest puffed, reminding Philip of a banty rooster. "How can I help?"

Philip motioned to her to be quiet, but Caroline shook her head. "No, Philippe, it's all right. Titus can be trusted."

By the time Caroline finished her story, Titus vowed to find the real killer of the murdered general. For once in his life, he would not tell Austin. Austin would kill Caroline, if he found out she was harboring a man. No, he would have to clear Philippe's name by himself. Then the man could go back to his regiment. Where he belonged.

# Chapter Eight

In the morning, Maeve was not surprised to again find a present on the log outside the door. She called aloud to Caroline, busy indoors knitting socks for men in the army.

"Look, lass. This time they left ye somethin' for yer hair."

Her first impulse was to tell Maeve to throw it away, but on second thought, Caroline decided she'd better inspect the gift, to see if she could discern some sort of message or meaning behind it. So far, the entire matter puzzled both of them. Perhaps Philippe would have a clue . . .

"Oh, Maeve, it is lovely, isn't it?"

The brow band, of slender strips of birch bark, was interwoven with gaily colored bits of feathers and pearlescent shavings from mussel shells.

"Aye. I don't mean to be scarin' ye, lass, but could it be they'd be wantin' your scalp adorned, before they'd be choppin' it off?"

"Maeve, that's truly horrid! What a terrible thing to—"

The sound of a horse's hooves pounding the ground stopped her. Maeve turned and looked, her eyes big.

"Get inside," Caroline ordered. *"Get inside!"*

Seconds later maid and mistress scurried about the cabin, bolting the door shut and running to find whatever they could use for protection. Maeve brandished the kitchen knife, slicing great paths of air like a mad genie, while Caroline ran to the flintlock on the wall. A frenzied pounding at the door nearly drowned out Austin's bellowing voice.

"Open up. Open up, I say! Caroline, Maeve, open this door now!"

Caroline ran to the door at once, raising the heavy latch. Austin threw himself against the door just as she pulled on the handle.

"It's an odd time for prayin'," Maeve muttered under her breath to Caroline.

"Shush, Maeve," Caroline admonished, smothering a smile. "Here, Austin, give me your hand. I'll help you up."

Scowling, Austin rose to his feet and dusted off his loose-fitting breeches. "I hurry here to save your lives, and you just happen to open the door the very moment I lean against it. That's the thanks I get. You're such—"

"Save our lives?" Caroline asked, sobered. "Are we in danger?"

Austin examined his fingernails. "I would say so. War's been declared."

Caroline froze. "War?"

"Yes, war. We have no time to waste. The British knew about it weeks ago, but some brainless ninny didn't see fit to send a courier to General Hull. Instead they sent the message by post. We just learned ourselves this morning."

"Will you have to fight?"

"Not likely. But I won't be able to come home as often.

I'll have to accompany General Hull on his sojourns. Your greatest danger is from the Indians. The British have bought their loyalty with spirits and firearms."

"And the Master Titus? Will he have to fight?" Maeve asked.

Arching a brow, Austin decided to answer the maid rather than upbraid her for her cheekiness in asking him a question. The day's announcement had set his blood to running. He had all he could do to refrain from rubbing his hands together. Now that war had been declared, he'd have even more opportunities to make money. A lot of money. "Master Titus is willing to risk his life for his country, if it comes to that. All the more reason to go on with your wedding, Caroline. If Titus dies in battle, at least you'll be left an independent widow. As General Hull's personal courier, however, I'll do my best to see that he is safe, at least until your nuptials take place. We wouldn't want anything to happen to your husband-to-be, would we?" He pinched Caroline's cheek.

"He's not my husband-to-be. I'm not marrying Titus."

Austin waved his hand as if shooing off a pesky fly. "Of course, you are."

"I'm not."

His eyes narrowed. "You're wedding him come September."

"No." She took a step backward. "We've spoken; Titus agrees."

Seeing his open palm come toward her, she braced herself for the familiar sharp sting.

"You're lying to me," Austin seethed. "I've seen Titus on several occasions. He would have told me—rather, *asked* me—if he'd wanted to change plans."

She glared at him, heedless of the welt rising on her

cheek. "He agreed not to wed, if certain conditions were met. He isn't aware of it yet, because I haven't had the opportunity to tell him, but the conditions have been met. Or they will be, soon."

"What conditions? What have you done to make Titus not want you anymore? *What have you done?*"

"I upped your ante, Austin. Titus doesn't want me, he wants a new printing press."

"Which he's going to purchase with your dowry."

"Not is, *was*. I'm buying it for him."

"You? Ha! Where are you going to get money, Caroline? Sell your body?" He laughed sarcastically. "The soldiers around here may be desperate, but not that— wait a minute." He paused. "Have you sold yourself to that—that idiot? That hovel *is* your animal shelter, isn't it? And you sold yourself to that poor excuse for a—"

"He's not an idiot! And I've never sold myself, never—"

Austin grabbed her arm and twisted it behind her back. "You'll wed Titus or I'll kill you. And you won't say a word of this to anyone."

Gritting her teeth, she ground out, "Go ahead, Austin. Kill me. Then explain how your sister died, and you weren't man enough to protect her. That ought to make you look good in your general's eyes, won't it?"

With a jerk he released her, shoving her to the floor. "I'm only trying to see you taken care of, before I get out of this hellhole. And I *will*, you know. You won't hold me back any longer." He pivoted on his heel and stalked out the door, slamming it behind him.

"Lass, when will ye ever learn? Ye get nowhere by defyin' yer brother. And ye know, if ye'd just let yerself cry, he'd stop. Why must ye act so strong?"

Rubbing her aching arm, Caroline replied, "Because he loves it when he thinks he's hurt me. He must never see me cry."

The regular pounding of approaching horse's hooves alerted Philip and scattered the animals to their hiding places outside. He peered around the corner of the building, thinking how ironic it was that in this secluded forest cove he had to identify his visitor in order to adjust his attire to suit their expectations. All he lacked were calling cards.

Ah, good. He'd surmised his guest's identity correctly. Stumbling forward, he slackened his jaw and affected a slightly blank stare.

Austin marched toward him and asked, "Have you something for me?"

Nodding, Philip uncurled his fist to reveal a crumpled piece of parchment. *Take it, you bastard. I'll be damned if I'm going to hand it to you.*

When it became apparent that the idiot would not drop the paper, Austin gingerly took it from his palm, then backed away. He turned to shield the missive from the fool's view. The man could not be totally without intellect, as he had managed to find his way to the British. Then again, even salmon, when they spawned, returned to their place of birth.

*My Dear Sir,* the letter began. *This Goode Man, apparently without Abilitie to Speake, has brought us your Message. Wee intercepted the Vessel and Received your Package. Although This Man seems without Wit, He has served Us Welle. We have Bathed and Clothed Him as a sign of our Seriousness in Accepting your Offer.*

Brows arched, Austin looked up. "Bathed him, eh? He certainly doesn't look it. Too bad you didn't shave him as well."

Philip's beard effectively hid the muscle twitching in his jaw.

The rest of the letter confirmed what Austin had hoped.

*The Fool seems unable to Talke naught but a Few Simple Words. Any further Communication may be sent on Paper Through Him. We have sent back with him a Token of our Esteem Upon receipt of your Letter.*

"Good." Austin strode to his horse, beckoning Philip to follow. "Apparently you understand much more than you speak. Do you have something for me?"

Philip nodded.

"Let me see. Now."

His hand trembling for Austin's benefit, Philip fumbled inside the pouch under his shirt and dumped out ten gold coins.

"Only ten?" Austin spat. "We're at war. That information's worth—or did you give the rest to a woman? A gray-haired woman?"

Confusion showed plainly on Philip's face. He shook his head no.

Austin shrugged. "I don't know. I tend to believe you more than her. I didn't actually see any of Caroline's money—maybe it isn't gold at all. She always has these strange ideas, and—oh, why am I bothering to tell you? Here."

He scribbled some words on another of Caroline's pamphlets. Philip thought he'd spied a few medical prescriptives, one about snakebite, and took it when Austin handed it to him.

"Tell them," Austin said, practically snarling, "that unless they send me double this amount, they'll get nothing further from me. Never mind. This missive tells them. As for you—you stay away from my sister! I swear, I'll kill you if you lay a hand on her. If I didn't need you to act as a messenger, I'd kill you now."

Philip widened his eyes in fear.

"Remember, fool. I'll kill you."

Philip nodded in response. Austin Swanson turned his stomach.

While he waited for Mad Bird, Philip tried to make sense of his encounter with Austin. The man had been livid to discover that Caroline knew about him. Then perhaps she wasn't a spy after all. But why had she told her brother about him, when she'd pledged to keep his identity a secret? Was it a classic case of a woman not being able to keep a confidence? Or was it something more?

As expected, Mad Bird, watching from the forest, arrived within minutes. The simple map Philip drew in the ground showed the destination of the British fort in Canada. Once he sealed the agreement with a handshake, Philip watched the Indian ride away. Then he went to the creek to wash away the dirt he'd smeared on his face.

"Philippe, Philippe! Where are you?" Caroline's voice echoed off the trees.

Donning his breeches and tossing his shirt over his shoulder, he advanced toward Caroline.

Relief washed over her as she looked into his ever-changeable eyes. "Oh, Philippe, I was so worried."

"Why, *chérie?*"

"Because there's a war going on, and the Indians are

helping the British, and oh, it's all too horrible to talk about."

So, the Americans had finally learned they were at war. He would have laughed if their predicament wasn't so pitiful. "Then, *madame,* I suppose I must leave here and head back to my regiment."

"Oh, no, you can't, you can't."

*Indeed,* he thought. *You toy with my brain, Caroline Swanson. For a moment I'd forgotten the Potawatomi took my boat to Fort Malden. Indeed I can't.* "And why can't I?" *Did she know about that, too?*

"Because, because—"

"Here, *chérie,* catch your breath. Did you gallop your horse the entire way here?"

"No, I ran. I left Derby at home. He never gallops; his knees are too bad."

"His knees are fine. You coddle him."

"I don't coddle him, I—" As Caroline struggled to catch her breath, she sank to the ground on the shirt he had just spread over the earth. Then she noticed.

He wore no shirt.

Standing, feet splayed, hands on hips, his scarred leg covered by his breeches, Philip reveled in her perusal of him. It would be so easy to take her, she was so willing . . .

She tore her gaze away and gulped. "There's no place safer for you to stay than here. You can't go back to your regiment. Unless you've found your general's real killer?"

"No."

"Then you see, you must stay here. It's not likely the British would attack on this very spot, at least according to Austin."

"Was it Austin who beat you, Caroline?"

"Beat me?" She laughed and touched her cheek. "Oh, this? I missed the bottom step of my ladder and fell."

"So that explains your face. What about your arm, Caroline? Did you also wrench your arm in the fall?"

"Oh, I'd forgotten about my arm. It hardly hurts at all." She winced as he touched her.

"Did Austin force you to tell him about me?" he whispered. "Is that why he beat you?"

She refused to look him in the eye. "I never told Austin about you. And I told you, he doesn't beat me." She fought to keep from crossing herself. "Now, you must stay here, but take care. We have another problem."

"Which is?"

"The Indians. They know you are here, and Austin says"—She did not notice his grimace. "Austin says they're sympathetic to the British. They've already killed your wife and son. What if they decide to murder you as well?"

"Not to worry, Caroline. I have my gun. Besides, the Indians will give me no trouble. You've only seen one Potawatomi, *oui?*"

*"Oui,"* she responded, pleased she'd answered him in French. Perhaps if she could learn his language, he'd feel more comfortable with her, confide in her more, and then, ultimately, trust her.

"Then it is safe, you see. The Potawatomi is frightened of me."

"Why?"

He invented a lie on the spot. "He says any man who survives a snakebite is special."

"So that's why they won't hurt you. I can understand that, but it's most puzzling. *I* didn't get bitten by a snake."

His brows arched. "You?"

"Yes. The Indians have been leaving gifts for me."

"Shawnee or Potawatomi?" he asked. Apparently he'd convinced Mad Bird too well that she was a Special One.

"I don't know. Do you think that if I showed you some of the things they've given me, you could tell me which tribe it is?"

"Perhaps. Or I could ask the Potawatomi who comes here."

"Oh, Philippe, would you? That would be wonderful." Without thinking, she jumped up and threw her arms around him.

It took Philip almost a minute to allow himself to respond to her, almost a minute before he returned the embrace, savoring the soft, feminine feel of her arms around his body. Sighing, he rested his chin in her hair and kissed the top of her head. It felt so good to have someone worry about his safety. Daphne had acted as if she'd cared, but he'd always had the nagging suspicion she only wanted to ensure he lived long enough to inherit Strathmore Castle. Despite evidence to the contrary, a small part of him that he had not listened to in a long time, told him not all of Caroline's anxiety was contrived. Some of it had to be real.

Caroline, treasuring the feel of his furry chest tickling her face, the masculine scent of him, the strength and security his arms offered as they encircled her and held her tight, leaned into him. A few drops of water dripped from his hair and beard, creating rivulets down his body. The temptation to catch them with her tongue, to feel his skin beneath her mouth, almost drove her mad, and her fingers worked their way into the thick, wavy hair.

He lowered his head to hers and opened her mouth, hearing her moan of surprise and pleasure as he thrust his tongue deep inside. His warming body pressed against her, driving his head to her face and breasts.

"Caroline," he murmured hoarsely.

"Philippe, please, oh, I mustn't do this, I mustn't." She pulled away, eyes rounded, breathing in shallow gasps, staring at him. "I—I can't," she said, but her words lacked conviction.

His answer echoed off the skies, a voice ripped in agony. "Why? Is it your beloved? Is it Titus?"

She gave her head an impatient shake. "Titus is *not* my beloved. He's my friend."

"A peculiar term to refer to one's intended."

"And he isn't my intended!"

He searched her face. "Much has happened while I was away from you. What happened exactly, Caroline? Did you discover Titus did not excite you?" He rose, strolled over to her, and stood, legs straddling a fallen tree trunk, hands on hips.

She dropped her gaze, her heart slamming against her chest. "I think it not seemly you talk to me in such a manner."

His laughter rang out. "Seemly? Lady Caroline, 'seemly' is the least of your concerns."

"Why are you talking to me so?"

"What is it, Caroline? Are you going to pull that famous woman's trick and cry?" His voice lowered, mocking her. "Or do I perhaps frighten you?"

She stood up, furious. "I am not afraid, and I never cry. No amount of pain can make me cry."

He took another step closer, and his breath tickled her ear. "Ah, but I'm not going to hurt you, Caroline. You play a wicked game. You know what you're about, don't you?"

She blinked and glared at him. "No, but I know what *you* are. You wish to make love with me."

He chuckled. "And you don't? Didn't you say you envied your animals? What do you really envy, Caroline? Their freedom? In all things?"

His hot breath caressed her throat.

"Do you envy them their ability to feel like this?"

She gasped as his hand plunged down her neckline, stroking her nipple. Her sweat-slicked skin seared like it was afire; her breasts strained and pushed against her shift. He sucked gently at the hollow in her throat, dipping his head lower, and her shift glided down past her shoulders. She caught her breath while he laved her nipple, and hot flame moistened the cleft between her thighs. She moaned and leaned into him, uttering tiny, mewling cries.

Then he pulled away. "We're both in this game, Caroline. Let's take from it what we can."

"Philippe, you—you talk in riddles, and I'm confused enough already. Please. Let me go home. I have to think."

Swallowing, he watched her walk away. He had been gone too long, much too long to hunger after this woman so, this flimsy excuse of a woman, this, this traitor who would turn him in at her brother's bidding without a second thought.

Thinking of all the reasons why he shouldn't want her, shouldn't have her, didn't work. He starved for her like a lovesick schoolboy. He crossed his arms and laughed harshly. He, Philip Masterson, who could one day own anything in the entire country of England, who could *buy* America if he wanted it, craved the one thing he must never have!

Caroline, head bent down, heard the bitter laugh echo through the woods, far, far away. "I've got to get home," she murmured to herself, her voice breaking. "Oh, dear heavens, I need to get home."

The next morning Caroline fled to the shelter, yearning to pet Willie or Fawn. She brushed past Philip, who'd come out to meet her, and went inside.

"Where are they?" she demanded, striding outside. "What have you done to them?"

"Your animals?"

"Yes, my animals! *Where are they?*" By the time she'd finished her sentence, Fawn had crept up within ten feet of the pair, peering around a tree, and Willie had sidled over to her.

"You see, *madame?* Your deer and raccoon are still here."

Somewhat placated, she stooped low, patting Willie on the head. "What of the others? Where are Robin and Crow? And why won't Fawn come near?"

Perplexed, Philip answered, "The birds, *madame*, have healed. I thought they should learn once again how to find their own feed."

"You! You had no right!"

At the harshness in her words, Fawn scampered off into the woods.

"I think you frightened her, Caroline. She was ready to come near you when you yelled."

Instead of responding, she stared at him with blazing sapphire eyes.

Philip hesitated before approaching, then took her hands in his. "Your object is to heal your animals, *oui?* And in so doing, you must let them go when they are well. You cannot keep them prisoners, *chérie.*"

A look passed over her face that terrified him, a look of such confusion, such disorientation, he barely recognized the calm, self-assured young woman who'd nursed him to health. "Oh, Philippe, I just don't know what's happening to . . . " Her words trailed off as she slumped against him.

"Come," he whispered in her ear. "Come inside."

She bowed her head and allowed him to lead her like a lamb to its slaughter. Once inside she sat primly, hands clasped in her lap.

"Tell me," Philip coaxed. "Tell me what troubles you."

"Say please." Her attempt at humor fell flat, and she quelled the first thought that came to her mind. She could never tell him *he* troubled her.

"I never say please, *chérie*. Now tell me."

"It's just that my brother's in the war, and I'm worried about him. And Titus is at the fort, aching to fight. And then I come to see my animals and find even they don't need me, and—and . . . "

"Is that it, Caroline? You need someone to need you?"

"Yes," she whispered. Then she looked into his eyes and read the distrust in them, and knew he still needed her to free him of his bonds of suspicion. Whether he knew it or not, he still needed her. "Philippe, it seems all we do is talk about me. Do tell me about you."

"We'll make a bargain."

"What kind of bargain?"

"I'll tell you more about me, if you tell me why Austin beat you."

"I told you, he didn't—"

"Then the bargain's off."

She sighed. "Very well. But you first."

"No, Caroline. You."

"You don't trust me, do you?"

"I trust no one."

"You win, Philippe." She paused. "Austin beat me because I told him I wouldn't marry Titus."

His brow arched. "Why?"

"Why is not important." She inhaled deeply. "Now it's your turn."

"I think not. There's more to the story that you're not telling me."

"How do you know that? I mean . . . " Her words came out in a rush. "Titus was only marrying me for my dowry. He wants a new printing press, and—and I told Austin I would find a way for Titus to get it."

"You?" His mouth turned up in a dry grin. "Were you planning to steal one?"

"No. I was—Philippe, I was hoping maybe—I found the gold behind the barrel."

He looked at her blankly. "There's gold behind the barrel?"

"Yes. You mean you didn't know?"

He shrugged. "No. Let me see." He walked over to the barrel, fumbled behind it, took out the pouch, and poured a few coins in his hand. *"Mon Dieu,"* he whispered. "British gold. Here, *chérie*, you take it."

Shaking her head, she said, "No. I mean, yes, I'll take enough for Titus's printing press. But you, Philippe, you take the rest."

"You don't want it?"

"No. Whatever would I need it for?"

Bemused, he watched her carefully count out a few of the coins into her hand.

"There. That should be enough. Now take the rest, Philippe. Later, after you're back with your regiment, maybe you'll find good use for it. Now." She looked at him expectantly.

"Now what?"

"Now it's your turn to talk. Tell me about your childhood, perhaps. That would be a good start."

So he talked, relaxing when he created fiction, tensing when he related fact.

"I am but a poor man."

"But rich in ways more important than money. You're honest and kind."

"How so?"

"You were most generous in giving me the gold. Austin would never have shared it."

His lips twisted. "I am a bastard son."

"That's ridiculous."

He looked at her in surprise. "No, it's true."

"Not the fact, the word. It's not the child's fault, if he was conceived out of wedlock. Why should he be so labeled?"

When he didn't respond, she asked, "Did your mother have a difficult time in raising you?"

"My mother abandoned me, when she realized my father wouldn't divorce his wife and wed her," he responded curtly. "What else do you wish to know?"

"I—I'm sorry. I didn't mean to pry."

"You have nothing to be sorry about, *chérie*. I agreed to talk. Now, since you seem to have run out of questions, let me tell you how I grew up."

With words he painted a picture of a young boy guiding the last of the fur trappers through the forests, returning laden with pelts that earned him acclaim among the citizens of the American settlement known as Frenchtown.

179

What would she think, if she knew he'd really grown up in boarding schools in England?

All the while Caroline was keenly aware of his eyes on her, of the way he looked at her, and she knew he felt the same thick tension in the air as she. Her every sense vibrated. She listened carefully to his words, but nothing in them was remarkable until he mentioned his pistol, his voice falling to a reverent hush. She could sense it meant more to him than he knew. And while she listened, she imagined his lips on hers, his hot breath against her throat. She knew he watched her out of the corner of his eye, waiting. He wanted to make love to her. If she let him, he would trust her, perhaps. He would know she'd given him all she could.

She crossed herself. "I have to leave, Philippe."

Swallowing the lump in his throat, this time he knew better than to try to force her to stay. Though he would sacrifice anything to have it otherwise, Caroline Swanson headed in only one direction where he was concerned. Away.

## Chapter Nine

For twelve days Philip waited for Caroline's visits, knowing he was exhausting excuses to justify his stay at the shelter. Even though the latest message from General Brock—delivered via Mad Bird—had said he could stay as long as he needed in order to convey messages from Austin, time was running out for him to remain near Caroline Swanson. He wanted her, ached for her, but felt as if she offered him the apple from the tree of Eden. Philip had never trusted anyone. Now he didn't trust himself. If he made love to Caroline Swanson, who knew what he would say to her, what secrets he'd reveal in the throes of his passion?

Titus paid a brief visit, stopping to see Caroline for little more than an hour.

"Look, Titus." She unfisted her hand, revealing the gold coins.

His mouth dropped open. "Where did you get these?"

"I found them. In the shelter."

He snorted. "You expect me to believe that?"

"Yes, it's true."

"They're British, Caroline. What would British coins be doing in the shelter?"

Shrugging, she said, "I suppose they're left from the Revolution. You've seen the shelter; it could easily have been built forty years ago. British soldiers probably hid the money there."

"I don't believe it. What does Mr. Desjardin know about this?"

"Nothing, Titus. I swear. I mean, I found the gold and took what I thought you'd need for the press. I gave the rest to him."

He looked at her gravely. "Caroline, I always thought you were a woman of virtue."

"I *am*, Titus! How can you think otherwise? I've never lied to you."

He watched her, and when she didn't cross herself, he grunted. "All right, Caroline. The wedding's off. I'll handle it with your brother. He won't be happy, though. He still wants to leave here, and with you unattached . . . "

"Oh, Titus, don't worry. I've already thought of something. As soon as Philippe's name is cleared, I'll offer my services at the fort. You said yourself many of the horses were in poor condition, and I could help them. Then I'd have employment."

"Where will you live?"

"Why here, of course! With Maeve."

"My mother won't hear of it. She sent me to tell you that she wants you and your maid to move in with her directly."

Caroline's face fell, then she brightened. "We'll go to your mother's in a few days, but we'll only stay until the war's over."

"What will you do then?"

"Don't worry, Titus. I'll think of something. I always do."

When she arrived, Philip felt the air charge, tantalizing him.

"Oh, Philippe, it's so dreadful."

"What now, *ma petite?*"

She eyed him, unsure as to how he would accept what she had to tell him. "You don't object to my telling you the war news, do you? It's just that once Titus clears your name and you return to your regiment, it will be easier if you know what's happened while you were gone."

"No, it's quite all right."

"You may not like this."

"Go on, Caroline."

"It appears we've made another dreadful mistake. Somehow General Hull's trunk, one containing all his secret battle maps and plans of attack, fell into British hands. Oh, Philippe, what will become of us?"

A bleak look passed over his face. "I do not know."

"Do you think we have a chance of winning?"

"A chance, surely. But, at the moment, things do not look good, do they?"

"No."

He cleared his throat. "Any word from Titus yet?"

"I'm sorry, I almost forgot. He was most grateful for the gold, but he's made no progress with uncovering the real killer's identity." Reaching over and patting his hand, she said, "I am sorry. I know how anxious you are to see this settled. Titus said men are moving around so much, it's almost impossible to learn anything."

"It's all right, Caroline." He sighed, rubbing a hand across his brow. "I'll manage somehow."

She reached out to him, stroking his shoulder. "Oh, Philippe, I *am* sorry. I have further bad news, I'm afraid."

"Go on."

"I have a favor to ask you, along with the news. Promise me you'll do what I ask, please?"

Philip mulled this over. He had never promised anyone anything in his entire life. Even his looming betrothal to Daphne had been implied. He'd never actually *asked* her to marry him. It was just understood.

"A promise, no. But I'll do my best."

Licking her lips, she stared down at her hands. "I'm not certain I'll be able to come back here after today. Not every day, at any rate. Mrs. Duffy told me I must move in with them. She's worried about me, what with the war and all. Besides, she says it's not seemly my maid and I live by ourselves with no one to look after us. And she says Austin wouldn't look kindly on Maeve and me living alone, either. Of course, he didn't say anything before he left, but I suppose he was too preoccupied and just expected I'd try to do the right thing. And—"

"And?"

"And she wouldn't look kindly on my coming here, Philippe. The Duffys live another five miles farther than I, and it will be very difficult to get here. I'll come as often as I'm able, but . . . "

The muscle in Philip's jaw twitched; his face offered no other hint of how this news affected him. Dismayed, Caroline watched him draw his invisible cloak around him. She felt like she'd coaxed and cajoled and encouraged an animal to eat out of her hand, only to snatch the food away from him at the last minute.

"So what is the promise you wish me to make, *madame?*"

"Will you take care of Fawn and Willie for me? As long as you stay here, I mean."

Stay here? Without Caroline? Suddenly Philip remembered that he had work to do, work that involved returning to Fort Malden.

Caroline sensed his withdrawal.

"Please, Philippe, don't—"

"Don't what, *chérie?*" he snapped.

She couldn't leave him like this. She couldn't let him go to face whatever demons he fought.

Her question, soft and anxious, floated on the summer's breeze. "Let's go for a walk, a short one. Please?"

"I thought you were in a hurry to go."

"No," she whispered. "Not now." *Not ever.*

Moments later they walked hand-in-hand to the maple that had become, by unspoken agreement, their sanctuary, their haven.

Caroline scrutinized his face, searching for clues as to what he was feeling, finding nothing but a studied impassiveness. Disheartened, she sat on the ground, crossing her feet at the ankles, and patted the earth next to her.

Philip sat beside her and cleared his throat. "As to your animals, I will watch them as long as I am here. But I cannot promise how long that will be."

Her brow creased. "But I've already told you it's not safe to leave."

"It's my decision to make. Not yours."

She sighed and nodded. Then, hesitatingly, "Will you tell me where you are going, when you are leaving?"

"No."

"You still don't trust me, do you?"

He looked off in the distance, trying to clear his vision of Caroline Swanson. "I trust no one."

"Why?"

A short bitter laugh was the only response.

Now she took his hand between hers, bringing it to her lips, kissing his fingers. A shiver ran through her at the feel of his skin against her mouth, and at her own daring, but she had started and would not stop now. It was the last balm she could think of, the last healing potion she had.

"Stop," Philip ordered.

She looked up at him, her eyes soft and liquid. "Why?"

"Because. You're only doing this because of some misguided belief that it will help me somehow. Don't do me any favors, Caroline. I won't have you offering yourself to me in sacrifice. I'm not some noble god, I'm a *man*."

She hesitated, then said tentatively, "Why do you think no one can love you?"

"Me? *Mon Dieu, madame,* who would want a penniless soldier, one with nothing to commend him? Neither honor nor wealth, with a scarred, twisted body besides?" The sarcasm in his response shocked her.

Taking his hand once again, Caroline bent her head to kiss it, her hair hiding her face from his view. Then she took his fingers and ran them along her cheek, pressing her lips against the center of his wrist. His other arm encircled her, drawing her closer to him, and she edged lower, leaning down past his hips to his leg. She knew how it felt to crave love. No one could help her, but she—perhaps she could help him.

She heard his sharp intake of breath as she tugged off his boot and folded down the top of his stocking. He stiffened.

"No, *chérie.*"

He'd said *chérie*.

She continued, ignoring his garbled protests, for surely if he wanted her to stop, wanted it truly, he was strong enough to overpower her. In seconds she freed the stocking, revealing the pitted, bumpy calf.

"Caroline, no, you don't have to—"

"What is it, Philippe?"

A wrenching pain filled him. *Not Philippe—Philip!* he wanted to shout.

When he did not respond, she caressed his leg. "It's a good, strong leg. It shows a great victory. Not many men live after such a snakebite, but you fought and survived!"

"It was because of you, Caroline," he groaned, his fingers stroking her hair. "You saved me."

"But you took the first step. You came to me."

She looked from his leg to his face, contorted in some deep, secret anguish that she had to pull out and throw away. *Come to me now,* she mouthed, but no words came.

At that moment, he didn't care if she was a skilled seductress, didn't care if she would kill him and personally serve his head on a platter. All he wanted was to make love to her once, whatever the cost.

He wrapped her hair around his fingers and gently pulled her to him. "Kiss me."

Obediently she responded, astonished at the feel of his mouth covering her lips, as if he would swallow her whole, of the crushing sensation as he kissed her like a starving man. His warmth and strength suffused her, his encircling arms holding her close, pressing her breasts against his chest. When he pulled away, she moaned softly. Her whispery cry acted like some magnetic propulsion, pushing him closer, and he kissed her deeply. Caroline thought she would die from the heat.

Holding her away from him, he freed his shirt with one hand. He emanated a warmth Caroline could feel even before she splayed her fingertips across his furry chest.

His hands roved over her shoulders, then dipped down the split neckline of her frock, finding her breast. She gasped with pleasure, and taut excitement skittered between her legs. A kiss of air skipped over her thighs. Weak and giddy, she let her arms fall from his neck, allowing him to slide her shift, then her chemise, over her arms. He laid her down gently on the mossy earth, watching her. She resisted the urge to cover herself with her hands, somehow knowing his perusal of her thin form was as important to him as her perusal of his leg. He gently tugged on her pantalets, skimming the fabric past her knees, her calves, her toes. She shivered; the heat mounting inside her and the wispy summer's breeze wafting over her created a tornado of passion. When she'd begun this, she never expected this rapture, never expected this torment of pleasure, remembering only the command: "Women, submit to your husbands." This was submission?

He stroked her arm, nuzzling his face down to her hardened nipples. He grasped one rosy tip and ran his tongue over it, then over the other. At her soft moan, he suckled lightly, teasing.

"Now, Philippe," she begged. *Let there be nothing between us, nothing . . .*

He stopped at her gasp of surprise and pain. Then, grunting, he thrust deeper, harder, and Caroline wrapped her legs around him, urging him to take all of her, despite the brief, flaming pain that seared through her as he broke her barrier.

The pain gone, she felt herself being lifted higher,

higher, amazed at the fever between her legs, of the wondrous, heady sensation of being filled with him, of the intense, blissful pleasure that rocked her time and again. Tears ran down the corners of her eyes. *Now there can be nothing between us, Philippe. I have given you all I have.*

When he was spent, he pulled away. Then he noticed the moss, a deep earthy red where it should have been green. Swallowing, he looked at the woman beneath him, the last of her tears dripping to the earth. "Caroline. I—"

"Now do you believe me, Philippe?" she whispered shakily. "Can you trust me now?"

When he did not answer, the meaning of what she'd done slammed into her. Her cheeks reddened; she crossed herself. She bit her lip and looked at him directly, the moistness in her sapphire eyes once again threatening to spill over. "I always thought," she whispered, "I always thought it would be so—special. And it was, for me. I trusted you, Philippe. But you still don't trust me, do you?"

"Trust. Is that what this is about, Caroline? Trust?"

"Yes. I'd given you everything else I had. I told you things I never told anyone. I brought you here, to the one place no one else ever came to. And then it was no longer mine, when Austin and Titus came here because of you. I opened my heart to you and gave you everything except—the one thing you asked for. And I wouldn't have minded, not if it would have helped, but—"

"Caroline, listen to me. This wasn't supposed to be about sacrifice, or even trust. It was supposed to be about love."

Her eyes widened. "Love?"

"Yes." Blast Britain, blast Daphne, blast his damned lies, and that, that *creature* he had created. Blast *Philippe!*

"I love you," he said suddenly, amazed that he meant it.

"I don't believe you."

"Why?"

She eyed him warily. "How can you love someone you don't trust?"

A strangled laugh rose in his throat. "Caroline, look. I do trust you." He didn't mind lying to her, because he did trust her. Not completely, but did it matter when he loved her so much that he would gladly hang for her? "Caroline, marry me."

Her mouth dropped open. "Marry you?"

"*Chérie,* do you love me?"

She blushed and looked away. "Yes, I suppose I do," she whispered.

"And can you trust *me*, Caroline? Trust me not to hurt you again?"

She hesitated, and looked into his eyes. "Yes."

"Then marry me, my love."

"But—but Austin—"

Philip's jaw clenched. "Listen to me. If I could make it right with Austin, would you marry me?"

Her heart rose; she thought it flew from her body and danced in the heavens. "Yes. Oh, yes." Then, doubtfully, "How will you make it right with him?"

"You said he'd do anything for money."

"Yes."

"Perhaps a few gold coins could make him change his mind."

"Oh, yes, that would work!"

Philip knelt before her, grasping her hands, begging her.

"*Chérie,* listen to me. I have to leave, but I'll be back in four days." *Mad Bird should be here at any time. I can make it in four days, if I convince him to go with me and we row like hell.* "When I come back, I'll have many things to tell you, but for now you have to trust me. And then I'll make things right with Austin."

"But what will you do, where will you go?"

Touching a finger lightly to her lips, he could only think of their soft sweetness, of the taste of them, like rich, berry-sweetened cream. "I'll be safe, love."

"You'll straighten out your name somehow?"

He almost laughed out loud. If she only knew how close to the mark her question was.

"Yes."

There were so many things she wanted to ask him, but he had talked about trust. And she would trust him. He fastened the pouch around his neck, and she saw that he was preparing to leave immediately. Trying to keep him near her a moment longer, she groped for something to say. "What am I to do while you're gone?"

He drew her to him and held her tightly. "Just wait for me. When I come back, the first thing I'll do is find Austin and make things right with him."

She pouted. "The first thing?"

"All right, I'll come see you first," he answered with a grin. *"Then* I'll see Austin. But I have to leave. The sooner the better."

She looked to where her hands gripped his arms, and smiled. "Do you really want to go?"

His voice cracked. "No, never. But I must, so I can come back."

She couldn't understand why her eyes felt so moist; her lips trembled. "Then hurry, Philippe. Hurry back to me."

"I will, *chérie,*" he whispered, kissing her hair. "Four

191

days. I promise. Now, go home. It's not safe for you to see where I'm going."

She whirled, her eyes bright with fear. "But you said there was no danger!"

"Not for me, Caroline. I just don't want you to know my whereabouts. Look, I can't explain it all now, but I will when I get back." He hated to see the doubt in her eyes, but he would make it all up to her. When he returned, he would tell her all of it, and spend the rest of his life making it up to her, the lies, the deception. He would never deceive her again.

After she'd donned her clothes he helped her to Derby, wishing for once the horse would take off in a hurry. He couldn't bear to see her disappear into the woods so slowly. He wanted her gone, their goodbyes over with, so he could get back to Fort Malden, relinquish his commission, and come back to her.

Once she'd mounted the horse, she looked down at him, eyes shining with unshed tears.

"I'll be waiting for you, Philippe."

"I'll be here. Four days, when the sun is high, come here and show me the way to the Duffys. It will be all right, m'love." He didn't blame her for the disbelief in her face; he scarcely believed himself. But he meant every word of it. And as she went off in the distance, looking back over her shoulder at him, he whispered over and over.

"I'll be back, I'll be back, I'll be back."

## Chapter Ten

When Caroline returned home, she threw her arms around Maeve and twirled on her toes, performing a little pirouette of joy.

"Oh, Maeve, I wish I could tell you. The most wonderful thing happened to me today!"

Smiling, Maeve answered, "Aye? Well, then, why don't ye tell me about it?"

"It's a secret, and I don't think I should, but you're my dearest friend, and I know I can trust you. Besides, if I don't tell you, I think I shall burst!"

After Caroline had told Maeve everything except her tryst with Philip, the maid's delight was almost as palpable as her mistress's.

"So, when are ye goin' to be tellin' yer brother the news?"

Caroline sighed, but her melancholy did not last long. The memory of Philippe asking her to marry him rose unbidden, and a smile played about her lips. Four more days. Four more days, and he would return!

\* \* \*

When Genevieve and Howard Duffy arrived at the Swansons' to take the two young women to their home, Caroline was overcome with guilt.

"I'm so sorry you're not going to be my daughter-in-law," Genevieve said, grasping the girl's hands within her own. "I do think it would be good for Titus to wed, but I'd never want the two of you to enter into a union you'd come to regret. But I've been thinking . . . "

Caroline followed her meaningful glance in Maeve's direction. The Irishwoman had bent over to pick up a bit of bread that had fallen to the floor, and seemed oblivious to their conversation.

In another time, in another place, a union between a serving maid and a printer's son would never be permitted, but so few women lived in Michigan Territory, that such a liaison would not be impossible. Caroline looked at Genevieve and nodded thoughtfully. The possibility of Maeve falling in love with Titus had never occurred to her before, but there had been telltale signs. The sidelong glances, the way Maeve's voice softened whenever Titus visited. And Titus, Caroline realized, was much better suited to Maeve. A match between the two merited consideration. Perhaps with a gentle push or two . . .

By the next morning, Caroline tried to push the butterflies in her stomach away. Three more days. Three more days and Philippe would return, and soon after she would become Mrs. Philippe Desjardin!

Early morning on the day after he'd left Caroline, Philip and Mad Bird finally landed near Fort Malden, and headed to Gen. Isaac Brock.

Walking past soldiers busy sharpening swords, counting balls of lead shot, and rolling barrels of foodstuffs to the supply house, Philip noted that the place swarmed with men. Then he spotted the general's slender back, as Brock entered the log enclosure that served as his office.

"Over here." Philip gestured to the Indian, ignoring the curious glances of the soldiers. Though he recognized many of the faces, no one greeted him. They'd been trained well.

He entered the small, dark room, Mad Bird at his heels. Brock looked up from his makeshift desk, a pine-planked table, and Philip thought the man's curly brown hair had receded somewhat since the last time they'd spoken.

"What's wrong?" Brock asked, rising. "Why are you here? Have you been discovered?"

"No. Relax, sir; nothing is wrong and no one's been discovered. But there is a matter that needs discussing. A private matter."

The general's blue eyes studied him. "Get some food and drink for the native," he ordered an aide watching the exchange. "Mr. Ainsley and I are not to be disturbed, unless there's an emergency."

Once they were alone, Brock said, "Well, Ainsley. Tell me the bad news."

"There's no bad news," Philip answered, careful to keep his voice evenly modulated. "And the name's Masterson, not Ainsley."

Brock's eyes narrowed. "I'm well aware of that," he replied. "But you know the rules."

"Yes," Philip snapped. "I know the rules, and I'm done with them."

Brock tipped his chair back, tamping his pipe against the table. "Done?"

"Yes. I've served you well, and I wish to sell my commission."

Carefully the general responded, "Very well, Philip. I can see where you might need a rest. We've kept you very busy in extremely trying circumstances. You probably haven't had time to recover properly from that snakebite, either. Let's say we give you two weeks. At the end of that time, if you still retain this notion, you can train someone else, be an advisor of sorts. In the meantime, of course, we'll need you to continue your duties. Much of our success at Mackinac is due to the information you acquired for us. We're preparing to attack Fort Detroit in two weeks." He chuckled. "Stroke of genius, your pretending to be an idiot. Swanson's been a reliable source of information, thanks to you. Who knows what else he might have for us?"

Rising, Philip paced the small room. "You don't understand, sir. I wish to leave entirely. I don't want to train anyone. Besides, by the time the new fellow would be trained, this war will be over. I'll sell out my commission and—"

"No!" Brock lowered his voice and glowered at him. "We've come too far. The idea of posting advertisements for your return—then taking them down, as if we'd *found* you—was inspired. If my guess is correct, none of the colonists think you're still around. We've begun rumors that we've sent you back home, and it appears they believe us. Besides, the Potawatomis trust you implicitly, and we need you to continue dealing with them; they admire you. You represent Britain to them. If you abandon us, they'll see all of us as traitors."

Easing back in his chair, the general waited, tenting his fingers.

After several long minutes Philip turned, arms folded across his chest. "I fear," he said, his voice steely, "I haven't made myself understood. It's not simply my post I wish to resign. It's the army. And as I initially bought my way *into* this position, I can buy my way *out* of it. As we are both perfectly well aware, I came into this for adventure, not out of some undying patriotism to a cause I've never understood from the beginning. As you seem to have forgotten, *we* have been impressing *their* sailors. It's they who should be attacking us, not the other way around. You knew my circumstances from the beginning, and you agreed to them. Now, General, I want out." He flung the parcel of gold on the table, where it fell with a thud.

The general rocked back in his chair. "What is it, Masterson? A woman?"

"What it is, sir, is no concern of yours. A woman is involved, yes, but there's more to it than that."

"Such as?"

Philip rubbed his hand across his chin, wondering how honest he could be. He and Brock had been friends ever since his enlistment. And he'd gone this far. He might as well finish it. Perhaps he wouldn't be allowed to resign honorably, but at the moment it didn't matter. They could throw him out, for all he cared.

"My allegiance has changed."

"*What?*"

Sighing, Philip pulled out a chair and straddled it, facing his former friend. "What you know of my background is incomplete."

"What are you saying, man?" Brock thundered, past caring who heard him. "You're wealthy with a fine future in front of you. I know that much. His Majesty would

197

never allow a traitor to lay claims to a British inheritance. And you're betrothed to a beautiful woman back home. Why would you throw it all away?"

"No one ever asked me if I wanted this fine future, as you mistakenly call it. My life's been controlled by other people from the time I was a lad. I'm done with control, Isaac. Do you understand me? In all walks of my past life, I am done. That includes Britain's efforts to control the colonists' future. It would have been easy enough for me to escape and live among them; the country is large enough to hide me well. But I can't abide a liar, and I trust our friendship will stand me in good stead. I'll not betray your presence or your plans. This isn't political, it's personal."

"You're damn right it's personal," Brock roared, throwing the pipe to the ground. "It's not just your home you're denying, it's your country! And how do I know you wouldn't betray us?"

Philip's eyes narrowed. "You've known me for two years now. If I give you my word, which I do rarely, I keep it."

The general sneered. "Apparently I haven't known you well enough, Masterson. But perhaps in the next several weeks, we'll get better acquainted."

So deftly Philip couldn't anticipate it, Brock shoved a pistol against his temple and yelled. "Miller, Price!"

The guards, alerted by the discordant words coming from the quarters, rushed in and grabbed a stunned Philip by each arm.

"Chain him and see that he doesn't escape. I want him under constant watch. The man knows too much; he could do us great harm. He is to stay under constant surveillance, until either such time as I feel he listens to reason, or until we win this damnable war and return home. And if he won't capitulate of his own accord, do whatever's necessary to see that he does."

On the fourth day since Philip left, Caroline thought she would shatter in half. Her agitated pacing nearly drove Genevieve to distraction, until finally the elder woman said, "Why don't you take the air? Or a ride on your horse? But stay nearby, and take Maeve with you."

"Oh, may I? Thank you so much, Mrs. Duffy."

Genevieve chuckled. "I do hope my company isn't so disagreeable to you that you can't wait to get away from me."

"Oh no, not at all. And I do hope we can remain friends always."

Caroline walked to the door, Maeve in hand. When she reached the exit, filled with a strange sense of foreboding, she turned to say something to Genevieve, but the right words failed her. She only waved a feeble goodbye and went outside.

Once Derby was saddled, Maeve eyed him in distrust. "I don't think he kens what a saddle is, lass."

"Not a sidesaddle, at any rate," Caroline agreed. "But we don't dare ride him bareback. If Mr. or Mrs. Duffy saw either of us riding bareback—"

"Ye mean, if they see *ye* ridin' bareback. I'm not that fond of ridin' with the aid of a saddle and a beast what knows what he's doin'. Let alone this one. He's eyein' me like a nosebag of oats, he is."

A twinkle shone in Caroline's eyes. "Derby? You're frightened of Derby? The worst he'll do is lay down on the ground and refuse to get up. Come on, do hurry. Here, I'll give you a leg up."

After Maeve mounted Derby, Caroline swung herself easily into the saddle on Buttercup, Genevieve's horse, and grimaced. "I wouldn't know I was on a horse, if I didn't see it with my own eyes," she muttered. "A saddle just does not feel natural."

Unlike Derby, Buttercup liked to gallop. The golden mare, excited at having a rider who urged her to run, tore off.

"Where are we goin'?" Maeve shouted.

Caroline yelled over shoulder. "Just let Derby follow; he'll find the way."

"Ye mean to the shelter? But that's too far!"

Pretending she didn't hear, Caroline dug her heels into Buttercup's side and leaned low in the saddle.

Her exhilaration quickly changed to disappointment, when she discovered that Philip hadn't arrived. She'd hoped they could snatch a few moments of privacy, before Maeve reached them. Convinced he would come at any moment, she debated whether she should go south, toward Frenchtown, to see if she could see him in the distance, then reluctantly decided to stay put. If Maeve found her gone, she'd likely assume her mistress had been carried off by Indians. Maeve would head right back to the Duffys, who would surely come looking for her. She had to keep her animal shelter a secret from *someone*.

Caroline hummed softly, searching for Fawn and Willie. Within minutes the doe peered out from behind a tree, and Willie sidled up to her, rubbing his wiry fur against her ankle. Try as she might, she couldn't encourage Fawn to come any closer. "It's all right," she coaxed. "It's only

Now you can get Heartfire Romances right at home and save!

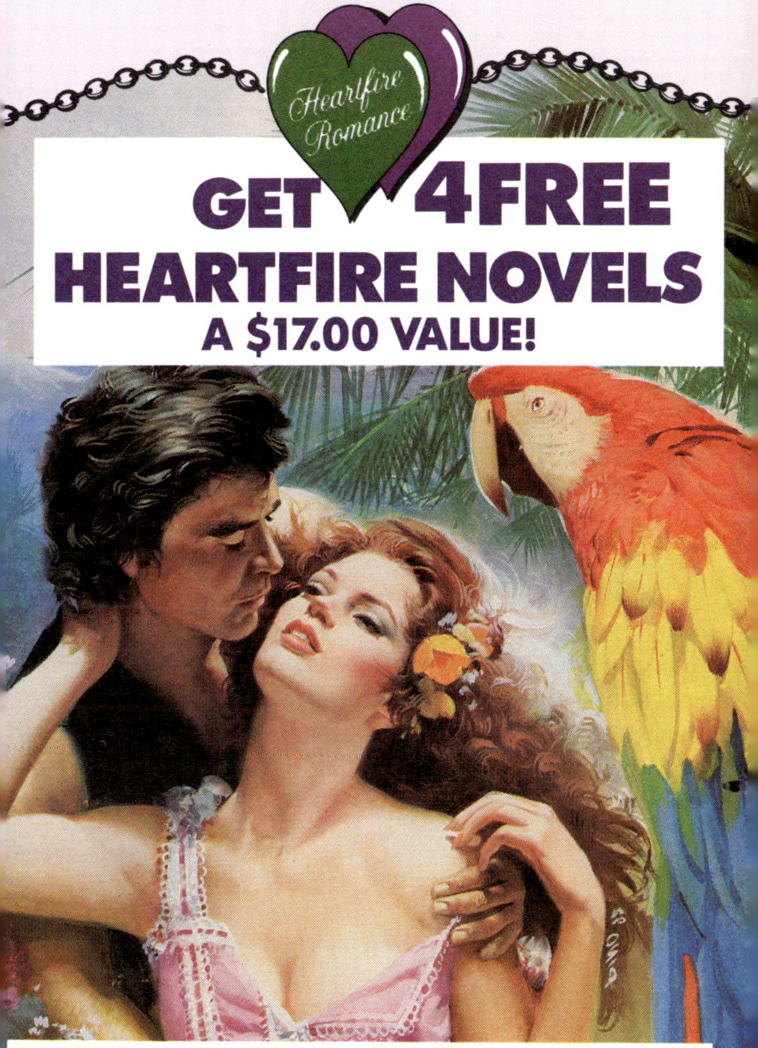


Home Subscription Members can enjoy Heartfire Romances and Save $$$$$ each month.

TO GET YOUR

# 4 FREE BOOKS

MAIL THE COUPON BELOW.

## FREE BOOK CERTIFICATE

*Heartfire Romance*

## GET 4 FREE BOOKS

**Yes!** I want to subscribe to Zebra's HEARTFIRE HOME SUBSCRIPTION SERVICE. Please send me my 4 FREE books. Then each month I'll receive the four newest Heartfire Romances as soon as they are published to preview Free for ten days. If I decide to keep them I'll pay the special discounted price of just $3.50 each; a total of $14.00. This is a savings of $3.00 off the regular publishers price. There are no shipping, handling or other hidden charges. There is no minimum number of books to buy and I may cancel this subscription at any time. In any case the 4 FREE Books are mine to keep regardless.

NAME ______________________

ADDRESS ______________________

CITY ______________ STATE ______ ZIP ______

TELEPHONE ______________________

SIGNATURE ______________________

(If under 18 parent or guardian must sign)

Terms and prices subject to change.

Orders subject to acceptance.

ZH1293

## GET 4 FREE BOOKS

HEARTFIRE HOME SUBSCRIPTION
SERVICE
120 BRIGHTON ROAD
P.O. BOX 5214
CLIFTON, NEW JERSEY 07015

me, surely you haven't forgotten already?" But the animal bounded off into the woods.

Disheartened, Caroline went back inside, Willie tagging along after her, and did what she could to tidy up the surroundings, studiously avoiding the barrel in the corner. She didn't want to know if the gold was still there or gone. If Philippe took it, he had to have a good reason. Perhaps he wanted it near him, so he could take it directly to Austin when he returned.

After a long time, she heard a complaining Maeve dismount from Derby. Caroline rushed out just in time to see her maid waddle, bowlegged, to her.

"By the saints in heaven," Maeve gasped. "If ye ivver be wantin' to go fer a ride, I think ye should be goin' by yerself, if ye don't mind me sayin' so."

Caroline bit back a smile. "Was Derby too hard on you?"

Straightening her shoulders, Maeve snapped, "Of course not. Too wide is all." She drew a couple of deep breaths before she spoke again. "I take it yer man hasn't arrived yet, or ye wouldn't be out here by me."

"You're right. But I'm sure he'll be here any minute; in fact, he's probably approaching even now. Would you mind staying here, while I go to greet him? I'll take Buttercup with me in the event Philippe's regiment didn't give him a horse; he's probably exhausted from all that walking."

"I'll stay as long as there's a spot to sit."

"There's a plank bench inside."

Maeve settled herself on the bench, resting her back against the wall. "How far is Frenchtown exactly? Is that where his regiment is?"

Pursing her lips, Caroline replied, "I presume so,

though he didn't really say. And I'm not certain exactly, but I think Frenchtown is about thirty miles or so away."

"And he said he'd be walkin' there and back? His leg must have healed right fast."

"It did, but I presume they'd give him a horse."

"But didn't ye say he planned on walkin'?"

"I know what I said, but, well, I just want to have everything perfect for him when he arrives. And while I'm certain he has a horse, I just want to be prepared, is all. And I could ride alongside him with Buttercup. Now, make yourself as comfortable as you can; I'll be back shortly."

The minutes turned into hours. Leading Derby, Maeve eventually found her mistress almost a hundred yards away, slumped on the ground against a tree, Buttercup standing alongside.

"Something must have happened to him," Caroline mourned. "Something to hold him back. But I'm sure he'll be here tomorrow, or maybe even tonight!"

"Come on, lass. It's time we be gettin' back. If we don't, Mrs. Duffy will be sure to have some folks lookin' for ye, and ye don't want her to discover this place now, do ye?"

Biting her lip, Caroline shook her head. Like a limp doll, she sank into the saddle, following Maeve all the way back to the Duffys.

"Oh I'm so relieved to see you," Genevieve said, fluttering about them when they arrived. "I was just about to send Howard after you, but he said to give you a few more minutes." Seeing the dejected look on Caroline's face, Genevieve turned to Maeve. "Is she all right?"

"Yes'm. Just a little—oh, ye know she's been keepin' pets and all, and one died." Without thinking, Maeve crossed herself at the lie, then, appalled, looked at her

202

arm, as if it had flown from Caroline's body and affixed itself to her side.

"We'll talk about this some other time," Genevieve whispered to the maid.

Hours later, after lying fully tensed, waiting for Philippe to knock on the door and announce his intentions, Caroline finally fell into a fitful sleep.

On the eighth day of his captivity, Philip eyed his breakfast rations suspiciously. As a change from the usual dry biscuit and water, a fresh, steaming loaf of warm bread, a small beaker of honey, and a jug of fresh milk rested on the tray in front of him. Better yet was a mug of warm cider, a decent apple, and a slice of dried beef.

Ignoring the chains around his wrists, he picked up the bread, sniffed it, and examined it. He began to place it next to him on the ground, then thought better of it and brought it to his lap, to give him a better chance of swatting the incessant flies away until he decided whether or not to eat it.

He repeated the process with the apple, inspecting it closely for signs of tampering, then dipped a finger in the milk. No trace of poison there that he could detect, nor in the cider. It was peculiar that suddenly Brock had decided he merited a passable meal. The general must have had a change of heart.

Wincing, Philip rubbed the spot around his ankles where the chains chafed with one hand, while eating his bread with the other. His boots stood in the corner, mocking him, as if knowing he'd never reach them. He saw the toe of one wiggle, and guessed it provided a home for one of the mice that had scurried around last evening. Chuckling, he remembered wondering where they went during the day. Now he knew where at least one lived.

His meal done, he squinted, looking out to where sun streamed through a tiny crack in the log structure's corner. By his reckoning it was nigh nine o'clock in the morning. He wondered what Caroline was doing at this time, if she had lost all faith in him because he hadn't returned. Pushing all thoughts of her from his mind, he decided the morning's meal could be a good omen. Perhaps Brock had reconsidered and decided to set him free after all. If it wasn't so soon after he'd given the message to Mad Bird, he'd think Daphne had sent the money he'd requested—money of his own, to buy out his commission. But he doubted any ships had even departed yet with his packet.

One thing was certain. Brock would either release him, or he would have to escape today. Caroline waited for him.

He drained the jug of the last drop of cider, just as the door rattled and his two guards entered, brandishing weapons. Or improvised instruments of torture.

"Why, good morning, Cyrus. John. How nice of you gentlemen to come calling. Sorry I can't get up, but . . . " He looked at his chains, grinned, and shrugged.

"You can stand, Ainsley," the shorter one, Cyrus, barked. "The chains aren't that short."

"You're right, of course," Philip answered, speaking quietly to distract John's attention from the nail-studded board the guard waved in the air. "I say, as long as we're treating me so well this morning, what with a hearty breakfast and all, why don't we just—*uumph!*"

John grinned, swinging the board toward Philip.

Philip doubled over, clutching his stomach. Dots of blood seeped through the front of his shirt.

"Sorry we forgot our calling cards," John said. "But we thought you'd remember us better, if we gave you this instead. We'll be back, Ainsley. To remind you of who we are. And who *you* are."

"The name—the name's not Ainsley," Philip groaned as the door closed behind them.

Every time he heard footsteps he tensed, waiting, trying to anticipate what they'd do next, what they would want him to say. The blood had stopped flowing, sticking his shirt to his wounds until he tore it away, gritting his teeth. Not even the pain could keep his thoughts from Caroline, waiting for a promise he couldn't keep. "Just give me more time," he whispered to the sun, hoping a beam would carry his message to her. "I'll be back, Caroline. Just give me a little more time."

They fed him a fine supper of bread and fresh-churned butter, a slab of pork, and another mug of cider.

He waited for them to turn on him when they picked up the tray, but they looked past him, took the earthenware plate, and left.

All night Philip struggled to stay awake, his eyes fluttering open whenever he heard a strange sound. But they didn't come back.

Three days later Philip saw two candles light the way for his guards. Cyrus and John stomped in; Philip exhaled in relief. No nail-studded board was in sight.

"Who are you?" John demanded, holding his candle high.

"Philip Masterson. Why? Did you chaps take the wrong prisoner?"

His head snapped as a fist slammed against his chin. He tasted blood.

"Wrong answer, scum. *What's your name?*"

Struggling to keep his head steady, Philip smiled and said, "Why don't you gentlemen tell me?"

The guards exchanged glances. Cyrus nodded. John stepped forward. "Your name's the Ferret, British spy loyal to His Majesty King George III."

"His Majesty's a raving lunatic," Philip sneered.

Cyrus drew nearer. "So you're not simply a traitor, you're a heretic, besides."

"A realist," Philip said staunchly. "If you'd only use your heads, instead of your balls to think with—"

John ripped the sleeve from Philip's shirt. Philip looked at the green shredded fabric tossed in the corner, then back to his captor. "What do you want?"

"You've got one more chance. Brock's orders. Tell us you're the Ferret now, Ainsley, and save yourself grief."

"I don't understand," Philip said, stalling. "If you know I'm the Ferret, why do I have to tell you?"

John nodded to Cyrus, who lifted the candle and tilted it sideways above Philip's arm.

Philip saw the hot yellow wax pool, before it dripped onto him. He closed his eyes a second before the scalding fluid touched him, focusing on places other than this dark, dank cell, concentrating on a cooling glade in the forest and the feel of satin fingertips upon his skin.

\* \* \*

Six more days went by with no sign of Philip. Caroline and Maeve made daily pilgrimages to the animal shelter, but could find no trace of any human visitor. Though the weather was beastly hot, Caroline felt a definite chill in the air.

On the twelfth day after Philip had left, Titus returned home for a visit.

"It's good to see you, son," Genevieve greeted him, as he stepped in the door.

Titus pecked his mother on the cheek and turned to Caroline, avoiding Maeve's eyes on him. "Caroline, we have to talk."

She followed him outside. The two walked side by side for several moments, until Titus said bitterly, "It's about Philippe."

Caroline's heart leaped in her throat. "Has he been cleared of any wrongdoing? Is he back at the fort in Detroit? Maybe that's why he hasn't come. Maybe he was so busy he couldn't get away!"

Titus cleared his throat. "No one's heard of Philippe Desjardin."

Puzzled, Caroline fixed him with a questioning stare and waited for him to continue.

"You're not thinking clearly where the man's concerned, Caroline. He's not even American."

"Of course, he is," she argued. "Just because he's from Frenchtown, doesn't mean he isn't American."

"Caroline," he explained evenly. "There's no such man as Philippe Desjardin."

"Then who is he?" she challenged.

"I believe he's the Ferret."

She choked back laughter. "No, Titus. You've been listening too much to Austin. Philippe's no spy."

"No American general has been killed, Caroline, at least not before we knew war was declared."

"Perhaps—perhaps the murdered general was from another fort. Perhaps Mackinac."

"I've checked. No generals or senior officers of any sort have been killed by friendly fire. Certainly not before the war. Not in the entire Michigan Territory."

"Philippe made friends with a Potawatomi," she argued. "After his family was slaughtered by Indians, he made friends with them so they wouldn't murder him as well."

"The British have befriended most of the Indians. You know that."

Her shoulders straightened; her jaw set. "He speaks fluent French."

"As well as English. A great many British speak French, too, Caroline. Residents of Frenchtown don't have a monopoly on the language."

"And he knows too much of our soldiers and the land . . ."

Titus arched a brow. "And the Ferret wouldn't? Where is he now, Caroline?"

"He—he went to the fort."

"Fort Detroit?"

She nodded.

"I've been there for the last several weeks. There's been no Philippe Desjardin."

The color drained from her face. "What makes you think he's the Ferret?" she managed to say.

Hesitating an instant, afraid she would faint dead away

208

in front of him, Titus replied, "Too many things to go into now. But I have to know one thing, Caroline."

Numbly, she waited for his question.

"What did you tell him?"

When she did not reply, he grabbed her by the shoulders, shaking her. "Caroline, *what did you tell him?* The British know too much, they know our battle plans, our strategies. You've been—" he choked, *"consorting* with someone I can't identify. *What did you tell him?"*

Sickened, she looked at him and shook her head. "Nothing, I swear."

"Are you certain? Austin is always complaining that you listen to his conversations, offering your opinions. What have you heard that you've told the Ferret, Caroline?"

She wavered, and he caught her in his arms before she could fall. Pushing him away, she retorted, "I swear to you, I told him nothing." *Only,* she thought, *that I loved him.*

Half-convinced, Titus stepped back. "For your own sake as well as mine, you must tell no one of this man. If anyone finds out you've sheltered the enemy, they'll hang you as a traitor. It won't matter that you're a woman. They'll hang you, Caroline. Do you understand?"

She nodded, eyes glimmering. "And you—" she choked.

"That's right. They'll hang me, too, for suspecting his identity and not turning him in. Maybe I'd get away with it, because I didn't know who he was in the first place, but now that I suspect and haven't turned him in . . . Yes, Caroline. We'll both hang."

She clung to one last hope. "But the British have him back. Your mother told me they'd taken down the posters offering a reward for his return long ago."

"Probably a decoy. My father and I print things, especially now, in the war, to mislead the British. I'm sure they do the same."

She turned away, burying her head in her hands. "I won't tell anyone about him," she murmured brokenly.

"Not even Maeve?"

Her wounded look told him all he needed to know.

"You've already told her, haven't you?"

"Yes," she whispered.

"Now you've implicated two people you care about. You *do* care about us, don't you, Caroline? That, that *spy* hasn't so blinded you to reason that you only—"

"Oh, no!" The wail tore from her heart. "He's vile and horrid, and, of course, I care about you and Maeve! I wouldn't do anything to hurt either one of you. I'm sorry, I'm so sorry." Though tears pricked behind her lids, she refused to cry. Philippe had taken all from her, but he could not take a pride she hadn't known she possessed until now.

"What are you going to do?" she asked dully. "Surely you can't let him run free . . . ."

"No. I'll turn him in, of course. But it will take some time. There are things I know in my gut, hunches if you will, but I have to prove them. And I have to figure out a way to do it without involving you or Maeve."

His sincerity convinced her. Though she would never love Titus, as she had once loved that despicable, vile man, she knew she could respect him. And that was one thing she never could feel for Philippe, ever again.

Philip had lost count of the days he'd been held captive. In his rare moments of lucidity, when his body wasn't racked by pain from the increasing forms of torture Brock's thugs devised, he worked on plans to escape. He'd have to persuade Mad Bird to help, but he was no longer certain of the Indian's loyalty.

Mad Bird had tried to reason with him, but Philip would hear none of it. The more the guards and the Potawatomi tried to persuade him, the more convinced he became to work for the Americans. If he ever got out alive. At first he'd clung to the belief that Brock wanted him alive, or he wouldn't have been fed so well. But the days went by and his tortures grew worse: first the candle wax, then the fire itself, burning away the hair under his arms, then snuffed out just when it reached his skin. For variety, his guards sometimes brought the flame to his inner thighs, his buttocks. Then they proceeded to the board, pounding him with it, the nails just long enough to pierce his skin, but too short to damage his internal organs. They tended his wounds, so he knew they only prepared him for more, and for the first time in his life, he tasted fear. Still, the more they hurt him, the more he knew he could never belong to any of them again.

Today they returned. Philip struggled to bring himself to a standing position, resting his weight on his good leg, for the cell's dampness soaked into his damaged calf, making it ache continuously.

"Change your mind yet, Ainsley?"

He licked his lips and shook his head. "Name's not Ainsley," he mumbled.

John raised the board. Philip focused on it, trying to feel the pain before the impact so that the actuality of it would lessen. Then he noticed that it was a different board, without nails, but rounded, and his stomach churned. It was a club, the kind they used to batter men senseless, and he steeled himself for this new, raw agony.

John swung the board forward, and Philip eyes widened as he followed John's gaze. He heard a crack, felt blinding agony as his good leg felt like it had been severed in two. Looking down, he distantly wondered why it jutted out at such a peculiar angle. Then darkness devoured him and pulled him into a black whirlpool dotted by hot, piercing stars.

## Chapter Eleven

By September, Caroline's crossings became more and more frequent, her guilt competing with the gratitude she felt since discovering no child grew from Philip's seed. Why God had been so good to her, the worst sort of woman, was beyond her comprehension, but she vowed to face the remainder of her life with a newfound maturity. Though she missed her animals, she would not go to see how they fared. No mature woman engaged in such foolish pursuits. The shelter she'd once run to for safety had been tainted by the traitor's presence, and the haunting memory of what had occurred within and beyond its walls. She fervently hoped a bolt of lightning would set it afire, explode it in a cloud of smoke.

For years she'd defied her brother and disdained tradition, but now she saw the error of her ways, and resolved to become the very model of a lady.

Despite her best intentions, she woke up at night breathing heavily, having dreamed of Philip's kisses, of the feel of his fingers stroking her flesh. And when she sometimes stopped and noticed a bit of moss under her feet, remembering a similar velvety piece stroking a beard-covered cheek, her conscience pricked only a little. She knew the solution was to stay indoors, away from her memories. Along with her prayers for forgiveness and absolution, she prayed Titus would uncover undeniable evidence confirming the Ferret's identity, as quickly and safely as possible.

"Lass, I think ye ought to have picked a fabric more sunnylike. This is doin' nothin' for yer complexion. Are ye certain ye be feelin' well?"

Caroline smoothed down the sides of her dress, noticing the frock's color for the first time. She hadn't been able to conceal her apathy towards the upcoming military ball, which the Duffys insisted she attend with them, so Genevieve had selected the pale apricot fabric for Maeve to sew into a dress. When Caroline had been equally disinterested in a style, Genevieve had also chosen the design of overly embellished tiers that Maeve found as trying to create, as Caroline did to wear.

"I feel like a stuffed peacock," she complained.

"Ye look more like a sick hen," Maeve remarked honestly. Eyes darting to make sure Mrs. Duffy could not overhear, Maeve lowered her voice. "Any news yet on whether Master Titus has found any more about that— that man?"

Caroline sighed. "Yesterday I received a message, but he took such pains to write it in code, I scarcely could make any sense of it. As near as I can decipher, he's still working on proof as to the Ferret's true identity. I do wish he'd hurry!"

"Why, lass? It can hardly make any difference—"

"Oh, but it can! I don't think I'll feel fully at ease, until

214

the Ferret is dead and buried." She sniffed. "Actually, I think burying's too good for him. Quartering him's more his due. In fact, I'd feed his remains to Willie, if I wasn't afraid my poor animal would sicken."

Despite herself, Maeve chuckled. "Ye are out fer blood, aren't ye?"

Caroline's face hardened. "The Ferret's probably bloodless. Hearts pump blood, don't they? And he hasn't got one. Maeve, can you shorten this just a tad, and lower the neckline just a little? I'd like to show these condescending ladies tomorrow that I can be every bit as fashionable as they. It may be rather tasteless to have a party in the middle of a war, but as long as I have to attend, I might as well make a good impression."

Both Titus and Austin arrived in the evening. Shortly after learning of Philip's true identity, Caroline had submitted to Genevieve's earnest requests to discard her deerskin frocks. Maeve had sewn Caroline's dress, a lilac gauze creation.

Austin refused to comment on her appearance. "You will behave at the ball tomorrow, will you not?"

"Of course. I wouldn't want to embarrass you, would I? May I fetch you a glass of cider?" she asked, changing the subject.

Before the stunned men could reply, she left the parlor to get a tray.

Austin turned to Genevieve. "I think I owe you a good deal of gratitude, Madam. I scarcely recognize my own sister. Perhaps all she's lacked these many years is a woman's guidance."

"Really," Genevieve replied, "she's been quite docile.

I'd prepared myself for the worst, but other than the first week or so—"

"The first week?" Austin asked.

Genevieve studied him a moment before answering. "Yes. She was quite—agitated—for the first few days, then seemed to be ailing. Just when I prepared to send a message to a physician, she recovered quite miraculously."

"Miraculously? Was she that ill?"

"No. I'm afraid I misspoke myself. It was nothing, really, probably just a case of feminine exhaustion." Just then Caroline reentered, carrying a silver platter holding a crystal decanter and glasses. As the men watched speechlessly, she poured them each a glass, then sat down opposite them.

Testing her, Austin said, "There are rumors of another battle heating up."

Caroline stifled a yawn, looking quite bored.

He tried again. "The plans can't be divulged, of course—"

"Oh, Austin," she said, laughing. "Why would we want to know of war plans? Not that they're not important, I'm certain, but we've been so busy, we've hardly had time to think of the war. We were distressed when Fort Detroit was lost, but there's many battles to be fought yet. It can still be regained."

Not believing a word she spoke, Austin's lips set in a grim line, while Titus's eyes never left Maeve, dusting the china figurines on the mahogany shelf in the background.

"That's right," Genevieve said, looking pointedly at her son, who turned his attention back to his mother. "And Caroline's been such a dear. She's helped me so much around here. And Buttercup seemed to have the colic, but Caroline cured her. Your sister's most amazing."

Relaxing in his chair, Austin replied, "Yes. Most amazing. But now I'm afraid I must leave. I'd like to be at the fort before dusk."

There was something about soirees and galas, Caroline decided, that prevented her from working up much enthusiasm for them. Even now, when Maeve helped her pull the apricot gown over her head, something niggled at her. She brushed her apprehension aside, telling herself it was only superstition that gave her such an uncomfortable feeling. This gala was bound to be better than the last one she'd attended, for it was there that she'd first heard of the Ferret.

"Ye look lovely, lass."

Caroline stepped back, satisfied. The last time she'd donned the garment, two days ago, she and Maeve had laughed for hours over the frilly tiers and puffed sleeves. Between the two of them they'd devised some alterations. Now the gown, bereft of its flounces, skimmed lightly along the planes of her body. Floor-length, the hem rose slightly at the back in a delicate ruffle. The sleeves came to points over her hands, while the neck . . .

"Maeve, don't you think this is a bit too low?" Caroline clutched her hands over the plunging neckline, edged by a bit of white lace.

"No, lass. Ye did ask me to alter it. Though I think I may have misjudged the depth just a bit. Well, it's too late now. Just make certain no tall men stand next to ye, arching their necks for a better peek."

"Maeve!"

Just then Genevieve stepped into the bedroom. Caroline wished she'd locked the door, but she couldn't bring herself to close it completely.

"Why, my dear . . . " Genevieve stopped, puzzled, then walked around Caroline, inspecting the dress from every angle. Caroline didn't move. "That's not the same design we'd settled on, is it?"

Maeve answered hastily, "No, ma'am. It's my fault, I'm afeared. I love to sew, I do, but certain designs are not so easy for me to copy. This was the best I could do."

Caroline shot a glance of appreciation at her, and waited for Genevieve's verdict.

"You did a fine job. Yes, this suits Caroline much better. I have to confess," she said, addressing Caroline, "I'd never thought of you as the sophisticated type, but you look much more—grown up—in this. And the neckline—" she blushed slightly, "it's *de rigueur* in Paris, according to the latest plates I've seen. Unfortunately, if my frock were cut along the same lines, it would dip clear to the waist."

Caroline averted her gaze from Genevieve's sagging bosom, afraid if she looked at Maeve's face, she would break into laughter.

"Now, dear, here's a shawl sent to me many years ago by an aunt in France." Genevieve handed Caroline a shimmery fabric square, deeply fringed around the circumference. "Wrap it around your shoulders on the ride to the gala, so you don't catch a chill. By the way, Howard will escort us. Titus sent a message that he'll be a bit late."

They arrived at the scene of the party a little over an hour later. A makeshift canopy, comprised of a bark roof lashed to log supports, provided a covering in case of rain. Festoons of late summer flowers, goldenrod and ivy, draped over support posts and around tables, lending a festive air. Silver glittered everywhere. Coffee and teapots on silver trays, gilded silver punch bowls and cups, and gleaming pitchers of cider, lemonade, brandy, and rum appeared, most held aloft and proffered by liveried waiters. Linen tablecloths covered the tables, crisscrossed in the middle by strands of ivy and roses. Heavy Persian carpets covered the dirt floor, so with a little imagination one could almost imagine the location was the middle of a thriving European city instead of the wilderness.

Caroline wished Maeve hadn't suddenly felt ill and decided to stay home. Genevieve had graciously invited her, and it would have been fun to see her reaction to the luxurious surroundings. "Where did this all come from?" she whispered to Genevieve.

"The generals brought as many accoutrements with them as they could. It's difficult for them, you know, living in such untamed surroundings. They do a much better job when they don't have to worry about drinking from a muddy stream instead of a tankard, and when they can sleep in comfort instead of on the hard earth."

Caroline clamped her mouth shut, resisting the urge to retort that the army might be able to move a little faster, if they didn't have to cart such frivolities around. Then she remembered Austin telling her that the generals sent their personal belongings ahead, and wondered how the enemy could not know an attack followed a veritable convoy of items snaking through the forest.

But the vow to act the part of a good, mindless woman remained uppermost in her mind, and she determined to get through the evening as honorably as possible.

"Where on earth did they find all of these waiters? And

am I wrong, or are some British in attendance?" Caroline asked.

Genevieve waved her fan, stirring up a slight breeze in the already warm tent. "You're entirely correct. Some of our diplomats are meeting with their senior officers, hoping to work out terms for a cease-fire. Even a few of their wives attended, in hopes of smoothing things over. As for the servants, I'd hazard a guess we had to send for them from somewhere. I'm certain there's not this many servants in the entire Territory.

"Come dear, let's circulate," Genevieve said.

Mr. Duffy had already gone on ahead to see what news he could gather worth printing. Caroline looked for any sign of Titus, but could find no trace of him or Austin. The faint strains of a dance began, and within moments she found herself besieged by several uniformed young men. Before she could deny him, one whisked her away from the crowd of admirers.

Caroline stumbled and fell against him, conscious of the curious stares of couples on the sidelines.

"Say," her partner said. "Y'all don't dance, do you?"

Shaking her head, Caroline struggled to follow his feet. "No. I've never had an opportunity to learn." For the remainder of the dance, she said nothing, concentrating on following the man's footsteps.

"What's your name?" he asked, leading her away from the carpeted dance area and toward the punch bowl.

She looked up at him, a tall, dark-haired man with heavy brows. She supposed some women would find him attractive, but his black-brown hair only reminded her of . . .

"Caroline," she answered softly. "Caroline Swanson."

"Hmm. Are y'all any relation to Austin Swanson?"

"Yes. I'm Austin's sister."

"That's right," the man said, handing her a mug of syllabub. "Ah remember Austin saying he had a sister."

"Do you know my brother well?"

"Yes. Ah'll have to tell him Ah had the pleasure of dancing with his sister."

"And your name?" Caroline asked politely.

"James Thompson. Ah'm a private. Tell me, how is it a beautiful young woman like y'all is unattached?"

Caroline looked down at her feet. "Actually, I was betrothed to Mr. Titus Duffy, but we—the wedding was called off."

"Titus?" James grinned. "He's a good sort, but not as bright as I thought he was, to let someone like you slip away. Say, why don't Ah give y'all a private dance lesson or two?"

Nodding her agreement, Caroline listened and watched carefully as James showed her the elementary steps. He'd had the reputation, he told her, of being quite a good dancer back home in Kentucky.

"Kentucky? How is it you came here?"

James shrugged. "This is a national war, not just a local one. Ah expect several of our regiments will come to the Territory in time. We aim to help our countrymen."

"Of course."

He released her from his arms. "You're a quick learner. Now, let's go inside. Ah expect your brother will be here any time now."

"Thank you," Caroline replied. "I'm sorry to have taken so much of your time."

"The pleasure was mine, Miss Swanson." He smiled widely. "Mah only regret is that Ah didn't have the opportunity of meeting y'all at another time, before this crazy war. But that's mah lot in life. Always a day late."

His open, nonthreatening friendliness warmed Caroline. "I'm certain a young lady must await your return, Mister Thompson."

James shrugged good-naturedly. "Ah haven't had the good fortune yet of meeting a lady like y'all, Miss Swanson. Y'all wouldn't mind waitin' on a certain Southern soldier when he gets out of this war, would y'all?"

Averting her eyes, Caroline responded, "I'm sorry, Mr. Thompson. I just—I'm not able to wait."

James looked at her in understanding. "So, another man's in the picture. Well, ah can understand that. Now, let's go inside."

Thinking it better not to correct him, Caroline took his arm. As soon as they strolled past the tent's flap, James bid her goodbye and left her next to Genevieve. Caroline watched his retreating back. Though she'd felt none of that engulfing pull she'd felt when near Philip, neither had she felt the strange sense of detachment she always felt when near Titus. Though she might never love a man like James, she could share a laugh or two with him. And trust him, unlike . . .

She brushed the image away, refusing to waste any more of her time on that traitor.

"Oh, hello, Caroline," Titus said, approaching her. "By the way, don't you think you should cover up? Didn't my mother give you a wrap of some sort? I can't believe she'd let you out of the house looking like that."

Caroline swallowed her sharp response. "Yes, she did. It's rather hot in here, though."

Titus snorted. "You should feel naught but a draft; you're scarcely clothed."

Bowing her head meekly, she muttered, "You're right.

222

I'll go get my wrap." She waited a few minutes, expecting him to say he'd fetch it for her, but when he waved at an acquaintance in the far corner, she sighed and went in search of Genevieve.

Moments later she'd fought her way through the crowd, ignoring the suggestive comments of the men, pretending she didn't hear the invitations to dance that came at her from all directions, wishing she had a blanket to tie around her instead of the flimsy shawl. Whatever had induced her to change the frock's design to this revealing style?

By the time she again reached Titus, deeply engrossed in conversation with several heavily accented soldiers, some French, some British, the tension of the evening threatened to undo her.

"Titus," she whispered. "Ask me to dance."

"Pardon me?"

"I said, ask me to dance. I've already been asked by someone, and I turned him down, saying I'd already promised you. Please, Titus."

He looked at her in surprise, setting his glass down on the tray of a passing waiter. He raised his arms, bent at the elbows, palms facing her.

An hour ago she would have stood puzzled for a few minutes, before figuring out what he wanted her to do, but the brief lesson with James had made a lasting impression. Caroline mimicked Titus's pose, touching his fingertips lightly with her own, ignoring the perspiration stains under his jacket.

As her tutor had said, she learned quickly. It helped her to hum the melody in her mind, and though she didn't know the exact tune, she anticipated the notes with reasonable accuracy. Her innate musical sense lent fluidity and grace to her movements, contrasting vividly with Titus's stiff precise steps. Several observers who'd known the Swansons for years commented on Caroline's metamorphosis, the men nodding approval, the women more reluctant to compliment the young woman who'd previously been no threat to their femininity. Even the servants noticed the slender young lady with the silver hair.

When the music stopped, Titus bowed low, then led Caroline to the sidelines. "Where did you learn to dance like that?"

"It's nothing, really. By the way, when we were dancing, I thought I heard a fight break out?"

Titus shrugged. "Tempers are high. This is the first outing for many of the men since the British released them. They're drinking more than they should, and the heat doesn't help."

"It *is* stifling."

"I just saw someone I have to talk to. It's private business. Excuse me, will you?" He searched her face for understanding.

Something in the tone of his voice, the dogged determination, told her the business had to do with the Ferret. A shutter fell over her face. "Do go. I'll look for my brother."

"I'm sorry, I meant to tell you that Austin said he didn't think he'd be able to come. Find my mother or father instead. And get yourself something to drink. You look flushed."

A quick scan of the tent told her that Genevieve and Howard must have stepped out of the enclosure for some air. Fresh air sounded like a good idea.

She heard harsh words exchanged in the opposite corner. The promise of another skirmish worked like a magnet, drawing most of the people toward it. Taking advantage of the diversion, Caroline headed outside.

Even outdoors people milled about, couples strolling arm-in-arm, men, some uniformed, others in civilian clothes, talking in small groups. She waited until a couple rose and left one of the few benches, then sat down, smoothing her skirt under her. No sooner had she folded her hands in her lap, than a striking blonde with hair piled high and green eyes that slanted upwards from the corners waved off the two men flanking her and sank down on the bench.

"You don't mind, do you?" the woman asked, pulling a fan from the folds of her gown and opening it.

Caroline recognized the woman's accent as British.

"I'm American, you know," Caroline said.

"Well, I should think you won't kill me for sitting next to you. I'm Daphne Westmoreland from Britain. This war's a terrible nuisance, isn't it?"

Caroline looked at her, thinking how ironic it was that the first woman she met from Britain should be named Daphne. She told herself it wasn't fair to hold Daphne's name and nationality against her, and decided to behave with decorum.

"I've never thought of it as that. I always thought war was much more than a nuisance."

Daphne tapped Caroline on the arm with her fan, and smiled. "I'm sorry, my dear. Of course, it is for you, what with it being on your land and all."

Wincing, Caroline thought the woman sounded like a spitting cat.

"Of course," Daphne continued, "we're bound to win, and then you'll all be British, so we might as well be friends right from the start. What's your name?"

"C-Caroline," she sputtered.

"Ah, Caroline. And tell me, where did you get such a quaint gown? It's quite an old design, isn't it? But your taste is good, it befits you well. Perhaps I'll have to adopt the style, after I birth this babe."

Caroline's gaze dropped. Inwardly berating herself for not noticing before, she saw the gown's billowiness resulted from the woman's advanced state of being with child. "What are you *doing* here? When did you come here? Shouldn't you be home in case the child decides to come tonight?"

"Oh, you truly are amusing! I'm not ready to birth the child just yet." She leaned forward conspiratorially. "Actually, part of this is the result of too many bonbons. Though bonbons didn't put me in this predicament. 'Twas something else I ate."

Appalled at the innuendo and the woman's sly smile, Caroline rose, but Daphne pulled her down next to her.

"Have I offended you? I do apologize, but before you go, could you help me? I've just arrived in this country, you see, and I'm looking for a man."

Caroline swallowed the retort that Daphne had obviously had enough men for a while. She cleared her throat. "I don't think I'd be of much help." She wouldn't even offer her brother to this—this man-eating vulture. "The British are either here at this gala, or at Fort Malden."

"Oh, but my man isn't. Not here, that is, and I don't expect he's at Fort Malden. You see, he sent me a letter and told me to come at once."

"In your condition?"

"Oh, but he didn't know, you see. And he needs money desperately. Sit down."

226

Although she'd had every intention of escaping the woman, Caroline obeyed.

"You see," Daphne whispered, "my Philip's very important."

The hair on Caroline's nape stood on end. "Philip?" she asked weakly.

"Yes, Philip. You see, he wants to sell out his commission, and I can't tell you what it is, but it's very important. I have to tell you, his letter didn't surprise me at all. I *knew* Philip didn't come to America to win it for our country. He's never had a loyal bone in his body in his life." She poked Caroline twice in the chest. "And in his letter he told me to meet him near Lake St. Clair in Michigan Territory, but I have no idea where Lake St. Clair is. I just arrived here, you see, and as you can tell, I've been in no condition to travel much. If I gave you a message, do you think you could locate him for me? Tell him I'm at Forsythe's Tavern."

"No, I don't think I'll be fit to tell him," Caroline said, standing. "I—I'm very ill, you see. Very, very ill, and suddenly I don't feel well."

Daphne stood, alarmed. "You are? Can I help?"

"No! No, get your arm off me! It could be a new form of the yellow fever, a variation of one in the south, and the physicians think it might be catching."

"Oh!" Daphne shrank back. "Oh, get away from me, get away!"

Hearing the commotion, Titus hurried toward the women. "Caroline, what's the matter?"

She rubbed her hand against her brow and sagged against him. "I'm not well, Titus. Please, fetch the carriage. I need to go home."

227

# *Chapter Twelve*

Through a haze of pain and exhaustion, Philip could hear Cyrus and John argue with General Brock, as they approached what he'd come to think of as his cell.

"For God's sakes, you fools," Brock thundered. "What good is a spy with *two* bad legs?"

"We only broke one. Besides, you told us to do what was necessary to bring him around," Cyrus protested.

Keys clanged and the door creaked open, admitting the men. Philip shrank against the wall, shielding his eyes from the sudden shaft of light.

Brock swore softly. "Good God." He stooped to Philip's level. "Ah. I see you recognize me."

Philip winced when Brock touched his broken leg. The general turned to the guards.

"How long has he been like this?"

John shrugged. "Three, maybe four weeks. Don't worry, it's healing already. Don't know where the bloke gets his ideas, but by keeping that leg straight it appears—"

"*Exactly* how long!" Brock roared.

"Four weeks."

"How are you, Philip?" Brock asked, concern in his voice.

Philip's words came out dry and cracked. "I've been better." His eyes closed.

Looking over his shoulder, Brock called John to him. "He's no use to us now. Our most valuable spy, and you ruined him."

Philip's eyes fluttered open; he grinned weakly, careful to keep his leg straight, as he remembered Caroline did with her animals when they broke a bone. "I'm not ruined, sir. I've got some life in me yet."

"You do?"

"Aye. What day is it?"

"September 15th," Brock answered, trying to smile reassuringly. "By the way, Fort Detroit surrendered while you were in here. It's ours now. That's why I wasn't here to—never mind. If you weren't such a hardheaded fool—"

"Then I wouldn't be the Ferret, would I? And I am, you know. The Ferret."

Brock exhaled in relief. "You will be all right, won't you? You've come to your senses. Do you think you could handle a boat ride to the fort?"

"After what I've been through, I'd feel like a baby in a cradle. Why?"

"I want to go back to Fort Detroit for a while, and the best physicians are there at the moment. I'd like to take you there, if the journey wouldn't tax you overmuch. Or we could send for a doctor to come here?"

"No," Philip said hurriedly. "Detroit would be much to my liking." He licked his dried lips. "Tell me. Have we taken prisoners?"

"We did, but we've released most of them. We didn't

have enough food to feed them all. Besides, the Potawatomis will keep them in line, in case they think of causing an uprising. But enough of this for now. I can see you're getting tired. I'll have someone move you to my quarters immediately."

Closing his eyes again, Philip nodded. "The sooner we get out of here, the better. I'm eager to work with Mad Bird again. Did you capture Swanson?"

"No. My one big disappointment."

Philip mustered a smile. "If you get me out of here and get this leg on the mend, I can deliver him to you."

"Are you certain?"

"Yes. If you get rid of your thugs for a few minutes, I'll tell you what I have in mind."

Later, when Philip had told Brock what he'd planned, the general clasped his hands together. "Capital idea! But how do you intend to accomplish it? You'll never be able to walk that soon."

"Not walk, perhaps, but I should be fit to ride. I'll need a horse. Surely you managed to acquire some, when you captured the fort."

"Some, yes. But none very good, I'm afraid."

"I can manage. Now let's get me out of here."

Brock clapped a hand on Philip's shoulder. "Masterson, I just want to say I'm truly sorry this had to go so far. I knew you'd come around sooner or later." He hesitated. "You are sure about what you plan to do, aren't you? It could be dangerous. There's no regrets? About the woman?"

Philip met the general's probing stare. "What woman?"

Wordlessly Titus steered Caroline outside and into the carriage. "Stay here. I'll be back in a moment. I'll have to tell my parents to find another way home."

After he left, Caroline replayed Daphne's words in her mind over and over. *My Philip's very important . . . I knew he didn't come to America to win it for our country . . . he's never had a loyal bone in his body . . .*

It couldn't be a coincidence. It just couldn't. But then, what did she expect from a spy? Total honesty? And what kind of woman was she, that Philip's betrayal of *her* hurt worse than the knowledge he had betrayed her country?

The carriage's walls suddenly closed in on her, suffocating her. She scrambled out next to the driver, clutching her skirts around her just as Titus came outside.

"Caroline," he said. "I couldn't find my parents. I left a message with some friends; they'll let Mother and Father take their carriage. Now get in the carriage before someone sees you."

Staring straight ahead, she ignored the gape-faced look of the driver next to her, as well as Titus's threatening voice. "If I have to stay inside that thing, I'll scream. Now let's go home."

Muttering under his breath, Titus ordered the driver to start. "And hurry. Before anyone sees my friend here sitting outside like some kind of—man."

After they arrived home, Caroline went to bed immediately, leaving Titus to pace the floor in the family's living quarters. His parents arrived soon after. Maeve clicked her knitting needles in a chair in the parlor, attuned to her hosts' strained mood. The candle's glow shed barely enough light for her to see, but Maeve wouldn't have missed this conversation if she had to paste a candle to her forehead. Keenly aware of her status, she knew she needed an excuse to stay near the Duffys. Knitting required more candles than the lone taper burning in Caroline's chamber; no one would object to her working late. She sat quietly in the far corner, well back from the family gathered near the fireplace.

Howard and Genevieve, sitting side by side on the pine settee, cast worried glances from one another to their son.

"I suppose," Titus said, twisting his hands, "that I ought to try to talk to Caroline."

Genevieve shook her head. "I wouldn't advise it. You can speak to her in the morning, after she's had some sleep."

"Things can't get much worse, can they?" Titus asked mournfully. "Caroline's distraught over something, and she won't tell me what it is. I learned this evening that General Hull's up for a court-martial . . . "

Howard started. "A court-martial? Surrendering to the British was an act of cowardice, I agree, but I hardly think it worthy of a court-martial!"

"It's not just because of the surrender, Father. Neither of you can breathe a word of this to anyone." He glanced over at Maeve, who'd fallen asleep in the chair. Convinced she was totally oblivious to the conversation, he continued.

"It seems the general saw fit to send our written battle plans and army statistics ahead of him, via schooner. Someone tipped the British off. They intercepted the ship, and, well, that's how they managed to overpower us so easily."

Maeve's eyes flashed open, then shut tightly. Stunned at the news, the elder Duffys did not notice.

Genevieve's hands flew to her mouth. "That's dreadful!"

"There's more bad news, I'm afraid," Titus said wearily.

"More?"

"Yes. I'm almost positive I've identified the Ferret, and Caroline knew him. If I turn him in, her honor, if not her life, is bound to be compromised, and mine along with it. If I don't . . . "

"Our country's in further jeopardy," Howard said, rising and pacing.

"Yes, damn it!" Titus retorted. He slumped back in his chair, cradling his head in his hands.

Genevieve's brows knitted together. "How did Caroline come to know the Ferret?"

"The less you know of the circumstances, the better. But believe me, if people use their heads, they're bound to wonder why she never told anyone of her, uh, association with the man. She's never fit in anyway, and they'll just look for an excuse to find fault with her. I don't know whether to tell Austin or not . . . " His voice trailed off in despair.

The little grunt of protest Maeve made, before she remembered herself and clamped her mouth shut, did not go unnoticed.

"What were you about to say, dear?" Genevieve asked.

Hesitating, Maeve set her needles down on the table next to her and came forward. "If I may be allowed to speak, ma'am?"

"Of course. You've become quite one of the family."

Maeve looked squarely at Titus. "Sir?"

"Speak your piece."

"Well, then, if ye don't mind me sayin' so, and it's apparent ye don't, I'm awonderin' how ye could be thinkin' just of yerself, Master Titus."

Aghast, Titus responded, "But I'm not thinkin'—er, *thinking*—of myself."

"Ye said yer life was compromised. Those were yer exact words, sir. If ye ask me, and ye did ask, mind, I'd be thinkin' ye ought to convince Miss Caroline to wed ye. Folks will start thinkin' of her as a Duffy, and you Duffys are all respectable. Besides, no one knows but you and me, sir, what went on betwixt the lass and the Ferret, as ye be callin' him."

Genevieve looked from Maeve's pale face to Titus's ashen one. "Exactly what *did* go on between them?"

Titus addressed Maeve as if the two of them were the only people in the room, his voice low and choked. "You must love her very much."

Maeve nodded solemnly, her eyes bright. "Aye, sir. I do. Don't ye care what happens to her?"

"Of course. Caroline's been a dear friend of mine, ever since we were children."

"Just as she befriended the stranger," Maeve whispered. "My mistress is kind. She'd do naught to hurt either one of us."

Howard tented his fingers. "I think the maid makes sense."

Genevieve, who'd watched the exchange between her son and Maeve with a mother's intuition, nodded thoughtfully.

"Then," Howard continued, "may I suggest you allow me to help?"

Titus swiveled in his chair, focusing his attention on his father. "How?"

"For one thing, the newspaper. I believe I can concoct a story that will allay any suspicions about Caroline's involvement with the Ferret. It should help if you decide to go to the authorities with your information. I won't print much, just a line or two. And you'll have to help me."

"Yes," Titus answered. "I'll do it."

Howard rubbed his hands together. "Fine. It will be easily believed that she couldn't see through the man. Women can be too trusting."

Genevieve and Maeve bristled, then looked at each other. Putting a finger to her lips, Genevieve motioned to the maid to keep quiet. Maeve retreated to her chair.

"At any rate," Howard said, "you're bound to be thought of as a hero, when you reveal his identity. How much evidence have you to prove it?"

"All of it. Just before the fracas broke out at the soiree, I learned his name, Philip Masterson. It seems Mr. Masterson had made some enemies of his own, who were all too eager to relay the information to me."

"Well, we must make the best of a difficult situation. If you're really concerned about Caroline, and I presume you are, you'll do your best to make her see she must marry you." Howard turned to Maeve. "Do you think your mistress would be agreeable?"

Maeve thought a few moments. "I think Master Titus should wait a few days, sir. Until she gets over whatever is upsettin' her. And then—I don't know. But I'll help ye all I can."

Titus sighed. "Fine. I'll do my best, but I won't be able to come back for at least two weeks."

"Where will you be?" Genevieve asked. "How will I send a message to you, in case something goes awry?"

"You can't. I'm working on something confidential, and I can't tell you my location."

Howard's eyebrows rose. "Are you part of a plan to overtake the fort?"

"I said I can't tell you, Father. I'm sorry. But if all goes well, I'll be back in time."

"If all goes well?" Genevieve croaked.

Chuckling bitterly, Titus responded, "Unfortunately, there's no way to anticipate what will happen during a war. But I'll see what I can do."

Caroline refused to entertain the possibility of marrying Titus, when Maeve broached the subject.

"I won't do it," she stated flatly. "Titus doesn't want it, and neither do I."

"But don't ye see, lass?" Maeve entreated. "He'd be savin' yer life. Yer in trouble. Big trouble."

"Maeve—don't you feel anything for Titus? I've seen the way you look at him, and he at you."

"But it's a time of war, lass. Nothing's ever been spoken betwixt Master Titus and me. Besides, it's only a dream, it is, this notion of him feelin' anythin' fer me. I'm but a maid. Besides, ye must think of savin' yer own skin."

"My skin?" Caroline laughed. "My skin's worth nothing, Maeve. And don't worry about me. I can take care of myself."

Late that night, after everyone had gone to bed, Caroline stared out at the night sky, knowing the faint horizon lay some miles yonder, beyond the dense woods. While she could see nothing, her soul reached far beyond her field of vision.

"Philip," she whispered to the blackness. "Wasn't it enough you broke my heart? Did you have to take the pieces with you when you left?"


Two days after General Brock brought Philip to his temporary quarters, he greeted him at daybreak.

"Philip, wake up. I've brought someone to see you, and have news to tell you."

Waiting till his head cleared, Philip slowly sat up. "What's the news?"

Brock sat down on the cot next to him, rubbing his palms together. "It's bad news, I'm afraid. It seems you've been identified."

A chill ran up Philip's spine. Certainly not Caroline . . .

"So it seems," Brock said, "the sooner we get on with this plan of yours, the better. A disguise should work, but this might be the last time you'll have such an opportunity."

"We'll talk about that later. Do you know who identified me? Did they say my name?"

Blowing air through his teeth, Brock said, "I'm not certain how bad this is, actually. The man said you were a Frenchman, and I don't know how much of a description he gave. Were you well disguised?"

Closing his eyes, Philip relaxed. "Well enough." Apparently a woman had not turned him in.

"Another man's been accused by the Americans of consorting with you. I believe it's Swanson, which shouldn't put you in danger. Swanson can hardly identify you without implicating himself."

"Maybe," Philip said thoughtfully. "Maybe not."

"Well, don't worry about that right now. I've brought someone to see you." He strode to the door and motioned someone to come in.

Philip looked up and grinned. "Mad Bird. It's you."

The Indian smiled back. "Brock says you want a horse."

"Yes. And I want you to help me on my next venture."

"Yes. Your horse is outside."

Philip grimaced. "I'm sorry, but I can't walk to the door just yet."

"It's all right, Philip," Brock said. "Stay there. We'll bring him in."

Within minutes, Philip stared with disbelieving eyes at the familiar roan in front of him.

"Well, what do you think?" Brock demanded. "Mad Bird chose him from the animals we confiscated from the Americans. Thought it was a poor choice myself, but the Injun swore none other would do."

"He'll do just fine."

The horse whickered in greeting.

"Good heavens, man," Brock said, laughing. "You don't have to look at him like he's Pegasus or anything. It's just a horse. And a nag at that."

"He'll suit me just fine. Give me a week, and I'll have him behaving like a baby. In fact, I have a notion to take him for his first lesson right now."

"With a broken leg?" Brock asked. "Are you serious?"

"Aye. Remember our plan. We've no time to waste. Besides, my leg feels much better than it has the last few weeks. Just help me on him, so we can get to know each other."

Philip patted the horse's velvety, soft muzzle. "We're going to do all right, aren't we, boy?"

When Caroline looked out the window, black, threatening clouds scudded in the distance. She heard the distant rumble of thunder, and hoped the rain would relieve the oppressive heat. Tucking a stray lock of hair behind her ear, she listened to a far-off sound. Looking closely, she thought she could see riders on horseback. Puzzled, she went downstairs, where Maeve set the table.

"Where's Mr. and Mrs. Duffy?"

Maeve looked up. "Mr. Duffy said somethin' was wrong with the old printin' press, I think, and he was goin' to fix it. Mrs. Duffy went with him, said the ride would be coolin'. Why? What's troublin' ye, lass?"

Pulling up a chair, Caroline bit into a juicy apple. She swallowed and said, "That must be them I saw from the window, then. I do hope they get back before it rains."

"Aye. They didn't leave that long ago. They must have seen the storm abrewin', and decided to wait until it clears."

Caroline waved Maeve into the chair opposite her, and spread a thick layer of peach butter over her bread. It tasted bland. She pushed the plate away and listened to Maeve tell her about the chores Mrs. Duffy wanted to accomplish the next several days, putting up pickles and apples, late summer berries, and plums.

Caroline commented at appropriate intervals, straining to hear the sounds coming from out of doors. She shook her head; she was imagining things. Lightning never struck in the same place twice. It would be just as unlikely that Indians would attack her home again—but then, this wasn't her home.

She pushed her chair back and strode toward the door, pushing it open.

"What is it, lass? What's the matter?"

Caroline exhaled in relief. "Nothing. Just my imagination playing tricks on me." She laughed giddily. "I thought I heard Indians, but it's only Austin and another man. They must be out on a drill. But—oh, dear God," she gasped as the riders came into focus. "Why didn't I realize . . . "

Maeve ran to her side. "What is it, lass?"

"Austin and Titus. They're on foot, and the other soldier's on horseback."

"But that wouldn't mean anything amiss, now, would it?"

"It would if the other man had a gun pointed at them. They must be in some sort of trouble. Quick, Maeve, we must help them."

"How, lass?"

"I don't know," Caroline said quietly. "We'll just have to wait and see."

It seemed like hours before the men were close enough for Caroline to step outside to greet them. She glided outside, head high.

"Austin, Titus." She tipped her head slightly in the stranger's direction. "Good morning, sir. For what reason do you bring my brother and intended here at gunpoint?" *Don't tell him, Titus. Perhaps I can protect you somehow, if they think we're to wed.*

"You didn't tell me she was your betrothed." The portly, balding soldier sounded accusing.

240

Caroline held her breath, but before Titus could speak, Austin said, "They're not. They were betrothed at one time, but that was before she gave Mr. Duffy the gold." He shook his head in despair. "I'm so sorry she's my kin, Dinsmore."

Caroline felt the color drain from her face.

"Is that true, Miss Swanson?" Dinsmore asked.

She looked at his face, focusing on his sagging jowls. "Yes."

"And who gave you the gold, ma'am?"

"No one. I—I found—"

"*Who gave you the gold?* Was it your brother?"

"No! No, Austin never gave me any—"

"It's as I told you, sir," Austin interrupted. "She gave the gold to me, but I had no idea—"

"*Quiet,* Swanson! If I want your opinion, I'll ask for it. Now, Miss Swanson, who did you harbor in the old shack about eight miles south into the woods?"

Her head swam. "I didn't harbor—"

"Did you or did you not aid and abet the traitor known as the Ferret?"

She wavered. "I aided him—I mean, I healed him from a snakebite . . . "

"And why would you heal a traitor, ma'am? So you could sell him state secrets for gold? So you could tell him what your brother did for us, Miss Swanson? So you could betray the filial secrets Austin Swanson told you?"

Thunder clapped; lightning cracked.

"Why don't we go inside, sir?" Titus suggested in a gloom-filled voice. "It's going to pour down, and Caroline looks like she's—good heavens, I've never known her to faint."

The portly man agreed. "Inside, then! But tie this

241

woman—this would be her maid, would she not?—to a chair, and bind Miss Swanson's hands together. I won't have either of them escape."

From the fort, Philip mounted Derby and nodded for Mad Bird to follow him.

"Hurry," he commanded. "We're going to attack the home I told you about."

"Kill the woman and the man?" Mad Bird asked.

Philip pressed his lips together in a tight line. "Aye. Kill them all."

## Chapter Thirteen

Not more than ten yards from the house, Philip raised his pistol in perfect synchronization to Mad Bird's hefting of his tomahawk, looked at the Indian, and with one deft move aimed straight for his heart.

Numb, Caroline sat at the table, staring past the faces across from her. She'd thought the thunder had stopped minutes before, but suddenly a loud *pop* ripped the air. She saw Maeve jump.

"Pardon me, sirs, but that wasn't thunder," the maid said, quaking.

Dinsmore looked outside and swore. "Indians."

Iciness surrounded Caroline. Indians. Just when she thought things couldn't get any worse.

"Quick! Follow me!" Dinsmore ordered the men. Get on my horse. We've got to get away!"

Austin looked at him doubtfully. "Three on a horse? Outrun Indians?"

"And what about them?" Titus asked, indicating the women.

"One's a maid and the other's a traitor. If they kill either one of the females, they'll just save us the trouble."

"But—"

"Don't argue with me, Swanson! Now that we know you're not guilty, we need you back at the fort. Alive."

"But we're supposed to take her back with—"

*"Out."* The officer shoved his gun against Austin's ribs. *"Now.* And you." He yelled at Titus. "Forget about tying the maid. We've got to get out of here."

The reality of the situation hit Caroline like the lightning splintering through the sky. To the right she saw Maeve run toward the cellar. "Come, lass. Follow me."

She got up, but with her hands tied, she could not lift her skirts. A horse galloped outside. Its hooves pounded the earth, thundering ever nearer. Her heavy skirt encumbered her, weighed her down, impeded her movements. Just as she reached the doorway, a brown hand grabbed her neck and yanked her outside, while she kicked and bit. She struggled and fought till a voice whispered in her ear, "At least your hands are tied, sweetheart. Otherwise, I'd never stand a chance."

"Philip?" She gaped at him. If it hadn't been for the mercurial eyes, she never would have believed it was him. His hair hung in braids on either side of his head; a leather-beaded band snaked his upper arm. His skin, stained brown from walnut hulls, glistened beneath the deerskin vest, and the Indian-style, skin breeches were tucked into the same fringed boots he'd worn before. He looked like nothing more than a . . .

"Savage!" she hissed. "Let me go!"

Abruptly he released his hold on her. "Fine. You're free, but how long before they come back to get you,

Caroline? Austin's involved you in his schemes, hasn't he?"

"And you haven't? You think I'd be better off with you, I suppose. You're a British spy, Philip. Why would I put my life into the hands of the enemy?"

His face remained impassive, except for a steely glint in his eyes. "By all means, stay here. From what I've managed to gather, you're scheduled to hang for selling battle maps."

"But I didn't sell them."

"And the only one who knows that right now is you, me, and who else?"

She hesitated. "Austin."

Philip shrugged. "Exactly. And if you think you're safer with him, by all means . . . " He turned Derby away from her and said over his shoulder, "Your dear brother's returning, Caroline. Make your choice."

Looking past him, she could see the officer's horse heading toward them, with Austin and Titus running behind him.

"I'd like to stay and greet them Caroline, but . . . "

He tapped Derby's sides lightly, and the horse took off.

She saw Philip retreating, Austin approaching. "Wait!"

In seconds Philip was beside her, scooping her up in front of him. "I'll untie you later, my sweet. Right now I'm in a bit of a hurry." Turning, he aimed the pistol at the other horse's hooves and fired. It reared, sending Dinsmore careening into Austin.

"You didn't hurt him, did you?"

"Oh, for heaven's sakes, Caroline . . . "

By the time Austin, Titus, and Dinsmore were in pursuit, they'd crossed the stream once, then back again.

"We should lose them easily," Philip muttered in her

ear. "That horse will never last with three astride. Still, we'll cross once again, just to make sure."

"But Derby hates water!"

"You haven't seen him complain, have you?"

"You—you're forcing him; you'll cripple him. First you stole him, and then you broke his spirit."

Chuckling, Philip said, "I don't think he's broken, Caroline. Derby seems in one healthy piece to me."

She opened her mouth to argue, but closed it. Derby galloped so fast, she gripped his mane to keep from falling. "Where—where are we going? Are you going to take me prisoner to Canada?"

"You're not my prisoner. If you want to get off, just tell me. I'll stop Derby and let you go."

"And leave my horse? Never!" She ignored another meaningful chuckle.

After another minute she said, "You haven't answered the rest of my question. Are we going to Canada?"

"No. I've no desire to lose my life."

Her head snapped sideways. "You? But you're one of them."

"That's what they thought. But they'll soon learn otherwise. There's a little matter of a dead Indian to tip them off."

Confused, she asked, "But where are we going?"

"Kentucky."

She felt all the air sucked from her. "Kentucky?"

"Save your questions, Caroline. We're going to ride for a long time, until I think it's safe to stop."

"But you'll tire Derby."

"Don't worry about Derby. I'll let him slow down in a little while. Now, be quiet. I can't concentrate with all your infernal questions."

Soon the woods and trees ceased to look familiar. Caroline could not tell if they moved north, south, east, or west.

At first she kept herself as stiff and straight as she could, but by dawn she was so exhausted, she could scarcely keep her eyes open. Eventually the horse's easy canter rocked her to sleep, slumped against Philip.

When Caroline woke long after the sun rose, she lay on the ground. A pillow of sorts, Philip's leather vest, was crumpled beneath her head. A light blanket, the design clearly Indian, covered her. She shifted slightly, stifling a groan as she felt her bruises throb. Every part of her body burned and ached, from her head to her shoulders to her wrists to her ankles. Turning her head, she saw Philip curled on his side about three feet away from her, the rhythmic rise and fall of his shoulders telling her he slept soundly.

She looked at the sky, trying to determine their location in relation to her home. But with no stars to guide her, she had to admit she was lost.

Wincing, she tried to sit, but her numb hands would not obey her commands to push her up.

With a sickening awareness, she looked down at her ankles, and saw a thin leather strap wound around them several times. As she tried to rub her hands together, all hope for escape fled. They were tied more tightly than her ankles.

Her fear turned to rage. Tossing and turning, she struggled to free herself of her bonds, so she could box her captor squarely between the ears.

Philip, hearing her efforts, turned toward her and opened his eyes.

"You, you heathen! I'm going to give you a piece of my mind."

"Not quite as nice a piece as I had before, but lovely just the same."

"You *bastard!*"

Philip chuckled softly. "My, my. Take away your virginity, and all hell breaks loose."

Reddening, Caroline turned away quickly, but Philip had already seen the tears spring to her eyes. Propping himself up on one elbow, he put his other hand on her shoulder.

"Caroline, I'm sorry."

"For what minor travesty? For betraying my country? For involving my brother in your schemes? Or for lying to me about Daphne, for taking—" her voice broke.

Philip grimaced and pulled away. He spoke quietly, patiently. "Caroline. Listen to me. My people think I went to capture Austin so that he couldn't identify me."

"Capture? Don't you mean kill?"

His voice turned steely, hard. "I *should* have killed him, for what he's done to you. He said you were the one who sold the maps, didn't he?"

When she didn't answer, he shook his head. "Even if you don't believe me, you're safer with me."

"How?" The cry seemed to wrench from her very heart. "My safety's none of your concern, Philip. You only want to add me to your harem, so Daphne and I can take turns bedding you. I met her at a gala, you know; why did you have to send for her? What have I ever done to you, Philip?" *What have I ever done except love you?*

Her pain ripped into him. "I'll explain in time, Caroline."

The rawhide strips cut into her wrists; she wanted to cross her arms in front of her to hide her heaving breasts. She lashed out at him.

"What time? What makes you think I'll stay with you? I'll escape the first chance I get, and there will be a chance, Philip. No one, not even you, can watch me forever. And what makes you think I would believe anything you would ever say to me? Telling falsehoods to people is your life, isn't it? You're a master at it. I know now. You're nothing but a liar and a cheat."

Philip's eyes flickered. "Don't be a fool. The Americans want you as much as they want me. Maybe more. Whether you want to admit it or not, we're in the same predicament right now."

She ignored his searching look. "Untie me."

He hesitated, then withdrew a small knife, and cut the rawhide strips around her ankles, then her hands. He turned and mounted Derby. "Well," he said, looking down at her. "This is the only time I'll ask you. Are you coming with me or staying behind?"

For two weeks they rode. Philip found riding much easier than walking, which Caroline remonstrated against at every opportunity.

"That leg will never strengthen unless you exercise it," she said to him.

"Oh, no? More than likely you just want me on my feet, so you can escape. You'd have a good chance to outrun a cripple."

"Oh, Philip, stop it. You broke a leg; that hardly makes you a cripple. Broken legs heal."

"Yes, twisted and ugly, more often than not. But then it will just match the other one, won't it?"

She turned and glared at him. "Nevertheless, you'll be

weak in addition to twisted, if you don't start walking on it."

"When I can trust you, sweet. When I can trust you."

She sat in front of him on Derby, his arms brushing either side of her. When her lids closed in drowsiness she slumped against him, then feeling the contours of his strong chest, she jolted erect, sharply awake. It took all her willpower to keep her eyes open. She wondered if he had drugged the morning tea he brewed for her over an open fire. She wouldn't put it past him.

When several minutes passed in which neither of them spoke, Philip said, "Seeing you have no objections worth voicing, let me tell you my plan. There are regiments of good soldiers in Kentucky, crack shots, with guns I've heard are the best around."

"Better than that?" she asked sarcastically, pointing to his pistol.

"Better than anything. At any rate, I've heard the Kentuckians are banding together to help the Americans at Frenchtown. I mean to go with them. They would never recognize me. Hard as it may be for you to believe, Miss Swanson, I came to an awakening while I was away from you. I have changed allegiances."

Silence and a vacant stare met his announcement.

"I can see you're dying to ask me why, so I'll tell you. I decided I rather like it here. My countrymen have impressed free men, they've—well, I can see all my reasons don't matter to you. At any rate, I like the people here, in this country. I like the land as well. So I've decided to stay and fight. On your side. It'll be safer in Kentucky." He laughed bitterly. "At least there I have a chance of getting killed by the British, instead of by the Americans. And then, providing I live through this, I'll become a citizen."

"Liar."

Folding his arms in front of his chest, he arched an eyebrow. "Excuse me?"

"You're a liar. But it doesn't matter, does it? You'll just keep lying, and getting people to trust you, and . . . " She choked on a sob, and refused to say more.

When she had to see to her personal concerns, he hovered nearby, alert to her every move. It seemed to Caroline her last vestiges of pride were gone as he watched her constantly.

"Why do you watch me every minute?" she asked at last.

"For your own safety. If you decide to run away, either the Indians or your own people will kill you. Oh, Caroline, stop crossing yourself. You don't need to."

She glowered. "My conscience is no concern of yours."

"Well, your hands are, if they're always batting the air and confusing my horse. But they do look red and cold. Here, let me warm them up a bit."

She wiggled and squirmed, afraid to kick him lest she miss and send Derby into a flying gallop. With grim determination she ignored the feel of his hands stroking the backs of hers.

By keeping well away from trails and paths, Philip managed to avoid meeting any settlers, though they encountered an occasional Indian. Caroline's stomach churned as he spoke to them, bribing them with gold coins. She knew they believed he was still a loyal Englishman. So did she.

\* \* \*

By the third week, frost nipping exposed ears and noses, Philip's leg had healed so well that the only irregularity in his gait stemmed from the leg with the snakebite, and Caroline gave up fighting him, even mentally. It seemed her entire life had been spent trying to please the men in her life—first her brother, then Titus, at some point Philip, under the guise of Philippe—while still holding on to some semblance of herself, of her own wishes and desires. Some small portion of her had always held back, forever defiant. And what had that defiance earned her? Derision. Punishment. And the loss of that last, most sacred part of her womanhood. Philip was only another link in the unending chain of men, who sought to bend her to their will.

They sat across from each other on opposite sides of a campfire, over which Philip roasted a hare he'd trapped. No moon or stars rose in the night sky, the only illumination came from the fire's glow. Caroline sat cross-legged, clothed in an Indian's deerskin shift Philip had brought with him.

Chewing on a slice of juicy meat, Philip stole a glance at her across the fire.

She sniffed at the piece of pork he'd thrust at her a minute before. Her hair hung in stringy waves around her shoulders, yet, seemingly oblivious to her appearance, she'd make no move to dress it with the tortoiseshell comb he'd given her. She brought the meat to her lips, tasted it, then dropped it to the ground at her side.

"You have to eat, you know," he said.

Staring at him vacantly, she answered, "I don't eat meat. I can't. Please." Her voice rose several decibels, and Philip was surprised that it sounded almost shrill. "I can't. I would do it for you, but I can't. Please don't make me."

Whimpering, she ducked her head down in the crook of her arm, shoulders shaking.

Appalled at the wildness in her reaction, he said, "It's not for me that I would have you eat, Caroline. It's for you. If you don't eat, you'll starve to death." A chill ran down his spine, as he saw a whisper of a smile cross her lips.

"Caroline," he said, as if coaxing a wild animal, "I don't want you to starve. It's too dark to search for berries, and I don't know if any fruits grow this late here. Besides, it's cold. You need to have some meat on your bones to help you through the winter."

She threw a horrified look in his direction, and he realized with a sinking sensation that she hadn't thought of the winter, or worse yet to her, that she'd spend it with him. His food stuck in his throat. She looked utterly terrified. Of him.

Wordlessly, he rose and walked over to her, then sat directly behind her, pulling her into his lap. He didn't expect her to welcome his arms around her shoulders, meeting in front of her breasts. He waited to see if she'd struggle, try to free herself. But she sat perfectly rigid, as if in a trance. He wished she'd fight.

He cleared his throat. "Caroline. After we meet the Kentuckians, we'll head back to Detroit. We'll get there, I promise you. And when we do, I'll aid the Kentuckians in freeing your land."

She didn't answer, staring straight ahead.

"Listen to me," he continued desperately. "We're wanted by everyone in Michigan Territory. We need to lose ourselves in a group. Otherwise, they'll identify and kill us."

"Do you think I care?" she replied tonelessly.

A loud sigh escaped his lips. "No. I thought you would, but I guess I was wrong." He waited for her to protest, to argue, but once again his words seemed to hang in the night, audible only to him.

Now his voice turned harsher. "I don't care if they kill me, Caroline." He paused. "I've much to be ashamed of in my life, all of it my fault, my responsibility. I can take any punishment I might incur."

His arms tightened around her, while he buried his face in her hair. "But I couldn't bear it if anything happened to you."

They sat that way for several minutes, Philip's arms clasped tightly around the stiff, unyielding woman. When she refused to acknowledge him further, he released her, rose to his feet, and spoke briskly, looking down at her.

"Tonight you may go to sleep hungry. But on the morrow, I'll have none of this, no more. You will eat, or I will force food into your mouth and hold you until you swallow. Wouldn't that be agony, Caroline?" A bitter smile showed on his lips. "To have me hold you for eternity?"

She blinked and looked up at him.

"Fine," he said. "I see I've penetrated that thick skull of yours."

She stared back at him. "You're a liar. You only mean to infiltrate my people, so you can betray them again. Well, I suppose I have no choice but to accompany you— for now, at least—but I'll warn them at every opportunity, Philip. I'll tell them who you are."

The next day, Caroline tore into her food, chewing vigorously at the late fall berries she had gathered.

"So, I see you're hungry," he said.

She shrugged.

"You can talk to me." He stooped down opposite her, and she wondered why such a deceitful man had been given such well-shaped thighs and a flat belly. A wolf in the guise of a shepherd, talking as gently to her as if coaxing a trapped lamb to safety. "I won't bite."

"No," she snapped, eying him warily. "Biting's the least you would do."

Sighing, Philip brushed back the lock of hair falling over his brow. No wonder she looked askance at him. Though her hair fell wildly around her shoulders, it gave her an eerie, ethereal appearance, like an untamed angel. On the other hand, Philip thought he must look something akin to a creature from the nether world. Yes, a haircut and shave would do him good. And if a bath would improve *his* temperament, it had to affect hers.

"Would you like to bathe?"

Her eyes lit up, before a cloud passed over them and her expression changed, shuttered, defensive. "No, thank you."

"Why?"

Though she tried to snip at him, she could not quite keep her voice from quivering. "What would you do, Philip? Watch my every move?"

"Better yet, I think I'll bathe you."

She rose to her feet, her trembling lower lip belying the defiant thrust of her chin. "You will not."

"Aye, Caroline. I will."

He grinned and took two steps toward her. "Take off your clothes."

"No!"

"Then I'll remove them for you."

"You will not! All right, wait, I'll do it." She took a step back and fumbled, removing the boots he'd brought for her. Licking her lips, she fought the tight frisson of excitement rushing up her spine. "Please. Turn around."

"No."

Arms folded across his chest, feet splayed, his grin grew wider. "I think I'll watch this time. For your safety, of course."

"Oh!" She averted her eyes, seeing his arousal press full against his taut breeches.

"What is it, Caroline? Are you afraid?"

"I'm never afraid." With that, she tore the shift over her head and stood, hands clenched at her sides. Her chin lifted. "So. Is this what you want to see, Philip?"

"Yes," he replied thickly. "Now come here." He pivoted on his heel and led the way to the water's edge, ripping his clothes off as he walked.

She stared, fascinated, at his tight, tensed buttocks. He turned and looked at her, eyes glazed.

"Get in," he ordered hoarsely.

"Pardon me?"

"Get into the water."

She walked to the water's edge, pointed her toe in, and gasped. "It's freezing." But like a bucket of ice water it cleared her head, lifting her out of the fog that had surrounded her ever since she'd escaped with Philip. It seemed like years ago.

Philip chuckled. "Good."

She raised her brows, but he evaded her searching look, pushing her gently into the water.

"I—I can't stand it," she murmured through chattering teeth.

Groaning, he replied, "Nevertheless, you'll bathe."

Then, so softly she could barely hear, he murmured, "I must have been crazed." He lifted her trembling body and cradled her in his arms just above the surface, scooping a handful of water over her. She squealed in shock. He repeated the action again and again. The erotic sensation of holding a supple and pliant Caroline in his arms, rubbing the length of her naked body while he washed her, caused a distinct hardening between his thighs.

For a moment Philip closed his eyes, relishing her slippery body pressed against him, caressing her soft, slick skin, while his hands stroked and probed every intimate part of her, from her rounded buttocks to the velvety spot behind her knees, to the cleft between her legs.

He'd noticed her wincing when she sat, and supposed her bottom was slightly bruised from the long days in the saddle. He turned her in his arms. The buoyant water half-supporting her, he turned her over and lifted her slightly aloft, kissing her bruises, gliding his lips across her tender bottom, tracking the crevice with his tongue . . .

A tiny, strangled gasp startled him.

"Please, Philip. Oh, please!"

Eyes glazed, he pulled her to him. Her legs straddled him and she writhed against him, her head arched back, the pulse visibly racing in her throat. His last vestige of self-control evaporated. He thrust himself inside her and swore softly.

"You—are—so—tight. Clasp yourself around me, Caroline."

She threw her head back and held onto his shoulders, feeling his fullness within her, the very core of her aflame as he rubbed against her, heightening the heady, exhilarating sensation of intense heat within her, of cool water over her. Thrills shuddered through her in perfect synchronization with his release. When they were done, she slumped against him, drawing one deep, steadying breath after another.

"Well," he said huskily. "I really meant to give you a bath."

She looked up at him through her lashes. "I—um, I think I'd better finish by myself."

Slowly he released her. When she stood on the sandy bottom, she was grateful for the water's buoyancy. Otherwise her weak knees would surely give way.

"When you're done, wait for me on the shore," he said tenderly. "I have a need to bathe as well."

Her ablutions finished, she hurried to the shore, donning her clothes over her still wet, shivering body. Philip strode past her, brushing her shoulders with his. Then, darting a glance at his back, she ran over to Derby, jumped astride, and kicked. The horse stood still.

"Go," she whispered. "Go, Derby. Run!"

She heard Philip's voice ring out. "In case you're thinking of escaping on Derby, don't bother. He won't respond to anyone's commands but mine."

"Oh, bother," she said under her breath. "He'll listen to mine. He's my horse, after all. And I'm the one with a way with animals."

But after ten minutes of pleading, cajoling, and commanding, she gave up. Derby would not move.

Frustrated, she returned to the water's edge and sat Indian-style, resting her chin on her hands, watching Philip through the brown reeds.

Caroline pressed her lips together. At a distance of some twenty feet, he turned and faced her, naked and proud like some heathen god. She had never seen shoulders so broad or hips so narrow. Suddenly she saw him looking at her, grinning. He stretched his arms overhead, yawned lazily, then arched his spine, and dove backwards into the water. It was some seconds before Caroline remembered that the water was only deep enough to reach beneath her arms, and she breathed in sharply, lest he'd broken his neck. Then she realized the bare buttocks and muscular calves rising from the water were displayed for her benefit.

*Philip was standing on his head.*

Her scream of anger and embarrassment reached Philip's ears, muffled by the water. Smiling, he lowered his legs and stood. He luxuriated in the knowledge that he was close enough to shore for Caroline to see his masculine endowments, yet too far away for her to be repulsed by his leg.

When he came back to shore, shaking himself off like a water spaniel, he ignored Caroline's mumbled sputters and pulled her to her feet, leading her to their campsite. She dragged behind him.

"Can't you hurry?" he asked.

"I could if I wanted to," she snapped.

"I'm not that much of a fool." With that, he lifted her into his arms and carried her rigid body to the campsite.

## Chapter Fourteen

Though the journey had been arduous, Caroline could not help admiring the beauty of the land. The gently rolling landscape shimmered crimson, orange, and fiery yellow, the blazing colors reflected in the trickling streams that coursed through the forested hills. Fallen leaves crunched beneath the horses' hooves, heralding their arrival to squirrels and chipmunks scurrying across their path in preparation for winter.

After crossing a treacherous river Caroline feared would swallow them alive, they met up with several bands of soldiers armed with the longest rifles she had ever seen. She had a mind to somehow sneak a message to the men that Philip was none other than the Ferret, but his look of warning left no misunderstanding between them. While she grudgingly admitted he had treated her kindly thus far, escapades of the Ferret were legendary, even here among the Kentucky militia men. If she betrayed him, she feared what he would do to her. And what they would do to him.

Now the Kentuckians stared at them, some with rifles raised, as Caroline and Philip entered the campsite on a high bluff overlooking the confluence of the Auglaize and Maumee rivers.

"What regiment might this 'un be, gentlemen?"

Caroline stared at Philip, wondering from which bag of tricks he'd pulled the Southern accent.

A tall, redheaded man strode toward them. "This here's Capt. Richard Hightower's Company, 17th U.S. Infantry. Ah'm Captain Hightower. We're one company of the Raisin Force. Who might y'all be?"

"Philip Mathews, suh. Ah aim to be a party to any company commencing to battle in Michigan Territory. And this here's mah wife, Mrs. Caroline Mathews." He ignored Caroline's glowering look.

"Then y'all have the right company," Hightower answered. "We're aimin' to help our brothers in Frenchtown. Hear tell they're in dire straits. We kin always use more men. But we don't cotton to womenfolk ridin' with us."

"To tell ya the truth, Captain, Ah don't, either. A war's no place for women. But mah home was jist burned to the ground by the Injuns, and she don't have no place to go, suh. If yer company doctor is agreeable, she could be useful in seein' to the care of any sick or injured men. She's even better with animals."

Hightower motioned, and a slight, blond man came out of the group of watching soldiers.

"This is our surgeon, Dr. Alexander Montgomery. Did y'all hear what this gentleman said, Alexander?"

"Aye. And Ah could use a good assistant." Remembering how his intended, Maria, waited for him at home, Alex knew he would allow this man's wife to stay on as his surgeon's mate, if she had even minimal skills. "If Ah may be allowed, Ah'll take Mrs. Mathews to assist me in tendin' Isham's hand. Ah'll report back to you, Captain, to give you mah impression of her abilities."

"Acceptable, Doctor." Hightower turned to Philip, as he motioned for Caroline to follow the physician. "As for you, Mr. Mathews," the captain stated, "ya'll might as well know Ah take only the best. We've no room for laggards or hangers-on. Kin y'all shoot?"

Philip's chin lifted. "Of course Ah kin shoot." He aimed his pistol at a falling leaf and sent it flying in a hundred tiny pieces.

One of the men in the crowd whistled, another clapped his hands.

"Impressive, Mathews. But kin ya'll do it as well with one of these?"

Philip looked at the long-barreled rifle. "Ah'm sure Ah kin."

"Not so fast. This weapon's not a'tall like a pistol. Look." Hightower showed Philip how to load the weapon, using loose powder to fire the round lead ball. Philip watched attentively before nodding, hoisting the gun to his shoulder, and firing at a squirrel in a tree.

He missed.

Keenly aware of the men watching him, he reloaded, aimed again, and shot at the crotch of a tree.

"Nice shot, suh. But kin y'all hit a movin' target?"

Philip pointed the gun at a slender limb holding a squirrel, and fired.

One of the soldiers walked to the dead animal, picked it up by the tail, and twirled it around. "Thar's not a mark on it."

"No." Philip grinned. "Ah hit the bark beneath him. The force killed him, not the ball."

Hightower extended his hand. "Welcome, private."

Just then Caroline, escorted by the physician, returned.

"Mrs. Mathews is as skilled as any surgeon's mate Ah've seen," the doctor said. "Ah'd be glad to have her as mah assistant."

"She's an accomplished rider, too," Philip said. "She won't let us down."

"Then why didn't she ride her own horse?" Hightower asked.

"Well, we're poor folk, and have only one horse between us, suh. If you've none to spare, Derby kin handle both mah lovely wife and me. Been doin' it ever since we started out."

"Well, then," Hightower said softly. "Mah lucky day. A crack shot, a surgeon's mate, and a good horse. It's nice to have y'all with us."


Hightower and the commanding officers from the other regiments decided to camp on the bluff, until the turbulent river froze thick enough to cross. Caroline settled into the routine of assisting Alexander with the soldier's minor injuries, while Philip learned all he could of the Kentuckians' battle plans. Whenever she had a spare minute she went to the horses, rubbing their legs with liniment, seeing to any scrapes they'd incurred while working on drills with their riders. At night, when Philip came to their tent, she rolled onto her side and pretended she slept, even when he pulled her tightly to him. She told herself she needed the heat from his body and braced herself for his advances, but he only smoothed her hair and planted a tender kiss on her cheek. Then he fell asleep, exhausted from the endless drills and planning.

One evening while they were seated around the campfire, she decided that this ragtag bunch of men, with their long scraggly beards and loathsome habit of spitting tobacco, were only one step removed from animals. Actually, animals were better.

She straightened her spine, squared her shoulders, and held her head high.

She willingly took the roasted wild turkey leg Philip offered her, noting his smug grin. Bending her head low over it, so it would appear she was eating, she addressed a man of about twenty-four with startling blue eyes and full lips displayed above a blue black beard. Caroline had noticed the animosity between this particular man and Philip, and guessed her "husband" was jealous of the man's primitive good looks and the admiring glances he sent her way. His name was Zebedee Mitchell.

"Have you heard of the Ferret, Mr. Mitchell?" Her voice melted like honey.

Philip paused mid-bite, then continued chewing as if she'd commented on the weather. No one but Caroline noticed his right arm steal behind her back, his fist pressed threateningly into the base of her spine.

Zebedee grinned. The woman had never condescended to speak to him before. "Aye. We all heered of him. Heered of him jist like we heered of all them Injuns supposed to be around us. Ain't seen none of them, either."

"And what do you think of the tales about him? The Ferret?" Philip asked.

Caroline's mouth dropped open at his sheer audacity, but he simply smiled at her, eyes twinkling.

"Think them's a bunch of bull. Pardon, ma'am."

Flabbergasted, Caroline fixed wide blue eyes on him. "Then you don't think there is such a man?"

Another of the men shrugged, spittle running down his chin mixing with the turkey juices. "Oh, there may be sech a man as the Ferret, but them stories about him—them's jist yarns."

She steadfastly ignored Philip's muffled chuckle. "Then you don't think he was responsible for capturing General Hull's trunks and compromising our safety? You don't think he's killed a hundred men single-handedly?"

"Why didn't you ask me yourself?" Philip growled in her ear.

Caroline muttered back, "Because I'm sure you would have claimed it was two hundred."

The last man who'd spoken, Caroline thought she remembered his name as being Ephraim, eyed her quizzically. "Ah ain't sayin' too much cuz Hull's on our side, but that there general's a brick shy of a load. And a yellow-livered sissy, on top of it all. Shoulda put him out ta pasture a long time ago. As for the Ferret killin' a hundred men, well, Ah dunno. He coulda, but Ah doubt it. Hear tell he's royalty or sumpthin'. Those kind don't got the stomach fer it. Or fer our rifles."

The others grunted their agreement.

"But what about the women?" Caroline persisted. "What if you found the Ferret right here, alive and well? Wouldn't you worry about your women?"

The men hooted, exchanging ribald comments.

Again the fist balled against her back, but Caroline smiled pleasantly.

Zebedee shrugged. "If'n he wanted Annie, he'd have to fight her fer it. She's as mean an' ornery behind a rifle as any man I ever knowed. And as good a shot. And I'll tell you what, little lady. I wouldn't worry about the Ferret if I was you. Why, if'n he was in our midst—" he shot a meaningful look at Philip. "if'n he was, mebbe he'd be wantin' to be on our side. And if he didn't, why we'd jist gut him alive, wouldn't we, boys?"

Guffaws answered him.

Suddenly Caroline felt herself being raised to her feet by Philip's strong arm at her waist.

"If y'all will excuse us, the missus and me, why we got some things we gotta do." He winked broadly at Caroline, making sure the men saw.

Gritting her teeth, she put one foot in front of the other as he propelled her toward their tent. As much as she wanted to fight him in public, she didn't know if she'd be better off at the hands of the Kentucky men, or worse. For one thing, she couldn't fight him any way but vocally; he was far stronger than she. For another, she'd seen the way the soldiers looked at her, like hungry mountain lions. Except for that one time at the river, Philip hadn't accosted her. But his remarks in front of the men . . .

"How *dare* you?" she snapped, as he shoved her into the tent. "How *dare* you talk like that in front of those— those barbarians, letting them think we came here to— oh! And what do you think you're doing, aping their ridiculous accent? Who do you think you're fooling?"

He dodged her kick to his shins and grabbed her wrists with one hand. The steely look in his eyes made her wonder if she'd gone too far. "Men hear what they want to hear, Miss Swanson. If I want to travel with them—and make no mistake, I do—then I must become one of them. I doubt they even noted my accent. As for barbarians, I'd wager they're smarter than the men you're so fond of protecting. Austin, for instance. An absolute paragon of virtue."

Ice filled his voice; his eyes became unreadable. "As for

how I dare talk to them like I did—how dare *you*, Miss Swanson? How dare you imperil your own life? Were they to kill me, you'd be nothing but a plaything to them, an amusement to be shared. Do you understand me, or do I need to go into more detail?"

Unable to refute his logic, she cried in frustration, "Oh, I wish you'd never brought me here!"

He studied her for several minutes. "So do I, Miss Swanson. So do I. Now, if you'll excuse me . . . " He grabbed his bedroll from the floor.

"What are you doing?"

Turning to her, he smiled bitterly. "Sleeping outside the doorway, my lady. So you'll feel safe." He pivoted on his heel and left her standing alone.


Three hours later, Caroline, still awake, listened to the night sounds. The mid-November air cooled quickly. She felt chilled, and rubbed her arms with her hands to warm them. Her toes tingled from the cold, and she wondered how she would manage to keep warm throughout the winter months, if Philip decided to spend every night across the tent's entrance. She'd never realized how much heat radiated from him, when he slept next to her.

Beyond the open flap she could see the embers of a small warming fire he had built; his huddled back and regular breathing told her he'd fallen asleep. Then his head jerked up and he was on his feet, a glint of silver reflecting in his hands. She wanted to call out to him, to warn him to be careful, but then he disappeared before she could speak.

She waited a few minutes, then heaved a sigh of relief,

seeing a distinctly male shadow approach the tent. As he pulled the flap back, she rose to her feet.

"Good evenin', little lady."

She screamed.

Zebedee clapped his hand over her mouth.

"Quiet, woman," he growled under his breath. "It's me, Zeb. I seen the way ya've been lookin' at me. Ya'd rather be with me than yer husband, now, wouldn't ya?" He leered at her. "Yep, pretty one, yer jist gonna love stayin' with me. I got plenty of tricks I'm gonna teach ya."

When he slowly released his hand from her mouth, Caroline licked her lips, her nails digging into her palms so hard she drew blood. She concentrated on that pain, willing it to distract her from her shaking knees. "How are you going to keep me? He'll fight you, you know."

Zebedee grinned widely, displaying several gaps where teeth should have been. "I ain't afixin' to fight him. He's gonna be dead. Two of my men are readin' to kill him right now, so's I kin git to ya. And after me, they'll take their turns with ya."

"You can't do that!"

Zeb jutted one hip out. "Why not, little lady?"

"Because—because he knows the way back to Fort Detroit. You can't kill him. He knows all kinds of things, like—like how to talk to the Indians. He's friends with them, even. They won't kill us as long as he's around."

"Oh? I thought ya hated him." Zebedee eyed her with open suspicion.

"I do, I do." Caroline rested her hand lightly on his arm. When she saw his eyes light up at the gesture, she swallowed. What more must she do to ensure their safety?

"But," she continued, "I don't wish to be killed. We met scores of Indians on the way here, and I was certain they were going to kill us. But he talked to them, and they simply let us pass."

Zebedee's mouth slowed chewing his tobacco. He studied her for several long, tense moments, while Caroline struggled to look at him calmly.

"What else is there about him ya kin tell me? Ah ain't trusted him from the beginnin'. He ain't all he's tellin' us, is he?"

It was a gamble. She knew it was a gamble, but she had to tell him the whole truth. If Zebedee ever thought she lied to him, she and Philip would never get out alive.

"He's British."

"What?"

"I said, he's British. That's why he's such good friends with the Indians. The British have been making friends with the Indians from the time this war started; you know that. So you see, after we get to Michigan Territory, you can kill him."

She laughed in a pitch slightly higher than normal.

Zebedee hesitated. "What about y'all? Can't y'all tell us the way back without him?"

She shook her head. "No. I'm not that good on directions. I'd never be able to guide you. But I do have a good memory for landmarks, streams and such. I think I'd know if we weren't retracing our steps." She hesitated. "There's one other thing."

"What's that?"

"My brother's an important general in Michigan Territory, a good one. If I were to return with child, he'd kill any man he suspected of using me ill."

Zebedee's brow creased. "What about the soldier? I thought the two of ya was wedded."

Eyes widening, Caroline forced out a fat tear. "Oh, no.

I was betrothed to another man, another general. I have no particular loyalty to him," she finished lamely, praying he'd believed her. From far-off she heard groans and grunts, and knew she had to bring the conversation to a close before they killed Philip. "Your men are hurting him. If you don't stop them, we'll never find our way back."

Still not entirely believing her, Zebedee called, "Daniel, Jabez, stop! Gotta talk to ya before ya do anythin' more."

From out of the darkness, Hightower marched in front of Caroline and Zebedee. "What's goin' on here? One of the sentries woke me up, thought he heard a noise."

"It's all right, suh," Zebedee answered. "The lady here, she was steppin' out, and thought she saw somethin'. A giant snake ya said it was, didn't ya?"

Caroline swallowed, feeling the tip of a knife blade against her back. "Y-yes, a snake," she echoed.

Hightower raked his hand through his hair, stifling a yawn. "Well, where's Mathews, then?"

"Jist stepped out to relieve himself, suh. And the missus got skeered. Daniel's goin' to fetch him right now."

"If yer sure yer all right," Hightower said, looking closely at Caroline.

The knife tip pierced her skin a fraction of an inch; she felt a wet drop of blood. "Y-yes. I guess I was just dreaming. I'm sorry to disturb you, sir."

With a wave of his hand, Hightower turned and walked away.

As he disappeared into the trees, Zebedee growled in her ear. "Ya done good, little lady. Now keep yer mouth shut, and y'all will live till mornin'. I got plans for ya, but they're gonna have ta wait."

* * *

Philip knew he heard it, knew he heard footsteps around his horse. Now the night was unnaturally quiet. Still, he sensed someone nearby.

He paused, listening for the telltale *whish* of a man relieving himself, for that would explain the noise he'd heard earlier. Instead, a twig snapped. It wasn't an Indian, then. Indians walked softly. His pistol felt comforting in his hand, the cold metal reassuring him. Hooking his finger firmly in the trigger, he took one noiseless step, then another, grateful for the training the Potawatomis had given him back in Michigan Territory. If not for their patient instructions, his chronic limp would give him away. Instead, when he walked, he lightly put his weight on the balls of his feet. To proceed in that fashion normally would impede his progress, but now speed was far less important than quiet.

He cocked his head, listening for the sound of breathing. A *shh* came from his left; he whirled to face it. A blow came from behind, but he heard the hand cutting through air in time to dodge, so it glanced off his shoulders.

From far-off in the distance, he heard a scream he knew in his gut was Caroline's.

He struck out blindly, trying to make out the shapes of the two men in the darkness. They chuckled at his attempts, but he felt the satisfying thud of his fist meeting stomach. Someone's teeth skimmed the back of his hand. Philip grabbed his assailant by the hair, landing a punch square in the middle of the man's mouth. The strangers had names now, as his eyes pierced the darkness. Jabez and Daniel were two of the Kentuckians, but as he swung and ducked, Philip racked his brain, trying to remember

271

if he'd done something to make them want to fight him. Or, as it looked now, kill him.

"Damn," he heard Jabez say. "He split my lip."

"I got him," Daniel answered, grabbing Philip's neck and turning him around.

Philip swung, but Daniel hit him at the base of his spine, then kicked the back of his knees.

Slumping to the ground, the air whooshed out of him as he tried to protect himself from the kicks and punches that brought pain from every direction. Right before he slipped into unconsciousness, he thought he heard a deep voice order, "Stop!" But maybe, he thought wryly, it was just wishful thinking. Then the night became blacker than before, dotted by a million sparkling stars.

It was dawn before Philip woke, rubbing the back of his neck to ease the relentless pounding in his skull. He brought a hand up to his head, flinching when he felt the size of the lump. On unsteady legs he rose to his feet, bracing himself against the tree trunk, blinking several times to clear his thoughts. He reached in his pant leg for his pistol, swearing softly when it wasn't there. Well, perhaps it was time to persuade one of the Kentucky men to let him have one of their long rifles.

The thick growth of pine and spruce trees blocked out the morning light, holding his vision to three feet at best. Within minutes he came to the site where the men were dousing their cooking fires, preparing to break camp. His tent had already been torn down. He searched their ranks for Caroline, but could not see her.

Gradually the sound of clanging tin, squeaking leather, and flicking straps faded away as the Kentuckians stopped their preparations to stare at him. Even their mouths ceased worrying chunks of tobacco between their teeth.

Philip smiled and took a step forward.

Guns jammed in unison. The Kentuckians circled him and shifted their rifles to their shoulders. Philip stared down the barrels, but never lost his smile.

"What's this about, mah good men?"

Zebedee strode into the center from outside the circle, the men parting to let him in.

Peering over the black-haired man's shoulder, Philip saw Caroline in the distance, her face turned away from him. Around her shoulders he saw the tattered orange blanket Zeb always clutched on chilly mornings.

"We ain't yer good men, British boy." Zebedee spit a mouthful of tobacco on the ground.

The light left Philip's eyes, but his smile remained easy. Caroline had told them about him. He'd thought he could trust her.

He turned his palms upward and shrugged his shoulders.

"Well, then, you've found me out. Aye, it's true I'm of British descent. So what are you going to do to me now?" His gut churned.

"It's what yer goin' to do fer *us*, soldier boy." Zebedee spat. "We're fixin' to head cross the Maumee and inta Michigan Territory. Need ta recapture the fort. Seein's how ya come from there'n all, we figure yer jist the guide we need. Specially since ya seem to have a way with the Injuns."

Philip's heart plummeted, now knowing beyond all doubt that Caroline had told the Kentucky men everything. If she'd told them he was the Ferret, they'd kill him as soon as he was no longer useful to them. He'd just have to make certain he stayed useful for as long as possible.

"It's true, I did learn something about the Indians. But I learned from the Potawatomi, and a bit from the Shawnee. I know nothing of your bands."

Zebedee studied him, measuring his words. "Ya better not be lyin' to me."

"I'm not." Philip nodded in Caroline's direction. "What about her?"

"She's stayin' with me. She came the same way ya'll did, and she'll tell me if yer leadin' us in the wrong direction. Truth is, we wouldn't be needin' you a'tall, if it wasn't fer yer way with the Injuns. Why, she'd be givin' me everythin' I need."

The men guffawed, clapping each other on the backs at this remark.

Philip's teeth clenched. "I'll take you, providing you don't hurt her."

The corner of his mouth turning up, Zebedee said, "Hey, I reckon I'll be jist as gentle with her as I kin be. None a' my women ever complained."

Philip's hand shout out, clipping Zeb's ear as he ducked to miss the blow.

Zeb's fists balled, ready to strike.

"Go ahead," Philip taunted. "Kill me. Call your men to help you, I'm outnumbered. There's no way I can fight all of you. Then let's see you get into Michigan Territory by yourself without getting slaughtered."

"All right," Zebedee said through gritted teeth. "I'll let ya go."

"Then the woman comes with me."

"Nossir," Zeb replied. "As long as I got her, I knew yer

gonna stay. Now plan yer course. We gotta lotta ridin' to do."

By now, Caroline's curiosity had gotten the better of her. She circumvented the men, her stomach flip-flopping when she saw Philip's bruised and battered face, and the way he kept rubbing his right arm with his left. Their eyes met, his reflecting his disappointment. Apparently he believed she wanted to stay with this vile man, believed she'd planned their assault on him. If only she could tell him she'd saved his life.

"Wait," she said softly, putting her hand on Zebedee's arm.

Philip's lip curled in disgust.

Lifting her chin a notch, she glared at the Kentuckian. "There's no way the man's fit to ride."

Sneering, Zebedee ground out, "Let 'im walk."

"He can't. You know he's a cripple; he'd never be able to keep up with the horses."

Philip's flushed face did not go unnoticed. Caroline wanted to cry out, *I don't think of you as a cripple. Don't you see? I have to make them think of you as weak, so you can escape.*

But he avoided her eyes, the rigid set of his jaw hurting her more than any physical threat.

She tried another tactic. "You're right, we need to go. But I can help him, so he can in turn help us. He'll owe us, you see."

"How can y'all help him?"

"I—I know of medicaments and such. Dr. Montgomery will vouch for me. And he's much too busy to take care of Philip. Besides, I used to make ill animals well again. If you let me go, I'll tend to your horse. I saw him this morning, and—"

Zebedee's brows shot up. "My horse don't need no tendin'."

"Yer wrong, Zeb," Daniel said. "I was jist saddlin' him up and noticed a limp. Went to check it and sure enough, it looks like Ol' Rooster got hisself in a fight. His left forelock is cut purty bad."

"I'll see to the animal," she said quickly, and walked beyond their sight to the horses. After glancing around to make sure no one was in earshot, she whispered in a husky voice, "I'm sorry, Rooster. I didn't want to hurt you this morning, truly I didn't. But it's just a flesh wound, it will heal . . ."

She threw her arms around the horse's neck and blinked back tears. "I had to do it, so they'd let me see Philip. I have to take care of him and—and I'll take care of you, too." She swallowed and straightened. "I have to go back now, or they'll become suspicious."

Fifteen minutes later she assured Zebedee the horse would heal, if he was led riderless behind them. The Kentuckian said grudgingly, "I guess y'all kin see to the man's wounds. But make short work of it."

As the company secured the last of their supplies on the horses' backs, Caroline and Philip knelt in the middle of the clearing.

A tense silence hung between them, until Caroline slapped a muddy mixture on a reddened spot on the back of Philip's neck.

He let out an oath. "What in God's name is that?"

She peered around him, smiling smugly. "A simple healing balm; it will clean your wound. Usually I mix it with something mild to make it sting less, but there's nothing to be spared."

Gritting his teeth, he replied, "What about the water in

the stream thirty feet away from us? Is that too far for your precious self to walk? Even this *cripple* could force himself to crawl over there, if he had to."

Caroline's fingers stilled their ministrations momentarily. But, she argued with herself, he'd treated her abominably. She poured a healthy dose of the Kentuckians' whiskey over the cut on his forehead, grimacing when she saw his involuntary shudder. The gooseflesh on his back, raised from the cool autumn day, stood out in bluish relief. A lesser man would have screamed, as the hot liquor splashed on his open wound. She couldn't even bear to have the biting liquid touch her lips.

"Are you quite finished now?" he asked hoarsely.

"No. Lift up your arms."

He hesitated, then raised his arms over his head.

Taking the length of bandage she'd hurriedly made from some strips of cloth, she pulled off his shirt and wrapped his chest, pulling so tightly Philip wondered if he was to be mummified. "Do you mean to cut off my air?" he gasped.

"Not at all. From the way you keep rubbing your sides, I'm certain your ribs are badly bruised. This will help you ride in some degree of comfort."

"Comfort?" he snapped. "The only comfort I'll receive is if I die for want of breathing."

"Are you quite happy we'll be staying with this bunch of ruffians for the next several weeks?"

"Actually, I rather am."

Tying off a length of bandage, Caroline gave a curt laugh. "I don't believe you."

She'd come around in front of him, and he fixed her with his stare, his eyes a cool, clear gray that echoed the color of the autumn sky.

"I know you don't, Caroline. But I've wanted to change sides some time now. Become an American." When she opened her mouth to snap back a hasty retort, he brought his hand to her lips, touching them briefly. "I know you don't believe me," he said gently. "Yet it's true. I don't know what will happen to us, but I will tell you this, and you will listen to me. You think you know me well, but there's much of me you don't know. I have little to commend me, but—" he paused, sighing. "I think I was tiring of my past before I even landed in America. Someday I'll tell you more, but for now just let me say that everyone I'd ever known was like me: shallow, manipulative."

"Like Daphne?" she shot back.

"You don't know the half of Daphne," he replied quietly. "But she's not important now. What is, is you. Caroline, at first I wanted to become an American because of you. But then, when I realized you might never grow to—care for me, I thought that if one good came of this, even if I you left me alone, I would serve my new country to the best of my abilities. These men convinced me my decision was right. They may be crude, but I doubt there's a dishonest bone in any one of them."

"What about Zebedee, Daniel, and Jabez?"

"All right, three out of how many? Eighty-six left alive in all the regiments combined? You'd never find such good odds in all of England. And," he said, grinning, "they're also the best shots I've ever seen."

The sound of approaching footsteps told them their time alone was coming to an end.

"Believe me, Caroline," Philip whispered. "I have much to offer my new country—"

Zebedee grabbed her arm and brought her up next to him before she could hear the rest of Philip's hushed sentence.

"And you."

## Chapter Fifteen

They camped on the bluff in the most miserable conditions Caroline had ever experienced. She no longer crossed herself. Her hands were kept so busy tending to ailing men and animals, she had no time to waste on such self-indulgence.

The regiments despaired of receiving the supplies promised them. They reduced their daily rations until they subsisted on a few ounces of flour, a mug or two of ale, and an occasional thin slice of dried beef and pork. Time and again men went out to reconnoiter the area, only to find the Indians had preceded them, torching fields of corn and wheat, burning houses, and slaughtering livestock in their pens. When they returned disheartened, they described cows and pigs rotting in the fields, their flesh picked free of their bones by hungry vultures.

Almost instantly, Zebedee succumbed to the dysentery sweeping through the camp, his body added to the scores they'd already buried.

Alexander said to Caroline, "Now that you're no longer in danger from Zeb, I'd like you to stay away from the sick men in the evenings. Go to either his tent or Mathews'. Get some sleep."

"No. The men need me."

Looking her straight in the eye, Alexander responded, "Yes. They do. But if you drop from exhaustion, you won't be any good to anyone, will you?"

"Then give me my own tent," she said staunchly.

"No, Mrs. Mathews. We've none to spare, unless you want to take over Zeb's."

She shuddered. "I couldn't do that."

Alex laid down his surgical instrument. "Mrs. Mathews, I don't know why you're so afraid of Philip."

"I'm not afraid."

"Then go back to him. Even if we had a spare tent, you wouldn't be permitted to stay by yourself. It isn't safe. I must insist. If you won't go back to Philip's tent for a good night's sleep, I'll notify him to come get you."

She knew she should argue, knew she should protest, but she was so tired . . . "I'll go."

When she walked into the tent, Philip masked his concern. He'd never seen her look so poorly, and wondered if she'd be the next to be buried. Over a hundred men had perished from cold, starvation, or illness. But not Caroline. He would see that she lived.

"Welcome home," he said casually.

"It's not home," she snapped. "As a matter of fact, I doubt we'll ever see home again. Michigan Territory seems a million miles away."

He added another chunk of grisly beef to the pot he stirred. "We'll get there, Caroline. Now tell me. Have you been near any of the ill men?"

"Ill? Ill means there's a chance of getting better. I've not seen one man recover of late. They're dying, Philip.

Dysentery, fever . . . Is there ever an end to it? There's nothing we can do, we have no supplies. They ask for help, and there's nothing I can do . . . nothing anyone can do." She buried her face in her hands.

Philip took one look at her and stood up, pot in hand. "I'm taking this outside to simmer. I just warmed up that blanket by the fire. Wrap up in it. I'll be back with something for you to eat as soon as it's cooked."

He returned an hour later to find her curled in the corner, fast asleep. He yanked the blanket from her shoulders.

"No!" she cried, instantly awake. "I—I'm freezing and tired! Let me sleep." She tried to snatch the blanket back, but he held on tight.

"You can have the blanket after you've eaten, Caroline. Now come. I've made us a hearty stew."

The hearty stew consisted of some flour mixed with ale, bits of beef, and salt. Caroline thought she had never tasted anything so wonderful. "Where did you get so much meat?"

"I thought you didn't like meat."

"I don't. But one has to eat it, if there's nothing else to be had. You haven't answered my question. Where did you get so much of it?"

"I saved it."

"Saved it?"

For the first time she looked closely at him, thinking that if he intended to disguise himself he could hardly do better. Though he, too, had lost weight, he appeared tougher than ever. His beard, long and luxurious, appeared neatly combed, and his hair, pulled back in a queue, hung past his shoulders. His eyes, reflected in the candlelight, were all that remained familiar. They changed colors according to the light, appearing green when the candle flame flickered, bluish when it burned brightly.

He wore a brown linsey fringed shirt, Kentucky jeans, and a leather belt which held his pouch. Across his shoulders a leather strap held a powder horn and two leather cases, one carrying the pistol Hightower had confiscated from Zebedee and given back to him. The other contained ammunition for the rifle. Once again Caroline thought that if not for his changeable eyes, she never would have known him.

"I've been saving it," he said again.

"Pardon me?"

"The meat. I've been saving it."

"Why? You're so thin."

"For you."

She couldn't stand him being so kind to her. "What arrogance! Were you certain I'd come back?"

"No. Not really. But I hoped."

As she tried to think of a sharp retort, two men she vaguely remembered seeing before entered.

"Lieutenant, James," Philip greeted them, standing.

"Dispense with the formalities, Philip," the lieutenant said. "Are you ready? Oh, excuse me, Mrs. Mathews. Ah don't believe we've been introduced. Second Lt. Ashton Garrett of Captain Hightower's Infantry at your service, ma'am."

"Sir. I'm pleased to meet you."

"And I'm James Gray," the other man said. "A volunteer like your husband." The men exchanged glances and laughed at a private joke.

"Don't worry, Caroline," Philip said. "These men know we're not married, though they're the only ones

283

who do besides Zeb and his cronies, and nobody listened to them anyway."

"Does she . . . ?" Ashton asked Philip.

"Aye. She knows."

"What do I know?" asked Caroline, feeling decidedly left out by the secrets the men shared.

"That I was the Ferret," Philip whispered, as James glanced outside to check for eavesdroppers.

"And you—you don't *care?*" she asked the men.

"No, ma'am," Ashton answered. "You see, the way Ah figure it, if General Washington's adjutant general could change allegiance, then so can Philip here. He's proven himself to us time and again."

"How?" she asked, incredulous. "It's not as if we've gone into battle."

"No, ma'am. But he has helped us with the Indians a couple of times already. They seem to trust him, believin' he's a British soldier we captured. And we've been practicin' shootin' from time to time. He's a crack shot, could very well have put James and me down if he wanted to. No, Philip's a good man. Ah'd trust him with mah life."

She looked from one to the other in total disbelief. "Where are you going now?"

"To scout, my dear," Philip explained patiently. "The Indians are just as dangerous at night as in the day. Maybe more so."

"Oh."

"Now you stay here while we go. Get some sleep. We'll be gone awhile."

"Philip?"

"Yes?"

"Would it be all right if I went to see Derby first? I

haven't seen him for awhile, and I'd like to check on him."

"Ah, Caroline, Derby's not—we had to let him go."

"Put him down? *You put him down?*"

"No, nothing like that. But there's not enough food for the horses, surely you must realize that. With so many men dying, we had a surplus. We had to let some of them go. And Derby was one of them."

"How could you?"

"Don't you see? If we'd kept him, we'd have had to slaughter him for food. He should be better off, he'll be able to forage—"

"Derby will never be able to forage!" she retorted, eyes flashing. "He'll starve. Oh, I should have never babied him so much, it's all my fault, it's all my fault—"

Philip grabbed her shoulders; his voice held the undercurrent of a threat.

"This is no time to get hysterical, Caroline."

Tears stinging behind her lids, she blinked, and looked at him as if trying to remember who he was.

"Now get some sleep," he commanded.

She bowed her head meekly and nodded.


As far as Caroline could determine, it was the first of January. The journey from Kentucky to Michigan Territory had taken three times as long as it should have, due to three ever-vigilant enemies: weather, Indians, and the lack of supplies.

The cold winter gnawed away at her fingers and toes, the lobes of her ears, the tip of her nose. She no longer felt her lips, even though Philip had given her his deerskin muffler to wrap around her face. She'd wanted to refuse it, seeing icicles form in the beard he'd grown to keep his face warm. But her pride had long since vanished, merging with the hoarfrost coating the brush in the morning, and the snow that drifted around them in mounds that could hide trenches concealing Indians waiting to attack.

They'd crossed the Maumee the day before, but it had frozen unevenly and a thin layer of ice gave way easily beneath their horse's hooves. Immediately after, her legs blue from where the frosty tongues licked at her above her deerskin boots, Caroline donned a pair of buckskin breeches beneath her frock. The warmth that penetrated her soon after dispelled all objections to wearing yet another object of animal skin.

She shifted slightly, looking at Philip out of the corner of her eye. He rode near the front of the line, to her right and slightly ahead of her, silent except for an occasional exchange with Lieutenant Garrett. Garrett always listened to him now, and the other Kentuckians' antagonism toward him waned, as they admired his unerring precision with a gun.

Caroline had come to the conclusion long ago that Garrett and Philip were a great deal alike. Neither one of them wanted to fight the Indians, which surprised her. From the first, she'd thought Philip would fight anybody at the slightest provocation.

"No," he said, when she remarked so to him. "That's why I earned their trust back in Detroit."

"I thought you earned their trust so they would help you fight us."

His features softened. "That was true at first. And still is, as far as the British are concerned."

At first she was going to remind him that *he* was British, then changed her mind. He didn't deserve that kind of

286

reaction, especially after what she'd seen the day before. There had been a skirmish with the Indians, a minor one that would have been much worse if not for Philip's intervention with the chief. Still, Caroline reflected, it was a matter of time before a fight ensued with some savage tribe. The Kentuckians were bloodthirsty and eager to fight, and most of them were furious at Philip for denying them the opportunity. But Hightower agreed with Philip, and with him on their side, Caroline knew they were safe.

"I have no quarrel with the Indians," Philip said to her patiently. "Rather, I feel sorry for them. This land is theirs, and we're taking it from them. They mean only to protect it. Besides, the British have prostituted them by buying their loyalty for a few barrels of rum."

Caroline grew pensive. Again he'd identified with the Americans. She didn't know if it was a ruse to make her trust him, or if he truly felt this way. "And you mean to help them?"

"No. I mean to convince them you are all my prisoners, that I'm taking you to the British for imprisonment."

Caroline gave a short laugh. "And you think they believe you? They believe one man could capture and hold dozens of American soldiers?"

Studying her, he said, "The Indians hold great store in legends and the words of Tecumseh. He's told them of me."

"Of Philip Masterson?"

"No. Of the Ferret."

Now as she looked at him, she wondered how she could have doubted him so much.

After that first skirmish, some of the Kentuckians had

attacked bands of Indians, compromising their safety and leading them all to danger. Philip had rushed into the foray, slaughtering the savages with a vengeance that showed no hint of any empathy with them. Like a fox defending its kits he attacked, emerging unscathed except for minor injuries. Perhaps on foot Philip could not compete equally with able-bodied men, but on horseback his years of training in fencing and dueling stood him in good stead. He wielded a tomahawk with an efficiency that amazed even the Indians. Soon the Kentuckians, too, flourished the brutal weapon, taken from the dead. And now Philip hefted the long rifle with ease, shooting with deadly aim and accuracy.

Once when Captain Hightower complimented him on his marksmanship, Philip replied, "Thank you, sir. In truth, I relish the feel of this weapon, though I still miss my pistol."

After tracking down the weapon, Hightower commanded Zebedee's cronies to return it.

Philip ran a finger down the barrel reverently, and handed the weapon to Caroline.

"It's something you can handle," he said.

She refused to take it. "I'll have naught of killing."

He shoved it down her bodice, and she gasped at the coldness against her bosom.

"You never know when you might change your mind, Caroline," he said bitterly. "Lord knows I've changed mine a thousand times, since I came to this land." Then he turned on his heel and walked away.

If Philip emerged outwardly unscathed from the battles, the same was not true of Caroline.

After the first one, when she sat under a tree trembling

288

and praying, eyes closed, he came to her and grabbed her roughly.

Startled, she screamed, certain an Indian had come to slay her.

He jerked her to her feet. "Wake up! There's men that need tending."

Wringing her hands, she stared at him. "I c-cannot," she whimpered. "Oh, dear God, I c-cannot."

He grabbed her hands, his fingers digging into her wrists. "Why do you think God gave you such skills, woman? So you might have pets for friends? These men have treated you well, and the physician needs your assistance."

"B-but all I know is an-animals," she protested.

"Don't play the poor whimpering female with me! You nursed me from a snakebite and from fevers. You nursed men on the bluff. Now go help these men. *Now*. We need to get out of here quickly."

And so she did, tentatively, bringing her hand to her mouth time and again to gulp back her anguish. Philip went to her side, helping her.

From that night on, when she awoke from nightmares and could not stop shaking, she slept in Philip's arms.

But the next time he refused to help her tend the wounded. "I have bodies to bury. There is more fighting to come, Caroline. We've yet to meet the British. And when we do, we'll need your help again."

Ah, yes, Caroline thought now. They'd lost many friends in battles, but she'd come to a bitter acceptance that this was the way it had to be, if they were to recapture her home. At one point she'd even thought, why Michigan Territory? Why not leave Fort Detroit to the British? She said as much to Philip.

"Don't you see?" he replied. "The British will stop at nothing. The land's the least of it. After they've taken one territory, they'll take another and another, and when there's nothing left to take, they'll take your soul."

"What do you mean?" Caroline asked, bewildered by his emotional response.

"Nothing," he muttered.

She meant to ask him again, meant to coax him to confide in her, but by the time their days ended, they were too exhausted to engage in anything but minimal conversation.

On the third of January, one of their scouts rode toward them, talking quickly to General Winchester, then Captain Hightower and Philip. The men exchanged words until Winchester raised his hand to signal them to stop.

Philip rode back to Caroline.

"We've been asked to hurry to Frenchtown," he explained. "It seems they're in need of our help immediately."

Caroline sighed. "Another battle?"

"Well," Philip said wryly, "this one offers some variation."

"How so?"

"It's not the Indians who are attacking, not by themselves, anyway. It's the British."

"And whose side will you fight on, Philip? Will you lead us like lambs to the slaughter?"

"That question doesn't deserve an answer," he retorted.

She watched him ride away. In truth, she no longer cared about the outcome of this battle or any other. If they all died, then so be it. She was tired of it all, tired of the fighting, of tending to the injured. She wanted everything to be like it was before war was declared. Even Austin's abuses of her paled by comparison to these horrors.

Philip turned his head, catching a glimpse of Caroline. Swallowing a lump in his throat, he saw her slumped shoulders, her air of surrender. No, worse than that. He saw total, complete indifference to what happened to her. Perhaps to all of them.

Instantly he regretted the harsh way he'd spoken to her. There'd been so much he wanted to say to her, but she always distanced herself from him—and indeed, from everything around her.

He shook his head, at a loss to figure out how to get through to her. He knew she needed it for protection, this detachment. Otherwise, she'd surely go mad, as surely as a half dozen of their men already had, as he felt he would, if this didn't end soon.

He thought back to that first skirmish with the Indians, remembering how he'd practically had to carry her over to the wounded and force her to tend them. But by the third battle, she'd risen to the cause, coming out of her shell just long enough to care for the wounded before retreating back into herself. That night she'd woken in her sleep, sobbing.

"What is it?" he'd asked, alarmed.

"Oh, Philip," she'd cried. "I can't help these men.

There's too many of them, and I know too little. It's all my fault. Six of them died yesterday; it's all my fault."

"There, there," he'd said, drawing her to him and patting the back of her head as if she were a child. She'd finally fallen asleep in his arms.

That was how she'd slept nearly every night since. She'd start out in her own bedroll, but she always awakened. He'd hear her stir, and he'd welcome her into his arms, much as he had that night in her animal shelter, when she'd raced through the storm to him. It seemed that only when he held her could she sleep. He knew it was only when he held her that he felt complete, whole.

As the fights mounted between the Indians and the Kentuckians, the American band behaved increasingly like savages. After one particularly brutal fight, Philip watched one of the men approach Caroline. The man's name was Elijah, and Caroline had bandaged his wounds in a previous foray.

"Look, little lady," Elijah had said. "I broughtcha somethin'. As a thank ya, fer helpin' me when I was ailin'."

Philip knew Caroline really didn't want any of the spoils of war, but she held out her hand gamely. "How nice," she managed to utter. "What is it?"

Elijah plopped the prize into her palm. "Why, it's a piece of skin from the leg a' that Injun leader we jist killed. We all took'n a little piece and—"

She looked at Elijah in sheer horror and Philip had run to her, damning his hobbled leg for slowing him. By the time he reached her, she was on her hands and knees, teeth chattering, rubbing her hands in the snow, scraping them against buried twigs and stones to cleanse them.

"Caroline, Caroline," he whispered, picking her up in

his arms and carrying her to their tent. "Put it out of your mind. Forget it happened, Caroline."

She looked up at him, grasping his shirt, and buried her face in his chest. He set her unresisting body down on the blanket inside their tent, trying to warm her, though he knew her cold stemmed more from shock than the winter air.

After that she drew more and more into herself. By now Philip understood that this was her defense, for she'd acted much the same when he'd first taken her away. Only there was a wounded, sad look to her eyes he'd never seen before.

As the news spread up and down the lines of the upcoming battle, war cries resounded in the air. Soon they would fight the British.

## Chapter Sixteen

Unable to sleep, Caroline heard Philip stir. Minutes later the telltale clicking told her he tested the rifle time and again. She rolled onto her side and made out his silhouette in the darkness.

"We attack today?" she whispered.

"The detachment leaves at daybreak."

She sat up. "Am I coming with you?"

He stopped, set the rifle on the ground, and stooped next to her. "I've been given permission to take you, but my better judgment says to leave you behind."

She traced a circle in the earth next to her with her fingertips. "And how many men are going with you?"

"Upwards of five hundred are to meet us, I understand. A good number. The detachment consists of men from every troop. Winchester, Madison, and Lewis will command us."

"How long will you be gone?"

He took her hand and answered her, "I don't know. We need to hold the town once we recapture it. It could take some time before we return."

"Then I'm going with you," she said quickly, before she could change her mind.

"No, Caroline. You're safer here. You have no idea of what it could be like. We've heard the place is surrounded by Indians—"

"Then I could help."

He sat back on his haunches and looked at her quizzically. "How?"

"On two accounts. First, I could help the physicians tend to any men who might get injured." *Especially you, Philip. If you get hurt, I must be with you.*

"Two?"

"Two, the Indians liked me, remember? They gave me gifts. If you need someone to talk to them, to reason with them, they might listen to me."

"They might. Or they might not. Not good enough, Caroline."

"Then," she continued stubbornly, "who will protect me here? If I'm with you, you'll watch out for me, won't you? But I'm nothing to the men here. If fighting happens here, they might think of me for a moment or two, that's all. But you, Philip. You wouldn't forget me, would you?"

His arm came around her and pulled her to him. "No, Caroline. I'd never forget you."

He kissed the top of her head and sighed. "All right, you can come. But you must do as I say. If I tell you to do something, you must do it without question. No protests, no arguing. Do you understand?"

"Yes."

Cupping her chin in his hands, he looked into her eyes. "And do you promise?"

"Yes, Philip. I promise."

His voice grew hoarse. "Then promise me with a kiss, Caroline."

She leaned into him, and his lips brushed against hers. He kissed her tenderly, gently, as if she would break into pieces if he pressed too hard. Her eyes shone. "Just do what you have to. Nothing more, nothing less."

A shadow filled the doorway. "Mathews, y'all ready?"

"Aye, Lieutenant. I'll be there in a moment. Have you an extra horse for my lady?"

Caroline heard the lieutenant sigh. "There are some we can spare, but none in as good a shape as your Socrates. Ah think it better she ride with you."

"Aye, sir. She'll ride with me."


They rode for eighteen miles, camping at Presquille, about halfway to their destination.

The night was colder than any Caroline remembered. While she dined on bread and a piece of meat Philip managed to slip to her, she wondered if the icy weather was a portent of things to come. She shivered. Philip noticed and crept closer, drawing her to his warmth.

That night she lay next to him, her arms around his neck. "Philip . . . "

"Yes?"

"Make love to me."

He buried his face in her hair. "Ah, Caroline. Not tonight."

"Why?" she cried, wounded to the quick. He put his fingers over her lips, so she would not wake the other men.

"Because. You want me because you fear what will happen to me, don't you?"

Humiliated, she mulled over his question. She'd never expected him to deny her.

"You don't trust me yet, sweet. I'll come back to you. You'll see. Besides, I wouldn't leave you carrying my child. We were lucky before. We might not be so lucky again. I won't leave a bastard as my legacy. After this is all over, when we can love each other in celebration, it will—"

"Celebration?" she asked bitterly. "Celebration, after you've killed people? Philip, I wanted you tonight when all is peaceful, not after people have been killed by your hand."

"If I kill anybody, it will be because I *have* to. Don't you understand?"

She shook her head. "I understand none of it. I just want it to be as it was."

"With your land safe and your animal shelter nearby."

"Yes."

"And you hiding from the world, with no one to love you."

"Oh, Philip. Why does it have to be this way? Why?"

Stroking her hair, he murmured over and over, "I don't know, Caroline. I just don't know."


In the morning they set out to cross the Raisin River. When they reached the river's far side, the Kentuckians charged through a boggy field of cane. A shot rang out; Caroline gripped Socrates' saddle, but the horse went forward.

Philip commanded, "Keep your head down," and she flattened herself against the base of Socrates' neck, while Philip steered and aimed his rifle, dodging pickets and fencing the British had hastily erected to forestall the attack. She heard him swear, but all she could do was hold on, eyes shut to block out the sight of men falling to her right, to her left. It seemed to her all semblance of order had disappeared, as each man fought for himself.

"Stay flat!" Philip ordered again. She felt something whiz by her left ear, as he swayed to the right. She wished she could block out the sounds as well as the sights.

By nightfall it was over. The victorious detachment formed into groups for roll call, learning that only twelve men had died. When Caroline heard fifty-five were wounded, she said, "I must go help them," but Philip told her the physicians would not want her help, until after she'd had a good night's rest.

In their tent, she turned to him and said, "Thank you, Philip."

"For what?"

"For not killing anyone."

"I wounded a few."

"Yes, I know. But you could have killed them, and you didn't."

He grinned. "You won't tell anyone now, will you?"

A smile lit her face. "No, Philip. Not a soul."


The next day they resorted to mixing boiled hay with flour to make their bread. Her stomach growling, Caroline thought longingly of the well-stocked pantry at home, wondering if any of her larder still remained and if Maeve had been able to lay in any foodstuffs before the winter. Although rumors circulated of women and children captured and scalped by the Indians, she refused to think such had happened to Maeve.

In the evening some of the citizens of Frenchtown combined with the militia to hold a celebratory ball. Caroline declined Philip's invitation.

"The wounded need tending, Philip. I can't go."

"Don't the doctors have things under control?"

"I suppose so, medically speaking. But I can offer some things they can't."

"Such as?"

"A woman's touch."

He looked at the fatigue in her eyes, and knew that neither dancing nor sleep would cure her. She'd been through hell the day before; she needed to work out her demons in her own fashion. "Very well. I'll stay here with you."

When they finally went to bed that evening, he didn't know who was the greatest hero: him, for keeping the enemy at bay, or Caroline, for tending men's spirits when their bodies were beyond repair.

Another week went by scarce in food, but rife with unconfirmed rumors that the British were readying to retake Frenchtown. Philip was the first to take such rumors seriously.

He sought out Maj. George Madison. "We've got to get General Winchester to believe us."

Madison chewed on a piece of hay, then, grimacing, threw it down. "Y'all that certain this is goin' to happen?"

Philip answered, "That I am. I know how the British work, remember? They've been too successful for too long. At this point, their damnable pride won't let them lose even one battle. They want to make us look like incompetent jackasses."

Madison considered Philip's words a few moments before replying. "Even if yer wrong, it would be stupid of us ta be unprepared. Have ya tried talking to General Winchester?"

"Yes," Philip exhaled loudly. "You know, he thinks I'm all right when it comes to fighting, but as far as strategy—a part of him can't forget I was born British, I guess."

"Well, then, Ah'll have a go at talking ta him. Don't know if it'll do any good, but Ah'll give it a try."

But when he returned with Lieutenant Garrett, who'd gone to lend his support to their argument, Madison was glum.

"Winchester wouldn't listen to anythin' Ah had ta say."

"Then," Philip said steadily, "we'll just have to prepare by ourselves."

The only person the rumors seemed not to bother was General Winchester. Philip paced the stockade's lookout points during the night.

"What do y'all think?" Garrett asked, as Philip climbed down from his lookout post.

"I know the Indians' habits. There's an increase in activity; I'm sure of it. I wager they'll strike before day-break."

"Well," Garrett replied. "In that case, Ah think Ah'll be takin' mah men around the fort."

Their eyes met; Philip grimaced. "I could be wrong."

Garrett waved him off. "Ah doubt it. Just make sure whatever happens, ya'll guard yer ladylove. And that special pistol ya gave her."

Swallowing, Philip spoke in hushed tones. "That pistol's not half as good a shot as your long rifles. Thanks for the one you gave me."

"Ours ain't as purty, though. And ya'll like purty things, don't ya?" He grinned and nodded in Caroline's direction, where she paced and wrung her hands.

Philip followed his glance and smiled. "My pistol and Caroline are the only two things I do care about anymore, Ashton. Other than winning this damn war."

"Why, then, win it for her." Garrett beckoned to his men to follow him, while Philip, Madison, and Graves stayed inside to defend the sleeping people.

With nary a backward glance, the band of militia men separated so as to surround the fort to protect it from attack. Philip and Madison exchanged knowing looks when they heard Indian war cries in the distance.

Caroline rushed to them. "What's happening, what's going on?"

"I don't know, sweet," Philip answered honestly.

Caroline tried to ignore the endearment. "There's going to be another battle here, isn't there?"

"I hope not. It depends on what we hear from Lieutenant Garrett. He took some men out to reconnoiter. As soon as we hear anything, I'll let you know."

"You won't have to. I'm staying here with you."

Philip's brow rose, the corners of his lips twitching. "You need my strong arm around you?"

"No. You need mine around you."

When the messenger came, their spirits fell.

"Lieutenant Garrett and sixteen of his men were slaughtered," Philip said tonelessly, repeating the French words in English for her benefit.

Her eyes misted over. She whispered, "I know. I could tell by your expression."

The sounds of men wakening from their sleep mingled with horrified cries when Philip sounded the bell announcing an attack. Without a leader, for General Winchester had not appeared, they spontaneously divided into small groups. Philip maintained his position at the rear of the stockade, peering through cracks between the logs, until he spied a band of Indians approaching from behind a grove of trees.

"Quick," he ordered. "Follow me. Our only chance at stopping them is to go out and strike from behind."

"Well, then," Caroline said briskly. "We'd better hurry, hadn't we?"

By the time they reached the back, the Indians had abandoned their attempt at scaling the walls to chase the men who escaped through the fort's front gate in droves.

"Psst!"

They turned their heads and saw Madison and Graves motioning for them to follow. After what seemed like hours, they came to a small frame house surrounded by a garden with a strong picket fence.

"They'll likely to burn the house down," Graves whispered. "But we can dig ourselves into the snow, and fire from behind the fence."

"Why will they burn the house?" Caroline asked, a sickening sensation starting in the pit of her stomach.

"Because," Philip answered, "the Indians have probably ascertained that our illustrious General Winchester is nowhere to be seen. He's boasted about sleeping in the comfort of a private home. It's likely someone, somewhere, told the Indians he's not with the rest of us. The savages will likely burn down any building they come across, in hopes of murdering Winchester. He's the most

302

incompetent leader I've ever met. Except maybe for Hull." His lips tightened in a grim line.

"Why," Caroline asked, "would you want to cast your fate with men you consider so worthless?"

"They're not all worthless," Philip answered, catching Madison's look of gratitude. "Besides, something's got to turn this war around."

"You mean *someone*, don't you?" she snapped. "So that's what this is all about. You want to be a hero."

"If y'all will pardon me, ma'am," Graves said. "Nothing could be further from the truth. Mr. Mathews, he gives everyone else credit for—"

"There's not time for that now, is there?" Philip interrupted smoothly. "We've got work to do. Caroline, go inside the house. See if there's any food. And if there's not, stay there anyway."

"Stay there? But you just told me that they'll burn it down!"

"Don't worry, I'll get you out if I see any trouble. Now go."

"I'm not worried," she argued. "I just think it's ridiculous to find food, when we're all going to die anyway."

"Then at least we'll die on a full stomach."

The men laughed. Graves said, "He's right, ma'am. You're safer in there. We'll protect you."

Once inside, Caroline scoured the shelves, finding a few crocks of peaches, a bit of flour, and some slightly rancid grease. She thought it was silly to make a cobbler while men outside fought to their deaths, but the flour between her fingers and the old ritual of mixing dough felt comforting. Some hot cinders glowed in the fireplace. She fanned them to make them hotter.

A sound came from outside; she ducked. Gunshots!

It soon became apparent that the garden had become a major battlefield. Peeking out the windows, Caroline watched in amazement as the three men held their assailants at bay for hours. Gradually a few more men filtered in to help them, but they buried themselves so deeply in the snow, she could make out no more than another half dozen. Despite her horror, she had to admire their marksmanship.

Beyond the fence line, Indians whooped, threw tomahawks, and waved bloody scalps, while the British returned the Americans' fire time and again.

One Indian, unnoticed by the others, broke free and ran to the back of the house just as Caroline opened the front door, threw herself to the ground, and crawled through the snow to the men.

"What are you doing here?" Philip shouted, never taking his eyes off his enemies as he paused to reload his rifle.

"I brought you some peach cobbler."

Bemused, Philip arched a brow and took a bite of the cakey dessert, while Caroline pushed the plate to the other men.

"Now, get back inside," he barked.

"I'm afraid there's nothing else to cook," she replied in a honeyed voice.

"Get inside!"

She was about to make a sharp retort, when she saw the back end of the horse belonging to that same lone Indian around the side of the house.

"Philip, there's an Indian in the house," she whispered.

"Oh, there is?" He turned his head calmly, rifle over his shoulder, and fired into the open door. "I guess you'd better stay out here with us, then."

In seconds Graves shot the Indian. Then he held up his hand for a cease-fire.

Peering through the slatted fence, Caroline saw an American officer approach. "Who's that?" she whispered.

"Major Overton," Philip answered. "He was captured by the British. They must be sending him over here to ask us to surrender."

He guessed correctly. After Overton told them that the Indians would massacre them if they didn't lay down their arms, he said, "Now, will you men please decide what your course of action will be? You can't hold off the British much longer."

Graves turned to Madison and Philip. "What do you think?"

"If we do surrender, the Indians will scalp us anyway," Philip replied. "They'd never let us go."

"Can't you talk to them?" Madison asked.

Philip shook his head. "This is a different tribe than the one I used to deal with. If I recognized any of them, I'd give it a try. But these Indians have never known me to side with any but you; they'd not believe me if I told them I was British. Besides, they're too caught up in killing to stop now."

"What about your old regiment? Are none of them here?"

"None. If they were, I wouldn't go with them anyway. Unless you want me to, to offer myself as a hostage?"

Madison laughed. "You're more valuable to us here, Philip."

"So what's your opinion, then?" Graves asked.

The muscle in Philip's jaw clenched. "I'd rather go down fighting. If we die fending them off, you and Madison will go down in history as two brave soldiers who managed to keep the British at bay for hours. If we surrender, they'll massacre us like all the others, and you'll only be two of hundreds of others who gave up."

"I'm with him," Madison said. "But what about her?"

Looking at Caroline, Philip wrapped a cold, wet arm around her and drew her to him.

"Have you listened to what we've said?"

"Yes," she replied tonelessly. "You want to die here so you'll all go down as heroes, instead of going to the British, where we have a chance of living."

"Then go with them, Caroline. You're right. We'll probably die, and you with us. Go."

But when Overton held out his hand to take her away, she refused it. "No. I'd rather stay here. I don't trust the British, either."

Philip looked at her, trying to determine if the remark was intended for him, but his question went unanswered. The fighting started again.


Graves, Madison, and Philip killed a total of 182 of the British, before General Winchester finally arrived and ordered them to surrender. The British General Proctor assured the Americans that after he told the Indians to stay away, the savages would leave the wounded alone, while the British marched the men able to walk to an encampment. There they would get physicians and litters to return and fetch the wounded. Winchester supported Proctor. Dispirited, the Kentuckians laid down their arms.

While General Proctor, with General Winchester his prisoner, gathered those well enough to manage the twenty-mile trek to Fort Malden, Madison and Graves urged Caroline and Philip to escape.

"My work's not done," Philip insisted.

"They don't even know you're here, man," Graves argued. "As an Englishman, you never enlisted with us, so there's no record of you. Besides, there's been rumors the Ferret has orchestrated a great part of this battle."

The corner of Philip's mouth lifted "And you don't believe them."

"You're one of us now." Graves clasped Philip's hand in his own. "You're a great man, Philip Mathews, whether American or British. And as for your true identity, I don't think anyone else suspects."

Philip laughed bitterly. "But my legend precedes me. They invent stories about my exploits, when I haven't been seen for months. It's true, though, that Brock's probably the only one who could identify me, and he's nowhere near here."

Now the soft-spoken Madison's voice rose. "I've heard rumors that the British still have a bounty on your head. They don't know whether you're dead or alive, but they'll pay one way or another."

"That settles it," Philip said. "Let me talk to Winchester. Alone."

When Winchester strode toward him, Philip shifted his weight to his bad leg, which emphasized his limp.

"Sir," Winchester said, holding out his hand. "I don't believe we've met. But you did admirably in the fighting the last couple days, admirably."

Ignoring the compliment, Philip said, "As you see, sir, my leg precludes me from walking the distance to Fort Malden. And as for the lady, she's quite proficient at doctoring. So many of our physicians died in the fighting, that it would behoove us if you could persuade General Proctor to leave her here to look after our wounded, until you return. Besides, I doubt she'd survive the twenty-mile trek."

Winchester looked at Caroline, huddled about thirty feet away, rubbing her arms to keep them warm. In the distance she looked small and pale.

"Yes," he said. "Perhaps I can persuade General Proctor to let you stay behind to guard the wounded. I don't think he'll object to leaving the lady here, either. A woman on the march could just present problems."

"If it will help your argument, sir, I've made friends with some of the Indians here. With a word from me, they wouldn't hurt anyone."

Winchester rubbed his chin. "You speak their language?"

"Aye, sir. I'm the only one they will listen to other than the British. In fact, I believe I can guarantee the safety of our men."

"It's done, then. I'll talk to Proctor."

After Philip relayed the information to her, Caroline walked to the fur warehouses belonging to Gabriel Godfrey and Jean Jerome, who'd offered their buildings as a temporary hospital. Immediately she began assessing the patients, while Philip stood guard outside.

The night dragged on. With few supplies and even less medicinals, Caroline could do little for her patients. They reached out their hands to her, pleading for her to end their suffering. And when she could do nothing to appease their pain, Austin's words drove home with booming consistency. *"It's all your fault, it's all your fault."*

Outside, Philip strode the perimeter of the building,

trying to do the work of four men. The other three guards had deserted their posts soon after Proctor left.

Philip paused and cocked his head in the direction of a sound coming from the woods. He raised his gun to his shoulder, but lowered it when he saw one lone Shawnee approach, holding up his hand as if signifying peace.

"I am known as Tecumseh," the Indian said, extending his hand.

"Philip Masterson," Philip replied.

"No. You are the one they call the Ferret."

Despite himself, Philip smiled. "They say you are a wise leader. They are correct."

Tecumseh nodded in acknowledgement of the compliment. "My men wish to kill your wounded."

Holding his breath, Philip answered, "And you will let them?"

"No." Tecumseh folded his arms across his chest, deeply offended. "It gives us no honor to kill men unable to fight. But the redcoats gave my men much rum. I do not know if my commands are stronger than the redcoats' firewater."

"Well, then, I'll just have to do the best I can." A thought struck Philip. "Do your people know I was the Ferret?"

"Yes."

"Then," he said excitedly, "perhaps that will help. If they think I'm still a redcoat, they will listen to me, and I will tell them not to—"

Tecumseh's eyes narrowed as he studied the white man. "No. You are without honor. My men hate you more than any other white man. They think you are a traitor to your people. So do I. They might murder your men to teach you a lesson." He spit at Philip's feet, turned, and walked away.

"Oh, my God," Philip said aloud, his heart thumping against his chest. "They hate me. They will kill us all. They'll kill us all because of me."

One o'clock, two o'clock, three o'clock went by with no sounds but the cries of the wounded. Philip finally gave in to Caroline's pleading and went inside the large frame building. He took one look at her pale, drawn face, and brushed her lips with his.

"You've got to sleep, sweet," he whispered. If she slept, she wouldn't know of the trap he'd unwittingly laid for her, for all of them. If she slept, perhaps she would never know what happened.

They sat there for nearly an hour, Philip at last putting down his rifle and enfolding Caroline in his arms.

Despite her exhaustion his disquietude unsettled her. Guessing his melancholy stemmed from the injured surrounding them, she said softly, "You tried to warn them the British would attack, but no one would believe you."

"I failed. With everything," he replied. The disconsolate chord of his answer tore at her heart.

Caroline chastised herself over and over for distrusting Philip. He'd fought valiantly in terrible conditions with men that, though honest and stalwart, were not of his social class. He'd risked life and limb to protect her, to protect all of them. She knew his allegiance to his new country was not a sham. Nor was his love for her.

While holding Caroline tightly to him, all Philip could think of was how he'd changed her life for the worse. The girl who'd once skipped gaily in the woods like a carefree wood sprite, now faced relentless atrocities. And he'd compromised her life by keeping her close to him. He had no guarantee he would be accepted by either American or British. Likely a bounty hung over his head on both sides. And hers, by association.

He swallowed around the tightening in his throat. Not that it mattered now. In hours it would all be over.

A short time later Caroline dozed in his arms. Lulled by her steady breathing, Philip relaxed a little. Perhaps his imagination had gotten the better of him, perhaps they would survive after all. Soon dawn would break, and their captors would arrive. As much as he dreaded facing the British, they wouldn't scalp and torture as the Indians so relished doing. He closed his eyes; his head nodded.

Whoops of war cries rose like a bloodcurdling hymn, a cacophony building to an unholy crescendo.

Philip's eyes flew open. He jumped to his feet, shoving Caroline toward the window at the building's far corner.

"I'll cover you. Run!"

Half-asleep she stared at him, not comprehending. "But they'll kill me if I run out there!"

"Caroline, for the love of God, get out now, while you have a chance. Get out, go out the back way. You promised me you'd listen to me. Go!"

"Philip, I can't lea—"

"If I mean anything to you, you'll leave. *Please.*"

She looked at him, swallowed, and nodded slightly.

Before she could change her mind, he picked her up, broke the glass with his rifle butt, and pushed her out the window.

"Philip, I love—"

"Caroline, *run.*"

He spun around, rifle raised high. She could not see the Philip she knew; she saw a stranger with crazed eyes, resembling a cornered wolf's. She threw her pistol to him

311

through the open window and ran through the thicket of trees.

The Indians yelled in glee, hacking and butchering the sick and wounded. Philip stood alone in the middle of the carnage, his long rifle knocked from his hand by a soaring hatchet. An Indian whirled and faced him, tomahawk raised high.

"No!" Tecumseh shouted, grabbing the weapon from behind. "He must live to see his people die. His pain will last longer than theirs."

After the slaughter was over, Philip shuffled through the bodies, staggering.

"I'm sorry, Joshua," to one scalped body.

Then, "I wasn't prepared, Jacques. I never should have closed my eyes."

And finally, "Oh, Hiram, it's all my fault. *It's all my fault.*"

But the lifeless eyes stared back at him, the silent mouths petrified contortions of pain. He sank to his knees, sobbing and crawled outside.

When the British returned, all they found were dead men. When they asked what had happened to Philip, Tecumseh replied, "Justice is served. His suffering will last forever."

They presumed he was slain with the rest of them.

# *Chapter Seventeen*

Caroline ran through the woods, her fingers and ears turning blue from the cold, her feet crunching through the snow so loudly, she knew the Indians would hear.

It wasn't long before she heard horses approach, advancing from all directions. Instead of fear, she was filled with a mounting sense of anger. Anger at Philip for pushing her away from him, anger at generals who wouldn't listen to reason, and anger at Indians for killing whatever and whomever stood in their path. Recklessly she fled, unwilling to believe her life could end now. It could not. She would not die without telling Philip that she loved him.

The raised barrel of a rifle brought her to an abrupt halt. She looked up.

Six Indians surrounded her, two with guns poised, four with unsheathed tomahawks.

"Well," she said, her fury mounting. "It takes six Indians, does it, to slay one woman? What mighty warriors you are!"

The one in the middle brought his horse a step forward.

"Squaw with moon hair. No wonder speak with special voice."

At his words Caroline stopped, looking up from the scar on his chest to his face. She remembered where she'd seen him before. This was the Indian Philip had argued with. Philip had said she was crazed in the head, so the Indian wouldn't scalp her. Well, if madness worked . . .

Mad Bird exchanged a volley of words with his companions, who laughed and smiled at her.

Her apprehension slowly dissipating, she watched the English-speaking Indian dismount from his horse, walk to her, then lead her in front of his men.

"She has the moon-color hair," he said in Potawatomi. "The Great One holds her dear. She is like those with flattened face and slanted eyes."

The others murmured their agreement, while Caroline willed their foreign words to make sense.

"She should fetch great prize," another of the Indians said, appraising her closely.

"Yes," Mad Bird answered. "But first she will answer my questions." He smiled at her with a mirthless grin. "Tell me. Where is the one they call the Ferret?"

After the Indians left their carnage behind them at Frenchtown, Philip instinctively made his way back to the tiny settlement outside Detroit, where he'd heard they took their living prisoners. Numb and sick over the massacre he'd seen, he noted with escalating horror the bodies of those who'd escaped Frenchtown. At one point he identified the body of a Navarrone, one of the generous brothers who'd lent the American officers his home. Then he perceived with sickening clarity that the wounded at the Raisin River were not the only ones who'd lost their lives. It seemed even those able-bodied Frenchmen who'd tried to escape were hunted down, tomahawked, and scalped.

At a fork in the road two scalped, half hog-eaten bodies laid side by side, one a woman of Caroline's build. Unnerved, Philip approached, swallowing the bile rising in his throat. With his toe he rolled her over, the stench curdling his stomach, the smell of death invading his soul. The woman stared up at him with lifeless eyes. Brown eyes.

Philip cried.


Soon Caroline found herself in a secluded corner of the Potawatomi camp, heartened to see she was not the only American taken prisoner. Women and children she'd presumed slain were gathered in the center, crying and moaning, sending up desperate prayers for salvation. None of them could see her, hidden away in a small enclave she learned belonged to the holy man. The Indians seemed to think she would become contaminated if she mingled with the others, so they kept her isolated from the white men.

Mad Bird persisted in asking her Philip's location. She only looked at him blankly, seeing his frustration give way to resignation. She wanted to kick up her heels and pat herself on the back: she'd convinced the Indian she was a Special One indeed.

After a few days, the Potawatomis appeared to think she was harmless. She managed to creep away to talk to that same Lydia who had been at the gala where her nuptials to Titus were announced. It all seemed so long ago.

"But don't you see?" she said, trying to reassure the older woman. "If they wanted to scalp us, they would have done so already."

Lydia stopped sniffling into her apron and looked up. "But they are taking us away, one at a time. Who *knows* what's become of those they've already removed from our midst? Perhaps they've raped or tortured or . . . " Her voice rose hysterically.

"Hush, Lydia. It will do us no good to lose our wits. Tell me what you know of the Duffys and my brother. Have you heard anything?"

Gossip appealed to Lydia where reason failed. "Rumor has it that Howard was killed in a skirmish, when the British tried to destroy his printing press."

Caroline's heart sank. "And Mrs. Duffy?"

"I don't know. I heard she took refuge in Frenchtown with some distant relations, but I never saw her there."

"How long were you there? Did you inquire after her?"

Voice quavering, Lydia responded, "I was there but two days before the first skirmish. I didn't think to ask about her. My, I wish I had."

Caroline bit her lip, wishing she could ask about Maeve, but knowing Lydia would pay little heed to the whereabouts of a poor Irish servant. "And Titus?"

"He was injured in the same skirmish in which his father met his end."

"What type of injury? And where is he now?"

"I don't know." Lydia's brow furrowed. "I seem to remember something about his being taken care of, but I can't remember by whom or where. Everything's so confusing."

She swallowed. "What of my brother?"

"The last I heard, he was scheduled to hang."

Caroline exhaled in relief. "But he was alive."

"Yes."

A bellow rose from where their captors had been steadily consuming the contents of a large barrel of rum. The Indians kicked the empty wood-staved container, and Caroline guessed their shrieks escalated in proportion to the quaffing of its contents.

"It frightens me when they drink so," Lydia said.

"Nonsense! When they're that far in their cups, they can do us little harm. I doubt they could find the right end of a gun, much less aim a tomahawk."

"You haven't been here as long as me," Lydia retorted. "After their drunken revelries, one of us always disappears."

Caroline was about to argue when an Indian approached them and beckoned to Lydia. His gestures left little doubt he wanted the woman to come to him.

"No, stay away!" Lydia shrieked.

The Indian stepped forward, weaving slightly, and beckoned to her again.

Cowering, Lydia curled herself up tightly, but the Indian dragged her away while a stunned Caroline watched.

Sickened, that night Caroline tried to sleep. The muffled cries and fervent prayers of the other prisoners mingled with her own. A little boy of perhaps eight years of age found her in her dwelling. He approached her, wide-eyed.

"What are you thinking, little one?" she asked softly, reaching out a hand to stroke his hair.

"I wish the Indians would take me away," the boy replied.

"You do? Why? And what is your name?"

"My name is Adam. They took my mother yesterday, and I wish they'd take me, too."

Her heart near breaking, Caroline thought how sad it was a child so young should wish for death. "You wish to be with your mother, then?"

"Aye." Tears welled up in his eyes. He wiped them away with a chubby fist. "They mustn't have thought I'd fetch a good enough price."

"Price?"

"Aye. I know a little of their language. My brother and I, he's bigger than me, we used to speak it together so my mother and father would not understand us."

"Oh." Caroline was not at all convinced she believed everything the boy told her. "What does a price have to do with their language?"

"Nothing, really, except I can understand them. The Indians, they're angry at the British. I think the British promised them more rum, but then they changed their minds. So the Indians, they figure they have to buy it. That's why they keep us, you see."

Now Caroline was thoroughly confused. "What do we have to do with their buying rum?"

Adam looked at her as if she was the most witless being he'd ever encountered. "Why, they sell us, of course. To get money to buy more spirits."

"Sell us? To whom? There's little of our coin the British would value."

The boy shrugged and turned away from her, as if exasperated from trying to explain such a simple matter to an idiot.

*It doesn't make sense,* Caroline thought. *It makes no sense at all.*

When Philip finally reached the settlement near Detroit, he found the people in dire straits. He patted the gold in his pouch. Gold would buy food, if there was any to be had.

"Save your coin, man," a withered, crippled man named Albert told him when he inquired as to the availability of foodstuffs. "The Indians sent a messenger. They're bringing a prisoner to sell again today, but none of us have much money here. If you're willing to part with any . . . "

Albert looked at the wild-eyed stranger with unruly hair curling about his shoulders, and wondered if the man had understood a word he'd said. Doubtless, the man had lost his mind. Probably didn't have gold, either.

"Prisoner?" Philip asked hoarsely. "Does anyone know whether it be a man or a woman?"

Albert shrugged. "Nay, but we'll find out in just a moment. Here they come!"

Philip sank back behind a tree, watching the Indians pass. In minutes they set up a circle of stones in the middle of a clearing, and Philip understood that it was a primitive sort of auction. He watched, appalled, as the Indians nicked at a tall, spare man with their tomahawks.

"What's their intent?" he asked.

Albert looked at him quizzically. "They'll increase the tortures until we save him. By the look on your face, I can see you've no stomach for this. And I thought one as hale and young as you would be a part of the militia."

Philip pressed a gold coin into Albert's hand. "Give it to them."

"Why? You don't know this man. Or do you?"

"No. But after he's been returned to his family and his wounds tended, find out if he knows of a prisoner named Caroline. A woman with silver hair."

Shouting in glee, Albert did what he was told, not in the least surprised when the prisoner said he'd seen no such person. Silver hair indeed! But if the crazed man would offer money in return for news about an imaginary woman, well then, Albert was only too happy to oblige.

Days went by. Though he gave Albert money for each and every prisoner brought to the settlement, Philip heard no news of Caroline. Convinced she was dead, he went to the animal shelter each night to feel her presence, to talk to her, for from the heavens she would surely listen to any desperate animal in need.

All he said was, "Forgive me, Caroline. Please, forgive me."


It didn't take long for Caroline to capitalize on the Indians' belief that she saw things they did not. Humming songs aloud with a far-off gaze in her eyes, she gave little knowing smiles at appropriate intervals. Above all, she cared for their animals, applying salves and poultices to cuts the Potawatomis maintained would never heal. When the wounds disappeared, they stared at her in awe, calling her Special One and bowing to her.

Adam became her constant companion. He, too, believed she was different, and she saw him take great pride in guarding and protecting her. He endeavored to teach her the Potawatomi language, but she feigned ignorance.

Then, when an Indian spoke to her, she'd let loose with a stream of Potawatomi words, sometimes in nonsensical order, sometimes in perfectly lucid sentences. This reinforced their conviction that she talked to the Great One.

When ministering to the animals she eavesdropped with a vengeance, trying to sort fact from rumors.

She learned food was scarcer than she'd realized. The white men had been too preoccupied with saving their lives to plant crops the previous spring. There had been little to harvest.

She learned some of the prisoners taken from camp were indeed killed, though she could never ascertain how many.

Others were taken to the settlements near the fort and offered up for bid, with the Indians torturing their prisoners in public while the good citizens scurried about, trying to gather together as much of their scant supply of coin and food as they could muster, to offer as a ransom.

At no time did Caroline hear Philip's name mentioned. She wondered if he had been killed back in Frenchtown, but told herself a man as devious and cunning as the Ferret would find a way to escape. But as time wore on, she had a harder and harder time believing it.


On Caroline's twenty-fourth day of captivity, with the rest of the adult prisoners now either slain or exchanged for gold, the Indians came for Adam. They scowled and pushed him about, angered that the young stripling would likely fetch little in the way of coin.

"Don't worry, Miss Swanson," he called over his shoulder as they hauled him away. "My scalp is too small for them. My mother's waiting for me; she will buy me."

Unable to bear seeing him taken away, Caroline turned her back and fell to her knees, praying Adam's wishes would come true. Only the day before she'd heard the Indians complain that either there was no more gold in Frenchtown, or the settlers had become tightfisted. The Indians decided to increase their tortures, so the Americans would part with their funds.

Later, while currying one of the horses, she sidled over to the Indians. One of them laughed and held up a lock of sandy brown hair the same color as Adam's. A wave of dizziness passed over her. Then she realized it was not a complete scalp, but a piece measuring no more than an inch square. The shiny coin in the Indian's hand confirmed her suspicions. Just as they'd tortured prisoners in the past to compel the settlers to accumulate their coins, they'd begun scalping Adam until his screams aroused the starving populace to scrounge up British silver. Though they preferred gold, the Indians supposed the British soldiers would accept silver in exchange for a hogshead of rum.

That night, as they imbibed steadily of the spirits, Caroline heard them mention her. In the still, dark night she tried to discern what they were saying, but their words were too slurred for her to understand.

Two days later a sleeting rain woke Caroline from her sleep. While the icy slivers rattled against the dwelling, she snuggled deeper under her hide blanket. She had no desire to get up, to face another day filled with deception, a day in which she'd have to remember to maintain her guard at all times. One slip of the tongue, one wrong action, and the Indians would know she wasn't as special as she pretended. Spring would come soon, and she would escape. She would steal one of the horses she'd been tending and escape. With that thought, she closed her eyes.

Suddenly her blanket was torn from her. She shrank back. A dark-skinned hand grabbed her by the shoulder and ordered her to rise. Even if she hadn't understood Potawatomi, she could not mistake Mad Bird's command.

Struggling to free herself from his wrenching grip, she rose to her feet. Before she could fight back, he flicked a leather strap over her hands and tied them tightly together. Infuriated, she spat out a stream of Indian invectives. Her captor slapped her sharply across the face. Caroline ducked, but not soon enough, and winced as his hand caught her eye. She could feel her lid swell, knowing from years of such treatment from Austin that it would soon turn black. The Indian took her chin in his hand, studied the darkening circle, and smiled.

The Potawatomis forced her to walk alongside their horses, while they rode. There were twenty Indians; too many, Caroline thought, to escort one lone woman, until she realized if fewer savages accompanied her, the settlers could overcome them. She struggled to listen to their conversation, as much to keep her mind off her aching wrists and throbbing feet, as to learn her destination. With dread she supposed it was Detroit, for if the settlers had as little left in the way of food and money as she'd heard, she faced a long and painful death.

At various times in her past, death had seemed appealing, but now she had no wish to die. It puzzled her, this strong, overwhelming need to live, until she thought of Philip. *I am not finished with life,* she thought. *I have to see Philip, have to tell him . . .*

The settlement came into view. A few settlers ran inside their homes and latched their doors tightly shut, as if they could not bear to face yet another of their own taken prisoner. Most of the Americans, however, clustered around, their expressions a disquieting mixture of curiosity and pain.

A fist in her back propelled her toward a stone circle. She searched the crowd for a familiar face, but saw no one she recognized. All the onlookers appeared gaunt, their cheeks hollow, eyes deeply shadowed. Swallowing, Caroline knew the tales of starvation were true. Then a short, dark-haired woman stepped smartly around the circumference, and Caroline's lips formed the name.

"Maeve!"

The Indians ignored the woman pressing through the crowd, knowing by her dress that this was a servant with no goods to buy the woman's freedom.

"Hush, lass. I'm here to offer whativer comfort I can."

Darting a glance at the Indians to make certain they were engaged in conversation, Caroline said, "What do you mean, comfort?" Her brows drew together. "Can't you purchase me? There must be some money somewhere. Austin will—"

"Dead."

Caroline paled. "Dead? My brother's dead?"

"Aye. He was shot in a battle. He didn't suffer long, lass, and before he died confessed it was he who sent General Hull's trunks into the hands of the enemies. Ye're no longer under suspicion."

Head reeling, Caroline asked in desperation, "Won't Titus buy my freedom? His family has money, plenty of it."

A cloud passed over the maid's face. "No more, lass.

Not since last winter. But I've sent for him. He'll be comin' here directly, and he'll think of somethin'. He always does."

Taking what little comfort she could from her maid's words, Caroline asked softly, "Have you heard anything of Philip? Any—" But before she could finish her sentence, her captor yanked her by the hands and pulled her to the circle, shoving a stick under her chin to force her head high.

"Look," Maeve managed to whisper, before the din swallowed her words. "Southwest, there's Titus . . . "

Titus and Philip, the latter hidden behind an ancient oak, stole into the outskirts of the village.

Philip peered around the corner of the tree and shrank back as if hit.

"They've already blackened her eye," he choked.

"What are we going to do?" Titus whispered back. "Don't you have any coin left, none at all?"

His shoulders slumped. "None," he answered helplessly. "I've nothing left after I spent the last piece on that boy. If I'd known Caroline was captured, I'd have kept some aside, but no one knew of her."

He sagged against the tree, bringing his fingers to his temples. "Perhaps I should offer them myself in exchange for her."

Titus stepped in front of him, blocking his way. Philip almost laughed. This was the first time Titus had left the confines of his own home since he'd been injured three months before. Though his face had a tinge of color, his arm was still bound tightly in rags; it had been nearly shot off in a battle. Philip knew all he had to do was give a gentle push, and the printer's son would fall over.

"Don't be foolish," Titus said. "They want rum, not

more prisoners to feed. All they would do is murder both of you."

Out of the corner of her eye, Caroline saw Titus, his pasty face only a shade less white than the bandage around his arm. As the Indians turned her slowly in the circle, she could tell he was talking to someone, but the object of his attention stayed hidden behind the trees.

"Scream, lass," Maeve hissed. "Don't hold in the pain. Scream."

Caroline heard the maid before she felt the burnt end of the stick touch her hand.

Her scream rang out, anguished and pitiful.

Philip took another step, clenching his fists. Titus again blocked his way.

"You can't fight them, man! There's too many of them!"

"I can't just stand here and watch, either."

"Listen to reason. You'll both die. If a fight begins, if you stir up the settlers, they'll be slaughtered; their empty stomachs have left them no will to fight."

Philip looked down numbly at the child tugging at his breeches.

"Please, mister. Can't you help her?"

Philip's eyes narrowed. "Do you know her?"

"Yes, mister, please. The Injuns, they call her the Special One. They were gonna kill her right off for her scalp, 'cause they liked her hair, and then one of them told the others she was mad, but I don't think she's mad at all."

Lifting the child under the armpits, Philip shook him, heedless of the bandage around the boy's temple. "Why didn't you tell me about her? Why didn't you tell me?"

"Because," the boy answered, whimpering, but a defiant look still in his eye. "I've never seen you before. My mother, she just described you to me, said you gave her the money for me, and I came around back and saw you here, that's all. Besides, I might not have told you anyway. The Injuns, they liked her. I didn't think they'd let her go."

Philip's lip curled. "How, exactly, did they 'like' her?"

Still lifted a good two feet off the ground, Adam looked at him blankly.

"He's right, Philip," Titus said, casting a worried eye on the new patch of blood seeping through the boy's bandage. "There's no way he would have known to tell you about her. Now let him go."

After he'd settled the boy back on the ground, an agonized look crossing his face, Philip stumbled back behind the tree, burying his head in his hands.


Caroline screamed again as the Indian pushed the burning stick against her other hand.

He took it away; she stopped. Tears streaming down her face, she scanned the crowd, praying someone in the watching faces would take pity on her. They'd never been her friends, not really, but neither had they been her enemies. Then she saw Adam run to join the onlookers nearest her.

His face contorted from trying not to cry. "I tried to talk to him, ma'am, I tried to talk to him and tell him to rescue you."

"Who?" Caroline breathed.

Adam pointed.

She mustered a half smile. "That man is a dear friend," she said quietly. "He has no money, I'm afraid."

Puzzled, Adam looked in her direction. "Not *him*," he said, seeing Titus. "There's another man with him, a very rich man. He's bought everyone's freedom; he bought mine."

"Another man?"

"Yes."

"Who is he?" Blood rushed in her ears.

"I—I don't know."

Caroline turned her head in short, jerky movements to where she saw Titus speak to someone behind the tree. *Philip*, she screamed silently. *If it's you, why don't you buy my freedom? Give them a gold coin, Philip. Surely I am worth one gold coin to you!*

Seeing no offers of money from the crowd, the Indian shoved her, tearing her shift from her body. Caroline stood, tears running down her face, eyes closed, lips trembling. The Indian turned her, displaying her naked body for the crowd.

*Philip, where are you?*


Shocked, Philip's face turned ashen. "They cannot do this to her," he murmured. "She'll die. God help me, this is all my fault."


A thin sleet started up again, pelting her like sharpened threads. Her nipples tightened in rosy peaks against the cold. She closed her eyes and heard the crowd shuffle home. Their fading footsteps heaped humiliation upon humiliation. They would rather see her die than rescue her. She imagined she heard Philip's irregular pace mingle with theirs.

"Why are they all leaving?" Philip asked, horrified.

"There is no money," Titus answered.

"Nothing of value?"

"The Indians like only shiny things, Philip. You should know. The British taught them that."

"This is all my fault," Philip began to chant again. "All my fault—"

"For God's sakes, Philip, pull yourself together! Your damned self-pity isn't going to help Caroline one bit. We must think of something, Philip. *Think.*"

Titus's command jolted Philip to reality.

*Think, Philip. Shiny things . . .*

The woman with the moon-color hair trembled. Mad Bird watched the people wander away, some of them with hands over their ears to block out the sound of her screaming. The woman's hair streamed down her back, mingling with the gray, wet day. But he knew two men watched from behind the far oak. They were too far away for him to see them clearly, but they were there.

Mad Bird licked his lips, not knowing if what he was about to do would bring him coin, or if the men would applaud him on. Still, he could think of no other way to get money.

Caroline almost fainted when she saw the Indian leer at her. She pressed her spine against the pole in the middle of the circle, the pole she'd heard the unransomed prisoners were tied to, so they could perish in fiery flames.

Now, when the Indian licked his lips and grinned at her, Caroline thought she'd rather burn.

He reached out and grasped one nipple between his fingers; she cringed and cried out. He grabbed the other; she whimpered and twisted, trying to get away from him.

He yanked at his breeches; she spat at him.

And then Titus was in front of them, gasping for breath, water running in rivulets down his forehead. "Here," he said to the Indian. "Take this for her."

The Indian turned the silver pistol over in his hands, as if weighing whether or not the shiny weapon would buy enough rum to make his chief happy.

"Where did the gun come from?" he asked.

Titus cleared his throat. "I—I found it on a dead man."

Mad Bird looked at him suspiciously. "The Ferret?"

"Yes."

"Where is his body?"

Looking at the ground, voice quivering, Titus said, "Eaten by hogs."

Mad Bird looked off in the distance, but the wild-haired, bearded man behind the tree bore no resemblance to the redcoat who had befriended him. And left him for dead. He grunted, shoved the weapon in his breeches, and strode away to where his men awaited.

Her eyes closed, Caroline collapsed against the pole, her body so cold she couldn't feel the bonds or the pole behind her, waiting for someone to untie her. In the end she saw Maeve, blathering over how she'd tried to scrape up some money, apologizing for leaving. Caroline was only vaguely aware of someone wrapping her in a sodden cloak and carrying her to the animal shelter. She knew it wasn't Titus. One of Titus's arms was in a bandage. He would never have the strength to carry her.

It was Philip. Philip was carrying her.

That was her last thought before losing consciousness.

# Chapter Eighteen

"Wake up. Please, Caroline. Wake up."

Peering through slitted eyes, she could see the indistinct shape of a man moving into and out of her line of vision, as if pacing, making it that much more difficult for her to bring him into focus.

She closed her eyes. His ceaseless walking back and forth made her dizzy. She felt for the edges of her bed, but her left hand met a wall, a wall with pieces of bark still clinging to the logs. Wrinkling her nose she inhaled the distinctive, cloying odor of rotted, musty wood. She knew this place from somewhere, but where?

Then she remembered.

"Philip?"

"Yes." He stooped on one knee, grasped her hand in his own, and brought it gently to his lips.

"Philip? Is that you?"

He paused and brought a hand to her brow. "It's me. Your fever's gone. Don't you know me?"

"Only by your voice. I'm not sure I would have recognized you otherwise. Philip, when was the last time you shaved?" Her hands brushed his beard, surprised by its grittiness. His hair hung down his back; she wondered when it had last seen a comb.

But the look in his eyes unnerved her even more than his appearance.

"I don't know. Weeks, maybe months. Does it matter?"

She'd seen that look before, seen it in dying animals. But Philip didn't look unwell, not physically. She swung her legs over the side of the plank, and gasped as unexpected dizziness engulfed her; she gripped the sides.

"Are you all right?"

Steadying herself, she looked him in the eye. "I don't know. Are you?"

"Of course. It's not I who's been abed with a fever."

She sneezed. He offered her a rag to wipe her nose. "I've had an ague," she stated.

"Yes."

The tension in the air played a staccato, prickly tune on her shoulders; her nerves vibrated. "Philip, did you care for me when I was ill?"

"Some."

"How odd. Then who cared for me the rest of the 'some'?"

"Maeve, when she was able."

Caroline scanned the inside of her animal shelter. "When she was able? Was she ill, too?"

Suddenly she remembered all of it, her turn at the pillory, the Indians torturing her. She looked at the backs of her hands. Blisters had formed over the places where she'd been burned. And no one had bought her freedom; Philip hadn't offered one measly coin. Her head jerked up; she eyed him with suspicion. "Did Maeve save me?"

"She nursed you over the ague as well as she could.

The rest she told me to do, when she wasn't here to tend you."

Remembering her prior nakedness, Caroline lowered her lashes, but now she felt the familiar deerskin shift skim her body. She wondered who'd clothed her. "What do you mean, she cared for me as well as she could? Has she taken ill, has something befallen her?"

He rose and walked to the opening, where he'd hung a makeshift door on leather hinges. He spoke, his back to her. "She's been caring for Titus. He was injured, you know, and his arm needs her tending. His mother's taken abed, and his father died some months ago, so Maeve is caring for him."

Unsteadily Caroline rose to her feet and walked over to him, but he still refused to face her.

"Did you give gold for my freedom, Philip?"

His answer was almost a whisper. "I had no gold. If I had, I never would have let them hurt you to begin with."

"None? What of the pouch you kept around your waist, and the one you hid behind the barrel?" Whirling, she stalked to the wooden cask and pulled it aside, only to find nothing but dirt and a nest of baby mice. "But you bought my freedom, I remember it." She concentrated; bits and pieces of her last waking moments came back to her. "Your pistol. You bought me with your pistol."

Philip smiled helplessly, but beyond the upturned lips Caroline could only see a vacant stare.

"Why not? There's no one left to kill. They're dead. Everybody's dead."

Horrified, she watched him sink to the floor, grinning like a fool. From his mouth garbled sounds escaped, old, wailing sounds of keening, and he buried his head in his hands, shoulders shaking.

"I see ye've recovered, lass. I knew ye would. It's him I'm not too certain about."

Caroline whirled. "Maeve! I didn't hear you come in. Oh, am I glad to see you. What's happened, what can you tell me?"

" 'Tis better we go outside, lass."

As soon as they were out of Philip's earshot, Caroline, acutely aware of his husky, wrenching sobs fading in the distance, asked, "What's wrong with him? What happened to me? Where's Titus? Philip said he wasn't well, either. Where are you stay—"

"One at a time. I'll be tellin' ye, if ye just stop to breathe."

The day was unseasonably warm for late February, with the promise of spring in the air. In unspoken agreement, the women took advantage of the rare weather by seating themselves on two of the endless tree stumps dotting the area.

When Maeve saw that Caroline was comfortable, she began. "You caught a chill. I suppose yer humors were also affected, what with all ye've been through."

"How do you know what I've been through?"

"Why, Master Philip, he told me about the two of ye travelin' to Kentucky and back. In fits and starts, mind, but I have a way of figurin' it out. Anyway, ye had a fever three days, not countin' today. But ye weren't so deathly ill I gave ye little hope. Figured ye just needed to get yer mind cleared of all ye've been through, is all."

Caroline nodded slowly. "That's so. And you took care of me?"

Maeve shook her head. "Nay, lass, not I. I just told ye, Master Philip, he watched over ye night and day. I've been carin' for Master Titus."

Choosing to ignore the pleasant tingle that skittered up and down her spine at the thought of Philip alone with her in the cabin, Caroline asked, "What's wrong with Titus?"

"Why, he almost died, he did, lass. A skirmish 'round about three months ago, the same one what took yer brother. His arm was nearly shot off, and I did all I could to save him. He'll mend, but he's still weak and tires easily, I fear."

Caroline swallowed her grief. She would mourn Austin later; she could not face his death, not now. "How did you know how to save him?"

Maeve's face softened. "Why, from ye, lass, and with all the good things ye did for yer animals. Combined with me mother's good sense, of course. She did tell me some things, before I left Eire."

"And Philip? Why is he acting so strangely?"

Maeve shook her head. "That I cannot tell ye, lass, except he's been like that since he came back."

"When was that?"

"A month or so, more or less. And a good thing it was he came here, too. The British are lookin' for him. They say he's the Ferret."

Shifting, Caroline looked away. "Where has he stayed, then?"

"Here, in the animal shelter. It's the only place where no one finds him. Titus visits him often, so if anyone was lookin' they'd think any disturbances would be caused by him. The two of them have become fast friends."

Maeve pulled herself up importantly. "Everyone thinks Titus is a hero, you know, havin' gotten himself so seriously injured, and livin' to tell about it."

"Yes," Caroline said, musing. "I suppose he is. But what about Philip?"

"Oh, he saved most of the prisoners who were brought here by the Indians, lass. All the Americans that were captured with ye, I presume. At first he was sayin' he needed to save some of his gold, in case ye showed up, but then as soon as the Indians started torturing their prisoners, why he couldn't bear it, and would part with a coin sooner than hear them scream."

Maeve shrugged. "Sometimes they weren't really screamin' from pain, if ye ask me. Sometimes they did it to get our sympathy. But Master Philip, he couldn't bear it just the same."

"But the Indians side with the British. Didn't they tell the British they had the Fe—Philip?"

"Master Philip hid all the time. He'd send the money through someone else. Besides, he doesn't look quite the same, from what ye told me before."

"That's so," Caroline said slowly. "From the sounds of it, you've done a fine job of keeping things together in my absence. It's nice to have you as a friend and not a servant. Besides, whatever would I have to pay you with?"

Maeve made a face at her remark.

"To tell ye the truth, lass, at the moment food carries more weight than money in these parts. And the supply ye set in the shelter is more than anyone else has."

"But surely it couldn't have been enough to last this long."

"No, but I managed to stockpile some more last autumn."

Caroline contemplated this news for a few moments, before speaking again. "Did the Indians ever see Philip? They think of him as their friend."

Maeve appeared surprised. "Nay, he says they hate him. Says they killed scores of men because of him. In fact, he always gave the money to Master Titus to buy the prisoners, as if he didn't want the Indians to see him. I don't know, lass. I know ye set great store by him, and so do Master Titus and me. But—he isn't himself anymore. I don't know what the two of ye saw to disturb him so."

Equally confused, Caroline replied, "We saw a great many battles, sights I would forget had I the choice. But Philip—why, he seemed unfazed by it all. In fact, when last I saw him, he was conducting himself like—like a true American."

"Well, then, perhaps he'll talk to ye about whativer's troublin' him."

"I don't know, Maeve."

The Irishwoman's brows arched. "Ye sound like yer not so sure of him. I thought ye loved him."

After several seconds, Caroline sighed. "Yes. I've always loved him."

"Does he know?"

Caroline smiled sadly. "I don't think so. I just found out myself."

"Then let's hope ye can tell him. He won't listen to Titus or me, that's fer certain."

Seeing Caroline rub the small of her back, Maeve said, "I think we'd best be gettin' back now, lass. The air feels warm, but it's coolin' down quickly."

On the way back to the shelter, Caroline said, "Maeve?"

"Aye."

"Is there anything you wish to say to me? As a friend, not a servant?"

Maeve coughed. "I don't know, lass."

Exasperated, Caroline stopped, hands on hips. "Please, Maeve. I've been through too much the past several months to waste precious time circumventing the truth. Are you and Titus in love?"

Coloring, Maeve answered, "I'd never set my cap for one what was my friend's betrothed."

"Oh, nonsense! Titus and me were always friends, nothing more. Besides, as I just told you, I love Philip. But Titus is a good man; I'd like to see him happy. With you."

Maeve shrugged. "Well, if that's how you want it . . ."

For the first time in months, Caroline laughed. "How many people know the animal shelter is here?"

"Why, none, lass, as far as I know. People have been too busy protectin' themselves and lookin' for food to eat, to go huntin' in the woods for such a fine palace as this."

Caroline ignored the sarcasm. "You mentioned hunting. It's possible if they've hunted around here, they'd have found it by accident."

"Beg your pardon, lass, but I doubt they'd hunt this far away from home, what with being afeared of the British findin' them and all."

"Are they afraid of the Indians as well?"

"I don't think so. There's no one here but ye and Philip."

Caroline looked in Philip's direction, where he'd been sitting with his back against a tree. He appeared totally unaware of their presence.

"How long has he been like this?"

"He's not always so distant, lass. Most of the time he appears right civil, but melancholy. If ye hadn't told me what he was like before, I'd have never known anythin' was wrong." She pursed her lips and looked at Caroline. "Are ye sure ye want to be alone with him?"

"I've been alone with him several times in the past few months. I've never had occasion to fear him."

"But people will talk."

"Let them!" Caroline snapped. "I'd think their minds would be far too occupied with more pressing matters—like food—to concern themselves about me."

"Ye need people, ye know, lass."

Resting her chin on her hand, Caroline replied, "I do. But I need Philip most of all. And right now, he needs me."


They'd been snowed in for six days, and Caroline didn't feel she understood Philip any better than she had the day she and Maeve had talked.

Becoming used to his silence, she brushed the powdery snow from a crack in the cabin and peeked between the slits. A pair of squirrels raced around a maple, sending puffs of snow down from the branches. A cardinal, flitting from branch to branch, sang cheerily. Without thinking, Caroline mimicked his call.

Philip rose from the plank bed, having taken to lying there during the day, so Caroline could use it at night. While she slept he always stayed awake, prowling like a caged cat, alert to any nocturnal prowlers who might disturb her safety.

"Why are you doing that?" he demanded.

"Doing what?"

"Singing. Like the bird."

"I—I was lonely, is all."

Though he thought he was beyond all hurt, her words gashed his heart. He'd been with her for days, and she was lonely. Granted he hadn't been much at conversation, but what did they have to talk about? "Hmm, let's see, I reckon almost two hundred people died because of me?" Oh, she'd love that, wouldn't she?

Philip sighed and rubbed his temple, regretting his proficiency in analyzing others' behavior, their unconscious facial movements. Even though he'd made mistakes before, he knew he wasn't making any now. He didn't know how much he himself could take, and he didn't want to hurt her anymore. Yet, as soon as she learned those men died because of him, she'd hate him. He deserved it, of course, but she didn't.

" . . . I was just wondering what's become of them," she was saying, and he realized she'd been talking for some time.

"Of what?"

She fixed her blue eyes on his. "Of the animals, of course. Haven't you listened to a word I've been saying?"

At his crestfallen look, she brought her fingers to his lips. "I'm sorry," she said softly. "It doesn't matter. It's not important."

"Of course, it's important." He took her fingers away from his face, then released her hand. "You always loved your animals."

"Yes, I loved them, I cared for them. They trusted me, and now they're likely slaughtered. Fawn, at least, for these people have needed food. And is that so bad, that some people were kept alive by my animals? I'm not a child anymore, Philip. I don't want any more people to die, none of them, and if it takes my animals to save them . . . " She bit the back of her hand.

How he wanted to go to her, to hold her in his arms and comfort her, to run soft kisses down her cheek, to murmur that it would all get better, it was over. But it wasn't. She still didn't know he was responsible for the massacre at the Raisin River. How could he inflict more pain on her?

"I think it's time I try to clear a path out of here," he said. "Titus will visit as soon as he can get through, and you'll want to see Maeve."

But it was two more days before the snow had melted enough for Titus and Maeve to reach the cabin.

"Well, look here," Titus said after stepping inside, Maeve clinging to his elbow. "You've managed to make the place look almost homey, Caroline."

Nodding, Caroline acknowledged the reference to the interior, the walls freshly scrubbed with handsful of snow, fresh pine branches strewn over the ground to perfume the air with their tangy fragrance.

Philip frowned; it seemed Titus was full of compliments this morning.

"In fact, Caroline," Titus continued, "you look better than I've ever seen you."

Philip's scowl deepened as Caroline blushed. And, he noted perversely, he'd been so preoccupied with avoiding any interaction with Caroline, he hadn't even looked at her except when she slept. And then there was so little light, he could only make out shadowy forms.

Now he had to agree with Titus.

Caroline's former gauntness would have blended in quite unobtrusively with most of the other women he'd seen recently. Months of little food had shaved pounds off their bodies, so they all looked like walking sticks.

But the Indians had treasured Caroline, and had fed her well. Though still slender, he now saw curves where there had been none before. Her breasts strained against the deerskin shift. Skin boots almost came to her knees, yet the outline of shapely calves showed against them. Her face, too, had changed. He found he rather liked it. Cheeks blushed by the cold weather had filled out, their hollows no longer sunken, but attractively sculpted against skin as white as alabaster.

Philip wondered if Titus was fickle enough to cast off Maeve in the wake of Caroline's beauty. But the maid seemed of little inclination to tear herself from the young man's arm, and Titus seemed quite comfortable to have her at his side.

"Thank you," Caroline answered. "Though it's hard to believe the past months have been good to my appearance. They've been so ghastly in more important matters. Now," she said, smiling and nearly clapping her hands together, "have you told your mother?"

A muscle in Philip's cheek tightened. He'd seen far more of Titus than Caroline, yet that the two shared some secret was quite obvious.

"Yes, I have."

"And?" Caroline prodded.

"She agreed!" Maeve finally let go of Titus long enough to wrap her arms around Caroline in a hearty embrace.

"Would someone kindly tell me what this is all about?" Philip growled.

"Step outside with me," Titus offered. "I think the women would rather talk alone right now."

Titus and Philip walked side by side for some time, before Titus said, "Maeve and I have decided to get married."

"I should have guessed. But how did Caroline know?"

"Maeve told her."

"And Caroline didn't care? I mean, I thought you two had some feelings for each other."

Titus stopped, panting from exertion. "We do. As friends, nothing more. In fact, as damnable as this war has been, it's been rather fortuitous in one respect. My parents, you see, would never have permitted me to marry a maid before, but now Mother is so glad I didn't die in the fighting, she'd agree to anything."

Philip gave him a measured look. "And it's obvious Caroline is happy at this union."

"Absolutely. Actually, we only agreed to marry each other, because her brother manipulated us. Does she ever say anything about Austin?"

Grimacing, Philip replied, "Very little. At night sometimes I hear little snatches of dreams, and I think she apologizes to him. I think she really loved him."

"Not the same way she loves you."

Philip stopped.

"It's obvious, old boy," Titus continued. "Look. I never used to talk this openly with other people, but when death's near at hand, you quickly discover what's important and what isn't."

Philip had a mind to pop Titus in the jaw. The young man's pomposity at surviving a war was beginning to get on his nerves. Still, he decided that with all the mistakes *he'd* made, Titus was entitled to a little bit of pride. "Yes," he said stiffly. "I know."

"Well, she loves you, and though you haven't said so, you love her. Don't look at me like that. I was pretty sure of it even before Maeve told me. Now you two—"

"It would never work," Philip barked. "She can't love me."

"Why not?" Titus scratched his head with his bandaged hand. "You've pledged allegiance to this country, after all, and—"

"I can't stay here," Philip interrupted desperately. "There are so many things you don't know."

"Oh, yes, that Ferret business. That is a problem. From what I hear, there's a bounty on your head from both sides. The British want you dead or alive, and the Americans want you dead. This wouldn't have been a problem, you know, if you'd told someone who you were to start with."

"Why bother? It seems everyone knows I'm the Ferret."

Shaking his head, Titus answered, "Only Caroline, Maeve, and me. And none of us are bound to turn you in. Your secret is safe with us."

"I'd already thought of an answer to my predicament before you came here. I'm going to sea as soon as the lake thaws."

Titus stared at him, confounded. "The sea? But we've scarcely got a navy."

"Yes. I know. And for the most part your admirals aren't much to boast about, either. But I have experience. I sailed here from Britain, and took many a turn at the mast when I needed a change of pace. I'm also competent at the sextant. At least I was."

"You don't have to convince me," Titus protested. "I'm not to be your employer. But what are you going to do about Caroline?"

"She can't love me, Titus. I'm no good for her. She might as well learn that now."

"How?"

"I'll—I'll fix it so she hates me. And then if—if I ever salvage my self-respect, I'll court her again."

"She could turn you down later."

"I know," Philip said bleakly. "But that's a chance I have to take. It's too dangerous for her to be involved with me now. In many respects. And there's one more thing."

"Yes?" Titus looked a shade more peaked than ever. He wasn't given to intrigue, and already regretted he'd sworn to help Philip.

"Once the time is right and I go, you mustn't tell Caroline what I've done or where I've gone. I won't have her life jeopardized again because of me. Do you understand?"

"Certainly," Titus squeaked. "What's one more promise?"

Soon Titus and Maeve departed amidst pledges to return as often as they were able.

Caroline and Philip waved goodbye from the doorway. After the couple had left, Caroline turned slowly, following Philip's shuffling pace, hoping he wouldn't crawl back into his former despair now that their visitors had gone. If he did, she'd just have to pull him back, step by painful step. She'd healed his leg almost a year ago. Now she'd have to heal his soul as well.

## Chapter Nineteen

From a corner of the cabin, Caroline watched Philip stare into space for hours, just as he had the past several weeks.

"The fire needs stoking. Will you do it, please?"

His head snapped up as if he'd forgotten another person was present. "Did you say something?"

"The fire. Look. It's going out."

He grunted, then folded his hands behind his head, and looked off into the distance.

"Philip, please!"

"Oh, very well. I'll stoke your damn fire. Maybe if we're lucky, this whole place will burn down."

Anger overcame Caroline's dismay. "Philip, follow me. *Now.*"

Only a little surprised that he obeyed her command, she yanked a cloak she'd fashioned from an old blanket from the peg on the wall and walked outside. Her toes curled at the cold ground beneath her feet, but she knew her deerskin boots would repel the moisture from the thawed snow. Not that it mattered.

When they were about twenty feet from the doorway,

she turned, arms crossed in front of her chest, and faced Philip. He stopped and mimicked her posture, his sleeves rolled back to the elbow, exposing muscular forearms. Caroline wondered how he could be so heedless of the cold.

He waited. She hesitated. Then she stepped forward, arms outstretched to embrace him, and he bent forward slightly to gather her in. He nuzzled her hair; Caroline gulped, forcing herself to remember her plan, hooked one leg quickly around his bad calf, and tripped him. She stepped back as he fell to the ground.

"What the—" He stared at her in disbelief.

"Philip, I don't know what is bothering you. You seem to think I'm incapable of understanding whatever it is that plagues you so, and I think you underestimate me. We rode side by side for months. For a while I wasn't myself, I'll grant you, but you have to remember you practically kept me prisoner. I've done nothing to you, Philip. You're not my prisoner; you're free to go at any time. But if you're going to stay, come to me. I can't stand your aloofness any longer. Please, Philip. Let me love you."

Philip heard the desperation in her voice. It spelled danger. Not for him—God, how he wanted her, more than anything in his life he wanted her—but for her. Her fragility had somehow metamorphosed into strength, but the transformation was much too new to withstand any shocks. It would crumble and fall away, leaving her exposed and vulnerable once again.

"Caroline," he said as gruffly as he could. "Do stop nagging. It's getting tiresome." He marched away, ignoring her pained expression.

* * *

When Philip came in almost two hours later, Caroline whirled on him, eyes blazing. Two hours had given her plenty of time to think.

"Sit down. We're going to talk."

Forcing a lazy smile on his face, Philip reclined on the bench as if he were in the middle of the finest tavern in Britain.

"What do you want to talk about?"

"Whatever it is that's changed you. You're not the same Philip I know, and I don't like it."

Caroline didn't miss the slight flicker in his eyes at her statement, and wondered what she'd said to inflict a dart in his Achilles' heel. But the haughty smile returned along with his arrogant words.

"You're just upset because I didn't accept your brazen invitation."

"Invi—I didn't mistake your reaction. You wanted me, you—"

Her voice broke along with Philip's heart. But if he softened now, all was lost.

Steeling himself, he ground out, "I don't need you sacrificing yourself again on my behalf."

"Sacrifice myself?"

"Don't play dumb, Caroline. That first time we made love, you offered yourself to me like a sacrifice. You thought your lovely body would help me somehow, didn't you? *Didn't you?*"

Mortified, Caroline turned away.

In one giant move Philip rose to his feet, grabbed her by the shoulder, and spun her around to face him.

"*You* asked for this conversation, Miss Swanson. Not I."

Caroline bit her cheek; she would *not* cry in front of him. "I—yes." She looked him straight in the eye. "I thought you needed to learn how to trust someone. You don't trust anyone, not even me. And I knew you wanted to make love to me. I wasn't trying to hurt you, and would never have turned you in—"

"What a bunch of rot. You didn't even know I was the Ferret then. And I didn't need your help then, nor do I now."

She swallowed back a sob. "Fine. I won't help you, because you don't need it. But tell me why you're so— distant. You were never this far from me before. Even when we weren't together, I felt closer to you than this. Is it Daphne?"

He gave a short, harsh laugh. "My cousin's the least of it, Caroline."

Her lower lip quivered.

"Perhaps I never was, as you say, this distant from you," he said. "But you were another matter. No matter how hard I tried to reach you, while we traveled to Kentucky and back, you were always miles from me. You wouldn't reach out to me for one instant."

"Yes, but you have to understand, I'd left everything that was dear to me. I missed my animals, my home . . ."

"And now," he said softly, "I miss mine. I must go back to Britian, as soon as I can make the necessary arrangements."

She refused to believe him. "How? How are you going to leave? The British don't trust you; they know you've turned traitor. You're safer here. The Kentuckians think you're a hero."

Again the flicker in his eyes. "I'm no hero. Get that through your head. And I'm counting on your help. I have no other place to go right now. I'll be leaving the shelter from time to time for several hours, perhaps overnight, but I need a place to rest, to get some sleep. This shelter is yours. You can have me leave, if you so wish. I'd rather stay, but there's to be no more lovemaking, none of any kind, between us. If you so much as purse your lips to kiss me, I'll leave!"

And if he left before he found safe passage to Britain, someone would find him and turn him in at the least, or more likely, kill him. And his death would be all her fault.

"No, Philip. You can stay."

It took two weeks for them to settle into a strained, unspoken truce. Patchy brown spots of earth glistened through the remaining patches of snow like a mottled snow leopard's fur, according to Philip. When Caroline asked him if he'd ever seen a snow leopard, he said no, but he'd read about them. Impressed, Caroline asked if there were free libraries in Britain, such as the one she'd heard Mr. Franklin had established in Philadelphia, so the precious tomes could be read by all. But Philip only replied, "The less you know of Britain, the better," and she knew she'd overstepped the invisible boundaries he'd set down for her.

Philip left only once, but he was gone several hours. When he returned, she knew better than to ask more questions, but noted his mood seemed somewhat improved. He didn't try to avoid brushing against her as she walked past quite as much as he did before.

Then Maeve and Titus came with Derby.

Philip hurried out at once. Her joy tempered by the awareness that Titus and Philip were engaged in a heated

351

discussion, Caroline ran to Derby. The horse whickered in greeting.

"Maeve, whatever gave you the thought to bring Derby? I hadn't asked about him, I was so certain he was dead." Caroline giggled as the horse nuzzled her neck.

"Philip said he must have wandered back here after ye let him go. And Titus, he decided Philip could use him to, umm . . ."

Philip's glare stopped her too late.

Caroline thought she'd be sick. "You mean you're going to take Derby away from me?" she asked Philip. "Do you give me everything, just to take it away?"

"I need him. I can't walk far enough to get where I need to go without a horse."

"You can't. He's *mine!*"

"You have no choice in the matter," he responded evenly.

"He's right, lass," Maeve said.

Caroline whirled. "You, too? What's going on here?"

Titus coughed. "Nothing, Caroline. While Philip makes his, er, plans to escape, he just thought it would be easier to go on horseback."

"He's right." Philip had vowed long ago never to use his bad leg as an excuse, but he knew he had to be honest with her this one time. She'd see through any falsehoods immediately, with that same uncanny perception she had when analyzing her animals.

"If I hope to return here safely at night, to lessen my chances of discovery I need a horse to assist me. My leg slows me just enough, that were it to come to an all-out run between me and a pursuer, I'd lose every time."

"Not only that," Titus interrupted. "It won't be long before people put two and two together, and realize the

Ferret has a limp. Philip's leg is like a talisman." He missed the warning look Philip shot him, but Caroline didn't.

Philip's life was at stake, and he needed a horse. "But why Derby?"

"Because, lass, there's not many horses left. There wasn't enough hay to feed both men and horses. 'Twas only Mrs. Duffy's kindness that let us keep Derby, in hopes ye'd return."

The maid's statement confused Caroline. "Hay? We had to eat hay once, but now? All the time? To feed men?"

"Aye," Maeve answered. "Some of the people have been eating boiled hay, lass. It's all they have."

"I thought Derby looked a little thin."

"Ah, but that's much better for him," Philip stated. "He'll be able to move that much faster."


Six more days, and a comfortable camaraderie existed between Philip and Caroline. Derby almost pranced when Philip mounted him, galloping away at his master's signal. Caroline thought it appropriate, that an animal so crafty it had managed to outwit her for years, had so readily transferred its allegiance to Philip. The two, it would seem, were kindred spirits, sitting on whichever side of the fence benefitted them more.

Gradually, Philip relaxed to the point that he could engage in conversation with Caroline, as long as she kept her questions to a minimum. He was grateful they could be comfortable with one another. Still, to maintain guard, he stayed up nights while she slept. Or tried to sleep.

Once she closed her eyes and several minutes passed,

and he was convinced that she was sleeping, he'd draw a foot nearer to her. She sensed his nearness in the same way she sensed the nearness of her animals when they approached, still hidden in the thick cover of the forest. She sensed that animal part of him, that wariness combined with eagerness, that insatiable curiosity that led so many animals to their end.

But though it took all her resourcefulness, she wouldn't lead Philip to his death. She wouldn't bait him and torment him so he'd come nearer, though every part of her body longed for him, from the deepest recesses of her soul to the tingling, heightened awareness of her innermost femininity. His very breath, as he watched her, seemed to spiral from his mouth to between her legs, flicking her womanhood like a moist feather. Still, it wasn't simply the gratifying fullness of him within her that she wanted to experience—it was the mingling with him, the cleansing of his worries and fears. She was convinced that if he would only open his soul to her, she would purge him of all his shadows. Then if he left, even if he left with no commitment to her, she would be content. It took everything she had to lie still, control her breathing, and feign sleep.

Philip thought she was the most lovely woman he had ever known. Physically, perhaps, there were others more beautiful, but in her entirety, Caroline was as close to perfection as he would ever come. He choked back a bitter laugh to think that at one time he'd entertained the silly notion of spending a lifetime with her. He'd let that chance slip through his fingers. His monumental ego had once again gotten in the way. He'd wanted so much to prove to her he was worthy of her, he'd had to try to play the hero. Even now, bloodied bodies tortured his dreams.

Sighing, he rubbed his temples. He'd make the best of the situation; he always had. But the best would simply not be good enough for him to offer to Caroline.

They'd been in the shelter for over two months, when Caroline managed to befriend a baby rabbit. It kept her company in the long days, when Philip left on a clandestine mission to a secret destination. Although he always headed to the north, she suspected he changed his direction at some point on the journey. He would not reveal the vaguest hint of where he was going.

One thing eased her mind. He was not engaged in fighting. He refused to take the musket Titus had lent him on one of his occasional visits, leaving it for her protection. When she insisted she could never fire a weapon, he only smiled at her sadly and walked away.

He was always tired when he returned, sometimes to the point of exhaustion, but he steadfastly refused her offer of the wooden plank bed. More and more often he sat on the floor, resting his head on drawn-up knees. Caroline never closed her eyes until Philip's slow, regular breathing assured her he had fallen asleep.

The time he spent away from the shelter increased. When he returned, he was preoccupied. Caroline didn't like to see him so consumed by his plans, and told him so.

"But it's good for me, you see," he explained.

"Perhaps, but it's bad for me," she blurted out, before she could stop herself.

"What do you mean?"

"It's just that . . . for instance, you don't even notice what's going on here."

"There's not much to notice, except Bunny chewing on

355

some roots. Maeve and Titus haven't paid another visit, have they?"

"No." She didn't want to say that she suspected Titus accompanied him, not wanting to give Philip an opportunity to lie to her. "But there are other things."

"Like what?"

"Like you haven't been down to the cellar in days, and we're running out of food up here. I have no idea how much is left. And I'll need to plant some spinach and peas, but I don't remember if I put any seeds down there. I've been away almost a year, and Maeve has her hands full, and . . ."

Philip shook his head, a sad smile on his face. "You have to learn how to go down into the cellar sometime, you know. I won't always be here to bring up your food for you."

She looked away. "How long, Philip? How long before you leave?"

He hesitated before replying, "Soon."

"But you can't go!"

His smile gone, he answered, "Aye, Caroline. I can. Now, you go down into the cellar. I'll wait up here."

"I can't."

"You must. It's time to overcome your fears."

She squared her shoulders. "What about yours, Philip?"

"I'm trying."

"Not enough."

"Listen," he replied, his voice gruff. "That's not what we're talking about. We're talking about the necessity of your securing food for yourself. I haven't spent months fattening you up, just to have you starve to death after I'm gone."

"What does it matter to you?" she shot back, voice breaking. "What does it matter how I fare, when you're so anxious to leave me?"

"Because you're all that matters to me." He grimaced and turned away. He hadn't meant to tell her that. Not now, not ever.

"Philip," she said quietly. "If I go down into the cellar, will you talk to me when I come back up? And answer some questions, honestly, without deceit?"

"This isn't about—"

"Then I'm not going down into the cellar. And after you're gone, I shall starve to death. Even if Titus and Maeve give me food, I won't eat a bite."

The muscle in his cheek twitched. "Fine. I'll answer your questions."

Dropping down into the cellar was like descending into the bowels of the earth.

Caroline whimpered and wrapped her arms around herself, feeling the thready brush of spiderwebs against her forehead. She shut her eyes, chanting silently, "Philip's upstairs, in the light. He's upstairs, and all will be well. Philip's upstairs, he's upstairs, he's up—"

"Caroline!" A familiar voice rang out, penetrating the darkness. "Are you all right? Caroline, answer me!"

She opened her eyes a fraction. "Philip?"

"Caroline, take it easy. Talk to me."

"I—I'm here, Philip. I'm all right, I'm all right, I'm all right."

Stooping, Philip grasped the edge of the cellar's opening and debated whether to jump in after her. She sounded on the verge of hysteria. He never should have forced her to go down; he should have talked to her beforehand. She deserved that much. He should have told her what thoughts plagued him, should have told her about the nightmares, should have told her the truth, told her what an egotistical, swaggering fool he really was, and how his cocky self-assurance brought death upon scores of helpless, wounded men. He should have told her his fears. Hell, he hadn't even understood what fear was until it strangled him at the Raisin River. And now he'd sent Caroline to face her worst fears alone.

"Caroline!" he ordered. "Caroline, open your eyes! I'm up here, Caroline. I won't leave you."

Biting her lip, Caroline heard him call to her, lying to her. Yes, he was going to leave her. Every day he made plans to leave her.

Sweat broke out on Philip's brow, as he heard her frantic whimpers, each one cutting him like a whiplash. He'd try one more time, and then he'd go down and get her.

"Caroline! I forgot to tell you, I couldn't feed Bunny yesterday or today. He's hungry. See if there's something down there for him to eat, will you? I think some turnips are hanging in the far corner." Then he waited for what seemed like hours.

Caroline's eyes flew open, her whimpers gradually dying away. Bunny was hungry! What had Philip said? Ah, yes, turnips. Her eyes adjusting to the darkness, she scanned the cellar. She saw enough food to feed one person well to autumn, scarce enough for two. If she were careful, it would be enough—but Philip wasn't staying. She fought back tears and bit her lip.

"Philip?" she called out tentatively. "What corner did you say the turnips were in?"

Exhaling, Philip smiled and relaxed his grip on the opening. She was going to be all right.

Caroline found a store of tallow candles, half-eaten by mice, in the cellar. After she'd climbed out of the cellar, turnips in hand, Philip brought the barrel from the corner to the center of the room and upended it. Caroline sat on the edge of the plank bed, while he sat on a block of wood opposite her, the barrel between them serving as a makeshift table. In the center the candle burned, casting flickering silhouettes against the walls.

"You promised me," she said.

"Ah, but you know I'm the Ferret, a liar and a cheat."

His bravado didn't fool her. "Don't play games with me, Philip. You may have been the Ferret once. But for a time at least, you were as loyal to this country as the bravest Kentuckian."

Rubbing a hand against his chin, he responded, "Yes."

When a few long minutes went by, she tried again. "Philip, you owe it to me."

"Yes. I do. But it's so, so—"

"It can't be any worse than my going in that cellar."

Philip pushed himself away from the barrel, but Caroline caught his hand between her own.

"No," she pleaded. "Face me, Philip. I'm not your judge, your executioner. Philip, you loved me once. Why can't you at least trust me now?"

Philip looked shocked by her statement. Caroline felt her cheeks aflame, wondering if she'd misunderstood his attentions to her. But he *had* made love to her. Maybe he'd think that's what she meant.

"You're right, Caroline. I did love you. That's why I'm going to tell you what happened after I sent you away

359

from the Raisin River. So you can put me out of your mind forever."

Again he tried to pull away, but at the gentle pressure of her fingers, he stayed seated, smiling wryly at her. "Here's the truth. And it's not going to be pretty."

Caroline watched him, listening to him pour out all the frustration and guilt that had tormented him since that day three months before. When he came to the part where he'd been helpless to save the wounded, when he described their screams for him to come to their rescue, when he told her the epithets they'd called down on him, she couldn't be certain which parts were his imagination, and which were reality. But she'd heard of the massacre, so she knew much of what he'd told her was true. As he talked his voice cracked, but like a soul tormented he could not stop, and Caroline felt his anguish. Once or twice she almost brought her fingertips to his lips to beg him to leave off, as much for the horror he described to her, as the pain she saw him go through. When he was done, his voice dull and resigned, he looked at her through weary eyes.

"So you see, I'm no hero."

"No," she replied softly. "You are a man, Philip. A man I love, imperfections and all."

Philip blinked and looked away. This wasn't love she felt. It was pity. He'd seen the look in her eyes when he'd told her what he'd done, and worse, what he hadn't done, and he'd seen her eyes soften, he'd seen her distress. Once, perhaps, she could have loved him, but never now. He'd never know whether she was with him because she felt sorry for him, like for an injured animal, or because she loved him as a man.

"Philip, listen to me. The massacre wasn't your fault.

You weren't an officer, for heaven's sake. Protecting the men was a noble thing to do, but it wasn't your responsibility. You were friends with the Indians at one time, yes. But whether you want to admit it or not, for months you acted, you fought, and you thought like an American. You did what you thought best. The savages only saw you as the enemy. Besides, when you were friends with them, it was before the war had escalated; the continued fighting whetted nearly everyone's bloodlust. *It simply wasn't your fault."*

When the look in his eyes told her he remained unconvinced, she got up and paced, wringing her hands. "Philip, I know whereof I speak. Ever since my parents died, Austin told me everything that ever went wrong in our lives was my fault. And after a while, through his beatings and because his was the only voice I ever heard, I believed him. Everything was my fault.

"But it wasn't, Philip. Austin—well, he was the last living member of my family, and I'm sad that we were never close, as brothers and sisters should be. But he wasn't an honorable man.

"I believe Austin did many bad and evil things in the course of this war. I don't think I even want to know what all of them are; I know too much already. And for a while, as it became apparent to me—as I would notice people stiffen when his name was mentioned and so forth—I thought, I should stop him. But I was so afraid of him, I couldn't, and then I began to feel guilty about *that.* Like all the wrongs he inflicted on people were my fault."

Philip looked at her quizzically. "But you shouldn't. He beat you, he made you too fearful. You were crippled by that fear."

"No." Caroline stopped, looking at him. "No one can

*make* anyone feel anything. No one is responsible for another's thoughts, another's actions. Austin could beat me, but I could have stood up to him. I allowed my own fear. And I became imprisoned by it."

Uneasy, Philip looked away.

"That's right, Philip. You tried your best. No one else wanted to watch over the wounded. The generals were all too eager to entrust them to your care. You made the best decision at the time; no one could have done better."

She wished she could wipe the pained expression off his face, wished she could bring back the carefree, easy countenance she remembered. If only he would laugh again, a sincere, easy laugh, not the bitter chuckle she'd heard lately.

In the tense silence their eyes locked.

Philip wondered if she could be right, though what she'd said defied everything he believed.

Behind her back, Caroline crossed her fingers.

He considered what she said. Maybe she was right. Even if she wasn't, if she believed in him still, then maybe all was not lost. Perhaps he could prove to her, to himself, that he deserved her. So far he represented everything she hated: vast wealth and senseless killing. But then she'd said she lov—

Just then two men burst into the shelter; they were British.

Still concentrating on Philip, Caroline stared at the intruders, wondering where she'd seen them before.

Philip rose to his feet. "News from Daphne?"

With a sinking sensation, Caroline remembered. These men were Daphne's guards, or escorts, or whatever they'd been, from the party.

"Aye," the taller man replied. "We've been looking for you awhile, mate. She had a fine boy, some time past."

Philip tossed back his head and laughed with pure, unadulterated joy, shaking hands with the men.

"Can you come back with us, mate?" the other man asked.

"Yes."

Laughing and clapping the men on the back, Philip sauntered out the door into the darkness. Then, as if an afterthought, he called over his shoulder, "The talk did help, Caroline. Watch over Derby for me, will you? I'll be back."

She stood in the doorway and watched him melt into the darkness. Blackness enshrouded her heart.

## Chapter Twenty

Hands folded, Caroline, with Maeve at her side, stood looking off into the distance, where she had gazed for two straight weeks. Spring had brought a lace of green to the trees, that would soon thicken to obscure her vision beyond ten yards or so. She would no longer be able to see the path from just outside the shelter.

"He's not coming back."

"What makes ye think so, lass?"

"The man's a liar, a cheat, and a scoundrel. He plays a wicked game, going back and forth between his countrymen and us, playing patriot to us all. He goes to whichever side his bread is buttered on." *And Daphne melts in his mouth.*

"Could it be there's something ye don't see here?"

Caroline whirled. "I'm not blind or deaf, Maeve. When Philip left me, he was happy for the first time in weeks. And all because of—" she choked, "because of Daphne." Her eyes glittered.

Maeve looked down, then at her mistress. "Would ye be thinking more of him if he was miserable that a child of his was born?"

"N-no. No, of course not. I just think he's the most self-centered, most selfish, most opportunistic man I've ever met."

"Oh, lass, I think ye're not judging him fair."

"She's right, Caroline," Titus broke in. He'd been standing off to the side next to his carriage, while Maeve tried to persuade Caroline to move to his parents' house until the wedding. Genevieve hadn't liked the idea of a single woman living by herself in the middle of the forest.

"It's not fair to judge a man ill, just because he comes from wealth."

Realizing Titus thought her negative feelings would extend toward him, Caroline almost laughed. From what she'd learned, his parents' wealth—or former wealth, since the war had taken most of it—couldn't begin to compare to Philip's.

"His wealth isn't the only reason I abhor him. Did you know that traitor sired a child to a woman from England? One who isn't wed?" *And he could have gotten me with child as well.* Caroline had never felt so soiled or dirty, since she'd learned the truth about Philip. To think she'd given herself willingly to him, to think she'd been ready to do so again, to heal him. Ha! The man needed no healing. He needed gelding.

Maeve stepped forward. "Please, lass, come back with Titus and me. I could be usin' some help for the weddin'. Mrs. Duffy intends it to be a respite from the war, providin' it isn't over by then, and she still hasn't gotten over Mr. Duffy's passin'. She thinks she ought to be waitin' till after the year of mournin' is up, but by then it would be so late, we'd never prepare things in time. I have no idea how to plan for such an affair, and—"

"And I do? Oh, I'm sorry, Maeve. That wasn't kind of

me. Of course, I'd be honored to help you. Just give me a few minutes to gather my belongings, and I'll be with you."

In truth, she had few belongings to gather. Her spare deerskin frock hung from the peg along with her cloak, and she knew it would take Genevieve no time at all to offer her the use of some of her garments. For years Caroline had thought she'd be eager to rid herself of the animal skins, but now she ran her finger lightly over the simple frock, remembering how it had soaked through the night she'd run through the rain to Philip, and how he'd warmed her with his smoldering look. She thought back to Fawn and Willie, and wondered what had become of them. Then she leaned over to gather Bunny up in her arms, loath to let go of him. Bringing him to her cheek, she rubbed her face against his soft fur. He was her last tie to Philip. Nothing like a baby, she thought ruefully, and kissed the animal and set him down.

"Farewell, Bunny," she said, smiling through her tears. "I suppose your name should be Rabbit now, for you've gotten quite fat and big. The garden I planted should feed you well, and there will soon be food aplenty in the forest. Take care, Bunny," she whispered.

Then she stepped outside. "I've just thought of something. Will you come in and take the food that's left? I'll hand it up from the cellar."

Maeve's mouth dropped open. "The cellar? But, lass, you don't need to, Titus would be happy to go down, oof!" She gasped as Titus elbowed her in the side.

"Oh, it's nothing, really," Caroline replied airily, waving a hand.

In seconds she dropped down into the cellar. She stood still a moment, giving her eyes time to adjust to the darkness, remembering how Philip had encouraged her to go down alone, preparing her for this moment.

*Well, Philip, you did a good job,* she thought. *I don't need you anymore. I don't need you. I don't need you at all, not at—*

"Caroline! Are you going to hand anything up here or not?"

"Yes, Titus. Just a moment, I'll lift it up to you."

They arrived back at the Duffys almost three hours later, Genevieve welcoming her with open arms.

"Oh, I'm glad to see you," the woman said, enfolding Caroline in a warm embrace. "I wasn't certain how you would feel about coming here, what with Titus's agreement with Maeve, but we do still love you, Caroline. And I could certainly use your help."

That night, from her straw-stuffed bed in the spacious house, Caroline knew exactly how her animals felt when caught in a trap with no room for escape.

The plans for the wedding kept the women busy over the next several weeks, while Titus returned to the fort. Genevieve was adamant that the affair should be as genteel as possible. Caroline wondered how the Duffys' dwindling resources would extend to cover all the expenses the celebration would entail, but kept her thoughts to herself. After all, her opinions scarcely mattered. Nothing mattered anymore.

Summer came in its heat and glory. The war seemed like it would never end. More and more battles occurred in Michigan Territory, after it became apparent that the Americans would have to control the Great Lakes. With the Duffys' home located almost ten miles from Lake St. Clair, Caroline felt landlocked. Several times she announced her intention to go to the water, but Genevieve wouldn't hear of it.

"I'm sorry, dear, I truly am. I know how much you'd like to go. But they're preparing for battle, you know, building a fine navy, and the place is crawling with men. It wouldn't do for you to go there at all, Caroline."

"But I need to see the lake. It was so much closer to my home, and I miss it."

Genevieve's heart swelled with pity. "I suppose the three of us might go, as long as we stay together. Sometimes I forget how difficult this all must be for you. First, to have your brother passing away, then, this situation with Titus and Maeve."

Caroline smothered the sorrow that always engulfed her at the mention of Austin's name. "But Titus and me—we really weren't suited for each other."

"I know," Genevieve sighed. "It's too bad we couldn't link you up with somebody, but there's such a dearth of men around here. They're all at the—wait a minute. That *is* an idea."

"What?" Caroline asked, totally confused.

"The last time he was home, Titus mentioned in passing that he was delivering messages from the fort to the navy. Perhaps he knows a young man who might be . . . interested in you. He'd said he knew no one in the army who would do, but I'd never thought of the navy. Yes, a sojourn to the lake might be just the thing you need."

Groaning to herself, Caroline repeated, "Yes. To see men. Just what I need."

That night Titus managed to visit. After she went upstairs to bed, Caroline heard him arguing with his mother.

"That's the worst place for you women to go right now. Especially Caroline. If she hears what's go—"

"Then you'll just have to see to it that she doesn't hear, won't you? And don't you know someone there you can introduce her to? I like Caroline well enough, but it would be uncomfortable for her to live here after you're wed. And she certainly can't live with you and Maeve. How awkward."

"Mother, are you telling me you want me to introduce her to a man? Don't you understand?"

Genevieve clucked her tongue. "What I understand is that she's a very lonely girl."

"Well," Titus muttered. "I don't like the idea of the three of you going there at all. If I have military business there tomorrow, I'll try to accompany you for a while. If they see you're my family, the three of you should be safe."

"Safe?" Genevieve questioned him. "What do we have to fear?"

"For the most part, these men have been without women for a long time, Mother," Titus explained through clenched teeth.

"Good. Then maybe we can find *someone* willing to wed Caroline."

Caroline heard Titus groan in exasperation. "And how do the three of you propose to get there? Have you forgotten we no longer have a horse to pull our carriage?"

"Why, we'll walk of course," Genevieve responded briskly.

"Walk! *You?*"

"Of course. We females aren't as frail as you think, Son. The exercise will do us good."

"But it's five miles away," Titus protested.

"A short stroll. Now, I'll hear no more of your arguments. I appreciate your concern, but we'll manage just fine."

Caroline blocked her ears to shut out the remainder of their conversation.

The next day they headed to the lake, with Genevieve chattering constantly and Maeve uncharacteristically silent.

When they finally reached the shoreline, Caroline was amazed at the hubbub of activity. Men shouted back and forth, hurrying to put finishing touches on the ships she could see. Even more amazing was the warm greeting given Titus by many of the seamen and carpenters. Caroline wondered if Genevieve had a clue to what her son was about. Obviously he came here often, if not daily.

Maeve clung to Titus's arm, smiling warmly as he introduced her to the men. Caroline hung back, until Genevieve called her to unpack the picnic they'd prepared. Titus approached a young, good-looking man with curly, dark hair and warm eyes. As the stranger pressed something into Titus's hand, Caroline stepped closer.

Titus quickly scanned the pamphlet and grimaced. "I certainly hope he knows what he's about," she heard him say.

Then the stranger's eyes lighted on her, and he said, in a voice Caroline thought a little too loud, "And who's this fine lady you brought with you, Mister Duffy? A sister, I presume?"

"No." There was an edge to Titus's voice as he held out his hand to Caroline. "This is a good friend of my family's, Miss Caroline Swanson."

The man's eyes flickered as if he recognized her name,

and Caroline wondered if he knew she'd been accused of being a traitor. She stepped forward and extended her hand. He bowed and kissed it.

"Admiral Oliver Perry, ma'am, at your service."

"Admiral Perry. What is it you're doing here?"

Perry winked. "Actually, it's a secret, but not a very well-hidden one, I'm afraid. We're building a navy, you see."

"Three ships? A navy?"

Grinning, Perry responded, "Another's being tested for her seaworthiness. And we've purchased some older vessels. Look yonder."

Looking to where he pointed, Caroline saw three schooners ply the crystal blue waters.

"They're lovely," she responded.

Perry laughed. "I should hope they're more workhorses than pretty to look at. Now, if you will excuse me, I do have work to do."

"Won't you sup with us?" Maeve asked, looking down at the basket she held in both hands.

"I'm afraid I haven't the time, ma'am. But thank you for the invitation. Now, if you'll excuse me, Miss Swanson, Miss Maeve, Mr.—"

"Duffy," Titus supplied.

"Oh, yes, Duffy."

Caroline wondered why Perry acted like he'd forgotten Titus's name. He knew it just moments before, and he'd greeted Titus like an old friend. It was no use. As attractive as Oliver Perry was, she'd felt nothing toward him. Besides, every man she'd ever known had a dishonest streak. Only Titus was sincere. Titus, to whom she could never feel anything other than friendship. Sighing, she wished she could change the circumstances, but knew such hopes were futile.

Over their picnic, Caroline tried to think of a tactful way to ask Titus about the pamphlet Perry had given him, but found she didn't have the heart to interrupt the intimate cooing and flirting between the young couple. Genevieve seemed oblivious to it all.

After they'd finished eating, Titus left yet again, accompanied by his mother whispering earnestly in his ear. Caroline folded the cloth over the top of the basket and cleared her throat.

"Um, Maeve," she began, as offhandedly as possible.

"Aye, lass?"

"Does Titus come here often?"

Maeve's jaw set. "My betrothed's business is of no concern to me."

"You're not answering my question."

"What do you care what Titus does?"

"Oh, Maeve, that won't work at all. You can't possibly be jealous. You know I only care for Titus as a friend. Now, why won't you answer my question?"

Looking away, Maeve answered firmly, "Because I can't."

"Why?"

"Titus made me promise."

"Oh, well then. We certainly wouldn't want to go back on a promise, would we?"

Maeve sighed. "You'll be wantin' to ask Titus about the pamphlet, then, won't ye?"

"Yes. I know he won't give it to me. Can you get it from him, Maeve? Can you? Please, Maeve."

"I'll see what I can do. No promises, mind."

But she was as good as her word. After Titus and

Genevieve returned, Maeve whispered something in his ear. He grinned sheepishly, handing her the folded paper. Caroline saw him whisper to Maeve, who shook her head, giggling. Crossing her arms in front of her, Caroline waited for the lovers to put an end to their long goodbye.

On the way back home, a weary Genevieve followed some paces behind the younger women. Maeve placed the brittle paper into Caroline's outstretched hand.

Squinting to read it—for the pamphlet was of inferior quality with the print blurred in several places—Caroline scanned the beginning. War news, all of it, but nothing she hadn't already heard. Until she came to a heading one-third down the page: *British Spy Believed To Be in British Navy*.

Caroline swallowed and looked away, then forced herself to read the remainder through blurred vision. The pamphlet confirmed her worst fears. *A worthy Source Recently Conveyed to this Printer that the Notorious British Informante, the Hon. Philip Masterson, is Said to be in His Majesty's Service on Board the Queen Charlotte. Upon Hearing this News, Lt. Oliver Hazard Perry is said to Have Declared that He Will Blow the Man Out of the Water.*

"It would serve him right," Caroline muttered.

"Let me see it, lass. Ah, where were ye readin'? Down here?" Maeve's brow furrowed. "That doesn't sound like him."

"Like Philip? Ha! You don't—"

"No, lass. Like Lieutenant Perry. 'Tis true I just met him today, but he doesn't seem like a man given to boastin', d'ye think?"

Grimacing, Caroline answered, "I'm not the one to ask, being such a poor judge of men, I'm afraid. Oh, please don't look at me like that. I'm not to be pitied."

"No, lass," Maeve answered softly. "But yer not always right, y'know. Could be Master Philip's been impressed."

Caroline laughed bitterly. "He's a spy, Maeve. One who makes a profession of lying to people. And he's very good at it, too. No, impressment doesn't ring true, not when it comes to Mr. Masterson. He's British, through and through. The enemy."

Seeing that Caroline could not be argued with, Maeve held her tongue.


Summer drew to an end. Caroline resolutely pushed Philip from her mind, filling her thoughts and time with preparations for Maeve's wedding. She watched her friend blossom as Maeve reveled at being the center of attention, becoming an apt pupil for Genevieve's instructions at acting ladylike.

Though Maeve insisted she could live with them after the wedding, Caroline knew such an arrangement would eventually prove awkward for all of them. She sent out inquiries to Philadelphia for a position as a teacher. When they all came back negatively, Titus suggested she apply herself to healing.

Caroline warmed to the idea. "But there are no woman physicians, are there?"

Titus shrugged. "I've never known you to be daunted by such a small obstacle. If you've had enough of tending men, perhaps you could work with horses. Would you like me to inquire into that possibility for you?"

"Oh, so very much. You would do that for me?"

"Yes. You're a good woman, Caroline. The war has changed you. As it has all of us, whether for good or ill."

Caroline looked wistfully over at Maeve, who pored

over the guest list with Genevieve. "Yet there is one who grows happier, even while the war wages on," she murmured.

"Maeve is not as untouched by this as she appears," Titus replied. "We have friends whose lives are at stake, you know." He rose, turned, and shuffled off to his room.

There were so many secrets, so many plans in this family, and she was part of none of them. Shoving her melancholy aside yet again, Caroline looked forward to her future. Animals would be her salvation.

September first arrived. Caroline and Maeve stirred a great kettle of apple butter hanging in the fireplace.

"I think the leaves on the trees will begin to turn color by the day of your wedding, Maeve," Caroline said.

"Aye, lass." Maeve blew on the wooden spoon to cool the butter before taking a lick. "Mmm. Try some?"

"No, thank you."

"Ye really should, ye know. It might whet yer appetite. Ye were looking so bonny for a while, but now yer clothes are hanging on ye once again."

Looking down at her much-too-large muslin dress, Caroline grimaced. "With a few tucks it should be all right, don't you think?"

"It's not the frock I be worryin' about, lass. But, yes, some tucks will do it good. Will ye be wearin' this for the weddin'?"

Laughing, Caroline answered, "I think you're deserving of more than my work dress. No, while you and Titus have been busy cooing at each other, I've been sewing a traveling dress. I expect I'll be wearing that."

"You'll do no such thing!" Genevieve remonstrated as

she entered, waving a fan in the air. "You'll be wearing some bit of finery for my only son's nuptials."

"But I haven't any means of paying for it, and I can't take advantage of your hospitality any longer. You've been much too generous."

"While you're living in my house, young lady," Genevieve said playfully, tapping the tip of Caroline's nose with her fan, "you'll do as I say. Consider it a parting gift."

Finally Caroline capitulated, though she wondered where all the money was coming from. She knew the Duffys had little left after the war, yet just the other day Titus had come in, face gleaming, announcing that his new printing press had arrived. A new one, and the finest in the country. *He could have spent his gold on food,* Caroline thought, shaking her head. Still, the situation had improved somewhat, thanks to a huge cargo of seeds that had arrived in late spring. No one had ever been able to find for whom the shipment was meant. After coming to the conclusion that the rightful owner had probably been slain by the Indians, the settlers made full use of their unexpected bounty, planting twice as much as they needed. A good thing, too, for the Indians still carried out intermittent raids, and the British still rode into the area on occasion, their horses trampling newly sprouted gardens.

In addition to the wedding, they had another reason to hope. Rumors flew about Perry's navy, though Caroline thought the optimism unfounded. From what she'd seen, Oliver Perry was much too young and inexperienced to go up against the British, and his makeshift fleet too small. Besides, she doubted the American lieutenant had the killer instinct inbred in the British. And with Philip fighting against them—ha! Her side hadn't a chance.

Yet even while she thought this, a part of her conscience niggled at her. She simply couldn't believe Philip's misery at the slaying at the Raisin River had been a masquerade. And how had his distress at the killings turned into a compulsion to wreak more death and destruction? Then she remembered his face, his pure, untainted joy at the news of his and Daphne's baby, and she wondered if the birth of a child could eradicate all memories of any previous sorrow. She sighed. That was one puzzle she'd never be able to answer.

The day before the wedding, dread seized Caroline's heart. From far-off in the distance, she heard the faint sound of artillery, of cannon and explosions. She listened to see if anyone else in the house was alarmed, but all was quiet. By nightfall, attributing her disquiet to memories of the battles she'd witnessed—memories that surfaced at the most unlikely times—she closed her eyes and fell asleep.

The morning of September eleventh broke warm and sunny, with the scent of autumn in the air. A wave of nostalgia overtook Caroline, as she recalled a similar day almost a year ago when Philip had taken her away. Then, focusing on the excitement around her, she concentrated on the scene at hand.

Arriving carriages brought guests from miles around. Titus beamed, greeting the visitors, as everyone helped set up the tables with crossbuck legs made from unpeeled tree limbs. Maids hired for the day brought out wooden trenchers and platters of food in abundance.

News spread, sending waves of jubilation rippling through the crowd: the evening before, against seemingly unsurmountable odds, Lieutenant Perry had defeated the enemy on Lake Erie. Losses on both sides were enormous, but the victory could well turn the tide of the war.

Dressed in a pink gauze frock that lent a soft glow to her pallor, Caroline wondered if Philip were among those killed.

The parson arrived; guests stood. The ceremony was about to begin. At Maeve's request, Caroline had agreed to sing a simple melody about two lost people finding each other in a world intent on keeping them apart.

Her voice rising like silver bells, Caroline closed her eyes and sang, her soul intertwining with the lilting notes. Birds chirped and leaves rustled, while she poured her heart into the song.

Philip, as yet unnoticed, stood behind the guests, off in the trees, watching Caroline. She was thin again, thinner than the last time he'd seen her, but more beautiful than ever, her hair hanging in a silver curtain behind her back. He heard every note, every word of the song, recognizing in the lyrics two people other than the bride and the groom. He smiled slightly, willing Caroline to look at him.

Her eyes opened, meeting his. She blushed and averted her gaze, as if wishing she could flee to the far corners of the earth.

"Not without me, Caroline," he whispered half-aloud. "Not without me."

Then the parson asked the bride and groom to unite in marriage, and the ceremony was over. While the guests exclaimed their approval, Titus whispered something in Maeve's ear. She nodded, and to everyone's amazement Titus reached out and grabbed Caroline's arm, just as she took a step in the direction of the house.

"I'd like to say something to my guests," he announced,

378

holding Caroline firmly on one side, a beaming Maeve clutching his opposite arm.

A hush fell over the crowd.

"Today," Titus said, "is the happiest day of my life. First, of course, because I've taken this lovely lady as my wife."

The crowd cheered as he kissed Maeve lightly on the tip of her nose.

"Then there is last evening's victory on Lake Erie, news of which reached my ears just prior to my nuptials. This battle has been long in the planning, and now Detroit is ours!"

Cheers and huzzahs rang in the air. When the cries died down, he continued.

"My part, I'm sad to say, has been slight. But I did manage to print some pamphlets intentionally designed to mislead the enemy. Some information was erroneous, but most of it doesn't matter now. There is one misconception I'd like to clear up, though."

The crowd cheered louder; he signaled for quiet.

"I could go into a long explanation, but instead, there is a guest present I'd like to introduce to you. A very special guest without which my day—and last night's victory—would not be complete."

As Philip strode forward, lines of weariness etched around his mouth and his limp clearly evident, Caroline clenched her fists and gritted her teeth.

*It's Maeve's wedding,* she thought. *It's Maeve's wedding day and you, Caroline Swanson, will not make a scene. You will get through this, and find out what's going on later. Or better yet, you'll get away from here.*

Head bowed, Philip reached the front of the crowd and stood next to Caroline. She stiffened.

At Maeve's entreating look, Titus spoke hurriedly. "Some of you may recognize Mr. Philip Masterson. For those who don't, let me say he was a British spy who changed allegiance and became an American citizen some time ago. He worked diligently for our cause, first on land, then on the Great Lakes. I printed some pamphlets stating Mr. Masterson rejoined the British, knowing all the while he resumed his commission in order to lead them into our hands. All the time his loyalty was with us. It is to him as much as to Admiral Perry that you owe your thanks for last night's victory."

Philip glared at Titus. "You weren't supposed to say anything of that," he whispered.

Stunned, Caroline watched the two men.

Titus smiled. "It's my wedding day. Would you deny me this gift?"

Someone from the crowd cried, "And how did he help? We thought he was the Ferret."

Reaching behind Caroline, Titus pushed Philip forward. From the expression on Philip's face, Caroline thought he looked like he was going to the gallows.

He cleared his throat and coughed.

Her brows drew together. She wasn't accustomed to seeing him so ill at ease.

"It's true," he began. "I was the Ferret. But early on, after a series of misadventures—" He stopped, catching Caroline's eye and winking, "I became quite enamored of this beautiful country and many of the people in it. I pledged my allegiance to your homeland. I carry on my person a letter from the President, should any of you doubt my word. I managed to devise battle plans for the British, convincing them I was securing information that would assure them of victory. Instead, I assisted Admiral

Perry in leading them into a trap. But I think this is enough about myself, and we should turn our attention back to the bride and groom. Ladies and gentlemen, may I present to you Mr. and Mrs. Titus Duffy."

The crowd broke into applause. Philip walked away, then turned to Caroline. *Will you come with me?* he mouthed.

Feeling the guests' eyes upon her, Caroline knew she had to prolong the charade a few moments longer—if she could just shove her heart back into its proper position. It wasn't fair that Philip should still have this effect on her, especially after she'd tried so hard to forget him. He might have convinced Titus and everyone present that he was loyal, but she wasn't as easily swayed. There was still Daphne.

They walked to the woods at the outskirts of the gala beginning to unfold. Struggling to concentrate on anything other than the man at her side, Caroline kept her attention fastened on Maeve and Titus. Through the throng she thought she saw a familiar gentleman arrive and approach the newly married couple; she smiled when she saw a tired-looking Oliver Perry turn and head in her direction. With another person joining them, she had a slim chance of eluding Philip's charms.

"Miss Swanson," Perry said, bending and kissing her hand.

Caroline curtsied. "Admiral Perry. Congratulations, and thank you on behalf of everyone for last night's victory."

"You know him?" Philip asked, scowling.

Caroline batted her lashes. "Admiral Perry and I have been introduced previously."

Perry bowed his head in acknowledgement. "And I am

381

equally pleased to know you are the lovely Caroline of whom my friend spoke so often."

Caroline's smile vanished. "Spoke? Of me?"

"Aye," Perry answered. "More than I can say right now, though I highly recommend, Philip, that you take Miss Swanson for a stroll and tell her everything."

"Yes," Caroline repeated. "Everything."

She wasn't at all certain she liked the proprietary way Philip took her arm. She was even less certain she liked her reaction to the feel of his muscles against her flesh, dismayed when a most pleasurable tingle coursed through her. She hoped Philip didn't notice.

"I'll explain, Caroline. But you must listen, and not ask questions until I've finished."

"I'm through taking orders from men, Philip."

He hid a smile. "So I've heard. But this I ask you as a common courtesy. Can't you grant me the same consideration you'd give Maeve, if she asked you for such a simple favor? After all," he whispered, "we were very close once."

She wanted to slap him for tickling her ear with his breath, with his warm, moist breath smelling lightly of rum.

She licked her lips. "I won't interrupt," she said, wondering why her voice sounded so faraway.

They sat across from each other beneath a tree that reminded Caroline of the shady maple under which they'd made love. She tried to withdraw her hands, but Philip held them tightly.

"No, Caroline. You must look at me and listen."

He swallowed, praying as he'd never prayed before. She had to believe him. His whole life rested in her hands.

"You know I held myself responsible for the massacre

382

at the Raisin River. For days and nights I could hear the screams, see the blood . . . I still do. And for days—no, weeks—the only thing that kept me from taking my own life was the need to know that you still lived. You must believe me, Caroline. If you had died, my life would have ended."

Inexorably, she felt herself drawn to him. He was telling her the truth. The pain in his face, the vulnerability in his manner, convinced her that this was no act. Her resolve crumbling, with the slightest of nods she urged him to go on.

"By the time I found you, I'd long been convinced you were dead. I can't describe to you how I felt when I saw you standing there in the middle of that circle—you were a miracle! And then I wondered why I'd been lucky enough to have this miracle. I decided that I'd been given another chance. As long as you lived, Caroline, I could hope that you would love me. But I knew in my heart there was no way you—who values life above all, in all creatures—could love me, who'd allowed so many men to be slaughtered."

"But it wasn't your fault."

"Perhaps. Perhaps not." He smiled, touching a finger to her lips. "You promised not to interrupt."

She tried to smile in return, but her lower lip quivered.

"At any rate, I decided that if I were to have a chance, not just so you could live with me, but so I could live with myself, I had to redeem myself. Yet I was hunted everywhere, by Indian, colonist, and Englishman. If I had any chance to succeed, it had to be at sea. Two years ago when I sailed here from England, I learned some about charting courses, as well as the workings of the ship itself. If a man went down, and for various reasons, one always did, whether from dysentery or some other ailment, I was called into service. So Titus helped me contact Oliver Perry."

"Then Titus knew all along."

He grinned. "You interrupted again. Yes, both he and, I presume, Maeve. We set it up so I became impressed by the British. I expressed as much gratitude as I could without causing suspicion, thanking them for saving me from the Americans, and they readily believed me. I learned as much as I could of their naval plans and 'advised' them how to attack the Americans. They didn't know it, of course, but my advice was designed to play into the hands of Oliver Perry."

Caroline stared at him, awed. "You led the British right into an ambush."

"Aye. And assisted in a few other ways, which aren't important right now. What is important is you. Caroline, do you believe anything I've told you?"

"I want to, Philip, but . . . "

"But what? Caroline, I risked my life for you."

"And you, so you could live with yourself," she pointed out.

"Yes," he agreed slowly.

"You always think of yourself somehow, don't you, Philip?"

"I don't underst—"

"Daphne! You were betrothed to her. Philip, you left me for her. I—I don't blame you for wanting to acknowledge your son, but—"

"But what, Caroline? You loved me?"

"You . . . moved me. In ways I never thought possible. I was—selfish. I wanted you for myself, but it wasn't meant to be. When her guards told you about the babe, you were happier than I've ever seen you."

Chuckling, he said, "Aye. I was happy the child was a boy. It solves a lot of problems, you see."

"No, I'm afraid I don't."

"Daphne's a distant cousin. Remember?"

Caroline racked her brain. "Yes, you told me that. But what has that to do with anything?"

"My dear Caroline, everything. You see, now that there's another male descendant on the Masterson side, *he* can inherit Strathmore Castle, and all the bloody responsibility it entails."

She blinked. "Strathmore Castle?"

"Aye. I knew you wouldn't want to go to Britain to live, your love of this country is so strong. And Daphne's wanted the castle forever. There were so many problems I had to surmount."

"But your babe—"

"He isn't mine, Caroline. No, it's true. Daphne had a feeling, woman's intuition, call it, that I had come here to escape her clutches. Which was partly true. And when I told her about you in a letter, she figured she'd soon lose it all—the castle, everything. So she told me the child was mine, but I wasn't in England when he was conceived. In fact, I'd never touched Daphne. But she thought I'd be proud to have an heir, and wouldn't want the babe to grow up a bastard. By coming here, she could play with the child's birthdate a bit, and convince people back in England that the child was mine. She thought all I needed was a male descendant to calm me down, make me stay with her. She thought I'd want to marry her, when all I really wanted was to be free of all my inheritance entails. So I told Daphne that her son could inherit the castle.

She, of course, will live there until the boy comes of age. And the man who got her with child was eager to wed her, so the boy will grow up with his father."

Caroline listened, breathless. "Then you never loved her?"

"No. Never. Daphne was always my father's favorite. Ofttimes I heard him say he wished she'd been his child."

Caroline's brow creased. "Then why didn't he just leave the castle to her?"

"Britain's laws are not as kind as your country's. A man must leave his fortune to a male descendant, and though it irked my father sorely, I was the only son he had."

"Why did he hate you so? Who could hate his own child?"

Smiling bitterly, Philip answered, "I was illegitimate, Caroline. Apparently my mother truly loved him, but he just—used her. He refused to marry her, even when she told him she was with child. When I was born, resembling him as I do, my mother was so bitter by his poor treatment of her, she couldn't stand the sight of me. I reminded her of him too much. She abandoned me soon after."

Caroline's eyes softened. "And your father?"

"He cared for me as he was able. Sent me to boarding schools, claiming I was the orphan of an old friend. And when I'd come home for holidays, he'd give all his attention to Daphne. She's the child of a second cousin with whom he'd grown up as a boy. He doted on her from the beginning. The only legal way he could leave Strathmore to her was to have her wed me. I was not even consulted."

Caroline thought a few moments, afraid she'd misunderstood. "And you gave the castle to her? And your fortune?"

"Only half my fortune, Caroline. Years ago I inherited a considerable sum of money from my mother's father, and retained that. But I'd give all of it up for you. All you have to do is ask."

He held his breath, seeing her eyes moisten.

"I'm not fond of money or large homes," she said.

"But you wouldn't have to wear animal skins for clothing," he argued gently. "I could afford to buy you cloth aplenty."

"And would you want to live in a big house in a city?"

"I couldn't imagine living anywhere else than here, Caroline. This is where I found you."

"Hold me, Philip. Just hold me."

She took a step forward and nestled in his arms, struggling to maintain some degree of control.

"Tell me," Philip said finally, "about Austin."

She swallowed. "He's dead, you know."

"Do you miss him?"

"Of course. He was my brother. I loved him, but I feel a strange sense of relief. I supposed I should feel guilty, but . . ."

"No, Caroline. You have nothing to feel guilty about."

"What was it all about, Philip? In the beginning? How did you know Austin would trade secrets for money? Was it because I told you how greedy he was? Did you use me to find out who would be an easily bought traitor?"

She saw him hesitate. "Don't lie to me."

He held her hands tightly, so she could not withdraw them, and looked her in the eye. "In truth, I was looking for Austin. But I didn't know who he was. I had no idea he could be your brother. He'd contacted the British first, you see, and dealt with another spy before I'd ever met him. The British knew there was a traitor in your area

387

willing to sell secrets for a price, because he'd done so once already. The problem was, no one knew his identity. I was sent to find him, so we could deal with him again."

Her eyes brimmed with tears. "Then you *were* using me."

Sighing, he said, "No. I didn't plan the snakebite, remember? I certainly didn't plan that you would find me and help me, though it was my good fortune that you did." He peeked out the corner of his eye at her, attempting to coax a smile, but she studied the ground.

"Once you learned he was my brother, how could you continue to be in league with him? Didn't you know it would destroy me?"

He didn't remark that she looked anything but destroyed. Indeed, he sensed a new strength about her beneath her fragile appearance, a sturdiness he'd never seen before. Weighing his words carefully, he replied, "In the beginning, I thought you were in league with him."

Her brows shot up. "Truly?"

"Truly."

Despite herself, she smiled. "I didn't trust you once I learned of your involvement with Austin, and—"

"I didn't trust you before," he cut in. "How *did* you learn I bought secrets from Austin?"

"Maeve told me he confessed all before he died."

Grimacing, Philip said, "I'm sorry."

"I don't blame you. You didn't force Austin's hand."

He paused, then said, "What will you do now, with Maeve and Titus wed? What are your plans for the future?"

"I'm bound for Philadelphia. I've been offered a position as an assistant to a physician. I'm to prove my worth with animals before human patients."

"But you can't live by yourself. You need someone to take care of you."

Hope radiated from every pore of him.

"No, Philip." She turned slowly and headed back to the crowd. "I need no one to take care of me. I can take care of myself quite well."

He opened his mouth to argue, but seeing the determination in her face, swallowed his objections. "When are you leaving?" he asked hoarsely.

"Two weeks. I've given my word, and promises have become very important to me."

Her words stung. He grabbed her and whirled her toward him. "But you hate Philadelphia!"

"How do you know? I've never been there."

"I know, you're only going there because times are so hard here. But I have money, Caroline. I can buy food, have it shipped in—"

"Food is a problem for some of the people, yes, but not me. I planted a large garden, you see. And there were enough foodstuffs put away in the cellar that I didn't go hungry over the summer. Why, we had such a bountiful supply, we were able to use some of it for the wedding."

He stepped back, his joy quickly becoming replaced by a cold, gripping emptiness. "How did you get everything out of the cellar?"

"Simple. I went down for them."

"By yourself?"

She laughed. "After being held captive by Indians, tending men with sickening wounds, and witnessing some of the most horrid sights a woman has ever seen, do you think a little darkness would frighten me? No, Philip. Thanks to you, I'm cured. Of everything."

Gulping, he watched her walk away. *Yes, Caroline. You're cured. Of even wanting me.*

## Chapter Twenty-one

The next day Philip arrived at the Duffys with a bouquet of goldenrod and Queen Anne's lace. "Will you go for a walk with me?"

"Oh, Philip—"

"Please, Caroline."

They walked side by side, Philip taking infinite care to keep his hands at his sides, away from her.

"I'm the one who sent the seeds, you know," he said suddenly.

She stared at him. "Pardon me?"

"The seeds, the shipload that was never claimed. I arranged to have them sent here, so your people wouldn't starve. Caroline, I love you. I didn't want you to go hungry. I knew you didn't like animal meat, so—"

"No, *don't!*"

All was silent for a few moments, silence gradually interrupted by the sound of her choking sobs. "Don't you see, Philip? I can't love you again. You'll only leave."

"No, Caroline. I won't."

"You *will*. And I couldn't bear it. I couldn't bear to

have you leave again." She turned and fled to the safety of the house.

For four days he camped outside the Duffys, with Caroline refusing to see him, until Maeve said, "Lass, he can't stay outside forever. Rain's in the air. He'll be freezin' to death."

"Nonsense!" Caroline retorted. "He knows where the animal shelter is. He can always go there."

"But he won't. Yer not addle-brained, lass. Surely ye know he means to stay until ye see him."

"And you and Titus aren't making matters difficult for him, are you? Why, you seem almost happy to have him here."

Maeve's eyes narrowed. "In truth, we are. We became close friends while ye were captured by the Indians. And yer not makin' my first duty as Titus's wife easy fer me. Even Mother Duffy says I should be housin' him as our guest, but yer stubbornness is interferin' with what my husband and me be wishin' to do."

Exasperated, Caroline replied, "Then by all means, do let him in. It's your home."

"No, lass. Ye go out and ask him."

"Surely you can't expect me to—"

Nodding, Maeve said sagely, "Aye, lass. I'm no longer a servant. Indeed I can."

"Fine!"

Philip's eyes lit up when he saw Caroline step outside.

"Maeve and Titus would like you to come and stay as their guest," she said stiffly.

"Will you walk with me first?"

"No."

He shrugged and sat down. "Well, then. Please convey my regrets."

"Philip, don't be childish! It looks like rain, and you're certain to catch a death of an ague if you don't come inside."

He cocked a brow. "Would you care?"

"Of course, I'd care! I'd care about any animal that was too stupid to come in out of the cold and rain."

"It's questionable who's acting stupid, Caroline. I only asked a simple favor."

Inhaling deeply, she steeled herself and said, "Let's walk."

"No," he said, his eyes boring into hers. "Let's ride. I've brought Derby back."

Moments later, on Derby, her arms around Philip's waist, she wasn't surprised to find them heading in the direction of the animal shelter. Philip made a few attempts at conversation, but the escalating wind made talking difficult, and he soon gave up.

Halfway there, Caroline shivered.

"Are you cold?" Philip asked.

"No. I feel like—like someone's watching us."

Philip pulled lightly on Derby's reins; the horse stopped. "You're right. Someone's out here."

They waited for one tense moment. Two, three, four. Philip dismounted with slow grace. "Stay here," he ordered, voice low.

He crouched and pulled a long-bladed knife from his boot. Caroline screamed, just as a figure leaped down from the tree above him, sending his knife flying.

Mad Bird stood, lips spread wide in an evil grin, the silver pistol aimed at Philip's heart. "Mad Bird do to you what you did to Mad Bird," the Indian said, his voice menacing. "Only I finish what I begin."

"No! Don't!" Caroline pleaded.

In an instant she stood in front of them, her hair in wild disarray, her eyes rounded and vacant. She spoke in a mixture of Potawatomi and English, collaring Mad Bird's vest with a death grip.

"You cannot kill this man," she said desperately.

Mad Bird folded his arms across his chest. "Why not, Silver Hair?"

"The Great Spirit tells me he is a spirit as well. Says this man was called back to life after he was killed at the River Raisin."

Mad Bird shoved her away. "Crazy, lying woman! Tecumseh said Man with Forked Tongue was left to be haunted by spirits."

Desperately, Caroline racked her brain in order to find a way to convince the Indian to let Philip live.

"That's true. But the spirits claimed him and brought his soul to themselves. Now his body is left to roam the earth. No one must interfere with the spirits, Mad Bird. Such a wise man as you certainly knows that."

Doubt replaced the suspicion on Mad Bird's face.

Caroline saw Philip look from her to the Indian, as if calculating how to get the knife before Mad Bird could fling his tomahawk.

*No*, she begged silently. *It will never work.*

As if hearing her, he stood still.

"How do I know if you speak the truth, crazy woman?"

"Simple," Philip said. "You remember her horse, Mad Bird?"

The Indian looked at Derby, then nodded his head slowly.

"You also remember the woman's way with animals."

Again, Mad Bird nodded.

"Ask the woman to ride away on the horse," Philip suggested.

Caroline's brows drew together. What was he doing? Was he sending her away for her own safety again? Well, she wouldn't go, she wouldn't . . .

"Crazy woman. Ride horse."

"I will not."

Pointing the pistol at Philip, the Indian said, "Ride or I kill him."

Caroline laughed. "Kill him, Mad Bird. The Great Spirit will rain sorrows on your people till the end of their days."

"Get on the horse. Ride," Mad Bird commanded.

Tossing her head, Caroline backed up, ran, and jumped astride Derby. The horse stood still, munching the grass beneath his feet.

Mad Bird thrust his pistol against Philip's chest and stared at Caroline. "Make horse go."

Swallowing the fear congealing in her throat, Caroline kicked Derby's sides, she slapped him with the reins, she begged, she cajoled. "Please, Derby," she whispered in the horse's ear. "Please. You must go." His ears perked up, but he stayed steadfast.

"See?" Philip said, smiling. "The horse is a Spirit Animal, too. We are all three favored by the Great Spirit."

Mad Bird's eyes rounded; he backed up, looking with horror at the gun. His hand curled; the pistol dropped to the ground.

Philip picked up the weapon and blew lightly on it. Then he mounted Derby and grabbed Caroline's arms, clasping them firmly about his waist. With scarcely a touch of his heels, he directed Derby toward the shelter. They galloped away, leaving Mad Bird, awestruck, staring after them.

By the time they reached the shelter, rain pelted down from the sky. Caroline was almost grateful when Philip reached out a hand to help her dismount.

Philip dusted off the top of the plank with the bottom edge of his vest, then removed it. They sat side by side for several minutes, before he spoke.

"I must mean something to you, Caroline, for you to risk your life for me. Thank you."

"You're—you're welcome."

Another several minutes of silence, before she said, "Well? I assume we came here for a reason."

"Yes. I have a little matter I was hoping you could help me with."

She eyed him suspiciously. "What do you want from me now? You can't keep Derby. I mean to take him with me to Philadelphia. I don't care if he never lets me ride him again. He's all I have left from here."

"No, it's not Derby. It's another animal. One I found, you see. It's very hurt, and I don't know how to help it. I fear it will die without your aid."

She surveyed the shelter's interior, but saw nothing but the same crooked barrel, the same moss-chinked walls. "What ails it? A wound?"

"A grievous one, I'm afraid. It's probably mortal." He sighed. "Well, I see you don't believe me. It's probably just as well. It's a fairly worthless sort."

"What a horrid thing to say! Everything's worth saving."

"Would you like to see it?"

He reached behind the plank, fumbling, before closing his fist over something she could not see.

"Why, yes, of course." She pried his fingers apart, her face showing her confusion. "Why, there's nothing here but—"

"My hand," Philip whispered. "Though you can't see it, I hold my heart in my hand. Take it. Please."

Tears sprang to her eyes. "Oh, Philip, this isn't fair."

"Would you turn your back on a simple animal, *chérie?*"

She fell into his arms, sobbing. "But what if it hurts me?"

"Ah, no. This animal's fangs have been removed, you see. And his claws as well. Look."

He pressed his lips against her. Her arms encircled his neck, and she felt the smooth, raw power of him, the heat and the maleness. His moist breath mingled with her own, and his arms stroked her back, drawing her closer to him, tighter. Her lips parted. His tongue parried with hers, and she drew him in, tears streaming down her face all the while. Finally, she drew back.

"What if you leave me again?"

He paused. "The truth is, Caroline, there's a war going on."

"You see, I knew it, I—"

"If you want me to, I'll stay here with you and stay out of it. Or go to Philadelphia. Whatever you want."

She ran her fingers across the planes of his face, memorizing him. "But you couldn't live with yourself, then, could you?" she whispered.

"It would be hard. But not as hard as living without you."

She fought back tears. "Then go."

"Marry me first."

"Truly?"

"Yes."

A wistful smile crossed her face. "I wish we could. But posting the banns, getting the preacher—"

"It's a time of war, sweet. The preacher would marry us without waiting for the banns."

She sighed. "Always so certain, aren't you, Philip?"

"More hopeful than certain. But I've already spoken to him."

Caroline listened to the dying rain and nestled against him, drawing his arms around her. "I wish I could be certain—about you."

Taking her fingers to his lips, he whispered, "Nothing's certain, Caroline. Take a chance with me. When have you ever been afraid to take chances? You took a chance when I asked you to come with me to Kentucky."

"But that was different. I would have been captured, maybe hanged, if I had stayed behind. Everyone thought I was a traitor."

"You took a chance when you cured me of snakebite," he persisted, nibbling at her ear. "You didn't know what manner of man I was, if I would hurt you or not."

She told the tingle at the nape of her neck to stop, but it teased her as he gently kissed her shoulders. "And you *did* hurt me," she said staunchly.

"What about now, Caroline? Am I hurting you now? You give even animals a second chance."

"You're not hurting me now, you're . . . " The blood rushed in her ears; the hotness between her legs seared toward her very center. For a moment she relaxed against him, relishing the sensations coursing through her, waiting for him to do more, in the recesses of her mind expecting him to take advantage of her moment of weakness. But Philip's hands only tightened on her arms, and he kept kissing, brushing his lips against the back of her neck, lightly caressing the tip of her ear with his warm, moist breath and the tip of his tongue.

Her eyes welled with tears at his gentleness. She struggled one minute, then two, then thought, *Let it go, Caroline. You can't spend the rest of your life wondering what might have been.* In that instant, she gave up fighting him. "Oh, I don't want you to let go of me, ever."

Still holding her tightly, Philip stepped around in front of her, a mischievous twinkle in his eyes. "We could fix that right now, you know." He kissed her hard, and her heart thumped wildly, but he pulled away, leaving her weak and giddy and yearning for more. "Would you come to me tonight, Caroline? As my wife?"

"Oh, Philip, if only it were possible. But—"

"If we head back to the Duffys' right now, I daresay Titus and I could have the preacher here by dusk."

"Do you think he would come?" she asked, half doubtful, half hopeful.

He grinned. "Aye, my love. I know it."


The ceremony took place in front of the Duffys just as the sun set. Titus, Maeve, and Genevieve served as witnesses. Then, Mr. and Mrs. Philip Masterson headed once more for the animal shelter on horseback.

When they reached the shelter, Philip held out his hand to Caroline, who dismounted lightly and rubbed her arms.

"Are you cold, my love?" Philip licked the lobe of her ear.

"Not at all. Just . . . nervous."

He grinned. "But this isn't the first time."

"No. But before it was . . . different."

"You didn't love me then?"

"Philip, I always loved you. Even before you opened your eyes."

"Then open yours, my sweet," he said with a throaty chuckle. "As I recall, the first time you endeavored to give your love to me. The second time, we came together out of physical need. Tonight, dear Caroline, let me give my love to you. Let me fill you with my love."

She smiled and took his hand. And as the moon rose in the sky, only the night animals heard their cries of pleasure.

BBC

DEADLY

MY ULTIMATE
LETHAL BEASTS

STEVE
BACKSHALL

BBC
BOOKS

# CONTENTS

# DEADLY!

**THERE ARE CERTAIN KINDS OF ANIMALS THAT FASCINATE US ALL. WE MAY NOT ALWAYS LIKE THEM, SOME OF US MAY BE TERRIFIED OF THEM, BUT PREDATORS LIKE BIG CATS, SHARKS, BIRDS OF PREY, LETHAL REPTILES, STINGING SCORPIONS AND BITING SPIDERS... WE JUST CAN'T LEARN ENOUGH ABOUT THEM. AND ONE AND ALL, THEY ARE DEFINITELY DEADLY.**

But what makes an animal Deadly? Is it how dangerous they are to us as human beings? If so, then only the humble mosquito is a serious threat when it comes to statistics about what harms us. Crocodiles, sharks, bears and big cats harm fewer people than household objects, puppy dogs or cows.

If we accept my idea, that it is much more interesting to ponder how dangerous an animal is to other animals 'in their world', then how do we define a creature as Deadly? Does it need to be a predator? Is it the biggest bite, the strongest, the fastest, the heftiest or those with superpowered senses? Is it all down to one awesome attribute like a dart frog's poison or a honey badger's attitude? Are some animals overpowered? Is deadliness essential for survival? Is an animal's Deadly success defined by how scary they are, how long they've been around on the planet or how common they are at any one time? And (huge question) what is or was the Deadliest animal of all time?

That leads me on to other questions... How much has biological competition between predators and prey shaped evolution? And when did animals first become Deadly? We're familiar with the great predator icons of today: the tiger shark, the peregrine falcon, the alligator snapping turtle, the piranha. Also with the things that make them Deadly: swimming, running, chomping and using venoms and poisons. But dinos couldn't swoop like a falcon or leap like a kangaroo... could they? How long have these lethal powers existed on our lethal planet? Were the dinosaurs venomous? Were early crocodiles the first animals with big bites? Did anything before the dinosaurs have a turn of speed like a modern cheetah or sailfish?

Turns out 'Deadly' might be the biggest subject in biology...

This book will analyse the greatest animal record breakers, and face them off against each other. I'll use my 25 years of experience filming animals in the wild to assess their superpowers and explore some of the Deadliest beasts to have ever lived.

## STEVE

# 1.

# THE EVOLUTION OF DEADLY

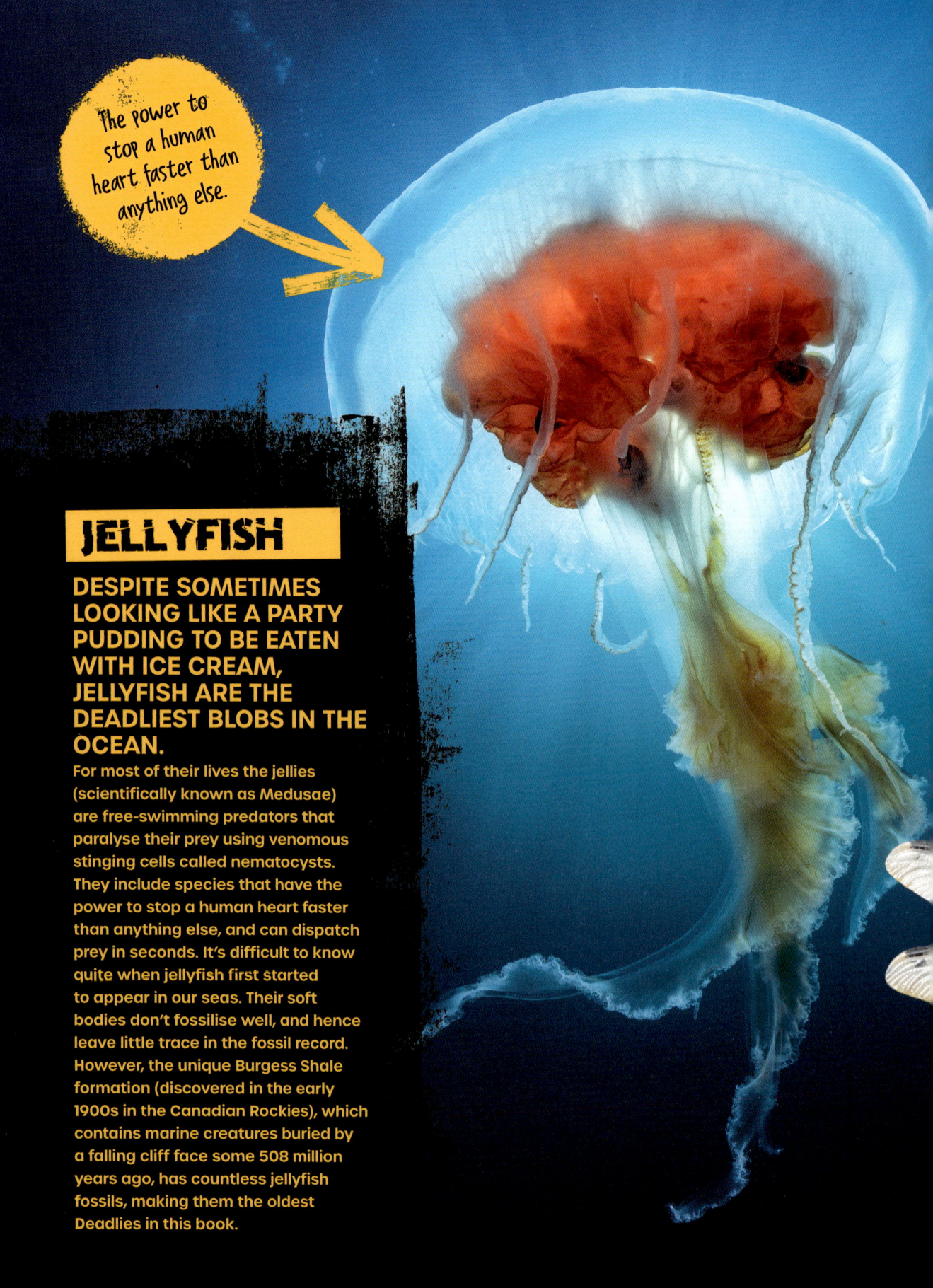

The power to stop a human heart faster than anything else.

## JELLYFISH

**DESPITE SOMETIMES LOOKING LIKE A PARTY PUDDING TO BE EATEN WITH ICE CREAM, JELLYFISH ARE THE DEADLIEST BLOBS IN THE OCEAN.**

For most of their lives the jellies (scientifically known as Medusae) are free-swimming predators that paralyse their prey using venomous stinging cells called nematocysts. They include species that have the power to stop a human heart faster than anything else, and can dispatch prey in seconds. It's difficult to know quite when jellyfish first started to appear in our seas. Their soft bodies don't fossilise well, and hence leave little trace in the fossil record. However, the unique Burgess Shale formation (discovered in the early 1900s in the Canadian Rockies), which contains marine creatures buried by a falling cliff face some 508 million years ago, has countless jellyfish fossils, making them the oldest Deadlies in this book.

# EURYPTERIDS

## TODAY'S SCORPIONS ARE RELATIVELY SMALL LAND-LIVING ARACHNIDS WITH A VENOMOUS STING IN THE TAIL.

Their ancestors could be considered the first ever active predators, savaging their targets before devouring them. The eurypterids were so-called sea scorpions found in the seas of 467 million years ago, and some were longer than the tallest men, with lethal biting mouthparts, though only a handful of the more than 250 different types had a stinger like modern scorpions. You would not have been wanting to go for a dip in the seas of the Devonian period, about 400 million years ago; there's no doubt you'd have been targeted by one of these giant armoured nightmares. Eventually the eurypterids started to move into swampy and fresh waters. They had complex stereoscopic vision and developed crab-like crunching claws, so would have been among the fiercest hunters of their day.

# DRAGONFLY

## THE GRIFFENFLIES OR GIANT DRAGON-FLIES OF THE CARBONIFEROUS PERIOD, ABOUT 300 MILLION YEARS AGO, LIVED IN FORESTS WITH A HIGHER CONCENTRATION OF OXYGEN THAN WE HAVE TODAY.

This enabled them to grow much bigger than they do now – into the biggest insects that have ever lived, with a wingspan of 75cm. Today, invertebrate size is restricted by the amount of oxygen that can be absorbed directly into their tissues (without lungs or gills). Back then, with this high concentration of oxygen in the atmosphere, this process could be more efficient, so dragonflies grew to be as long as your arm. While today's dragonflies are the most perfect and effective of all flying predators, they feast on soft-bodied flying bugs and are never of any danger to us. However, those giants of the past could have snipped off your fingers, with mouthparts like a set of gardener's shears.

Opposite: Jellyfish are found in all the world's oceans, this one in the waters of the Antarctic Peninsula.

Above: Illustration of Eurypterids in the ancient Silurian Ocean.

Left: A four-spotted chaser dragonfly at rest on a reed.

# CROCODILIANS

## THE CROCS HAVE BEEN AROUND SINCE BEFORE THE TIME OF THE DINOSAURS, AT LEAST 220 MILLION YEARS AGO.

They are descended from the ancient archosaur group, from which we also got the dinos and pterosaurs. However, they didn't always look like our modern versions. Before the dinos arrived, most crocs lived on land. There were some that climbed or even lived in the trees, and some species were herbivores (vegetarian)! A little later, there was even one marine croc species that lived in the sea and ate krill and plankton like a whale! However, in the heyday of the dinos, the Late Cretaceous, the crocodiles also bloomed, and got big and powerful. Really big, and really powerful! The biggest early crocs, like Deinosuchus and Sarcosuchus, would have been twice as long and weighed ten times as much as modern croc species. One named the 'shield croc', Aegisuchus, may have been coming close to 20 metres in length! These giant croc ancestors would have happily caught giant sauropods at the water's edge as they came down to drink, much as a Nile croc catches wildebeest today. Some scientists suggest that giant crocs like Sarcosuchus may have eaten sharks and other fish, catching fish under the water. They may also have eaten turtles and snakes.

## Croc survivors

It's long been a mystery how crocs survived the extinction event that wiped out most of the dinosaurs around 66 million years ago. We know that the asteroid that struck the planet created dust storms that blotted out the sun. Many other animals would have died soon after as they started to starve. This would have suited the crocs, which are not fussy eaters and would have delighted in all the decaying food. Then, as even the dying dinosaurs became harder and harder to find, the crocs' cold-blooded metabolism would have come into play. Modern-day crocs have very low energy demands and can go without eating for over two years in lean times. Huge ancient crocs with even bigger fat reserves and more efficient temperature regulation may have dealt with tough times even better. This would have allowed them to go for many years without eating, getting their energy from the sun's rays. When times got tougher still, they would have been able to essentially go into a period of extreme sluggishness, laying up in a burrow like a modern-day alligator for years at a time. If it was indeed the cold-blooded aspect of crocs that allowed them to survive, this gives extra weight to the idea that many dinosaurs may have actually been warm-blooded. This would explain why the conditions post-asteroid were too much for them to bear.

Giant croc ancestors would have happily caught the biggest sauropods.

Above: Illustration of a Deinosuchus, a crocodile-like reptile, attacking a Corythosaurus dinosaur in the Late Cretaceous period.

Below: Multiple Nile crocodiles seek shade in a hibernation cave during the dry season in Tanzania. They don't actually hibernate, but they conserve energy by entering aestivation, a state of dormancy.

It's long been puzzled over how crocs survived the extinction event that wiped out most of the dinosaurs.

# SHARKS

## THE SHARKS – WITH THE SKATES AND RAYS KNOWN AS THE ELASMOBRANCHS – ARE A FAMILY OF ULTIMATE SURVIVORS.

The first fossilised fragments of shark scales date from the Ordovician period 440 million years ago, although most scientists believe they are much older. This means we have had sharks on earth longer than we have had trees! In the early days, sharks didn't look much like those we have around us now; some had bizarre twisted mouths, spikes, spines and feelers. Others, like Stethacanthus, had what appear to be shower heads stuck to their backs (there is a suggestion that this might have enabled them to fit to the back of another animal, much as a remora suckerfish sticks to a shark today). They were hugely successful and some of the most abundant of all marine species. The first shark species that looked very like our modern sharks were the Paratriakis, around 190 million years ago. Then of course there is the true icon of Deadly, the meg, but our icons of today, like the great white, only turned up around 6 million years ago.

# HELICOPRION

## THE WEIRD TOOTHWHORL OF THIS MONSTER AMONG SHARKS IS FOUND QUITE OFTEN AS A FOSSIL, BUT ITS SOFT CARTILAGE SKELETON IS RARELY FOUND.

The biggest toothwhorls have been the size of a truck tyre and have been used to scale up Helicoprion, showing it grew bigger than a modern great white shark. How they used the buzzsaw jaw is something of a mystery. It's possible that it was some kind of funky mechanism for getting ammonites out of their shells. The few bits of skeleton that have been found have suggested that the Helicoprion had a similar shape to the fast fish of today, like mako sharks and sailfish. Imagine an animal with a buzzsaw jaw, the size of a bus, that swam as fast as a modern marlin. Now THAT is what I call Deadly!

Their closest relatives around today are the chimaera, also known as ghost sharks. We've dived with those at night time in the freezing Arctic waters of Alaska. They have such powerful reflecting layers in their eyes (to enhance their night vision) that your torch light bounces off them and creates a beam through the darkness!

Opposite: Illustration of two male Stethacanthus prehistoric sharks showing their odd hammer-shaped dorsal fins, thought to have been used for courtship display.

Above: Diving with a chimaera, also known as a 'ghost shark', the closest living relative of Helicoprion, usually found in deep waters.

Right: Illustration of Helicoprion showing the tooth whorl, a cluster of teeth arranged in a spiral.

# ANTS AND WASPS

**HYMENOPTERA (THAT'S THE FANCY WORD FOR ANTS, WASPS AND BEES) ARE SOME OF THE MOST SUCCESSFUL AND ARGUABLY THE MOST IMPORTANT CRITTERS IN OUR PLANET'S HISTORY.**

Today there are 180,000 different kinds, and oodles of those are Deadly. Think of the trapjaw ant, the giant spider hunter wasps, the African killer bee... Everything today, no matter how big and bold, is terrified of them! The Hymenoptera are also considered successful as they've been around so long: at least 250 million years, which is longer than even the turtles and crocs! While some slice and dice prey with giant jaws, there are others that use stingers for attack and defence. These stabbing syringes inject venom into the unlucky. Isn't it weird to think that dinosaurs like T Rex would have been bothered by wasps in just the same we are at a summer picnic!

Right: Close-up view of the mandibles of a trapjaw ant. These highly modified, spring-loaded mandibles snap shut with incredible speed and power.

Opposite, top: Bambiraptor is a birdlike theropod dinosaur from the Late Cretaceous period.

Opposite, bottom: With a secretary bird in South Africa, testing its predatory stamping ability on a rubber snake.

# RAPTORS BECOMING AVIAN RAPTORS

**SCIENTISTS HAVE KNOWN FOR A LONG TIME THAT DINOSAURS AND BIRDS ARE RELATED. HOWEVER, ARTISTS AND MOVIES STILL SHOWED THEIR DINO SUBJECTS IN THE SAME WAY: AS BIG TERRIFYING LIZARDS.**

Eventually they may have put the suggestion of quill-like feathers onto some parts (usually a crest) of dino representations, but little more was done to acknowledge this heritage. It does, however, seem that they should go far further, especially in the theropods (carnivorous dinosaurs that walked on their back legs). Some of these dinos may have been completely feathered, maybe with naked scaly feet. It's probable that they moved like birds, flocked together and made birdlike calls. It's also likely that their hunting was much more birdlike, catching things in the way a modern bird of prey might.

An example could be something like today's red-legged seriema bird from Latin America, or the secretary bird of Africa. These animals stalk the savannah before stamping on their invertebrate or reptile prey. We've even seen seriema plucking the legs off giant tarantulas.

Hollywood may have suggested that a dino raptor's claw was used to slice at the belly of their prey, but that doesn't really stand up to examination. If you use a claw like this to slice at armoured dino skin, it snaps and splinters without doing much damage. However, once you start to think of an atrociraptor or bambiraptor as being more like a flightless falcon or eagle, the use for those giant claws seems clear. Just as a modern harpy eagle will stab their talons into a sloth, or a bald eagle will use them to pierce a salmon, the claw is for stabbing, or for restraining and dominating wriggling prey.

ORCA

VS

SEA LIONS

Orca have 48-52 identical cone-shaped teeth.

## WHAT'S THE BIGGEST RISK YOU'VE EVER TAKEN TO GET DINNER?

I've eaten in a few places around the world that weren't that sanitary... but I can honestly say I've never risked a slow, painful death just to get a snack. In Patagonia, one population of orcas have developed a hunting strategy that does just that. The 'attack channel' is a narrow stretch of beach no wider than a tennis court. You can sit on the beach waiting for days on end and nothing will happen – other than sea lions splashing in the surf. But then, at the exact right time of the incoming tide, just before high tide, the orcas' dorsal fins appear. The sea lions seem totally unfazed by the giant predators lurking just beyond the break. On an unseen cue the orca come hammering in at top speed towards the shore, grasping the sea lions if they can. Often they target the young pups, trying to overwhelm them and grab a flipper or tail. In a startling display of bravery, the mother will often throw herself in front of the mighty orca, preventing them from getting to her offspring. Now is the most dangerous moment for the huge predator, beached on the sands where a stranding would mean certain death. The orcas banana themselves back into the spray, with or without their prey. I've watched it happen with my own eyes, and still kind of don't believe it's real!

## NOTHING GETS MORE AIRTIME OR INVOLVES MORE EXAGGERATION THAN THE 'BIGGEST EVER' ANIMALS IN A SET CATEGORY.

There are endless myths, legends and stories of leviathan anacondas 30 metres long, giant squid that ate a boat, crocodiles as big as double decker buses. None of these are ever properly, scientifically evaluated. This doesn't mean they definitely are not true – or possible. However, unless stated otherwise, all the records given here are for animals that were reliably measured under scientific conditions. This tends to mean that the animal was either dead or in captivity at the time.

## RECORD BREAKER?

## IT IS WORTH NOTING THAT WHILE THE INDIVIDUALS HERE MAY BE THE BIGGEST ANIMALS WE HAVE MEASURED, THEY ARE VERY UNLIKELY TO BE THE BIGGEST THAT HAS EVER BEEN.

Probably the best example of this would be the T Rex. There have only been around thirty decent skeletons of T Rex ever found. The most complete is known as 'Sue', discovered in South Dakota in 1990. At 12.35m long, Sue is a giant, and the largest T Rex we know of... yet some scientists believe more than 1.7 billion could have roamed the earth. The chances of Sue being the biggest of them all are approximately... well, 30 to 1.7 billion, and my maths isn't great but you get the picture! This obviously counts for the monsters of today as well. The biggest blue whale ever measured was a female caught in South Georgia, at 34m long. The heaviest was 220 tonnes. But there is no doubt that these are not the biggest that have ever been. This is also why I am always very careful to talk about the blue whale as being 'the biggest animal EVER KNOWN to have lived'. I want to make sure I allow for the possibility that we could one day discover something even bigger...

Opposite: Fossil skeleton of Tyrannosaurus rex, perhaps the most famous of all dinosaur predators.

Below: Standing cautiously in the 'safe zone' over Henry, a humongous Nile crocodile.

# CROCS

## THE BIGGEST SALTWATER CROCODILE RELIABLY MEASURED BY SCIENTISTS WAS LOLONG FROM THE PHILIPPINES, A MONUMENTAL MALE 6.1M IN LENGTH AND OVER A TONNE IN WEIGHT, MEASURED IN 2014.

He was caught alive after he had killed many local villagers, and amazingly the people built him his own enclosure and pool and took care of him until his death. The most notorious individual crocodile is Gustavus, a Nile crocodile living on Lake Tanganyika, who is rumoured to have killed at least 60 people. Many images exist of Gustavus, and he appears to be near to 6m, but all measurements were taken of imprints in the mud, or educated guesses based on comparisons to known objects nearby. Most sources suggest Gustavus is no longer with us, although it is entirely possible that he has just moved to another location. In captivity, Cassius was a legendary Australian saltwater croc, who was near a tonne in weight and 5.5m in length. I'm lucky enough to have stood right over the oldest crocodile ever known. Henry is a mighty Nile croc, captured in 1903, already a mature animal at a decent size and a confirmed man-eater. That would make him at least 124 years of age when I met him up close! Today he is at least 5.4m in length and is estimated to weigh three quarters of a tonne. Reminding me to avoid his 'danger zone', where the giant tail could sweep you towards his mouth, keepers encouraged me to step above him into a 'safe zone' where he couldn't reach. To see his extraordinary muscles and his gigantic feet next to my own tiny hands was the most starstruck I have been in my career.

124 years of age, 5.4m long and weighs three quarters of a tonne!

Left: Scuba divers taking photos of green anaconda in Formoso River, Bonito, Brazil.

Below: Zoo employees struggle to hold Barney, a 24ft reticulated python at Cotswold Wildlife Park.

Opposite: Holding a large reticulated python in Borneo.

# SNAKE

**IN 1910 AMERICAN PRESIDENT THEODORE ROOSEVELT, IN CONNECTION WITH THE BRONX ZOO IN NEW YORK, OFFERED A REWARD FOR ANYONE WHO COULD FIND A SNAKE OVER 30FT OR 9M IN LENGTH.**

In time that reward climbed to $50,000, an unimaginable fortune at the time. Explorers and fame-seekers launched countless expeditions to try and find a giant worthy of that reward, mostly searching for giant anacondas in South America... but without success. That reward stood for over a century until it was finally withdrawn. No one had ever presented a snake even close to that length, captive or wild, in all that time. The reticulated python is the world's longest snake, with the longest measured individual being one in captivity in the United States, at 7.67m or 25ft 2in. The biggest I was ever lucky enough to meet was Barney, who lived at the Cotswold Wildlife Park in the UK. He was over 24ft long, so in excess of 7m. On an episode of *Live and Deadly*, I stood shoulder to shoulder with eight zoo employees, each of us with a section of Barney in our hands. Every one of us was straining with his weight! Though probably not getting quite as long, the anaconda is undeniably the heaviest snake in the world. The heftiest females might be double the weight of an equivalent-length reticulated python. In 2024 Ana Julia was the name given to an anaconda filmed by biologist Dr Freek Vonk, said to be 26ft in length and weighing a quarter of a tonne, although Freek acknowledged he didn't get a chance to accurately measure her.

## CAT

## THE BIGGEST AND HEAVIEST CAT IN THE WILD IS THE SIBERIAN TIGER.

After a big meal, large males could weigh 300kg; that's three and a half times my bodyweight. In captivity cats may get heavier; especially liger, which are an artificial cross between lions and tigers. I met a liger in captivity that was at the time the biggest known cat in the world, at 450kg. He was, however, very overweight, slow and sluggish, and used to being overfed by his owner (Doc Antle, who featured in notorious Netflix documentary *Tiger King*).

Above: Remote camera view of a wild Siberian tiger walking in a forest in the Russian Far East.

Below: A very close-up encounter with a European grey wolf in Norway

Opposite: A male southern elephant seal rears up in a threatening posture, attempting to become the beachmaster in South Georgia.

## DOG

## THE BIGGEST CANID OR NATURAL MEMBER OF THE DOG FAMILY IS THE GREY WOLF.

The heaviest male ever recorded was 103kg, so quite a bit heavier than me. The dire wolf of the last Ice Age would have been bigger still.

# SEAL

**THE BIGGEST SEAL SPECIES IS THE SOUTHERN ELEPHANT SEAL, WITH MALES LOOKING (ON LAND) LIKE GIANT MAGGOTS WEIGHING UP TO 6 TONNES.**

Intriguingly, the female is tiny by comparison, perhaps only 200kg.

The number one macho male becomes the 'beachmaster'.

## APE

### THE BIGGEST APE IS THE MALE MOUNTAIN GORILLA.

When he matures, he gains a grey back that sets him apart as the senior male in the group, and is thereafter known as the silverback.

## CRAB

**THE TERRESTRIAL – SOMETIMES CLIMBING INTO PALM TREES TO GET THEIR FOOD – COCONUT OR ROBBER CRAB IS THE HEAVIEST AND CAN BE OVER 4KG.** The Japanese spider crab can have a leg span of 4m!

Opposite: A silverback mountain gorilla beating his chest, signalling dominance, in Rwanda.

Above: A coconut crab with large claws raised in defensive posture, Mozambique.

Left: A Southern sea otter standing upright...

Below: ... and kayaking next to one in Alaska.

## MUSTELID

**THE WEASEL FAMILY ARE WELL REPRESENTED ON DEADLY, AS ANIMALS THAT PUNCH WELL ABOVE THEIR WEIGHT.** The heaviest are the sea otters of the North Pacific, which can weigh up to 45kg, and the biggest are the giant river otters of Latin America, which can be a metre and a half in length. Though the latter's main diet is fish such as piranhas, we've filmed them hunting caiman and anaconda! These are all outdone in strength by the wolverine or glutton, which is no bigger than the UK's native badger, but has been filmed taking down reindeer and even moose!

Above: A graceful but huge blue whale in the Indian Ocean off Sri Lanka.

Below, left: The Goliath birdeater tarantula is the largest spider in the world, both in terms of mass and body length.

Below, right: Holding a Goliath birdeater tarantula carefully, although its venom is not lethal to humans.

Opposite: Kodiak bear sitting by a riverbank, Alaska.

*The biggest animal ever known to have lived!*

## SPIDER

### THE GOLIATH BIRDEATER IS VERY WELL NAMED, A TRUE GIANT AMONG ARACHNIDS.

Their legs could stretch out over a dinner plate and they can weigh 155g. We've filmed them hunting lizards, and Gordon Buchanan once filmed one killing and eating a fer de lance snake!

## CETACEAN

**THE BLUE WHALE IS THE BIGGEST ANIMAL EVER KNOWN TO HAVE LIVED.**

The longest recorded was 33.58m, in Grytviken in South Georgia. It was an emotional moment to be there where she was hunted and killed, an animal I had been talking about for many years as the largest ever known on our planet.

## BEAR

**ADULT MALE POLAR BEARS CAN WEIGH 600KG AND STAND DOUBLE MY HEIGHT – THOUGH THEIR WEIGHT FLUCTUATES DRAMATICALLY DEPENDING ON HOW SUCCESSFUL THEY'VE BEEN AT HUNTING RECENTLY.**

One male polar bear has been reported at 1,002kg. As for brown bears, one individual from Kodiak Island (in Alaska) weighed in at 907kg. Some of the brown bears we saw in Kamchatka, Russia, were also gigantic. Reports of those bears exceeding a tonne are common, but have never been verified.

**LION**

**VS**

**HYENA**

Outnumbered, even lions back down to the hyena.

**THE CONVENTIONAL IDEA IS THAT LIONS MAKE KILLS, AND HYENAS CLEAN UP WHAT'S LEFT WHEN THEY'VE FINISHED.** And this does happen. However, in many places in Africa, the leaner meaner spotted hyena is actually the boss. Not only are they likely to drive lions from their meal before they've finished, but big clans of hyenas are probably the top predator in the house, killing more prey than the lions and bossing them in every scenario. Hyenas will kill lion cubs, steal their breakfast, drive them out of their territory, not even give them peace to have a little nap in the shade. Their secret is teamwork and strength in numbers. The biggest clans of spotties could have 80 animals, whereas the biggest lion 'mega-pride' ever known had five males and around twenty lions in total. Battles between lions and hyenas can be short-lived, especially if the lions realise they're outnumbered and just do a runner. However, if the animals are more evenly matched, it can explode into a violent confrontation of dust clouds, flying claws and snarling teeth. Brutal battles like this almost always result in serious injuries or worse.

# 3.

# COLD-BLOODED KILLERS

# THE TERM 'COLD BLOODED' IS USED TO REFER TO REPTILES, AMPHIBIANS AND FISH THAT DON'T MAINTAIN A STABLE BODY TEMPERATURE BY BURNING CALORIES FROM FOOD.

Instead they absorb heat from the environment around them, sometimes by basking in the sun. The proper word for this is 'ectothermy'. I've measured the body temperature of crocodiles and snakes that have been basking the sun, and their blood has been up around 30°C, which is... well... not cold! However, that same animal could rouse after a long cold night and be just a few degrees above zero.

Being an ectotherm has big benefits for an animal. As they are not constantly burning off calories like us warm-blooded mammals, they don't have to eat all the time. Alligators have been known to go for more than two years without eating. I get peckish if I skip breakfast. However, the flipside is that ectotherms can be super sluggish if they're cold, and can run out of energy really quickly. When we're catching crocodiles for science, we know that they'll battle like crazy for a few minutes, then it seems like they give up. In reality they just have no fuel left in the tank!

# CROCS

## CROCS HAVE A LIFE THAT IS DOMINATED BY HEAT.

When you see a croc out on the riverbank with its huge mouth gaped open, it's not just sunbathing. Without the sun's rays, it simply won't have the get up and go, to get up and go! However, fascinating research has shown that the angle of their yawn when they're basking has another purpose. If a 3m croc is basking, and a 4m croc slides up onto the bank, the smaller one slightly closes their mouth, almost as if it's showing respect to the hencher herp hero!

Crocs cool down in the water, and have to emerge to bask.

# THEROPODS AND COLD-/WARM-BLOODEDNESS

## UNTIL RECENTLY DINOSAURS WERE ALWAYS THOUGHT OF AS BEING BIG, SLUGGISH COLD-BLOODED SCALY REPTILES.

However, some kinds of dinosaurs may have been able to generate or maintain their own heat, more like their descendants the birds do. Some theropods and ornithischians seem to have moved to colder climates in the Jurassic to follow food resources. Modern reptiles are totally dependent on their need for external heat, so wouldn't do this. However, giant sauropods stayed in places where the temperatures were warmer, even when there was less food around. This seems to suggest that heat was more important to them than food, so they in all likelihood were cold blooded. An extra element to this is that bigger animals lose less heat to the outside environment than smaller animals do, so huge sauropods may also not have needed to generate their own body heat.

Opposite, bottom: American crocodile underwater, Mexico.

Opposite, top: Nile crocodile with jaws fully extended, possibly to help it thermoregulate, South Africa.

Right: Illustration of what Deinonychus may have looked like. It was a study of this species in the 1960s that ignited the debate on whether dinosaurs were warm- or cold-blooded.

# TITANOBOA

**TITANOBOA, OR THE TITANIC BOA, IS AN EARLY AND SIMPLY HUGE MEMBER OF THE BOA FAMILY, WHICH INCLUDES SNAKES LIKE THE MODERN ANACONDA.**

This species was initially only known from chunks of its spine, until hero fossil finders located pieces of its skull and teeth. By looking at modern giant snakes, palaeontologists constructed models that show Titanoboa could have grown to nearly 15m in length – as long as two double decker buses. The biggest weight estimate is 1.8 tonnes, which is as heavy as a decent-sized car or twenty of me! Initially scientists reckoned it would have been much like a green anaconda, living in the water and feeding on things like crocodiles. Others have suggested, from looking at its teeth, that it may have been a piscivore (fish-feeding specialist). Titanoboa was found in South America 60–58 million years ago. Knowing about the existence of this gigantic snake, and what it would have needed in terms of heat in its environment, has been vital for science bigwigs, who used it as their main clue to figure out what the climate would have been like back then!

How would we have fared against a giant like this? Well, working with wild boas today, I wouldn't try and catch a wild snake of more than 4m in length on my own, as it would be able to overpower me. And a reticulated python or anaconda over 6m could swallow me whole. So a snake that's more than double that length and ten times the weight? They'd be able to catch, kill and eat a whole bison!

Opposite: Illustration of Titanoboa, one of the largest snake species that ever lived.

Above: Green anaconda on a branch.

Left: Swimming with a much larger specimen in Brazil.

## Swimming with anacondas

The murky waters of the Cerrado savannah in Brazil were a spooky film set for my dive with a demon.

Swimming through twisted tree roots beneath the surface, I caught my first glimpse of our target. She was huge – as long as a minibus and as thick as my thigh. As I watched, she came out of the undergrowth and for a few minutes was out in the open. She didn't swim, but moved along the bottom as she would move on land. As she went, she was tasting her way with her bifurcated tongue. The monstrous, marvellous snake nosed up to my camera, and I could see her eyes were white. She was 'in blue' – that is, about to shed her skin – and the transparent scale or brille that covers her eye was scuffed and pale. She probably couldn't see much of anything, but could sense me with that astounding tongue. As I lay on the bottom, not daring to breathe, she bounced her snout off my camera lens, before twisting back and moving off into the gloom. It remains one of the most 'Halloween' encounters I've ever had.

# GIANT SALAMANDER

**ALL AMPHIBIANS ARE COLD BLOODED, AND THEY RANGE FROM THE TINY FROGS OF LATIN AMERICA THAT ARE THE SIZE OF YOUR LITTLE FINGERNAIL ALL THE WAY UP TO THE BIGGEST AMPHIBIANS AROUND TODAY, WHICH ARE THE TWO KINDS OF GIANT SALAMANDER.**

One of these is found in the mountain streams of Japan; the other is on the brink of extinction but is found in China. They're absolutely enormous – a metre and a half in length, bulky and heavy too. They catch other animals with a snap of their broad jaws and by creating suction power that drags the prey into their gullet. Like all amphibians, they have damp skin that can exchange oxygen, kind of like breathing through it. Folds and wrinkles increase the surface area of the skin for just this purpose. It also helps that the waters in their mountain stream home hold unusual amounts of dissolved oxygen. While catching giant salamanders in Japan, I noticed that they had a faint rhubarb-like smell! Quite often certain kinds of alkaloid poisons have that same odour. I've been desperate to do the science and work out if the giant salamander is indeed poisonous, but haven't quite managed to get permission yet!

Opposite: Chinese giant salamander, the biggest amphibian alive today.

Below: A juvenile billfish, most likely a sailfish, famous for being one of the fastest fish in the ocean.

## FISH

### FISH HAVE A BROAD RANGE OF INTERNAL TEMPERATURES, MOSTLY DEFINED BY THE SEAS THEY LIVE IN.

Those living in the deep or freezing polar seas will probably have blood that is not much above 0°C. Those living on tropical reefs could be 30°C plus! However, there are some species that manage their internal temperature using neat tricks. One of these is what's known as a *rete mirabile* or miraculous web, a latticework of blood vessels that intertwine alongside each other. This enables blood that has been warmed through fierce activity to run alongside cooled blood, evening out the temperature between the two. One of the most profound examples of this would be the great white shark, which can raise its body temperature 10 to 15°C above that of the surrounding waters. Fast-moving billfish like marlin can specifically warm blood flow to the brain and eyes, allowing them to function in a different world of vision and processing than their prey.

# CROCODILE
# VS
# ANACONDA

A cold-blooded battle of snap vs squeeze.

**THIS BATTLE PLAYS OUT OFTEN IN THE GREAT WETLANDS OF SOUTH AMERICA.** It's a frantic wrestle between two amphibious ambush attackers and it could go either way. The anaconda has constriction on its side, the croc its formidable bite force. Ultimately the winner will probably be the animal that's larger – the biggest anacondas can easily devour smaller caimans whole, while the biggest black caiman or Orinoco croc would snap any anaconda clean in two. One of the biggest challenges for the snake, should it manage to constrict the caiman, is how to swallow it whole; snakes do not have the ability to take bites out of their prey, and need to get it down in one. There are cases of huge snakes literally bursting as they attempt to swallow a tough scaly croc. A dramatic case of someone's eyes being much bigger than their stomach...

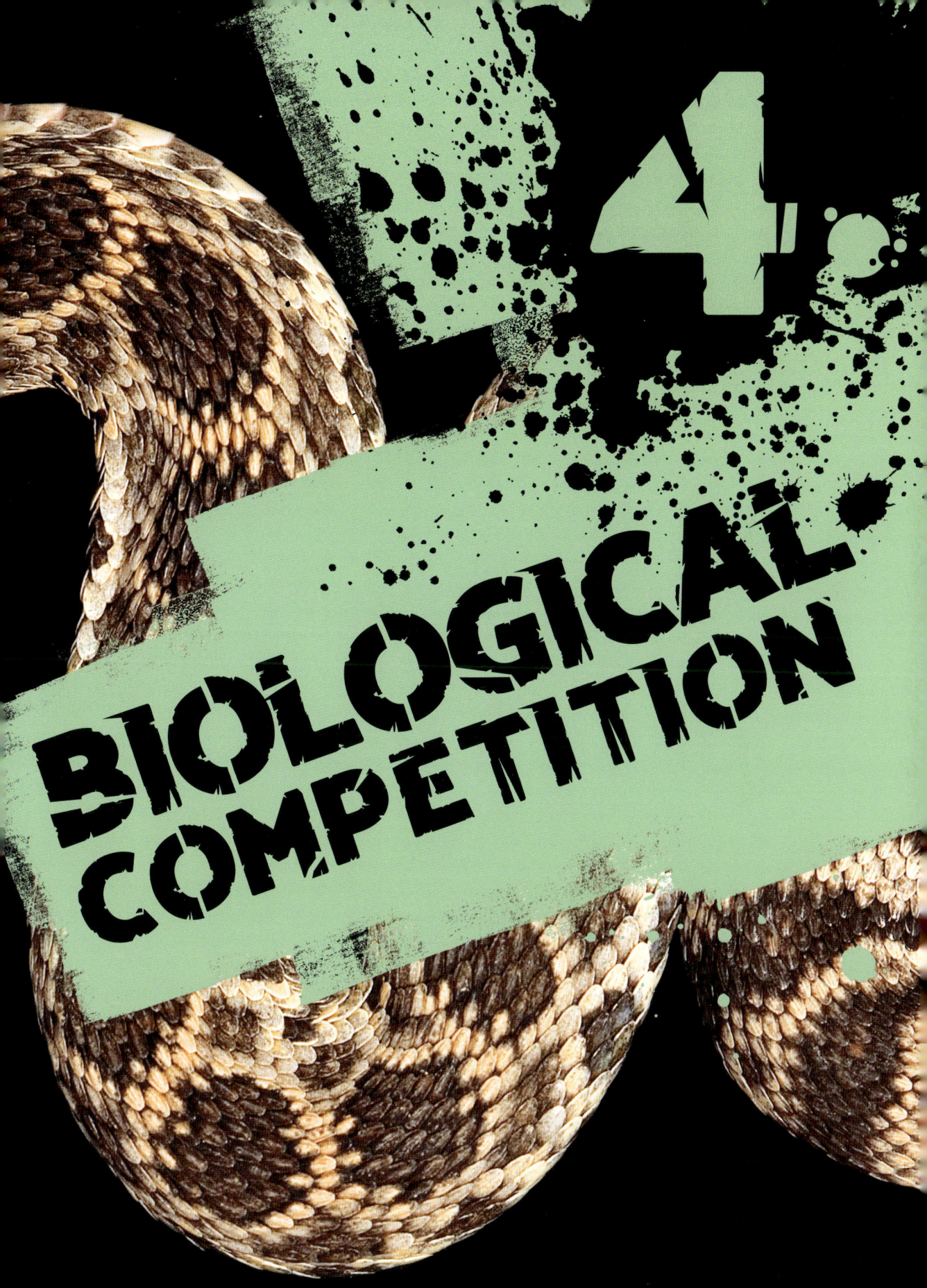

# BIOLOGICAL COMPETITION

**4.**

## THE IDEA OF BIOLOGICAL COMPETITION IS A REALLY IMPORTANT ONE IN EVOLUTION.

Imagine two animals that are both kind of bobbing along, minding their own business munching grass. One of them decides grass is boring and that the other animal looks more yummy. It decides to try and catch its pal and eat it. That species is now going to need some way of protecting itself... It might grow a hard shell, a lashing tail or a thrusting pointy horn. The animal that by now has become a predator is going to have to up their game. They develop wicked teeth, or super sprinting skills, maybe their spit turns into venom, or they develop eagle-eyed vision. Now the prey animal (I hate that they get called that. Can you imagine the indignity? 'Me? Yeah, I'm just food.') has got left behind and needs to get massive, or develop X-ray vision and laser-guided detachable fangs... well, maybe not that, but you get the idea.

Of course, the animals don't decide on these changes themselves and they don't happen overnight. They come about through natural selection and can take millions of years.

But this struggle and upscaling of abilities comes at a cost for both animals. A cheetah today may be the fastest land animal, but its lightweight skeleton is easily broken, and they are horrifically susceptible to overheating. They can't just keep getting faster and faster because eventually you'd have a fragile feline that could only sprint for a few seconds and then would collapse and die from heat shock. Something has to give. This is the idea of trade-offs, and is why we don't have a planet filled with stomping mega-carnivores the size of skyscrapers breathing fire and biting through buses for breakfast.

# FASTEST

## 10.

## CHEETAH

In terms of both acceleration and flat-out speed, the cheetah has no equal. They can go from 0 to 40 miles per hour in three big strides, and can top out at at least 60 miles per hour, possibly even 70. This speed is driven by their remarkable physiology: rangy limbs, lightweight skeleton, a super flexible spine that flexes like an archer's bow, a small streamlined head and a bobbing tail that functions as a counterweight to balance their movement. The feet are key: most cats have retractile claws that can be drawn back into protective pads when not in full use; cheetahs, however, have claws that are always extended like a runner's spikes. While the claws of a leopard may be sharp enough to tear through their victim's flesh, a cheetah's claws are relatively blunt, with the exception of the dewclaw, which sits high up on their leg. This is wickedly curved and sharp, and is used to slash at prey on the run.

## Racing a cheetah

I've had the great joy of racing a cheetah three times… I'm guessing not many people can say that! Each time it has been with an animal that was orphaned as a youngster and brought up to accept humans and not shred us. The most memorable was with a gorgeous female cheetah called Savannah about twenty years ago. It took her a good while to warm up and decide she wanted to run with me (not surprising really, as cheetahs generally lie in the shade doing nothing through the heat of the day). When Savannah did decide to run, it was the most explosive thing I've ever seen. She was at top speed in a stride or three and left me choking on her dust!

On several occasions I've been lucky enough to walk in a cheetah's footsteps for a few days and to see what their life is like in the wild. I have to admit to having been utterly shocked by how perilous their life actually is. Cheetahs rely on their vision to hunt and (other than very occasionally when there is a full moon) need to hunt in daylight. However, they are very liable to overheating. After a run of a

few hundred metres, the cheetah has to lie in the shade and pant for a long time to cool down. Should they hunt in the heat of the day, this cooling down period might last for hours. This means that the vast majority of hunts I witnessed were before the sun came up, or just after it went down. They had no more than an hour a day in which they could even attempt to hunt. Male cheetahs can catch things up to the size of an adult wildebeest, but females are really only good for attempting smaller antelope and gazelles (though I've seen them going after scrub hares, African wild cats, birds and babies of bigger beasts). If one of those doesn't wander near enough for them to approach in that hour of peak performance, then they're kind of stuffed. I followed one female on motorbikes with local conservationists for three days, and she made nine half-hearted attempts to hunt, failing at every one. Add to this the fact that cheetahs are killed by lions, leopards and spotted hyena and poached by humans, and theirs is a tough life indeed.

## 9.

### TRAPJAW ANT

These ants from the tropics have remarkable mandibles that open 180° (so they form a single line) and are locked in place. At their centre are sensory hairs. If triggered, they snap the jaw shut in 0.13 of a millisecond, which is several thousand times faster than the blink of a human eye. The force exerted is 300 times the body weight of the insect - like me snapping shut my jaws with 3 tonnes of force. A so-called 'Dracula ant' from Borneo was recorded snapping its jaws shut at 200mph, the fastest recorded animal movement.

## 8.

### SAILFISH

The fastest fish in the seas, the sailfish is the epitome of hydrodynamism - that is, streamlining underwater. The body is generally torpedo shaped, tapering from the most muscular section midbody to the thinnest section just before the tail. The crescent tail is the optimum shape for creating forward movement with the minimum amount of drag underwater. If you look at the tail of a mako shark, marlin, tuna... any fast fish, they'll all have this same shape. The one bit of the sailfish that doesn't seem to fit is the long sword-like bill at the end of the head. While in air, an arrow, javelin or spear is perfect for travelling far and fast, underwater this shape is not so effective. Think about the things we humans have created underwater for speed: torpedos and submarines have rounded ends, as this is the best hydrodynamic form. The sailfish's bill is actually used to swipe at small fish and separate them out from baitballs. Scientists have shown that sailfish that lose their bills can swim just as fast.

## Deadly sailfish encounter

To find the hyper-charged speedster of the seas, we first had to find the baitballs they feed on. These are located by looking out for birds like frigate birds and gulls, which circle over the baitfish – you can see them all the way out to the horizon. When you find a baitball, you drop in alongside it, and the sailfish come thundering in from the blue, using their rapier-like bill to separate small fish out from the baitball. After a while the small fish are desperately seeking shelter anywhere they can find it, and the only place to hide was behind us and our cameras. It was all we could do not to get turned into a swimming kebab, as the sailfish sought to skewer their dinner. It was one of the most exhausting and dramatic experiences I've ever had underwater.

## 7. DEATH ADDER STRIKE

The death adder is not actually an 'adder' (a kind of viper) at all but a member of the Elapidae (the cobra family). They're found throughout Australia and New Guinea, and are remarkably camouflaged: it's almost impossible to see them until you are literally right on top of them. The death adder is usually said to have the fastest strike of any snake, striking in less than a tenth of a second. With a highly toxic venom, the death adder literally kills in the blink of an eye! We've filmed a number of lightning fast snakes striking using the very finest slow motion technology, and it seems Africa's puff adder certainly comes close in their acceleration towards a target. Another interesting addition to the mix might be the stiletto snake, also of Africa. Their strike is completely different from that of these two straight strikers. The stiletto has bizarre fangs that it can slip out of the side of its mouth, and then it kind of reverses its head to snag its prey, injecting venom. The strike is unlike anything I've seen in any other snake species, with the whole serpent seeming to 'unwind' and twirl about, faster than the human eye can see. The moment of impact is pretty much invisible. As a side effect, the stiletto is one of the most dangerous of all snakes to handle, and even the most hardened snake experts steer clear of catching them!

### 6. PEREGRINE FALCON

The fastest creature ever known to have lived is the peregrine. In flat-out flight they can be outdone by many flying birds, swifts probably being the fastest bird in flight. However, their secret skill is to fly up high above their quarry, before tucking their wings into their sides and diving in what's known as a stoop. In stoop the peregrine gets close to 200mph. They have cones within the nostrils to baffle the movement of wind and stop the pressure on their brain from causing them to pass out. The body takes on a streamlined profile and they'll hurtle into prey such as pigeons on the wing, causing an explosion of feathers.

## Racing a peregrine

I've raced a peregrine in a fancy sports car, using high speed drones; we've even tested them against a fighter jet. However, the best race head to head against this speed demon was on a downhill mountain bike in the rugged landscapes of North Wales. My challenge was to hammer down the slopes as fast as possible, with a 200m headstart on our peregrine superhero. I had a lure attached to my helmet that the perry was trained to target. I simply couldn't go any faster, but the falcon would zip down in a second or two, make a practice pass and then BAM! Slam into my helmet. Despite the bird only weighing half as much as a bag of sugar, it nearly knocked me off my bike every time. The force generated was phenomenal. However, as with all speedsters, the peregrine is a finely balanced machine. If their weight is even slightly too high – over by even a few grams – they cannot fly and will not hunt. If their weight is too low, they are on a knife edge and HAVE to succeed in their next few attempts or they will simply not have the energy to try again. In the wild, this means they'd starve to death.

# RATTLESNAKE

The number one contender for the fastest moving muscles of any vertebrate is the rattle of the rattlesnakes – pit vipers found in the Americas. As babies, they develop buttons of keratin on the end of their tails, and when they shed their skin, more of these cusps are left behind, until the classic rattle is formed. Muscles in the end of the tail vibrate the rattle in an undulating motion at up to 90Hz, such intense speeds that it creates anything from a nonstop buzz to a sound like maracas being shaken. The more annoyed the rattler is, the more intense the rattle will be. Every animal that shares its territory with rattlesnakes knows that this sound means danger, and will leave the snake well alone.

### FROGFISH

One of the very fastest strikers underwater is an odd-looking fish indeed. Most of the time they just stand on the bottom, or wander along on their leg-like pectoral fins. They look like the slowest fish you could ever see. Right up until something swims into their field of view, and then – whammo! They drop their lower jaw at stupendous speed, creating a void that sucks the fish towards them, before powering forward and swallowing the hapless victim. It's all over in a fraction of a second.

### SWIFT

While much is made of the peregrine's record-breaking abilities on the wing, the truth is that the peregrine is practising controlled falling when it stoops. In flat-out flight, the swift is the victor, coming close to the peregrine's 200mph top speed. If you are lucky enough to be in a field as swifts soar low over the vegetation catching bugs on the wing, the sound of the wind whistling over their boomerang-like wings is incredible – like a giant's sword being sliced through the air.

## 2.

### SOLIFUGE

In order to figure out which bug is the fastest runner, scientists make tiny treadmills and put the creepy crawlies on them. Which sounds like a crazy amount of fun, and nearly impossible to make work! However, the victor was the solifuge or camel spider, the fastest runner of all invertebrates.

## 1.

### CHAMELEON TONGUE

Chameleons are silent stalkers, standing still or wandering slowly through the treetops, almost invisible to all but the most trained eyes. However, when they select a target, the eyes swivel to focus on it and the tongue explodes out in a millisecond to envelop their prey.

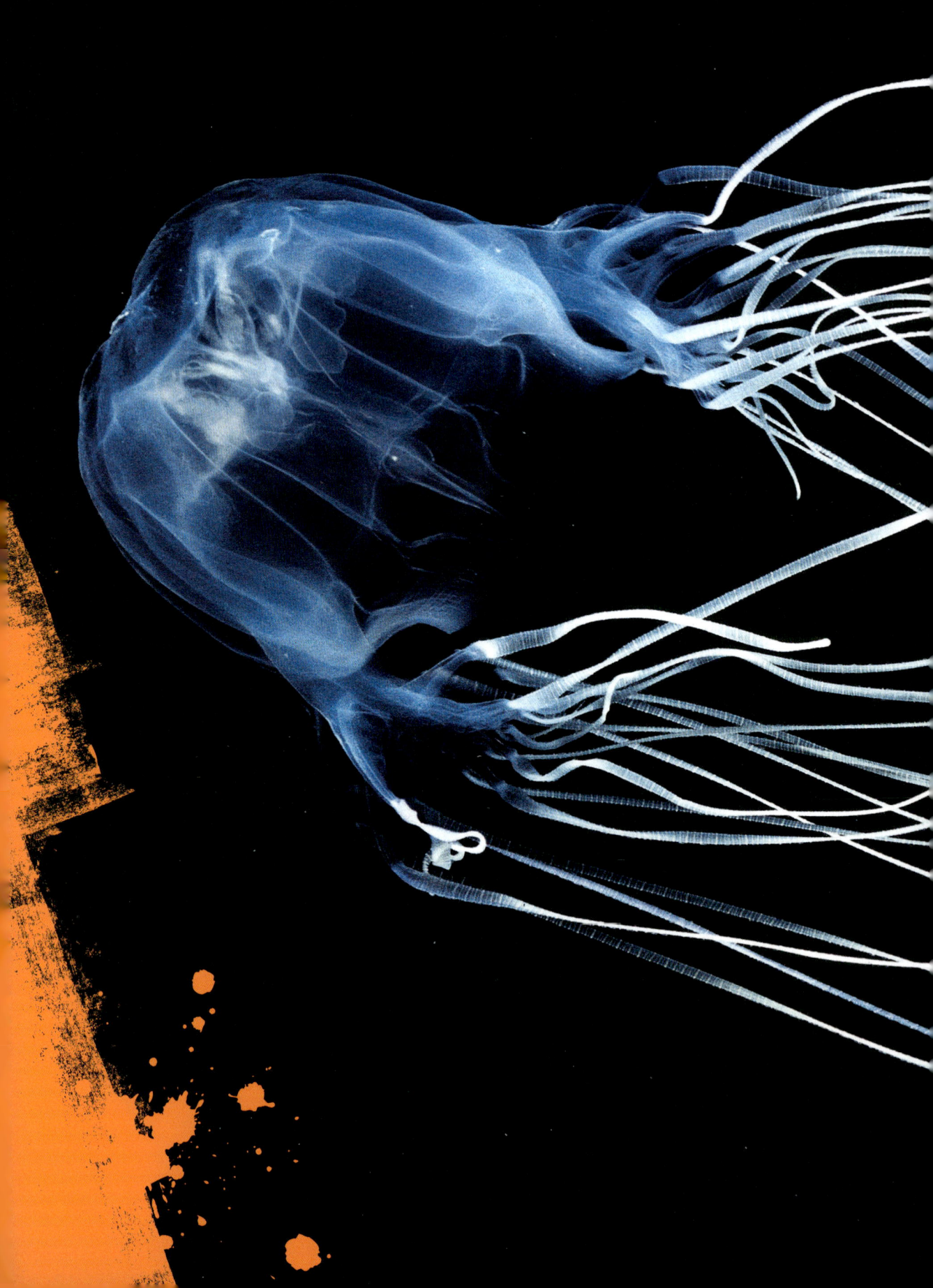

# POISON OR VENOM?

**NATURAL TOXINS HAVE BEEN AROUND FOR A VERY LONG TIME, WITH SCIENTISTS SUGGESTING SOME DINOSAURS MAY HAVE BEEN VENOMOUS.**

Poisons have to be eaten to have their lethal effect, while venoms have to be injected into the bloodstream using fangs, spurs, spines or claws. If an animal bites you and you die, it's venom, and if you bite an animal and you die, it's poison!

The blue ring is remarkably tricky to find for an animal that can be so colourful.

Above: Southern blue-ringed octopus at night, one of four highly venomous species of blue-ringed octopuses.

# BLUE-RINGED OCTOPUS

**DESPITE BEING THE SIZE OF A GOLF BALL, THE BLUE RING IS THE MOST VENOMOUS OCTOPUS ON EARTH, WITH ITS SPIT CONTAINING TETRODOTOXIN, THE MOST VIRULENT NATURAL TOXIN ON EARTH.**

In hunting, the octopus nibbles this solution into crabs and sea snails, killing them super quickly. Aquarium keepers have also learned, though, that if they keep blue rings in a tank with anything else, the poison will just leak into the water and kill everything! The bite is almost painless, and the very, very few human victims have not even felt the bite. The blue ring is remarkably tricky to find for an animal that can be so colourful. Those bright aposematic (warning) colours that give them their name are not always evident. For the majority of the time they are a drab brownish colour and match their environment. But if they feel threatened, they flash those neon blue rings all over their body and really stand out.

As a side note, tetrodotoxin is found as a poison in the skin and organs of puffer fish, making them the most poisonous fish in the world. Bizarrely, their flesh is a delicacy in Japanese restaurants, where it is sold as 'fugu'. Fugu chefs have to have licenses and extensive experience to prepare the dish. If it's done right, the customer should sense a light tingling on their lips, known as the 'brush with death'. If done wrong... well, several people in Japan die from fugu poisoning every year, proving you really shouldn't play with your food.

# GEOGRAPHY CONE SNAIL

## THE MOST VENOMOUS SNAIL ON THE PLANET IS A MARINE MOLLUSC THAT LIVES INSIDE AN ICONIC AND INSTANTLY RECOGNISABLE SHELL.

This protects the lethal beast within, which is armed with a harpoon that it can fire out of the narrow end of the shell into a fish – or a misplaced finger, should you pick one up. That harpoon is linked to a venom sac, and the toxic goo is injected down the hollow inside of the harpoon (more correctly known as a radula) and into its prey. This radula is single-use only, and replaced after each hunt. The venom is so potent that the fish will be dead in milliseconds. However, then the fun part happens! The cone snail envelops the fish in its tubular mouth outside of the shell, and digests the fish over several days.

# IRUKANDJI JELLYFISH

## THIS AUSTRALIAN SPECIES IS VERY SMALL, WITH A BELL NO BIGGER THAN THE END OF MY THUMB.

However it packs a punch - its venom can kill an adult human without treatment. The sting causes irukandji syndrome, a state where the victim is overwhelmed by a 'sense of impending doom', feeling as if the world is about to end, combined with extraordinary pain. The venom is not intended for this effect, but for stunning its prey, usually small fish and crustaceans, which will be instantly paralysed. Watching an irukandji hunt is absolutely hypnotic. Each tentacle is 'jinked' in the water, like a fisherman tweaking their lure. This intrigues aquatic animals that come in to see if they can get a free feed. Instead they get injected with enough venom to kill a small cow.

## BOX JELLYFISH

### THE SEA WASP OR BOX JELLY IS IN THE RECORD BOOKS AS THE MOST VENOMOUS CREATURE ON THE PLANET TODAY.

The biggest can have a bucket-sized bell, and tentacles that are double my height in length. These are covered with millions of stinging cells, and the venom affects the heart instantaneously. Under controlled conditions I administered a small portion of tentacle to my arm, and the effect was like having a white-hot iron pressed into my skin. When they use large amounts of stingers at the same time, the venom can kill large prey faster than any other creature. There is a defence though, in that the stingers only fire when they touch something organic (you or a prey animal's skin). A small barrier such as a wetsuit – or even a pair of tights – is enough to stop them stinging! And yes, I have gone into box jelly waters, wearing essentially lingerie!

Above: The Portuguese man o' war is not a jellyfish at all. It's a siphonophore, a multi-celled organism.

Opposite: Taking the opportunity to observe a Portuguese man o' war while in Wales. It's an infrequent visitor to UK waters.

# PORTUGUESE MAN O' WAR

## NOT TECHNICALLY A JELLYFISH, BUT A HYDROZOAN, A COLONIAL ANIMAL THAT CONTAINS DIFFERING BUT UNITED ORGANISMS ALL TOGETHER IN ONE VERY BEAUTIFUL PACKAGE.

It looks a bit like a purple Cornish pasty, but has the stopping power of a sledgehammer, with stinging cells all over its trailing tentacles. Unlike the box jelly and Irukandji, which swim actively towards prey and can even swim against tides and currents, the man o' war is very much borne by the winds, with its sail functioning like a... well... sail. Because of this they often end up stranded on beaches. If you find one, don't touch, as the stinging cells can fire off long after death.

# Deadly encounter

We were out at sea off the coast of West Wales, trying to film tuna and fin whales, when one of my crew shouted out, 'Stop the boat!' We saw this gorgeous blue and purple floating bell in the water and decided to get in and film it. Cameraman Mark and I both donned our wetsuits, making sure that not a single centimetre of our bodies was exposed. Mark put together a special camera rig that floats at the surface, giving us what's called a 'half and half' shot, enabling us to see the man o' war both above and below the waves. Swimming over carefully, we placed ourselves on opposite sides of the animal, its long tentacles trailing off into the water around us. It was hypnotically beautiful, a masterpiece of evolution. Looking closely underneath the bell, we could see several fish in the process of being digested. What a beast!

Looking closely underneath the bell, we could see several fish in the process of being digested.

# NEMATOCYSTS

## THE STINGING CELLS OF CORALS, ANEMONES AND JELLYFISH ARE CALLED NEMATOCYSTS.

These are found in the tentacles of all of these animals, and sometimes all over the whole animal. Each one of these is a cell, with a tightly wound-up tangled thread tipped with a harpoon. This connects to a small venom sac under pressure and with super potent toxins. Each one of these has a needle prick's worth of venom that would do next to nothing on its own, but the animal may have millions of these. The idea is that a very small portion of tentacle makes contact with a fish, a few thousand nematocysts fire out, the fish is instantly killed and then the tentacle draws the prey towards the mouth/bottom (it's the same hole). This is an elegant system that has worked for millennia. However, the problem occurs when a big clumsy non-aquatic animal like us stumbles into the path of a jelly. If a human swimmer blunders into its path, they can become entangled, stung all over their bodies, zapped hundreds of thousands of times. The overload of venom is so extreme that it can stop a human heart within seconds. It's this that leads the box jelly to be classified as the most venomous animal on earth.

# STONEFISH

**THE MOST VENOMOUS FISH IN THE WORLD IS QUITE A LAZY CUSTOMER, SPENDING ITS WHOLE LIFE LYING IN WAIT ON THE BOTTOM OF THE SEA FOR FOOD TO COME NEARBY.**

It does, however, have a row of hollow venomous spines running down its back, and if you were to step on it, that venom would inject into your foot and you'd be in for a very bad day. To show the venom apparatus in full effect, you can use a pair of tweezers to expose the bony hollow spines, which look like snake fangs. Then if you put some force down on the spine, the venom will literally squirt up into the air, as it's under such pressure. Despite the huge pain you'd be in if you stepped on it, the venom can be broken down using heat; just hot water is enough to start the process. For other elements of the process, there are antivenoms available, but from friends I know who've been stung, it appears to be about as painful an experience as you could ever have!

Opposite: Polyps, as seen on this coral species, have a ring of tentacles which are armed with nematocyst stinging cells. These are used to sting small prey as they move past.

Top: A stonefish with its venomous spines.

Bottom: A venomous hairy reef stonefish camouflaged on the sandy seabed in the Red Sea.

# MOST PAINFUL

### HORNET

The European hornet is a real bruiser, but not especially aggressive, and the sting isn't radically worse than its common wasp cousins. I was stung on the face while filming a paper nest the size of a football inside a British roof, and though it was sore, it doesn't compare to the others mentioned here.

**10.**

**9.**

### WEEVER FISH

When I was a kid, I remember my dad crying when he got stung on the toe by a weever fish. Found in shallow sands even in English seas, the weever is our equivalent of a stonefish, with venomous spines on its back used for defence. Dad was treated with very hot water, which helped to break down the protein in the venom, but... wow... he was in a lot of pain!

**8.**

### IRUKANDJI

My friend and mentor Dr Jamie Seymour of the Australian Institute of Marine Science was stung by an irukandji while studying them off the Queensland coast. I've seen footage of him in hospital afterwards, and he was in such agony that he couldn't stop screaming.

## FIRE CORAL

**7.** Swimming over shallow corals in Palau, Micronesia, I was doing my best not to knock anything, but then did a big swim kick and booted a fire coral into my ankle. The coral snapped out and stuck in my ankle bone. I started to swim for the boat, but within a few strokes my leg had stopped working completely. I was taken to hospital and treated with very hot water to break down the proteins in the sting... but for twenty-four hours the pain was intense, and I couldn't stand up at all!

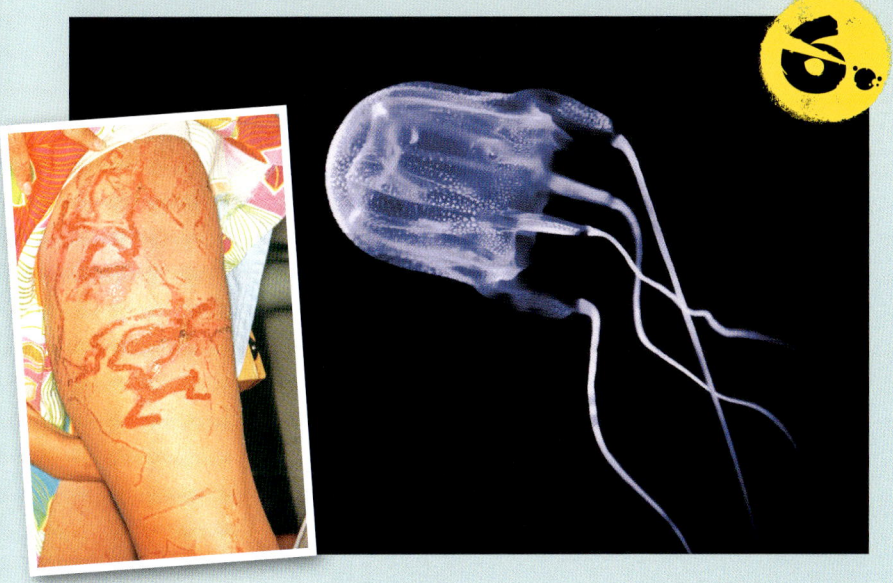

## BOX JELLYFISH

Deliberately getting stung by the world's most venomous animal may not sound smart, but I did choose a very small section of tentacles – so that I knew it would be painful but not dangerous – and placed it on my forearm. The pain was immediate and fierce, like pressing a heated iron on to my skin. It left a red welt and raised my heart rate for about ten minutes afterwards.

**5.**

## SCORPIONS

I have been stung by scorpions of several different species, and they are very different, but all cause severe pain that quickly spreads through the whole body. One of the luckiest moments of my career came when I was stung on the finger by a black forest scorpion in the forests of Brazil. This species can kill a human, and we were a long way from any help. However, fifteen minutes after the sting, I still had not experienced any pain at all. It turned out to have been a so-called 'dry' sting, where no venom is injected. Phew!

**4.**

## FIRE ANT

I put my hand into a fire ants' nest deliberately to see what would happen. Predictably, they attacked as a group, and I got stung maybe fifty times. Each sting felt hot and itchy and the pain persisted longer than you would expect from such a small ant. However, the real surprise was that the next day each sting came up in a perfect whitehead spot!

**3.**

## SCOLOPENDRA

These centipedes have a venom that they use to overwhelm their prey, which can be anything from a cockroach to a bat on the wing. I got bitten by one about half the size of this, and my hand swelled like a blown-up washing-up glove. I can't imagine what a bite from one as big as this would feel like!

## 2. TARANTULA HAWK WASP

Usually considered to be the largest species of wasp, and the insect with the second most painful sting, the female wasps paralyse tarantulas and lay their eggs on them. I have been stung several times to the fingers while catching them. The result? Like someone pushing a needle into your finger.

## 1. BULLET ANTS

The biggest ant, and aptly named – a single sting feels like being shot. I endured a rite of passage ritual where I wore a pair of gloves with hundreds of bullet ants woven in, and was stung over and over. For three hours I was so overwhelmed with pain that I couldn't see or hear the people trying to talk to me. An all-body experience!

# VENOMOUS SNAKES

**IN SNAKES, VENOM IS A MODIFIED SALIVA. IT STILL HAS SOME OF THE FUNCTIONS OF SPIT – THAT IS, STARTING TO BREAK DOWN FOOD SO IT'S READY TO BE DIGESTED.**

However, it also helps to kill prey, or cause huge pain in animals a snake might want to scare away. Drop for drop, all of the most venomous snakes in the world are in Australia, with the inland taipan number one, with a venom that could kill a hundred people. The eastern brown, coastal taipan and tiger snake all come in next. However, these are nothing like the most dangerous snakes on earth, causing few if any human fatalities. The snakes that have the capacity to be the most dangerous are the black mamba and king cobra, which can inject huge amounts of lethal venom deep into a wound. Untreated, these bites are almost always fatal.

However, even these snakes rarely harm humans. In fact, far less frightening and less venomous snakes, like the saw-scaled viper, and fer de lance snakes in Latin America, kill more humans than any other kind of snake. This is due to them being common, occurring near humans and striking readily should anyone step nearby. In parts of the world where they are common, people spend a lot of time barefoot, with no protection from footwear. Local hospitals may be a long way away, and may not have access to antivenoms. It's unknown how many people around the world die from snakebite, but in India alone it could be as high as 50,000 a year.

DEADLY 60

# MOST VENOMOUS SNAKES

**THIS LIST TAKES NO ACCOUNT OF 'VENOM YIELD', WHICH IS HOW MUCH VENOM A SNAKE HAS IN ITS STORES, AND HOW MUCH COULD BE DELIVERED IN ONE BITE.** The big vipers such as the diamondback rattlesnake, bushmaster, gaboon viper and the king cobra can deliver tablespoons of venom with every bite, ten times as much as any of the snakes on the top ten list, so will have far more lethal bites.

It is also not a marker of how dangerous the snakes might be. Of those listed here, only the Russell's viper and krait kill a significant number of humans.

**10. FOREST COBRA**

**9. TIGER SNAKE**

**8. COASTAL TAIPAN**

**7. COMMON KRAIT**

**6. BOOMSLANG**

**5. TIGER RATTLESNAKE**

**4. BLACK MAMBA**

**2. RUSSELL'S VIPER**

**3. EASTERN BROWN**

**1. INLAND TAIPAN**

# VENOMOUS SPIDERS

## OF MORE THAN 50,000 SPECIES OF SPIDER, ONLY AROUND 30 COULD HARM US.

However, those few have some really unpleasant venoms. The spiders with the longest venom glands are the wandering spiders of South America. They also have one of the most potent neurotoxins on earth. In addition, some nasty spiders like the recluse of North America have venom that can break down tissue. This means that wounds can start to rot away, leaving horrific scars. Some may lose limbs, fingers or toes.

# VENOMS AND MEDICINES

## THE SUBJECT OF MANY ACADEMIC STUDIES IS HOW VENOMS AND POISONS CAN BE USED TO TREAT HUMAN AILMENTS.

As these chemicals have been evolving since deep time, they are super complex and potentially some of the most powerful tools in medicine. There is already a drug made from the venom of cone snails that is used to treat pain and is far more powerful than conventional drugs, another for arthritis that comes from bees, one for diabetes from the Gila monster and others for heart conditions and issues with the blood.

Opposite: Only female black widow spiders are dangerously venomous. The much smaller males still have venom but their fang size is insufficient to penetrate human skin.

Above and below: Venom extraction, also known as milking, from poisonous animals such as snakes and spiders is crucial for developing antivenoms.

Milking spiders can provide an antivenom that saves thousands of lives.

# MOST TOXIC

**THE MOST POTENT NATURAL TOXIN IS BOTULINUM** (the animals described here kill with micrograms of toxin, while botulinum can kill in mere nanograms; one microgram is 1000 nanograms). Weirdly, botulinum is also the active ingredient in the cosmetic surgery procedure botox. Slightly less toxic are palytoxins, toxins found in certain corals, and ciguatera, which is found in the tissues of certain contaminated reef fish and can cause food poisoning. The data below are from animals that have toxins deliberately as a defence or to take on prey.

## 10.

### DEATHSTALKER SCORPION
Probably the most potent of all scorpion species, with teeny claws and a comparatively thick tail, they're small but definitely deadly.

## 9.

### SYDNEY FUNNEL-WEB SPIDER
The robustotoxin of the funnel-web is injected through giant fangs. The male and female are so different that they were originally described as separate species, with males having radically more potent venom. We've milked venom from their fangs using teeny vacuum cleaners, which is then used to make antivenom.

**DEADLY**

## HOOKED-NOSED SEA SNAKE

Experimental evidence shows sea snakes have a less potent venom than land snakes, but as the venom is usually tested on mice (which they never eat), that's hardly fair! Some sea snakes have enough venom to kill more than 20 people.

**7.**

## BRAZILIAN WANDERING SPIDER

The world's most dangerous spider has a truly horrible venom, which does all kinds of crazy things to the blood pressure. Additionally, they are big spiders with large venom glands and venom yield. This is why you never see me free-handling a wandering spider!

## GILA MONSTER

Until relatively recently the Gila monster and closely related beaded lizard were considered to be the only venomous lizards on earth. The venom is produced in glands in the lower jaw, and runs down grooves in the teeth. It is extremely painful, and seems to have evolved for defence – especially as the Gila monster's favourite food is eggs, which don't really need to be subdued with venom!

**5.**

## KOMODO DRAGON

For decades people had noted that when Komodo dragons bit a big animal such as a buffalo, it would quickly get ill and then weeks later eventually keel over dead. The Komodo's slobbery spit had always been thought to be full of nasty bacteria, and people reckoned it caused huge infections in the other animal, so eventually they just got sick and died. However, venom doc Professor Bryan Grieg Fry proved the Komodo does actually have venom: glands in the lower jaw secrete a toxin that prevents blood clotting and leads to shock.

## IBERIAN SHARP-RIBBED NEWT

The sharp-ribbed newt uses one of the craziest defences in nature. If threatened, it clenches its body so its sharpened ribs will pierce its own skin and go into the mouth of an attacker. One of the highlights of my academic career was working out that this is the first venomous newt or salamander, coating its own ribs with a toxin that makes the wound hurt more. Remarkably, the newt's own wounds heal almost instantly.

### 3. BLISTER BEETLE

The blister beetle secretes a caustic agent called cantharidin, which will blister your fingers if you pick one up (hence the common name). However, the real problem comes if they are eaten. It may seem bonkers to even think about eating a beetle that can scorch your skin, but they were once believed to have medicinal properties. Sometimes they can get mixed up in horses' feed, and then can be very dangerous indeed to dobbin.

### 2. GEOGRAPHY CONE SNAIL

The toxin injected by this most lethal of snails could theoretically kill a whole heap of humans.

### 1. GOLDEN DART FROG

The batrachotoxin found in the skin secretions of poison dart frogs is the most potent of all, and is used by local hunters to coat their darts. Even handling these frogs without gloves could kill you.

**6.**

# BEST BITE

# SALTWATER CROCODILES

**THE BIG CROCODILES, SUCH AS THE NILE, BLACK CAIMAN AND SALTWATER CROCODILE, HAVE THE HIGHEST RECORDED BITE FORCES OF ANY ANIMALS AROUND ON THE PLANET TODAY, WITH THE SALTIE BEING THE CURRENT WORLD RECORD HOLDER.**

We have bite-tested nine different species of croc on *Deadly 60*, with the biggest saltwater crocodile recording a bite force of 3700PSI, at least double what is needed to crush a human skull! There are several mechanisms that lead to this massive bite force. First of all, the skull itself is incredibly heavy and solid. The bone has all of the sutures (joints) firmly sealed, and is especially thick. It's like trying to pick up a skull made of rock. Then the muscles that drive the jaw shut are extremely thick and robust; however, the corresponding muscles that open the jaw are weedy and small. That explains why, even on a huge croc, you can hold the jaw shut with downward pressure from one hand. The bite force is accentuated by the teeth. If anyone ever describes their teeth as being 'razor sharp', they are far off the mark. Instead, the teeth are cone shaped; even the ends are not especially pointed. The benefit of this, though, is that they can withstand the enormous forces generated in the bite without breaking.

The muscles that drive the jaw shut are extremely thick and robust.

## Bite force

It was while filming the second series of *Deadly 60* in about 2009 that I came up with the Deadly bite test gauge. These were a series of loops of extra strong rubber, with fluid or gas inside under pressure. Then in the middle of the loop were pressure gauges, usually in the old-fashioned PSI – pounds per square inch. The challenge was to get a variety of biting beasts to chow down on the loop, and get a sense of how potent their bite force was. At the time, very few animals had been tested by

scientists around the world, and we were making science with every test. We had a small gauge effortlessly punctured and destroyed by a moray eel, and a lemon shark swam away with our bite test gauge. However, of the animals we successfully tested, we had me at 60PSI, hyenas at about ten times that, then the alligator, mugger croc, black caiman, American crocodile, Nile croc and finally the saltie at the top, with a hundred times my bite force before they wrecked the gauge!

# SARCOSUCHUS

**THE MEGA CROCS OF THE PAST SHOW ALL SIGNS OF HAVING A BITE LIKE MODERN CROCS, BUT JUST SUPER-SIZED. SARCOSUCHUS COULD HAVE BEEN 12M LONG AND WEIGHED 8 TONNES, SO DOUBLE THE LENGTH AND SEVEN TIMES THE WEIGHT OF MODERN CROCS.**

However, they may not have been the biggest biter; its snout is comparatively thin, suggesting they did a lot of feeding in or under the water, and thus would not have been the king of chomp. However, other early crocs like Deinosuchus may have had the biggest bites and Purussaurus brasiliensis got a little bit bigger, but was a bit broader and stouter than Sarcky.

# DUNKLEOSTEUS

**THE FIRST BIG BITER WAS THE FIENDISH FISH DUNKLEOSTEUS (I'M RELIABLY INFORMED THIS SHOULD BE PRONOUNCED DUNKLE-OS-TEUS), A PLACODERM THAT ORIGINATED WAY BACK 380 MILLION YEARS AGO IN THE LATE DEVONIAN.**

Up until this point in time there was no evidence of any animal having teeth, with very few having any bite at all. Dunkie then was a revolution in the big bite stakes. They also had no teeth, but a sturdy bony plated skull, and sharpened edges to their bony jaw. This would have allowed them to smash through shelled ammonites and other armoured fishes. They sucked in water to draw food into their mouths, the mouth opening and shutting in fractions of a second. As the biggest may have been 10m in length, they were one of the biggest biters of all time, certainly the biggest of any fossil fish.

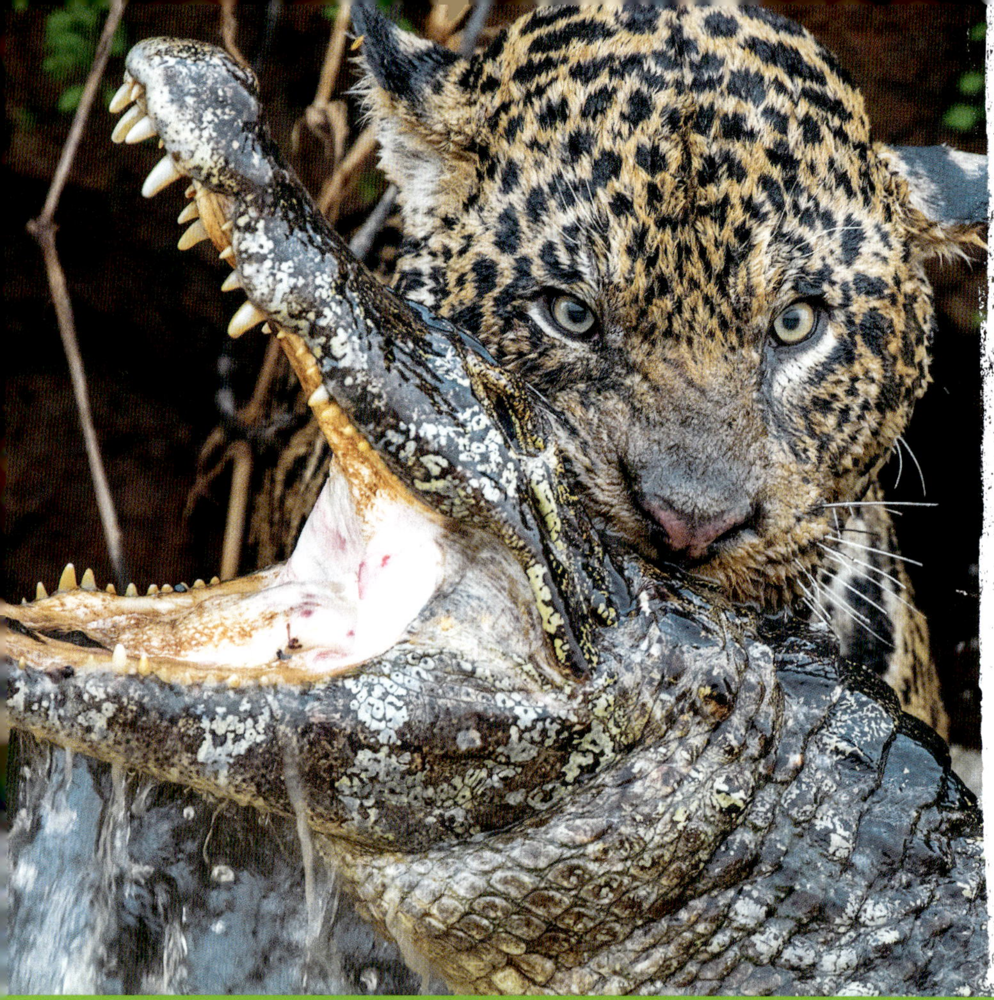

# JAGUAR

**THE JAGUAR IS THE CAT WITH THE BIGGEST BITE, EVEN BELIEVED TO BE MORE POWERFUL THAN THAT OF A LION OR TIGER, WHICH MAY BE DOUBLE THEIR SIZE AND WEIGHT.**

It's all down to the jaguar's choice of prey, and their method of dispatching it. Most cat species will bite to the throat of their target, but jaguars bite clean through the skull. Having the force to penetrate thick bone is formidable. Even more so when you consider some of the things jaguars will feed on. In Costa Rica, when it's turtle nesting season, the jaguars have learned to come down onto the beaches and savage the female turtles as they lay their eggs. The cat can bite clean through the turtle shell. Then in the vast wetlands of the Pantanal, the jaguars specialise in feeding on the caiman – super common crocodilians that can be two and a half metres in length. The jaguar will pierce clean through their bony skull and then run away with the croc in their mouth. On one shoot in Brazil, where we managed to film a female jaguar catching and killing a caiman, we also filmed another female picking up a whole cow in her mouth, which must have weighed a third of a tonne. And these were both girls! The males can weigh half as much again, and be much more powerful. It blows my mind what they must be able to do.

# SPOTTED HYENA

## THE SPOTTIE IS VERY DIFFERENT FROM ITS OTHER HYENA COUSINS.

Their reputation is that of a mean, cowardly, grisly scavenger, which is hugely unfair. In some places, spotties may kill almost everything they eat. They have the biggest groups (called clans) of any good-sized predator, which may reach up to 80 animals, and working together, they can take on things up to the size of hippo and buffalo. Whether they catch prey, steal it off lions or cheetahs, or find it dead and decomposing, they devour everything. This includes hide, sinew and bones. Using their stout carnassials, or cheek teeth, they crack right into the biggest bones, even crunching through giraffe thigh bones to get at the marrow within. Because of this, you can spot hyena poo a mile away; it's bleached white from all the calcium. Tortoises will munch hyena poo to get calcium for their shells, and porcupines love it to help them generate their ever-growing rodent teeth!

You can spot hyena poo a mile away; it's bleached white from all the calcium.

# SHARPEST TEETH

## VAMPIRE BAT

**THE ORIGINAL BLOOD-SUCKING VAMPIRE IS A TRULY REMARKABLE ANIMAL, WITH MAYBE THE SHARPEST TEETH ON THE PLANET TODAY.**

The upper incisors lack enamel so are sharper than scalpels – so sharp that when they land on or near an animal and bite, the host doesn't even feel it. Rather than sucking blood, the vampire laps the blood that pools in the wound. Despite their reputation, they are caring parents and giving pals. They roost communally, and if an individual returns to the roost without having fed, other bats will regurgitate their meals to enable the individual to feast (known as reciprocal altruism). A less sciency way of saying this would be that bats will sick up blood to their hungry pals!

DEADLY

Upper incisors lack enamel so are sharper than scalpels.

## LEECH

**LEECHES ARE THE ONLY WORMS WITH SHARP TEETH, HOUSED IN THREE JAWS.**

Their spit contains a mild anaesthetic and anticoagulant, so you don't feel the bite, and the blood keeps flowing so they don't have to suck. They appear to be attracted to the carbon dioxide we breathe out, and the sneaky little suckers head for dark secret places like armpits and bottom cracks till they can get stuck in!

## CONODONTS

**CONODONTS WERE EEL-LIKE VERTEBRATES THAT LIVED AROUND 500 MILLION YEARS AGO.**

They had no jaws, but probably had the sharpest teeth of all time, with the cutting edge one twentieth the width of a human hair. They sliced from side to side rather than up and down; what they chowed down on is anyone's guess.

# PIRANHA

**A PIRANHA HAS SETS OF TRIANGULAR TEETH OF EXCEPTIONAL SHARPNESS, WHICH INTERLOCK PERFECTLY WITH THE CORRESPONDING JAW.**

Their bite force is unusually powerful for an animal of this size. I should know, as I have been bitten three times, and lost two fingertips to piranhas! The image of piranhas churning water as they strip an animal down to the bone doesn't happen under normal conditions. However, about twenty years ago I was in Venezuela during an unusually dry season, and in some of the pools where the fish were concentrated, any meat in the water would cause them to go into a total frenzy!

LION
VS
CROCODILE

A croc crossing land is super vulnerable to lions, while a lion crossing waterways is at risk from big Nile crocodiles.

**THIS IS NOT A CLASSIC AFRICAN DEATH MATCH, BUT ONE THAT MUST BE STAGGERINGLY IMPRESSIVE TO SEE.** The victor is determined entirely by where the two predators meet. If the battle happens when a crocodile is crossing areas of open land between water courses, and lions happen upon it by chance, then there will only ever be one winner. Even a massive croc - if it can't break for the security of the water - will end up as lion food. In the water, however, it is a different story. There are plenty of cases where lions have been trying to cross a river, and opportunistic crocs have piled in to take on this top cat when it's swimming and vulnerable. Out of their environment, the tables are turned, and the lion - unless it gets lucky or can leap from the shallows - is going to come off second best.

**7.**

# TEAM PLAYERS

# DOLPHIN

## THERE ARE SO MANY WAYS THAT DOLPHINS CAN BE THE ULTIMATE TEAM PLAYERS.

They work together to gather fish into shoals and trap them against a barrier – like the sea surface or an underwater cliff. One of the most dazzling of their hunting tactics has so far only been recorded off the coasts of the Bahamas. On open shallow sandy banks you may happen upon what looks like craters from the surface of the moon. These are formed by crater-feeding bottlenose dolphins. I've been lucky enough to swim alongside them as they perform the technique – they swim a metre from the bottom, sending echolocating signals into the sands. When they encounter something solid, such as a sand eel or razor fish, they perform a perfect left-hand turn, go vertical and plunge into the sand to excavate the fish buried beneath, with a near 100% perfect success rate.

# ORCA

## AS THE LARGEST MEMBER OF THE DOLPHIN FAMILY, THE ORCA IS THE MOST FORMIDABLE PREDATOR ON OUR PLANET TODAY, AND POTENTIALLY THAT HAS EVER LIVED.

They have the largest range of prey, from the smallest fish and squid, all the way up to the biggest creature that has ever lived, the blue whale. Their team tactics are all driven by the most complex languages in the natural world. I say languages advisedly, as different 'ecotypes' or tribes of orca have not only different dialects but languages. Orca have a range of hunting styles, from swimming in unison to make a bow wave and wash an Antarctic seal off an ice floe, to thundering up onto a Patagonia beach to drag seals back into the surf.

Opposite: A crater-feeding Atlantic bottlenose dolphin hunting for fish on the seabed, Bahamas.

Below: A pod of Antarctic orca hunting a Weddell seal using co-ordinated wave washing technique.

Their team tactics are all driven by the most complex languages in the natural world.

# HARRIS'S HAWK

## THERE ARE RELATIVELY FEW RAPTORS KNOWN TO HUNT TOGETHER AS A TEAM.

The Harris's hawk is by far the most highly adapted. One individual may flush a jack rabbit out into the open and the second Harris's may chase it into the path of the finishers, which then hammer in and seal the deal. Though the kill is undertaken as a team, they are rubbish at sharing the spoils, and fight to get the food all for themselves. Because of their social nature, they are far better at tolerating other birds of prey, and also better at socialising with falconers. For this reason the Harris's is the most common bird of prey in falconry in the world.

## WOLF

**THE GREY WOLF IS ONE OF THE FINEST TEAM PREDATORS ON EARTH, AND WAS ONCE THE MOST SUCCESSFUL AND WIDESPREAD PREDATOR, FOUND RIGHT ACROSS THE NORTHERN HEMISPHERE.**

They have so many hunting strategies, and working as a unit allows them to take down prey much bigger than themselves – all the way up to bison and musk oxen, the biggest wild animals found in the frozen north. Like all the best team players, the wolf connects to others of its kind using vocal communication, bringing the team together with a howl.

## HONEYGUIDE AND HONEY BADGER

**A LEGENDARY KILLER COMBO IS THE CONNECTION BETWEEN THE WORLD'S MOST AGGRESSIVE ANIMAL AND A CANNY BIRD.**

The honey badger loves nothing better than... well... honey. However, it struggles to find it all by itself. The honeyguide will find a bees' nest and fly towards a viable powerhouse. That can sometimes be a human, but classically will be a *ratel* (the local name for the honey badger). The honey badger will shred the nest, and the larvae and wax that are left are a meal for the bird.

The honeyguide will find a bees' nest and fly towards a viable powerhouse.

# GALAPAGOS RACER SNAKE AND LAVA LIZARDS

**ONE OF THE MOST FAMOUS WILDLIFE FILM SEQUENCES OF ALL TIME SHOWS RACER SNAKES SLITHERING OUT OF THE ROCKS ON ISLANDS IN THE GALAPAGOS, THUNDERING AFTER NIFTY LIZARDS.**

Whether the snakes are actually working together as a team or just happen to be together in the same place is arguable, but it is worth a mention as the greatest reptile race ever.

Cannibalistic red devils in the dead of night - nature's spookfest!

## HUMBOLDT SQUID

### DIVING WITH A HUMBOLDT SQUID IS THE FREAKIEST AND MOST FRIGHTENING ENCOUNTER IMAGINABLE.

At 3m long they are a formidable foe, but it's their pack-hunting abilities that make them so sinister. On one expedition filming Humboldts in the Sea of Cortez, we captured an animal, then put a harness on its mantle with a tiny camera attached. When we released it, the squid swam straight down 400m and rejoined a platoon of other Humboldts; there might have been hundreds of them. What was especially impressive was that they were all equally spaced, moving in total unison, like a squadron of bombers heading out during the Battle of Britain. A squidron if you will...

Opposite: Group of alert Galapagos racer snakes, on the lookout for newly emerged baby marine iguanas.

Opposite: With a red devil off Baja California, Mexico. These squid hunt together in their hundreds.

DEADLY DEATH MATCH

Wild dogs are slighter and have unmatched endurance.

WILD DOG

VS

HYENA

Female spotted hyenas can be nearly triple the weight of a hunting dog!

**THE TWO BIGGEST TEAM-PLAYER PREDATORS ON EARTH DO NOT OFTEN RISK A CONFRONTATION.** Wild dogs are the most persistent and statistically one of the most successful predators on earth, while hyenas are arguably the most versatile and the least fussy. Wild dogs are slighter and less robust animals than sturdy female hyenas, and are more likely to flee than risk injury in a full-on battle. However, sometimes running isn't possible – especially if the dogs have pups. Other times hyenas will try their luck and raid the dogs' food while they're still feeding. In such situations, the scrap is extraordinary, very noisy, and someone is getting a beating.

8.

LETHAL LURES

# GREENLAND SHARK

## MOST GREENLAND SHARKS LIVE THEIR WHOLE LIVES WITH A WRIGGLING COPEPOD LIVING ON THEIR EYEBALL!

This was originally considered to be a parasite, but many now believe it acts as a lure, enticing prey towards the sluggish shark's ample jaws. By dating crystals in the eyeballs, scientists have shown that Greenland sharks can live to be over 400 years of age, making them the oldest living vertebrate animal by far. Studies suggest that Greenland sharks may not even mature until they are 100 years old. This is problematic, as it means that if you take a Greenland shark from the ocean before that age, they will not have had a chance to give birth to pups.

Scientists have shown that Greenland sharks can live to be over 400 years of age.

Opposite: Greenland sharks are often seen with copepods on their eyes. These are crustaceans that can grow up to 8cm long and act as a lure for prey.

Above: The spider-tailed horned viper is an incredible mimic. Its tail resembles a spider and the snake can also move it to attract prey, such as birds.

# SPIDER-TAILED HORNED VIPER

## THERE ARE MANY KINDS OF SNAKES THAT USE SO-CALLED CAUDAL LURING AS A WAY OF ATTRACTING PREY.

Caudal refers to the tail, and this process involves a snake twitching its tail tip around to mimic a worm, a tasty treat for any hungry bird or mouse. When the animal approaches, intrigued, they are met with the fangs of a venomous snake! The spider-tailed horned viper is by far the most out-there example of caudal luring. Their tail is twisted into a strange shape that looks like – you've guessed it – a spider! The viper tweaks the tail tip around to create the impression of a moving arachnid, and birds come to investigate. The rest of the viper is beautifully camouflaged – so much so that if you film the lure, you probably won't be able to see the actual snake, right up until the moment of strike!

Right: Surinam toads have a small lure on their chin to attract potential prey.

Below: A great blue heron uses this feather to attract fish to the surface of the water.

Opposite: A deepsea dragonfish with a bioluminescent lure hanging below its fearsome jaws.

## SURINAM TOAD

### A CONTENDER FOR THE WEIRDEST ANIMAL ON THE DEADLY LIST, THE SURINAM TOAD LOOKS LIKE A NORMAL FROG THAT'S BEEN RUN OVER BY A STEAM ROLLER.

It's incredibly flat, with elongated limbs – webbed feet at the back and long spindly fingers on the front feet. Their method of raising their young is just out-there odd: they take their spawn onto their back, and they sort of soak down into the skin, until the tadpoles are living, wriggling and visible, within the flesh of the adult. Grim! However, on catching one of these bonkers toads in a pool in Suriname, we noticed that it has a wriggling lure on its chin, enticing aquatic bugs to swim towards the mouth. The toads can then open their mouths quickly, dragging the prey into their gob with suction force.

## HERON AND FEATHER

### TOOL USE AMONG ANIMALS IS EXTREMELY RARE, WITH EVERY NEW EXAMPLE FOUND IN NATURE RECEIVED WITH EXCITEMENT BY THE SCIENTIFIC COMMUNITY.

It was a big deal then when some heron species were seen to collect feathers at the riverside and drop them onto the water's surface. As fish swam up to see if that might be a meal, the heron would lunge with its stiletto dagger beak and scoff them down. The story gets even weirder, as some crocodilians have been observed deliberately draping twigs and branches across their snouts during prime bird breeding season. When something like a heron comes in looking for nesting material, they land on the snout of our sneaky snapper, and end up as breakfast!

# ANGLER FISH

**THE ANGLER FISH IS AS ODD AS IT GETS. LOOKING LIKE A PARTLY DEFLATED RUGBY BALL, WITH TINY MILKY EYES AND A COMEDY TINY TAIL, THEIR BODIES ARE COVERED IN WEIRD LITTLE BUMPS AND LUMPS.**

And then dangling over the top of their head is a fishing rod they can move around, with a lure at the end that can glow with bioluminescence, tempting wee fishies to swim right up to the angler's mouth. This is just the entry-level oddness though. It's when it comes to mating that the angler is the queen of bizarre. The familiar big puffball is the female. The male is the size of my little fingernail. In the infinite darkness of the deep, if a male finds his potential partner, he will attach himself to her side. Eventually he just gets absorbed, and gets all his food from the female, never swimming free again!

# ALLIGATOR SNAPPING TURTLE

**WHEN LYING ON THE BOTTOM OF A MURKY SWAMP, THE ALLIGATOR SNAPPING TURTLE'S CRYPTIC COLOURATION AND UNEVEN SHELL MAKE IT AS GOOD AS INVISIBLE.**

With one exception. Inside the mouth (also camouflaged) is a pink wriggling worm, which jumps about and twitches from side to side. This inevitably attracts the attention of fish, which swim right into the turtle's mouth to investigate... with inevitable consequences. The lure is actually a part of the tongue, but one of the most effective enticements imaginable! The alligator snap is a true icon of Deadly. Way back on series one, we put traps out in a Louisiana swamp and collected them up early the next morning. We had no results until the very last trap, which had two inside, one of which was almost too big and heavy to lift.

Below: An American alligator snapping turtle uses a vermiform (or worm-like) tongue to lure its fish prey.

Opposite: With a huge alligator snapping turtle in the swamps of Louisiana.

The biggest alligator snapping turtle we ever found was heavier than me!

9.

# SUPER SENSES

# SHARK SUPER SENSES

**THE NORMAL SENSES OF A SHARK ARE LEGENDARY: THE NARES OR NOSTRILS ARE CAPABLE OF DETECTING A SINGLE DROP OF BLOOD IN AN OLYMPIC SWIMMING POOL-SIZED AREA OF WATER AND FOLLOWING IT TO THE SOURCE.**

Their eyesight is good, even in low visibility or low light. However, it's their two super senses that set them apart. The first is the lateral line: an organ that runs down the flank of the animal, a channel filled with microscopic hairs that are moved by the water around the shark. If a fish or seal swims behind the shark, it creates a wake or turbulence in the water and the shark can sense it using the lateral line. However, this pales into insignificance when you compare it to the power of the ampullae of Lorenzini, pores filled with jelly and linked to highly sensitive nerve endings, found in the shark's snout. They're especially good at detecting the weak electric fields given off in the moving muscles of their prey. A nuzzling hammerhead can perceive a ray buried in the sandy seabed purely by picking up on the minute amounts of electric field given off as their heart beats!

The hammerhead's cephalofoil spreads out its sensory organs.

# SNAKES AND THERMAL PERCEPTION

## SEVERAL KINDS OF SNAKE HAVE HEAT-SEEKING ABILITIES.

Some species of python have labial pits – holes in the lip scales. Pit vipers have loreal pits, which occur between the eye and nostril. These pits are like a funnel, and within them are tightly packed nerves that can detect the faintest of temperature change. Scientists have shown that even without their other senses, a pit viper can still strike warm-blooded prey with pinpoint accuracy, based entirely on this thermal superpower. It's also worth mentioning the snake's other super sense, which is surely its tongue. The forked tongue has two endings that can function independently, and when we film a snake's tongue flick in super slow motion, you can see the glossy tongue go up into the air and wave about, then drop down onto the ground and do the same. The sticky saliva is hoovering up scent molecules, which it then returns to the mouth. In the roof of the mouth is a special organ called the Jacobson's or vomeronasal organ. Here those scents are run through the testing machine, to find out if there's anything around worth hunting. As the two lobes of the tongue function on their own, the snake is smelling in stereo, and can move towards the stronger smells.

Opposite: Illustration of how a hammerhead shark uses electroreception to locate prey hiding on the sea floor.

Right: Coastal python using its forked tongue as a sense organ (top). The thermogram (bottom) shows the difference between a cold-blooded snake (dark) and warm-blooded mouse (light).

# TASTE

## TARANTULAS

### OK, SPIDERS DON'T HAVE TONGUES... SO HOW DO THEY TASTE?

Sounds like the set-up for a bad joke. However, spiders can actually taste, using hollow hairs (called setae) on the base of the feet and on their palps. They also have extraordinarily sensitive hinged hairs on their legs that can pick up vibrations. Watch any spider hunting in a web, and you'll see its legs daintily touching the silk, to pick up any wobbles and tremors from insects that have blundered into their sublime silken lair. Raft spiders use the same mechanism to pick up vibrations on the water from bugs that have plopped onto their pond.

Opposite: Goliath birdeater tarantula in defensive posture - raised front legs, large fangs on display and potentially releasing urticating hairs from its abdomen - in Suriname.

Left: Coloured SEM (scanning electron micrograph) of tarantula hair. These are irritating to human skin but they are also used to sense motion and noise, vibrating to alert the spider.

# SMELL

Polar bears can smell food from 20 miles away.

## POLAR BEAR

**BEARS IN GENERAL HAVE SOME OF THE MOST DEVELOPED SENSES OF SMELL OF ANY ANIMAL, WITH THEIR BIG DOG-LIKE SNOUTS CONTAINING A HUGE AMOUNT OF SPACE IN VAST NASAL CAVITIES.**

That space is crammed full of turbinates (boney structures) that further increase the surface area where smells can alight and be processed. The polar bear's phenomenal abilities are further emphasised by their Arctic pack ice environment. Their close cousin the brown bear lives in a temperate environment filled with smells, from flowers and honey to other animals' droppings and scent sprays – a busy bustling superhighway of scents. However, the polar bear lives in a place with very few smelly distractions. Because of that, they have been seen walking in a dead straight line for 20 miles towards food they can only have smelled. From 20 miles away. That's like someone cooking up doughnuts on the English side of the Channel, and someone on the French side being able to smell it!

# DASPLETOSAURUS

## IT'S ALWAYS TRICKY TO LOOK AT DINOSAURS AND FIGURE OUT HOW DEVELOPED THEIR SENSES WERE.

However, there are hints in fossils of the tyrannosaur Daspletosaurus that it was the bloodhound of its day. Like the bears of the modern era, its snout had large cavities with complex turbinates inside, and studies of the brain case suggest that the olfactory lobes – the bit of the brain dedicated to smelling – was unusually developed. This means that Daspletosaurus could have tracked down its prey using smell, even in low or no light conditions.

Opposite: Young polar bear using its highly sensitive nose to track smells on the sea ice, Svalbard Archipelago, Norway.

Above: Daspletosaurus skull showing large cavities within the nose, like modern-day bears, meaning it had a super keen sense of smell.

Right: Illustration of how Daspletosaurus might have looked like back in the Late Cretaceous period.

# VISION

## WE HUMANS ARE INCREDIBLY RELIANT ON OUR EYESIGHT, TO SUCH AN EXTENT THAT WE SOMEWHAT NEGLECT OTHER SENSES LIKE SMELL AND TOUCH (WHICH CAN BE FAR MORE PROFOUND IF WE FOCUS ON THEM A BIT).

However, our human vision is not unusually good when you compare it to other animals. Our colour vision is based on just three pigments, while certain crustaceans may have ten, and even humble spiders may be able to perceive ultraviolet light.

Left: Head profile of a golden eagle, a species with exceptionally sharp eyesight. They can spot prey from 3 miles away!

Opposite: Philippine tarsier showing large, specialised eyes which are packed with photoreceptor rods, enabling it to see well in low-light conditions, ideal for hunting at night.

## EAGLE EYES

## WE MAY TALK ABOUT SOMEONE WHO SEES WELL HAVING 'EYES LIKE A HAWK' OR BEING 'EAGLE-EYED', AND THIS IS ABSOLUTELY APT.

Eagles on the wing can see prey from 4 miles away. While we have one fovea or focal point in our eyes, eagles have two, giving them unparalleled depth perception. If you watch a bird of prey perched and looking for prey, you will see several things before they fly. First they'll ruffle their feathers up (the rouse) to align them perfectly. Then they'll bob their head around almost comically. This is a way of bringing those two fovea into play, assessing the distance to prey from two different perspectives. The last pre-flight check is to do a big squirty poo, lightening the load before taking off. All these signs make it easier for us as filmmakers, because if you see this sequence then you know a bird of prey is about to take flight!

# TARSIER

**THE GREMLIN OF THE FOREST, THE NOCTURNAL TARSIER HAS THE BIGGEST EYES COMPARED TO BODY SIZE OF ANY MAMMAL. IF OUR EYES WERE AS BIG AS A TARSIER'S, THEY'D BE LIKE A COUPLE OF HONEYDEW MELONS IN OUR NOGGIN!**

These huge eyes suck in vast amounts of light, enabling them to see the twilight world as we would see broad daylight. They leap and spring about in the treetops with formidable power – something no animal with lesser eyesight would attempt as they'd inevitably miss their target branch and topple to the ground below. Interestingly, though, when you watch a tarsier hunting at night, it seems their satellite dish ears are just as important, twitching around ceaselessly, listening out for the squeaks of crickets, the wing beats of moths and the footfalls of stalking praying mantises.

# BIGGEST EYE

## THE GIANT SQUID WAS ALWAYS CONSIDERED TO HAVE THE BIGGEST EYE IN THE NATURAL WORLD.

It is the longest invertebrate, with one that washed up in Newfoundland being measured at 16.8m in length. The deflated eyes on those forlorn dead squid were gargantuan, some as big as a watermelon. This is quite curious, as giant squid hunt at around a kilometre in depth, where no light ever penetrates. It is possible that they migrate upwards into shallower waters for some of their hunting, or that they are experts at perceiving the bioluminescence of certain deep sea prey species. The giant squid was considered to be the record breaker until in 2007 a related colossal squid was caught, still just about alive, in the Southern Ocean off the coast of Antarctica. Its eye which would have been 30–40cm in diameter, bigger than a basketball!

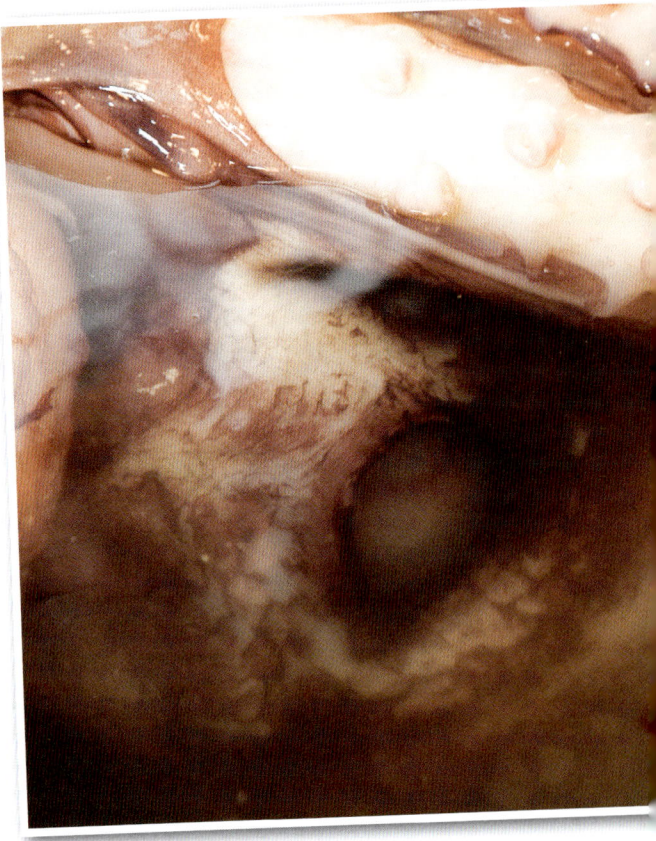

# BARRELEYE

## IS THIS DEEP-SEA DENIZEN THE WEIRDEST CREATURE ON OUR PLANET?

The barreleye has a unique glassy visor across its head, which almost looks like the windshield on a helicopter. It's possible to see right inside its fluid-filled head, to the brain and nerves. Its eyes, which are capped with bright green lenses, sit within this transparent head, and are mostly aimed upwards, possibly enabling it to see the silhouettes of fish that swim over its head. It's thought they may feast on deep sea jellyfish.

# TELESCOPEFISH

## THERE APPEARS TO BE SOME KIND OF LAW OF NATURE THAT ANY ANIMAL LIVING IN THE DEEP SEA HAS TO BE: A) A NIGHTMARE OF NATURE; B) DOWNRIGHT ODD.

The telescopefish obeys these two laws precisely. The telescope eyes that give them their name are tubular, with giant lenses. It's believed that they use these formidable eyes to pick out the silhouettes of fish against the weak light that penetrates down into the depths. However, as telescopefish are found down to 3,000m, where no light penetrates at all, they must surely also be spotting weak bioluminescence in their prey.

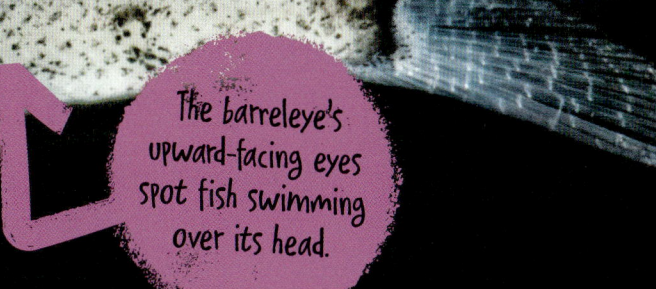

The barreleye's upward-facing eyes spot fish swimming over its head.

# MANTIS SHRIMP

## THE MANTIS SHRIMP IS A JOYOUS FIND ON A CORAL REEF OR IN THE MUCK OF THE SANDY SEABED NEARBY.

Peacock mantis shrimps have some of the most luminous and abundant colours of any marine critter. There are two essential kinds of mantis shrimp. The first is the spearer, which lunges from its burrow to impale close-swimming shrimp. We filmed these all the way back on series one off the coast of Borneo. We waited at night, lying on the bottom near their burrow, with a wee bit of food on a stick, until eventually one emerged, springing up to skewer the food like a kebab!

The other kind are the wandering boxers, which have different shapes of palps. Instead of spearing, they punch, smashing their palps into crabs and shells. This punch can shatter bulletproof glass. The scientific name for the group is the stomatopods, and they have better colour vision than any other animal. Their eyes look like the compound eyes of dragonflies, but are on stalks, giving absolute all-encompassing 360° vision, more complete than any other animal. Their visual system is based around ten colour pigments compared to our three, meaning they can see a whole different world of colour from us lowly humans. It's a conundrum why they have vision that is so much better than any other animal; why, when we humans can get by perfectly well with just three pigments? One part of the puzzle might be that they have distinctive colour patterns on their 'elbows' that they show to each other prior to battles, and perceiving the different colours might help them avoid or choose their opponents.

DEADLY

# OGRE-FACED SPIDER

## THE OGRE-FACED OR NET-CASTING SPIDERS HAVE THE BIGGEST EYES OF ANY SPIDER, AND ARE SUPERB AT PERCEIVING MOVEMENT AT NIGHT.

They use these big old eyes to target insects that are wandering below them, before entangling them in a net of silk. Like most spiders, their eyes reflect green or silvery under torchlight. I've tried to film the process so many times and it's amazing how sensitive they are: if the spider senses a little light or movement, they simply eat their web and disappear. However, on one shoot in Australia, I did manage to sneak in relatively close and set up a little light to try and see the spider in action. We waited for hours for something to wander into the firing line, and finally a bush cricket strolled up the branch and towards our spider. Then, at the very last second, our cricket did not keep walking, but sprang fully up into the spider's net, resulting in a sticky end, but not the one we were prepared for!

Opposite: Close-up view of harlequin mantis shrimp compound eyes, which provide the very best colour vision in the entire natural world!

Below: Ogre-faced spider ready to throw a web-net over potential prey at night, Madagascar.

# HEARING

## FENNEC FOX AND BAT-EARED FOX

**THE FENNEC AND BAT-EARED FOXES BOTH HAVE ABSURD EARS THAT MAKE THEM LOOK SUPER CUTE AS BABIES, AND RATHER RIDICULOUS AS ADULTS!**

Surely ears this big must be a hindrance to them? Well, it would appear not. If you film these animals on a thermal imaging camera, you can see the ears are boiling hot, radiating heat away from the animal's core in their burning-hot desert home. However, super hearing is surely the number one function of these colossal lugholes, the whole ear twisting around and about to detect the rustling footfalls of desert rats and scorpions.

deadly

With a satellite-dish face, the great grey owl can hear through solid snow!

Opposite: Fennec foxes have huge ears, not just for incredible hearing, but also to help regulate their body temperature in hot desert habitats.

Above: Great grey owl about to swoop down on some unsuspecting rodent under the snow, Finland.

# GREAT GREY OWL

## THE GREAT GREY OWL IS ONE OF THE MOST IMPRESSIVE BIRDS IN THE WORLD.

Inhabiting the icy forests of the taiga, Northern Europe and the Americas, the owl has a huge circular facial disc that is composed of unusually stiff feathers. It's convex, so the opposite of a satellite dish, which diverts sound to its centre. The great grey diverts sounds out to the ears at the outskirts of the disk. These ears are offset, not at the same height on either side of the skull. This allows the owl to judge the difference in time between sound arriving at one ear and the other. With minute micro-adjustments (done subconsciously in their teeny tiny brain), the great grey can locate a lemming scurrying along underneath the snow, and they will fly over, then punch through, to nab a lemming lunch in their talons.

# TOUCH

## SEAL

### ALL OF THE MANY SPECIES OF SEALS AND SEA LIONS HAVE EXTRAVAGANT WHISKERS KNOWN PROPERLY AS VIBRISSAE.

These thickened hairs are incredible at sensing movement and enable them to hunt in zero visibility. Possibly even more impressive are the whiskers of the walrus. Much shorter and stumpier, these bristles are almost their sole method of finding food. The walrus dives down to the murky seabed in Arctic waters and uses its whiskers like fingertips to locate clams buried in the murk. It then uses the exceptional suction power of its rubbery lips to suck the clam clean out of its shell. A day's hunt can garner 3,000 clams! Some fishermen also report seeing walrus catch smaller seal species, grabbing them in a deadly embrace and then using their rubbery lips to suck their brains clean out of their head!

Below: Walrus showing short, stumpy vibrissae, which it uses to feel for prey on the sea floor.

Opposite: Close-up of alligator skull showing holes in the jaw where nerves link to dermal pressure receptors.

Vibrissae, or whiskers, allow seals to sense movement in zero visibility and dark seas.

# CROCODILES

## IF YOU EXAMINE THE SKULL OF A BIG CROC OR ALLIGATOR, YOU'LL SEE WHAT LOOKS LIKE HOLES THAT HAVE BEEN DRILLED INTO THE BONE.

In life these would be packed with highly sensitive nerves, and on the scales on the outside are small black dots. These are known as dermal pressure receptors. They are incredible at detecting minute ripples in the water around the croc. If a bird falls into the water, it will struggle, making vibrations that travel out in waves, and the croc can pinpoint them. The croc has third eyelids or nictitating membranes that enable them to see underwater... but they are not completely see-through, and even in crystal-clear water, the croc probably only sees shapes and movements. However, with their awesome ancient super sense, a croc still has the edge over struggling prey. This is the main reason why, when diving with crocodiles, our number one rule is to be cool and calm.

# SUPERPOWERED SHARKS

## 10. BLUE SHARK: THE LONG-DISTANCE SWIMMER

The most migratory of all sharks, the beautiful blue undertakes huge journeys every year following its prey. They'll cross entire oceans, travelling up to 6,000 miles in a year! What is less known is that they also undertake daily migrations down and up through the water, from the surface to several hundred metres down, also tracking their prey.

## 9. GREAT HAMMERHEAD: THE SUPREME STINGRAY SENSOR

Sharks have special sensors in their heads with the fancy name of the ampullae of Lorenzini – pores filled with a special jelly, super sensitive to the weak electrical fields given off by the moving muscles of their prey. The great hammerhead's mallet-shaped noggin spreads out those ampullae, giving the shark the ability to sense rays buried in the sand merely from the electric pulses given off by the beating off their hearts.

## TIGER SHARK: THE SHELL AND SINEW SLICER

The tiger shark is a pugnacious pitbull of a predator. They're big, they're powerful and they have remarkable teeth. The can-opener curve in each tooth is lined with serrations like a saw, and each tooth is comparatively short and incredibly hard, able to withstand the pressure of biting and slicing through sinew, bone and even turtle shell.

## OCEANIC WHITETIP: THE BLOODHOUND OF THE SEA

A shark's sense of smell is legendary, using its nares or nostrils to detect a single drop of blood in an Olympic swimming pool-sized area of water, and then follow it to its source. The thing that's always bothered me about that is… what happens if a shark gets a nosebleed? Do they just swim around in circles? The true wizard of whiff has to be the Oceanic whitetip. Living exclusively in the big blue desert of the open ocean, they have to be able to find any potential food before other animals snaffle it. They have a reputation for being the first shark species to find sinking ships and can detect a floating whale carcass from many miles away using smell.

## GREAT WHITE: THE BIG BITE

The most famous set of JAWS on earth, the great white has the most impressive teeth of all. Each tooth is triangular, with wicked serrations down its cutting edges, and can fill the palm of your hand. They have 300 of these weapons, with five rows of teeth that will roll forward to take the place of the others as they fall out. A big great white might get through 50,000 teeth in a lifetime. Shark teeth fossilise readily as they are so hard, and therefore are super common in the fossil record. This explains why we know so much about extinct shark species.

**5.**

## REEF SHARK: THE LATERAL LINE

The lateral line is another sharky supersense that detects movements in the water around the animal. It's essentially a canal or channel filled with modified hair cells that is exceptional at detecting pressure changes and movement in the water around the shark. So if a fish swam behind the shark, it would create a wake or turbulence that the shark could detect, thus knowing the fish was there even if it couldn't see it.

**4.**

## LEMON SHARK: THE BENDY WONDER

The lemon shark is named for the surprisingly bright yellow colour the adults exhibit. With fish-hook teeth, they specialise in catching rapid slippery fish, and to enable them to snaffle them, they need to be as flexible as a yoga teacher! The lemon can snap around to grab hold of its own tail – not that it does, but it could if it wanted to!

## THRESHER SHARK: THE WHIPPERSNAPPER

The first person to suggest that the thresher shark uses its tail as a whip was the Greek philosopher Aristotle in his *History of Animals*, written around 350 BC. Everyone thought that seemed like a good idea and went along with it. However, it was two millennia later, in 2013, that it was filmed happening for the first time. Interestingly, the tail most often slices up through the water, with the narrow leading edge receiving less drag or resistance. It appears to create a pressure wave that stuns fish, and then the shark comes back to finish them off.

## WOBBEGONG: THE AMBUSH ASSASSIN

The wobbegong is one of the underwater world's great cryptic killers, hiding in plain sight with tassels over its body breaking up its outline and swirls of different colours to help it blend in. Even the eyes are camouflaged. The wobbegong can lie completely still for an entire day, biding its time. They don't strike until an unwary fish is hanging literally over their nostrils, and then they explode into action so fast that the human eye cannot even take it in. As they strike, they open their mouth super fast, creating a vacuum that sucks the victim in.

## CHIMAERA: NIGHT SIGHTS

The most ancient sharks we know of were probably related to modern chimaera or ghost sharks. Still around after more than 400 million years, these often bizarre-looking creatures haunt the ocean's depths, but sometimes come up into the shallows at night following the food. Off the coast of Alaska we were diving at night in seas that were filled with chimaera, which had one unexpected effect. Their eyes are superbly adapted to sucking in the maximum amount of light from the murky depths, and at the back of the eye an intense *tapetum lucidum*, a layer of cells, acts like a mirror, reflecting light through the retina a second time. A mere sweep of your torch across the eye, and light reflects back out from the eye, like a laser beam through the water!

# GOLDEN EAGLE

# VS

# FOX

## POUND FOR POUND, THE GOLDEN EAGLE IS ONE OF THE MOST POWERFUL PREDATORS.

They're also super successful, with their range covering much of the northern hemisphere. Female golden eagles have been known to dispatch antelope, goats and deer... and then fly away with them! And in the mountains of Kazakhstan, people will hunt from horseback with their trained eagles, hunting things up to the size of wolves! That said, there are occasions where canids (species in the dog family) will turn the tables on this aerial assassin. If the eagle is engrossed in prey on the ground, a fox might even attempt an opportunistic attack, and if they can evade the mighty talons of the eagle, there is a chance of success. However, knowing what they're capable of, if I was a fox, I'd be tucking myself away somewhere safe till the eagle was long gone.

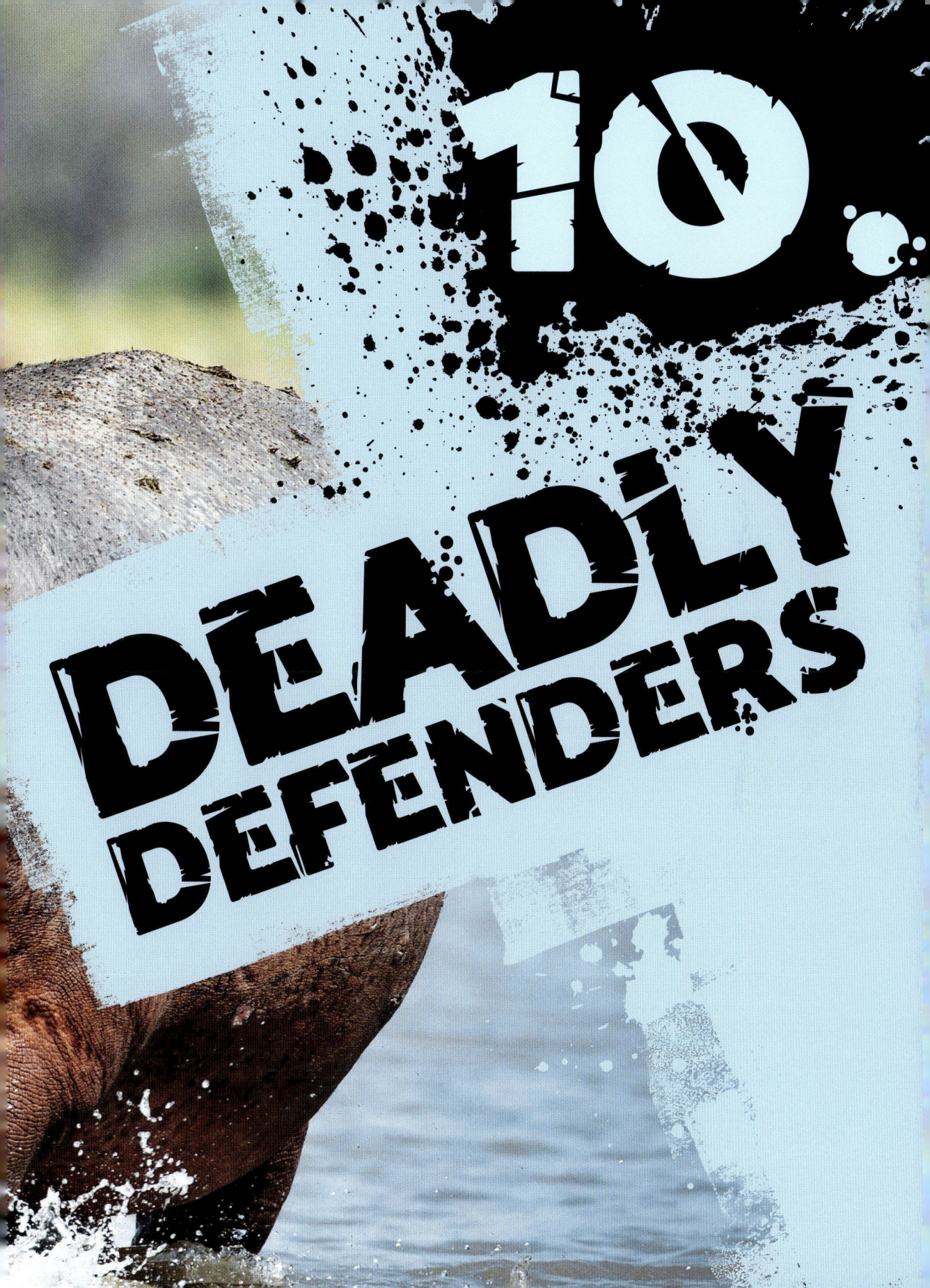

10.

DEADLY DEFENDERS

# PROTOCERATOPS

## ARGUABLY THE FINEST FOSSIL OF ALL TIME IS A WONDER OF PALAEONTOLOGY, A DEATH STRUGGLE FROZEN IN TIME.

A Velociraptor and Protoceratops were caught in a lethal embrace, battling to survive as they were swept away, probably by a landslide. The Velociraptor was desperately trying to overwhelm the ceratopsian, but Protoceratops was not giving in, using its superior weight and defences to battle the fierce feathered fiend. Even though the tableau is inanimate stone, you can see the terror on the face of the defender, the intent in the physique of the hunter. It's almost sad that this epic combat was to end with neither animal victorious, but it has given scientists so much information about the times. It could be a still image of a lion and buffalo in full turmoil, except this was from around 74 million years in the Late Cretaceous. You can take a look at the fossil on page 248.

Above: Illustration of Protoceratops, which lived in Asia during the Late Cretaceous period.

Opposite: Musk oxen pair, native to the Arctic, seen here on Wrangel Island, Russia.

# MUSK OX

## THE ARCTIC TUNDRA IS ONE OF THE MOST CHALLENGING ENVIRONMENTS FOR ANY ANIMAL TO MAKE A LIVING IN.

Through the winter months the temperature never rises above zero, and the little food that can be gleaned is scratched from frozen soils beneath the snow. Brutal storms can thunder through, with winds raging at a hundred miles an hour. Musk oxen gather tight together, their dense shaggy fur coats probably the thickest on earth. Younger animals huddle within the mass, protected by the windbreak bodies. In the summer months, they have savage mosquitoes and blackfly to deal with. However, none of this compares with the attentions of their number one predator: the wolf. Wolf packs will only take on musk oxen if they are in good numbers – or especially desperate – as this is one of the great deadly defenders. They are low slung and brilliantly balanced. In a charge they can accelerate as fast as a sports car and they carry half a tonne of bulk behind their sharp horns and solid bony boss (top of the head). A single musk ox bull could hold off half a dozen wolves and injure or kill any that misjudge their attacks.

# LAPWING

## THE BROKEN WING DISPLAY OF SPECIES LIKE THE BLACKSMITH LAPWING WOULD HAVE TO BE ONE OF THE BRAVEST DEFENCES IN THE NATURAL WORLD.

These birds are ground nesters, and, not surprisingly, eventually a predator or person will wander too close to the nest. Some lapwing species will just fly nearby, making a huge amount of noise and dive-bombing the interloper to drive them away. Others will go one step further. The lapwing approaches as close as they dare, but doesn't fly. Instead, they stumble along the ground, holding one wing beneath them as if it is broken. For carnivores like foxes, which are irresistibly drawn to weakness and signs of injury, this is just too much temptation. The fox will chase the lapwing, which takes a route as far away from the nest as possible, always staying just far enough out of reach to keep the fox's attention. Then, when the danger is good and gone from their nest and chicks, the lapwing takes off and returns to parenting duties. Deadly, no. Daring... indubitably!

Below: Blacksmith lapwings are very aggressive and will attack any perceived threat to their nest and young, no matter the size – including this African fishing eagle.

Opposite: Swimming beside a sperm whale, the largest of the toothed whales.

Swimming alongside a sperm whale is one of the most overwhelming animal encounters.

# SPERM WHALE

## THE SPERM WHALE HAS HAD MUCH TO DEAL WITH IN RECENT CENTURIES.

Their only natural predator is the orca, and the sperm whale's defence against them is to get into a wagon-wheel formation, with their calves protected within. However, when commercial human whaling started to target sperm whales, this strategy did not help. Soon sperm whales learned that they could beat whalers in sailing boats by swimming upwind, where the boats couldn't follow. Once new methods took over in whaling, the wondrous whales learned to dive deep to evade capture, though this did mean sacrificing their calves.

# HIPPO

**I OFTEN TALK ABOUT THE HIPPO BEING THE SCARIEST ANIMAL IN THE WORLD TO BE UP CLOSE TO, AND ARGUABLY THE MOST DANGEROUS TOO.**

There are lots of reasons for that. They tend to live in murky waters, so they could be right under your canoe and you'd never know until it's too late. They protect their territory, are very protective of their calves and both males and females can be hugely aggressive. One of the worst scenarios is walking along a waterway by night and accidentally getting in the way of a hippo that wants to get back into its safe zone of the water. They will barrel right through to get past! Ultimately, though, it's all down to their remarkable attributes. The biggest hippos can weigh 3 tonnes, so more than your average car. They can have tusks that are as long as your arm, with a sharp slicing point at the end. And they are fast. Way faster than you would ever believe possible. I'd been saying for years that they could run 'faster than an Olympic athlete' without ever believing it. However, in Zambia for our last series, we saw one spooked at night, and it ran and ran and ran, far faster than a human ever could. Yet more reasons to treat this Deadly defender with absolute respect.

# 11. WEIRD WEAPONS

# ARCHER FISH

## A DEADLY CLASSIC THAT WE HAVE SOMEHOW NEVER MANAGED TO FILM IN OUR MANY YEARS SEARCHING!

These innocuous-looking fish swim near the surface, eyeing up overhanging twigs and branches. When they spot a bug wandering about above them, they will gulp in water, before coming up to the surface and blasting a super-soaker squirt up to the branches. Their accuracy is phenomenal, and inevitably they hit the bug square on, knocking it into the water to be devoured. The whole process is even more extraordinary when you remember that light is bent when it enters water (known as refraction), so the archer fish has to precisely allow for this when calculating exactly where to squirt.

Nature's finest marksman, the archer fish is a bullseye dead shot.

# BOMBARDIER BEETLE

**THESE BEETLES STORE TWO QUITE NORMAL CHEMICALS IN THEIR ABDOMEN, BUT WHEN ANNOYED THEY MIX THEM TOGETHER WITH AN ENZYME AND FIRE THEM OUT OF THEIR BACK END AT HIGH SPEEDS.**

The mixture can be 100°C and be fired hundreds of times in a single second. The accuracy is such that they can target an inquisitive lizard and send them scampering in agony.

# VELVET WORM

**NEITHER WORMS, NOR MADE OF VELVET, THESE REMARKABLE AND ANCIENT INVERTEBRATES HAVE A SUPERNATURAL AND STRANGE SUPERPOWER.**

Either side of the mouth, the creepy crawly has slime glands that secrete a kind of glue. They can fire this out over many times their own body length to ensnare potential prey. Much like the spitting cobra and spitting spider, this squirted goo spirals in the air. Spiralling (or rifling) in the barrel of a gun makes a bullet twist in the air, which enables it to stabilise and travel further. It's likely that this spiralling functions the same in the squirts of these beasts!

# SPITTING SPIDER

## SPIDERS IN THE SCYTODID GROUP ARE PROPER WEIRDOS, AND PROBABLY THE INSPIRATION FOR SPIDERMAN!

They have the vague look of a human skull on their body, and the most remarkable ability: they are capable of spitting goo all over predators. They mix a kind of gloopy glue in modified venom glands, before firing it out through their fangs. It contains both liquid silk and venom, and entangles other animals, making them an easy dinner for the spider. The whole process can only be captured on very special high-speed cameras as it happens too fast for the human eye to recognise, however in super slow mo you can see the 'spit' swirling around in strange circles before hitting its target.

The spitting spider unleashes venom and silk onto prey such as silverfish.

# SPITTING COBRA

## THE TRUE SPITTING COBRAS HAVE EXIT POINTS AT THE FRONT OF THEIR HOLLOW FANGS (RATHER THAN AT THE BASE, AS IN OTHER COBRA SPECIES) AND CAN PUT HUGE MUSCULAR PRESSURE ON THE VENOM GLANDS TO SQUEEZE VENOM OUT AND UP TOWARDS AN ATTACKER.

It's a bit unfair talking about the cobra's spat venom as a weapon. After all, this remarkable mechanism is purely used to defend the cobra from attack, and never against prey. I've worked with all the species of venom-spitting cobras, as well as snakes like the rinkhals that almost flick venom from their fangs, and while the amount of venom spat varies tremendously, and the distance travelled can be from 1m to 3m, the thing that is constant is accuracy. On some encounters with spitters I have worn sunglasses and the venom pretty much peppers the lenses, where my eyes would be. If I wasn't wearing glasses, then the venom would start to break down the cornea, eventually resulting in blindness.

## Snake defences

The spit of a cobra is just one of a multitude of different defence displays that snakes have, which enable them to frighten off animals that are too big to eat. The first of these, found in every kind of snake, is the hiss. This is not a continuous sound, but delivered on the out breath, with the body of the snake working like an accordion, opening and closing to drive breath out through a constricted throat. Next up would be the rattle of the rattlesnake, buttons of dried skin that flick together, driven by one of the fastest moving of vertebrate muscle groups. Every animal that lives in rattler territory knows that means trouble. Next is the hood seen in many members of the cobra family, and a fair few other unrelated snakes too: flexible ribs spread wide to make the whole head end of the snake look huge. Then there's mock striking, standing up tall, tail flicking and finally venom spitting. All of these mechanisms are used to make the snake seem more frightening, to drive away other animals so they don't get too close. Most snakes will do absolutely anything to avoid biting you – a defensive bite is the absolute last resort.

The mongoose is all attitude and fearlessness.

SLENDER MONGOOSE

VS

BOOMSLANG SNAKE

The boomslang is a venomous African snake that inflates its neck when defensive.

**THE CONFLICT BETWEEN SNAKE AND MONGOOSE WAS CAPTURED IN RUDYARD KIPLING'S *THE JUNGLE BOOK*, WITH THE HEROIC UNDERDOG RIKKI-TIKKI-TAVI BESTING HIS EVIL SERPENTINE COMPETITOR.** In the wild world, this is also often how this fight ends. The two foes appear irresistibly driven to take each other on, even though it will surely be a fight to the death. The mongoose bounces from side to side and straight up in the air, the snake lunges forward looking to get its venomous fangs into its mammal tormentor. Should the snake land a bite, it is not the end. Mongooses have a mutated gene that makes them especially resistant to an element of the snake's neurotoxic venom. That doesn't mean they're immune, and they can still be killed by snakebites, but it does give them an advantage. (Interestingly, this is the same mutation the snakes themselves have, meaning they also are resistant to snake bite!) While the snake keeps facing the mongoose down, it has a chance, but once it retreats, the mongoose will leap in to deliver the finishing bite.

# 12.
# SUPER SKILLS

# AYE-AYE

## THE AYE-AYE IS A CURIOUS BEASTIE, A LEMUR WITH THE EARS OF A BAT, THE BODY OF A SQUIRREL AND THE EYES OF A DEMENTED MONSTER.

Each hand is adorned with one extra-long bony digit like a witch's finger. They use it to tap on trees, and their adept hearing then enables them to pinpoint the grubs wriggling around inside the wood. They use chisel teeth to excavate the bark, then the long finger with its creepy fingernail to hook the larvae out into the open. All in all, a living nightmare of a beast.

# CHAMELEON

## THE TONGUE OF THE CHAMELEON IS A HYPER-CHARGED MARVEL AT GRABBING HOLD OF BUGS LIKE LOCUSTS FROM NEARBY BRANCHES.

The chameleon's eyes are held within volcano-shaped turrets and they can swivel around independently. When they spot prey, they swing around until both eyes are focused on it, giving them depth perception. Once they have this, they slightly open the mouth, priming a tongue that can be as long as the chameleon's body. The muscles of the tongue are compressed, like a spring being pressed down and then released. The firing takes mere milliseconds. The end of the tongue is a sticky cup that affixes to sorry bugs, before drawing them in for a messy and noisy munching.

The chameleon has the ultimate X-Men superpower: an elastic tongue that can fire out at prey!

Opposite: The aye-aye is the world's largest noctural primate and one of the most strange with its elongated middle finger.

Right: This veiled chameleon has a tongue that is twice as long as its body to catch insect prey.

# GIANT ANTEATER

**ANOTHER ODDITY OF AN ANIMAL, THE GIANT ANTEATER'S HEAD IS A BONY TUBE WITH NO TEETH INSIDE.**

The tongue, though, is extraordinary, up to 60cm in length, with teeny backwards-facing spikes all over it to prevent its ant prey escaping. It is always covered with slobbery spit and can hoover up ants, whizzing out at up to 160 times a minute. They are generally speaking timid beasts, with almost invisible eyes but a phenomenal sense of smell. However, their claws are hyper-developed for tearing apart concrete-hard termite mounds, and there are plenty of tales of them defending themselves with a death hug and ripping, shredding slashes.

# ALLOSAURUS

**IT WAS ALWAYS ASSUMED THAT THE ALLOSAURUS WAS A BIG BITER, MUCH LIKE OTHER THEROPODS, CHOMPING WITH A HUGE AND VIOLENT BITE FORCE.**

However, when more modern techniques and knowledge were applied to Allosaurus fossils, scientists realised that the bones that would affix biting muscles were extremely weak, whereas the neck muscles were superior. The new idea is that Allosaurus used their upper jaw like an axe, swinging it down onto hapless prey to chop into them.

# STOPLIGHT LOOSEJAW

**THIS STRANGE DEEP-SEA DRAGONFISH HAS THE ABILITY TO PROJECT ITS JAW FORWARD TO ALMOST HALF ITS BODY LENGTH, SNATCHING AT OTHER FISH.**

The resistance that would come from having a jaw covered in flesh as other animals do is lost in the stoplight, as they have only bones there, thus allowing the jaw to grab prey at lightning-fast speed. In addition these fish have a remarkable ability to create red bioluminescence. As most fish at this depth cannot perceive this light, it's as if they are hunting with an invisible spotlight.

Opposite: A giant anteater baby's tongue will grow to up to 60cm in length by the time it has reached maturity.

Above: Illustration of an Allosaurus with a fiercesome set of teeth and incredibly wide-opening jaws.

Right: Northern stoplight loosejaw is a deep sea species with an extendable jaw, which lives below a depth of 500m.

# DEADLY DEATH MATCH

The giant river otter is a pack-hunting savage, and will take on anything in its waters.

## GIANT RIVER OTTER

# VS

## CAIMAN

Caiman may be armoured and have a potent bite, but stand no chance against smart and organised otters.

## THE GIANT RIVER OTTER IS THE LONGEST MEMBER OF THE WEASEL FAMILY, A GROUP KNOWN FOR PUNCHING ABOVE THEIR WEIGHT.

While most of their diet is made up of fish like piranhas, they seem to know no fear and will gang up on animals many times their own size, quite often taking on decent-sized caimans. I've been lucky enough to have a ringside seat at one of these events, and the swings in fortune were phenomenal. To begin with, as the otters advanced, the caiman (which was as big as me) sank silently beneath the water in among the tangled branches of a fallen tree, and it seemed would just slink away. However, the otters almost immediately found it, and the caiman returned to the surface. Now the croc began lashing with its tail, baring its vicious teeth and hissing like a huge snake. It seemed the otters had taken on way more than they could handle. The tables turned again and again, as an otter would leap in, come millimetres from being savaged and leap back. Throughout the exchange, the otters squealed, whistled and gargled, making an unholy racket. Finally the croc bid a hasty retreat, with its tormentors following. We missed filming the final knockout, but the otters triumphed and the caiman became dinner, eaten with the same outrageous noises in the background. Just like I'd say to the guy who stole my luminous trainers, 'You can run, but you can't hide.'

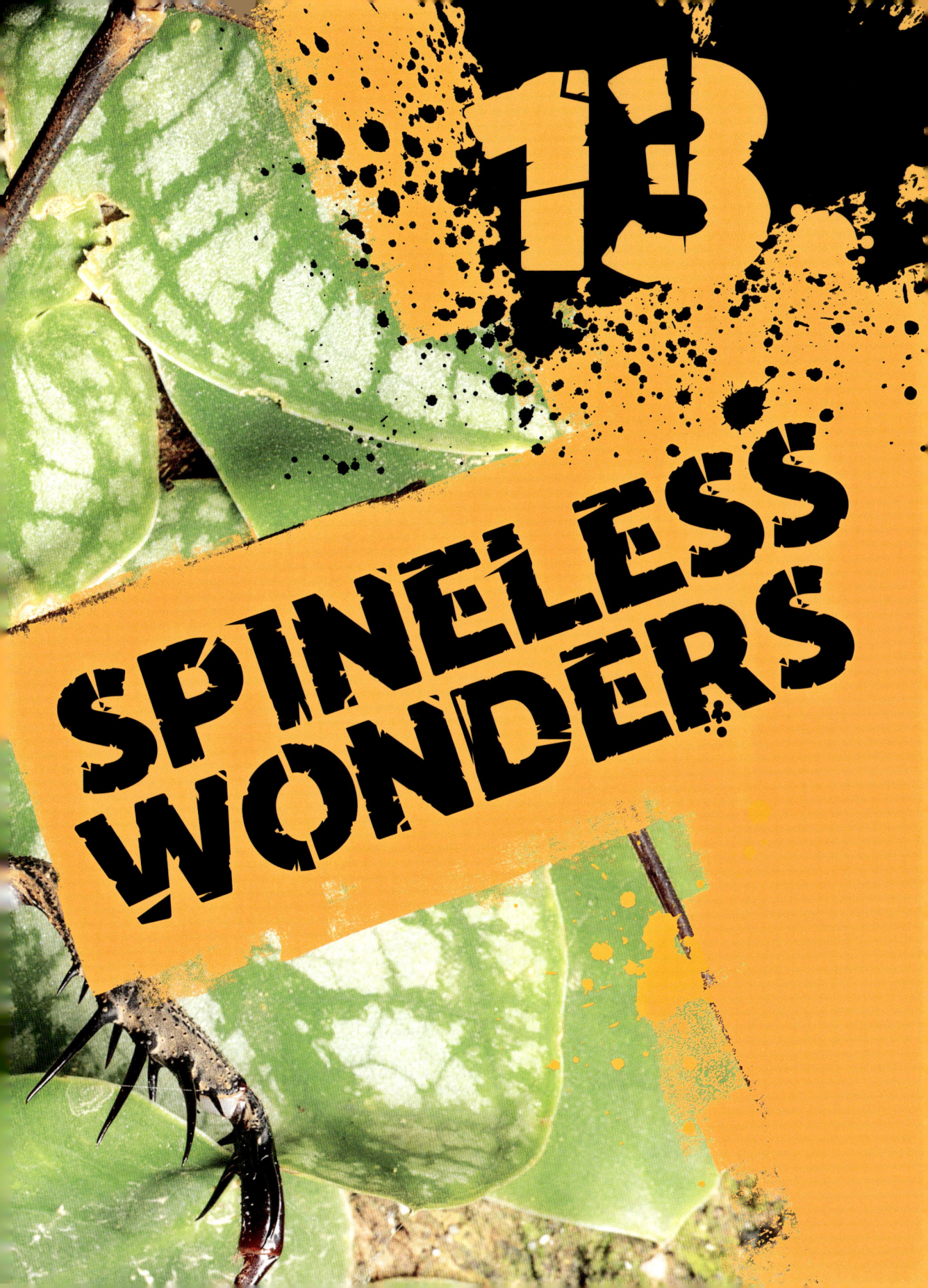

# 13

# SPINELESS WONDERS

# SCOLOPENDRA

## HANDS DOWN THE CREEPIEST CRITTER ON THE PLANET, THE LONGEST SPECIES OF CENTIPEDE IS A LIVING HORROR SHOW.

Scolopendra gigantea, the giant centipede, can be 30cm long – that's the length of my forearm. The front pair of legs are modified into venom-injecting claws, and their venom has a neurotoxin that can create phenomenal amounts of pain in anything that gets bitten. A pal of mine got bitten to the hand and it swelled up like a blown-up washing-up glove. These huge centipedes can catch and eat rodents, lizards, birds... and there's one cave in Venezuela where they've picked up the ability to wander out on the cave ceiling, hang down in waiting and catch bats on the wing as they fly out in the evening.

Right: Giant centipedes have diets that include lizards, toads and bats as well as small invertebrates.

Below: The solifuge – also known as a wind scorpion, sun spider or camel spider – is neither spider or scorpion; it is a separate arachnid group entirely.

Oppposite: The bobbit worm ranges in size from less than 10cm to nearly 3m!

# SOLIFUGE

## THE CAMEL SPIDER OR SOLIFUGE IS ANOTHER CREEPSTER OF HALLOWEEN PROPORTIONS.

With long hairy legs, they scurry around relentlessly at great pace, snapping at prey with four slicing dicing mandibles. They are most often found in arid desert environments, and in Southern Africa are known as Kalahari Ferraris for their sheer pace. Solifuges are not true spiders (though they are arachnids) and don't have venom, but they do have quite a nip and don't hesitate to use it.

# BOBBIT WORM

**YET ANOTHER NIGHTMARE OF NATURE, THE BOBBIT OR BRISTLE WORM, ALSO KNOWN AS SAND STRIKER OR TRAP-JAW WORM, CAN BE TRULY GIANT, GETTING UP TO 3M IN LENGTH.**

This bulk is hidden in a long, thin burrow down on the seabed. When their five antennae are triggered by fish swimming above, they snap out at impossible pace, to grab hold of prey with their slicing mandibles. The force of their bite is so intense that they might chop a fish clean in half with one snip.

Ancient, and a nightmare of nature.

# WHIP SPIDER

## AMBLYPYGI (AS THEY ARE MORE PROPERLY KNOWN) ARE ANOTHER ARACHNID THAT COULD GIVE YOU NIGHTMARES.

With giant spiked club-like appendages that function as grabbers, but look like mediaeval torture devices, and great elongated limbs for scampering around sideways like flattened crabs, the whip spider is a creep-show supreme. With poor eyesight, they are either nocturnal or live in dark habitats like caves or inside giant hollow trees. The front pair of legs are especially long and tap around in the dark, functioning both as tactile sensory organs and as a specialised tool. As they are so long, they tap a good distance in front of the whip spider's claws. Often they'll tap on the back of an unsuspecting bush cricket, which will charge forward to its doom.

# SCUTIGERA

## ANOTHER SCUTTLY TERROR THAT HAUNTS THE DARKEST PLACES AND COULD SEND A SPECIAL FORCES SOLDIER RUNNING SCREAMING FOR SAFETY!

The scutigera is a group of venomous centipedes that contains the common house centipede, whose bite is said to be no more painful than that of a honey bee sting. However, when working in the famous Gomantong caves in Borneo, we met with local bird's nest collectors who feared these scuttly centipedes more than anything else. They claimed one of their number had been bitten by one of these and had died in terrible pain just days later...

Opposite: A tailless whip scorpion devouring a katydid, in tropical forest in Ecuador, and on a man's arm to show size, Tobago.

Right: European house centipede (Scutigera) found on the ceiling of a limestone cave in Croatia.

The scutigera is arguably the creepiest creature around.

DEADLY DEATH MATCH

The world's largest wasp has a sting to die for.

TARANTULA HAWK

VS

TARANTULA

168 DEADLY

The world's largest spiders are a living larder for the wasp's offspring.

**MURDER IN MINIATURE HAS NEVER BEEN MORE SINISTER.** To many people, the tarantula spider is the most freaky, creepy thing on earth. However, they have a sworn enemy. Wasps in the family Pompilidae (the spider hunters) specialise in exploiting them. These huge wasps – some of which are the biggest wasps on earth – have fiendish females who are always looking for somewhere to lay their eggs. As adults the wasps lap nectar for food, but their spider foe is the perfect host for their growing babies. The female wasps course around using their sensitive antennae to smell for the presence of tarantulas, and once they find one, battle begins. The spiders are far from defenceless, rearing up and baring their giant fangs, but the wasps scuttle around, jabbing between their legs with the giant stinger at the end of their abdomen. I've been lucky enough to see these battles in action several times, and the wasps have always won. A potent sting from the wasp, and the spider is paralysed, unable to fight back any more. The wasp will then drag the lifeless spider to a burrow, where she lays her single egg on its body. In the most grim example of parasitism (when one organism lives on or in another) in nature, the wasp's larva will hatch out and feed inside the body of the spider, doing all it can to eat around the vital organs, so the paralysed spider stays alive. It's enough to give you nightmares.

14.

TOUGH NUTS

# TARDIGRADE

ALSO KNOWN AS WATER BEARS OR MOSS PIGLETS (I ONLY JUST LEARNED THAT AND AM BEYOND CHARMED!), TARDIGRADES ARE A GROUP OF EIGHT-LEGGED TEENY TINY ANIMALS THAT ARE IN THE RECORD BOOKS AS BEING THE TOUGHEST CREATURES ON EARTH.

They can be found in all sorts of places, but you won't see one unless you have a microscope. They can withstand highs and lows of temperature, enormous pressure, desiccation (removal of water), starvation and radiation. They have even been blasted into outer space. They're found in 'easy' environments like tropical forests and moss, but can also be found in hot springs and glaciers, and on the highest mountain peaks. If they go without food and water, they retreat into a state known as the 'tun', where they can basically have a kip for ten years or so. Then add a drop of water and they bounce back to life like nothing ever happened. They can live for 30 years at -20°C, a few days at -200°C, and for a few minutes at 150°C. Wow!

# MANTIS AND WIDOW SPIDER

**ARGUABLY THE MOST GRISLY ELEMENT OF NATURE IS THE MATING RITUALS OF CERTAIN INVERTEBRATES, ESPECIALLY WIDOW SPIDERS AND PRAYING MANTISES.**

On occasion, they practise what is known as sexual cannibalism. Essentially, the girl eats her boyfriend before, during or after he tries to woo her. Some people think this is all down to mistaken identity, with the female just thinking her suitor might be a light snack. Others suggest that he is so keen to pass on his genes that he sacrifices himself, and the female gets a nice protein meal before having babies. Either way, it's not something you want to think about too much! This happens most often in species where the female is much bigger than the male (sexual dimorphism) and has also been witnessed in anacondas.

Opposite: Tardigrades, or water bears, can live in extreme conditions such as hot springs, deep underwater and even in high levels of radiation!

Below: Female mantis feeing on male immediately after mating, an example of sexual cannibalism.

# RED-LEGGED SERIEMA AND SECRETARY BIRD

## EVEN THOUGH THESE TWO BIRDS OCCUR ON DIFFERENT CONTINENTS, I'VE PUT THEM BOTH IN HERE TOGETHER, AS THEY ARE SO UNBELIEVABLY SIMILAR.

South America's seriema stalks the long grasses of the savannah, often in pairs. Their long legs hold them up high enough to spot things wandering around in the grass from an elevated position. We've watched them catching massive tarantulas and just plucking off the legs like twiglets to munch on them. They will stamp on the most venomous snakes found in their environment and slurp them down like spaghetti. The secretary bird is very similar, but found in Africa. The name is thought to refer to the quills they bear on their heads, which look like the quilled pens secretaries would once have carried behind their ears. When two very different animals from different parts of the world evolve the same attributes or ways of dealing with problems, we call this 'convergent evolution'.

Left: Secretary birds, found in Africa, are known for their hunting technique of delivering a series of forceful kicks on prey.

Opposite: Red-legged seriema threat display, Brazil.

# MEERKAT

**THE MONGOOSE FAMILY IS HARD AS NAILS. LIKE MANY OF MY ERA, I GREW UP WITH TALES OF THE JUNGLE BOOK AND RIKKI-TIKKI-TAVI THE MONGOOSE, WHO TOOK ON A COBRA AND WON.**

Well, these tales are built around real events – mongooses will absolutely take on cobras many times their size, and often triumph. Meerkats are a member of the mongoose family, super social, working together as a gang or mob, and worthy of immense respect. They live in places like the Kalahari Desert where water is scarce, and they smash scorpions by biting the ends of their tails off, before munching them down like crisps.

The meerkat to me sums up what Deadly is all about: they look cute - especially the babies - but will happily assault a 2m long highly venomous Cape cobra, or savage a scorpion that could kill an adult human!

deadly

## STELLER'S SEA EAGLE

**MY FAVOURITE BIRD IN THE WORLD, NAMED AFTER THE LEGENDARY NATURALIST GEORG STELLER, THE STELLER'S SEA EAGLE IS A SOARING SUPERHERO.**

I've been lucky enough to film them hunting fish out on the ice floes north of Japan and scouring beaches in Kamchatka, Russia, for washed-up salmon. They are the biggest and most impressive of all eagles: on the wing they look like a flying dinner table, on the ground they look as if they could fly away with the giant brown bears they hunt among. They have to endure extremes of Arctic cold, fierce winds and then searing summer suns, and have an air of superiority and menace beyond compare. I adore them and would cheerfully have one as a pet... if I didn't fear they'd fly away with my dog. Or one of my children.

# ARCTIC FOX

## YET ANOTHER ANIMAL WHOSE CUTE DEMEANOUR BELIES A TOUGHNESS BEYOND IMAGINING.

In their brown summer coat, they look like a scrawny miniature wolf, and wander the tundra stealing birds' eggs and chicks. However, it's during an Arctic winter that they excel. Active throughout the months when the sun never rises and temperatures are regularly colder than the inside of your freezer, Arctic foxes just keep going. They may follow in the footsteps of polar bears, munching the food they leave behind, or nip in to steal some food off bigger wolves or huskies. Their dense coat keeps them warm in the iciest conditions and their furry tail wraps around their face to act like a fur hood. They don't even start shivering until it's -30°C. Respect!

Opposite: The Arctic fox can also be called white, polar or snow fox, and can smell a seal's den from a mile away even in the depths of the Arctic winter.

Left: Headlight elaters, also known as headlight beetles, are one type of click beetle known for their bioluminescence.

# CLICK BEETLE

## THE HIGHEST AMOUNT OF G-FORCE UNDERGONE BY ANY ANIMAL IS EXPERIENCED BY THE HUMBLE CLICK BEETLE.

When flipped onto their backs, they pop a peg out of a groove on their underside with a click and are catapulted straight up into the air with a force of 400G, and a peak of 2,300G. To give you an idea of what this means, I underwent 5G in a tight turn in a fighter jet, and went bright green and was violently sick! Some click beetles, known as flashlight or stoplight click beetles, additionally have bright fluorescent patches on their head and abdomen, making them look even more like a fabulous explosively leaping kids' toy!

Officially the world's most aggressive animal, the honey badger has met its match.

HONEY BADGER

VS

PORCUPINE

The deadliest defender can drive away and even kill lions.

**HONEY BADGER DON'T CARE.** The honey badger is officially the most aggressive animal in the world. A single honey badger has been known to drive lions off their kill, using pure force of attitude. This is a beast with no fear, but that doesn't mean they always triumph. The porcupine is Africa's largest rodent and one of the greatest Deadly defenders on the planet. They don't fire their quills, as has often been believed, but will back into an attacker, peppering them with their detachable spines (actually modified hairs). I've had a few spines in my leg from a friendly but boisterous tame porcupine. They hurt like crazy and were surprisingly hard to take out. Imagine trying to do the same thing if your entire face was stuck full of them... and you didn't have fingers to take them out with! This is one *ratel* who will never mess with a porcupine again!

# 15 PARASITES

# EMERALD COCKROACH WASP

## SOMETIMES KNOWN AS THE JEWEL WASP, THIS IS ONE OF THE MOST BEAUTIFUL YET MOST SINISTER KILLERS IN THE WHOLE NATURAL WORLD.

They appear to have been made out of emeralds and rubies. The male is small and indistinct, the female larger – and, as so often, more deadly! The female will find a cockroach far bigger than she is and sting the insect with extraordinary precision, paralysing its front legs. As the wasp is so much smaller than the roach, she can't carry it to her burrow, so instead the second sting is into the brain, and appears to take out the cockroach's sense of free will and desire to escape. The wasp then leads the cockroach like a dog on a leash to its doom. She will lay her egg on it, and it hatches out and feeds on the still living roach. If that doesn't give you nightmares...

# TSETSE FLY

## COULD THIS BE THE MOST SIGNIFICANT ANIMAL ON EARTH TO HUMAN HISTORY?

For when explorers started to move into sub-Saharan Africa, they found themselves afflicted by a strange malaise – sleeping sickness. Even the toughest just found themselves crashed out in the shade, unable to move, taken over by impossible lethargy. Untreated, it would lead to death. Because of this, huge areas of Africa were just left, and people travelled around them to make homes and lives in places without the dreaded sleeping sickness. Now we know that this is down to simple organisms called trypanosomes found in the saliva of tsetse flies. Weirdly, the fly is attracted to the colour blue, so in places today where the illness is rife, big blue traps will be hung alongside rivers and roads to catch them.

Above: Jewel wasp leading American cockroach prey by its antennae to her nest, where she will lay her egg on it.

Left: Here a tsetse fly is swollen with blood after feeding on unlucky human...

Opposite: ...but it is the mosquito that is the biggest killer of humans, responsible for several lethal human diseases, including malaria.

# MOSQUITO

## WITHOUT QUESTION THE MOST DEADLY ANIMAL ON THE PLANET TODAY TO US AS HUMAN BEINGS IS THE MOSQUITO.

In terms of how they affect us, and have done since our ape ancestors came down from the treetops, mosquitoes have been our biggest killer ever – more than all the human wars and strife combined. It's not the mossies themselves: they are just small female flies searching for a blood meal to raise their babies. Instead, it's the diseases carried in their spit. Dengue fever, Japanese encephalitis, yellow fever and of course malaria are just a few of the mosquito-borne diseases that kill more than a million every year.

'If you think you are too small to make a difference, try sleeping with a mosquito.'
– Dalai Lama XIV

# CORDYCEPS

## THE MOST DEADLY FUNGUS IMAGINABLE, AND INSPIRATION FOR THE GAME AND TV SERIES *THE LAST OF US*.

This lethal parasite is eaten by bugs while still a spore. The spore then matures and the fruiting body erupts out of the host. When fully mature, the fungus can be incredibly beautiful, but it's a creepy thought... What would it be like if it could infect a human?

Right: Cordyceps fungus parasitising a spider. The fungus alters the behaviour of its host before killing it, ensuring the insect will die in a high place, enabling the spores to be spread easily.

Below: Cookiecutter shark, found in deep water off coast of Hawaii, Pacific Ocean.

Below (inset): The lower jaw of a cookiecutter shark, showing its circular row of sharp teeth which leave a perfect circular scar.

Opposite: A land snail infected with a parasitic flatworm, causing its eyestalks to swell with pulsating sacs that resemble caterpillars.

The cookiecutter is the sneakiest of parasite sharks, slicing neat chunks from its host.

# ZOMBIE SNAIL WORM

## THE GREEN-BANDED BROODSAC IS A KIND OF FLATWORM THAT HAS TO PASS THROUGH TWO DIFFERENT ANIMALS TO COMPLETE ITS LIFECYCLE.

First the eggs will be eaten by snails, and they transform in the eye stalks of the snail to create weird pulsing shapes that look a bit like caterpillars. Birds will spy these and come and chow down on the snail, thus swallowing the worm within. The adult worm then transforms again inside the bird, and emerges as eggs in its poo. As if this wasn't weird and macabre enough, the parasite affects the snail's behaviour: those that are infected will take themselves to high, well lit, prominent places, so they are easier for birds to spot.

# COOKIECUTTER SHARK

## THIS WEIRD CIGAR-SHAPED SHARK IS A SNEAKY PARASITE, CHOWING DOWN ON LARGER ANIMALS, OFTEN AT NIGHT.

It has astonishing dentition (teeth) and slices perfect circular plugs of flesh out of its target. If you ever see a round scar on the body of a whale, tuna, sailfish or seal, think cookiecutter. There are even two cases of them biting people, and the wounds have been horrific.

# VAMPIRE MOTH

## THIS BIZARRE MOTH FROM MALAYSIA HAS A SHORT, STOUT, SHARP PROBOSCIS AND JABS THROUGH THE SKIN OF LARGE MAMMALS TO SUCK THEIR BLOOD.

Whatever next, a cannibal butterfly?! It seems the ability developed from related moths that would suck on sap from leaves, or puncture fruit to get at the juice within. Some are even known to lap at the liquid dribbling from certain animals' eyes. However, the ability to actually drive the proboscis through the skin to drink blood has only occasionally been recorded.

# COWBIRD

## THE TEAM AND I WERE IN SURINAME FILMING *DEADLY 60* WHEN WE WITNESSED THIS PHENOMENON FOR THE FIRST TIME.

A tapir was standing at the riverside, covered in black crow-like birds. As we watched, he lay down and the cowbirds proceeded to bounce all over his body, picking off ticks and lice and munching them down. The tapir rolled over onto his back so they could clean his belly. It was then that we witnessed one of the birds opening up a wound on the tapir's tummy so it could lap the blood that flowed out, making the bird not a kindly servant, but a potential parasite! Our scientific paper on this behaviour was published in the winter of 2024 – new science discovered by us on *Deadly*!

# FLEA

## IT STARTS WITH A LITTLE FLEA, THAT JUMPS UPON A RAT...

The rat flea was carrier of the Black Death or bubonic plague, which resulted in the deaths of tens of millions of people – arguably the most lethal pandemic our world has ever seen. Fleas feed on blood, and though they may specialise in one particular host (such as bat fleas or the house cat flea), they can spread from one to another really easily. Plague is not the only disease they carry, and their bites cause itching and discomfort. Even writing this paragraph has me itching, even though I don't have fleas. Well, I don't think I have fleas...

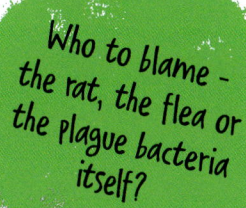

Who to blame – the rat, the flea or the plague bacteria itself?

16.

STRENGTH

# CONSTRICTOR SNAKES

**THE BIG PYTHONS AND BOAS MAY HAVE 800 BONES, AND EVERY ONE HAS MUSCLES ATTACHED, MEANING THAT FOR THEIR SIZE THEY ARE FORMIDABLY STRONG.** The technique of constriction is overpowering – literally. It was once believed that constriction was all about strangulation or suffocation, but it now seems it's more subtle than that. Prey animals may not have broken ribs, but their organs may simply have burst. The most reliable way these snakes kill is by blocking the vagus nerve that serves the heart. Once the heart has stopped beating, the constrictor stops squeezing so they don't waste any energy on a prey that's already dead.

The boa constrictor is the only animal whose scientific and common name is the same!

## The cave of hanging serpents

Fancy kneeling on your own in total darkness on the floor of a cave, knowing you're squidging into centuries of bat poo, listening with keen ears to the fluttering wings of bats that occasionally fan your face as they fly past? How about if you knew that somewhere out there in the pitch black, dozens of snakes were slithering down from the ceiling, getting themselves into position, priming themselves to strike? La cueva de las serpientes colgantes is as creepy as place as you could ever find yourself. And I should know: I've spent four nights of my life totally on my own in its darkened interior. Why alone? Well, through trial and error, we worked out that the snakes would not emerge and start hunting the bats if there was even the tiniest bit of light or noise. Even the little green light on my camera that shows it's switched on had to be taped over. I couldn't use light of any kind; even to get into position I had to feel my way across the bat-poo floor. I then set up an infrared camera on a tripod, pointed at a likely spot, knelt down (the ceiling is chest height so you can't stand) and waited. For hours and hours on end. Finally, a number of Mexican night snakes slithered down to hang like socks on a washing line, snapping at the bats if they grazed them with their wings. They have to be incredibly strong to hold up a portion of their body while hanging from the cave walls, so they can actively strike at the bats. Once and only once have I managed to capture a hunt. Interestingly, once the snake has the bat in their mouth, they don't mind the light at all, and I managed to snap a shot while the dangler scoffed the flapping bat down in one go!

# INVERTEBRATE STRONGMEN

## AN INSECT'S EXOSKELETON IS COMPOSED OF A REMARKABLE PROTEIN CALLED CHITIN.

This can be tanned, hard and tough, or much more flexible. The alignment of these chitinous limbs, plus their musculature and method of breathing limits how big bugs can get. However, it does lead to extreme pound-for-pound strength. A worker leafcutter ant can carry many times its own body weight in its mandibles for long journeys. A bit like us trying to run a marathon with a horse in our mouths.

# HERCULES BEETLE

## HERCULES WAS A LEGENDARY STRONGMAN, SO THE HERCULES BEETLE IS DEFINITELY WELL NAMED!

They can resist 850 times their own body weight, carrying it upon their back. That's like me carrying a jumbo jet! This incredible strength is used in tussling with other male Hercules beetles as they battle over females. However, they don't need anything like this amount of resistance and it's probably a side-effect of their formidably robust exoskeleton.

In the record books as the strongest animal for its size on earth.

Male polar and grizzly bears are the largest land carnivores, and preposterously strong.

## GRIZZLY BEAR

**IN REAL TERMS THE BIGGEST BEARS ARE PROBABLY THE STRONGEST OF ALL PREDATORS.**

They've been seen effortlessly lifting rocks that are hundreds of kilos in weight to get at the bugs beneath. The closely related polar bear has been seen dragging beluga, narwhal and walrus from the water and is staggeringly powerful.

# Polar bear encounter

While filming in Svalbard inside the Arctic circle, we saw many sides
to the polar bear in one single expedition. The first of those was a
sight of a bear that had clearly caught and killed a huge bearded
seal and dragged it up onto an ice floe to eat. His pure white face
was stained red with the blood of the seal, which had been stripped
to the bone. My next encounter was considerably more frightening.
Out among the ice floes in my kayak, all alone and a mile from the
main boat, I got a call on the radio from my team. 'Steve, Steve,
there's a polar bear swimming straight towards you!' At this point
I couldn't see it, and I soon figured out why... The bear had noticed
me from a distance and was stalking me! He was putting the
icebergs in between me and him so I couldn't see him and he could
approach unnoticed. All the time the crew were talking to me. 'He's
diving underwater, Steve, we can't see him...' I have never felt so
alone and so vulnerable in all my life. And then out of nowhere,
there he was in front of me. Knowing now that I saw him, he swam
past, then suddenly I made three or four explosive paddle strokes
and he came after me, doubtless thinking I could be breakfast!
Needless to say, I have never kayaked faster in my life!

# ELEPHANT

## WITHOUT QUESTION THE STRONGEST LAND ANIMAL IS THE AFRICAN ELEPHANT.

The record-breaking specimen was a male measured in Angola, who weighed 9 tonnes – as much as a double decker bus. I've seen both Asian and African elephants lift tree trunks that must have weighed tonnes, and they did it as if they were matchsticks. Probably even more remarkable is that they do that lifting with their trunk, which is an extension of their nose! It's also one of the most sensitive and adaptable of all tools, able to pick up small objects with a daintiness that belies their size.

Below: An African elephant is without doubt the strongest land animal in the world – capable of lifting its own body weight, up to 6,000kg!

Opposite: Keeping a wary distance from an adult African elephant, complete with tusks.

## Ellie encounters

Over the years the elephant has given me so much joy, and so many heart-lifting moments. They are social and caring but can be playful or petulant. They have, however, also given me a few utterly terrifying moments. The first was on my first ever wildlife series in 1999. The crew and I were on foot on the Mozambique/Zimbabwe border, trekking through a scrubby forest, when we came face to face with a lone bull ellie. He was huge and clearly didn't like having us around. Trumpeting loudly and flapping his ears, he charged at us. There were no big trees to climb or hide behind, no jeep to get into and drive away. The massive male stopped no more than five metres away from me. It had been a 'mock charge', one designed to frighten us, but without any lethal intent.

A decade later, we were filming in Nepal, again on foot, and we saw a male elephant sprinting towards us over the plains. He was a good distance away, but our guides reacted with utter terror, dropping everything and sprinting for our vehicles. The male's charge was silent and directly towards us. As we got in the vehicles and drove off, he was hot on our heels and didn't stop running, even after we were clearly going to get away. My guides told me afterwards that he was a 'rogue' elephant, who had killed several people in a local town just a few days before.

As a side note, some scientists suggest that this habit of older elephants to go rogue could be down to their teeth. As they age, an ellie's teeth wear right down, and for many of them the teeth and gums get horribly infected, swollen and filled with maggots. The pain must be unreal. It's suggested that it's this very pain that turns normal elephants into killers.

Megaraptor was a theropod with the arms of a bodybuilder and claws to match!

# MEGARAPTOR

**WHILE MOST OF THE THEROPODS WE KNOW OF HAD STUMPY LITTLE FOREARMS, MEGARAPTOR IS AN EXCEPTION.**

Its giant muscular arms would have been capable of lifting a tree trunk, or of tackling substantial prey. Perhaps the question really is not why Megaraptor had these arms, but why other theropods did not. Surely they would have been more effective with weapons like these? One species in this group is Maip, relatively recently discovered. It looks as if it had arms like a bodybuilder, and could have used these as one of its main weapons.

Opposite: Illustration of what Megaraptor may have looked like – including terrifying long hand claws.

Above: Harpy eagles are one of the world's largest and strongest eagles, with rear talons the same size as a grizzly bear's claws.

# HARPY EAGLE

## THE WHOLE HISTORY OF FLIGHT HAS BEEN ALL ABOUT REDUCING WEIGHT.

The harpy eagle, however, is a bird that can weigh up to 9kg and fly away not only with its own huge weight, but with a monkey or sloth in its talons. This is one seriously powerful bird. The harpy has a rear talon that is as stout, curved and pointed as a grizzly bear claw. It is used as a stiletto dagger, stabbed into its target. When climbing trees to film harpies coming back to their nest, we have to wear the kind of body armour that the military wear, to prevent them from flying in and stabbing us. One of my ropes access heroes was attacked by a harpy while rigging a giant rainforest tree, and the talon went right through his stab vest! He says that without it, he would have without doubt been killed.

# CHIMPANZEE

## CHIMPS ARE OFTEN UNDERESTIMATED AS THEIR YOUNG ARE SO UTTERLY ADORABLE, AND THEY TEND TO BE THE ONES WE SEE MOST OFTEN ON TV.

The reason why we see only baby chimps looking cute is that the adults are absolute horror shows! The adult male chimp looks plain frightening – like a hairy bodybuilder, with overlong arms, bald head and a look that says, 'I am trouble.' I guess because we are also so often shown chimps eating bananas in kids' books, we tend to be less aware of the fact that they can be hunters. On *Deadly* we've filmed them hunting red colobus monkeys, and we were also the first crew ever to get footage of one catching a tortoise in Gabon, Africa. The animal that found the poor tortoise carried it away in one hand, before smashing it open on the buttress roots of a tree. Adult chimps may be smaller than humans, but their strength is almost unbelievable: they can bend metal bars and smash up furniture... Let's just say they're far from the perfect house guest.

Deadly was the first TV crew to film chimpanzees catching tortoises to eat - the perfect takeaway food in its own tough lunch box.

The great white can only get the upper hand when the light is low but it isn't dark!

## FUR SEAL

# VS

## GREAT WHITE SHARK

The fur seal is agile, with great eyesight and tactile whiskers.

**AT FIRST SIGHT, THIS WOULD BE THE DEADLY DEATH MATCH WITH THE MOST OBVIOUS OUTCOME.** The wide-eyed fur seal – cuter than a bag of puppies – against the most menacing animal on our planet. There is no doubt that often the great white does indeed dominate the cuddly-looking marine mammal. Around some seal colonies, great whites will patrol at dusk and dawn, and when the seals' eyesight is compromised in low light, the shark will come thundering up from depth, smashing them at the surface, only for momentum to carry them up and out of the water in what's known as a breach. Often this first lunge is lethal, leaving the seal mortally wounded. However, in many places around the world, seals and sea lions will gang up on their attackers, with dozens of nifty seals using their superior dancing skills and lion-like teeth to give the sharks a proper pasting.

## 10.

### BOLAS SPIDER

The bolas is an ancient Latin American weapon: balls on twine that can be twirled and flung by horse-riding gauchos (South American cowboys) to take down animals by tangling their legs. The bolas spider kind of does the same thing! Using a capture 'blob' on the end of a string of silk, they swing and twirl and aim the weapon at flying moths that get within range. The spiders emit sex pheromones from their rear ends, which attract the moths to get closer, and some look like bird droppings in order to evade capture by their avian predators.

## 9.

### BROWN RECLUSE SPIDER

The brown recluse is one of the very few spiders in the world that justify people being arachnophobic (scared of spiders). Their bite injects a venom that can rot flesh and cause nasty injuries. However, probably the thing that makes them scariest is how... average they look. They're not like a black widow or funnel-web that is instantly recognisable. They just look like a normal spider, and that leads people to kill loads of harmless spiders, just because they look like recluses.

## 8.

### TRAPDOOR SPIDER

The different species of trapdoor spider spend their days within burrows, where they can escape from predators and hide from potential prey. Some species make a door to their lair, fashioned from a plug of silk and earth, moss and twigs. They hold the trapdoor shut, and if anything should trip their silken trip lines, they come flying out at insane speed to snatch their dinner.

## 7.

### GLADIATOR SPIDER

This spider goes by many names. It's sometimes called the gladiator or net-casting spider, as it holds a 'net' of silk, much like Roman gladiators might have held a net to snag their foes. They are also known as the ogre-faced spider – for the grotesque, ogre-like appearance of their heads, dominated by HUGE eyes which give them astounding vision, even in low light. When an insect wanders below them, the spider lunges forward and entangles them in the net, before injecting them with venom and trussing them up in a silken shroud.

## 6.

### FUNNEL-WEB SPIDER

The funnel-web spiders are hands down the most venomous on earth. The newly described Newcastle funnel-web is the biggest found so far, and it's a real brute, with fangs that could pierce a shoe and venom toxic enough to stop a bison. Well... probably. The male venom is many times more powerful than that of the female, and there are some animals (like dogs) that really don't seem that affected by it.

# 5. MOUSE SPIDER

The mouse spiders have some of the biggest jaws and fangs for their size of any arachnid. Some of the males have bright colours, with red jaws and blue bodies. Like the trapdoor spiders, the females spend their whole lives within long burrows, with trapdoors at the entrance. Though they look pretty terrifying, mouse spiders are neither as venomous nor as aggressive as funnel-web spiders, but should still be taken very seriously.

**4.**

## RAFT SPIDERS

The raft spiders live in freshwater wetland habitats and can be as big as your hand. They stand at the water's edge, with their front legs stretched out, feeling for the vibrations of bugs at the water's surface and aquatic critters beneath. They've been known to catch small fish and even frogs.

**3.**

## SKELETON TARANTULA

The skeleton tarantulas are some of the most handsome of all spider species, with white lines running down the centre of the limbs, which look like the bones of a Halloween skeleton costume. Many of their relatives solely live in the trees, but the skeleton tends to be terrestrial, hunting from a burrow for anything small that wanders nearby.

## 2.

## WANDERING SPIDER

The wandering spiders have the worst reputation of any bugs, and it's not surprising. Arguably the funnel-web has more powerful venom, but the wanderers are definitely the most dangerous to us as human beings. This is down to their habits. Wandering spiders got their name from their habit of travelling around at night looking for food. Come morning they'll hole up anywhere they can, sometimes in people's clothing or shoes. When that person wakes and puts on their boots, they squash the spider and get bitten, and the venom is very strong indeed.

## 1.

## WIDOW SPIDER

The black widow, red widow, brown widow, New Zealand Katipō and redback are all closely related and super-toxic spiders, with a distinctive shiny pea-shaped abdomen, where the females often have dramatic red markings. For their size they have unusually large venom glands, and potent toxins. A bite is excruciatingly painful, and can in some cases be fatal. The name comes from the habit many females have of eating their male counterparts!

**17.**

# BIG BRAINS

# DOLPHIN

## IT'S USUALLY ASSUMED THAT OUR PRIMATE COUSINS ARE THE SMARTEST ANIMALS OTHER THAN US, BUT THAT IS FAR FROM TRUE.

In fact, using scientific analysis it can be proved that many members of the dolphin family have far more effective brain power than any ape. The bottlenose dolphin is one of the most exceptional, so it's not surprising we've seen them using so many stunning techniques for catching their prey. One population is known to protect their snout with natural sponges when they're searching for food. Another that we filmed off the coast of Florida practise 'mud-ringing', where they drive small fish into shallow water and then encircle them in bubbles. As the fish try and jump out, the dolphin catch them mid-air.

# SPERM WHALE

The biggest brain of any animal belongs to the male sperm whale, which can have a brain weighing 10kg – the same as a sack of spuds! What is fascinating, though, is that while the much smaller females do have smaller brains, the bit of their brain that deals with complex processing is radically bigger than that of the boys. This is because the females are much more social. They hang around together at the surface chattering in a dialect called 'coda', which sounds a bit like Sellotape being ripped off a roll, or the static on an old-fashioned radio.

Being in the water alongside a socialising sperm whale is like sitting on an electric cow fence: their sounds zap through your whole body and you can feel it from your toes to your ears!

# ORCA

## THE ORCA RIVALS THE SPERM WHALE FOR THE TITLE OF BIGGEST BRAIN ON EARTH, BUT THEY ARE MUCH SMALLER ANIMALS.

With their brain to body weight ratio far exceeding any other animal, they are the kings of smarts. Or rather the queens of smarts: orca society is all about girl power. Due to their astounding brains, orcas have developed shedloads of ways to catch prey. They might swim together in a line to create a mini-tsunami that could sweep a seal off an ice floe and into the water. They might even come ashore, risking beaching themselves on the sands to snatch an unwary fur seal in Patagonia. They even have fashion: certain orca groups one day started wearing salmon as hats, and pretty soon the craze caught on!

Right: This chimpanzee is using a branch as a tool to dip in honey and drink from.

Opposite: Ravens can demonstrate remarkable cognitive abilities including making and using tools, solving problems and even forward planning.

## CHIMPANZEE

**A CHIMP'S BRAIN IS AROUND 400 CUBIC CENTIMETRES – THAT'S A BIT MORE THAN A CAN OF FIZZY DRINK.**
They have often been observed using tools. One of the most primal experiences I've ever had was sitting behind a cohort of chimps as they used sticks to fish bees out of a nest, before filling their faces with the honey within.

# RAVEN

## MOST BIRDS HAVE PRETTY SMALL, LIGHTWEIGHT SKULLS AND NEED MOST OF THE ROOM INSIDE THEM FOR BIG EYES OR HIDDEN EARS, WHICH DOESN'T LEAVE MUCH ROOM FOR BRAINS.

The owl group has both huge eyes and ears, hence their brains are teeny tiny; the wise old owl sadly is actually one of the least bright birds! The crow family or corvids are the exception to this rule. They are tool users, creating fishing hooks and lines out of twigs, and can drop nuts onto roads so passing cars will drive over them and crack them for the birds to eat. They even appear to understand the idea of water displacement, being able to drop things into water to make a boat float higher and give them their reward. Much of what I've seen in this area is from a tame raven named Bran owned by a pal of mine. Bran takes one look at a puzzle and figures it out almost immediately, gaining a reward of tasty grubs or meat. When Bran looks at you, you can tell he is sussing you out!

# GIANT PACIFIC OCTOPUS

**THE GIANT PACIFIC OCTOPUS IS CONSIDERED TO BE THE CLEVEREST INVERTEBRATE, WITH A CENTRAL DOUGHNUT-SHAPED BRAIN AND THEN A SMALLER ONE FOR EACH OF ITS EIGHT ARMS, MEANING THEY CAN MOVE INDEPENDENTLY.**

They have about as many neurons in their brain as a dog does – far more than any other invertebrate. Despite rarely living longer than two years, and being related to slugs and snails (Mollusca), they can learn from each other, solve mazes, figure out ways to open jars and form relationships with keepers, both good and bad. They can recognise the keepers they like when they come to their tank, and swarm up to greet them, whereas the ones they don't like get blasted with water from their siphon (a funnel-shaped tube more usually used for jet-propulsion or breathing)!

Right: The brains in each arm of the giant Pacific octopus contain more neurons than the central brain!

Opposite: This veined/coconut octopus is one of only a few cephalopods known to use tools. Here it is using a coconut and discarded plastic lid as a mobile home.

# OTHER OCTOPUSES

**ON *DEADLY 60* WE FOUND A COCONUT OCTOPUS ON THE SEABED, AND DROPPED TWO HALVES OF A SCALLOP SHELL IN FRONT OF IT. THE OCTOPUS PICKED THEM UP, PULLED THEM TOGETHER AND MOVED IN, THEN WANDERED AROUND WITH ITS OWN MOBILE HOME!**

All octopus species have the ability to pucker their flesh and change their colours to resemble their seabed home, but one takes this to another level. The marvellous mimic octopus has the ability to twist its form into a variety of other shapes, to resemble a sea snake or a lionfish, depending on what kind of predator may be nearby. Octopus mums will look after their broods and sacrifice their life to dote on them. One in particular, the deep-sea Graneledone octopus, was observed sitting over her brood for four and a half years, the world record for any animal.

The hippo takes no prisoners - a bull can bite a croc in half!

HIPPO

VS

CROCODILE

Even the biggest Nile crocs need to watch themselves around hippos.

## HIPPOS AND CROCODILES LIVE ALONGSIDE EACH OTHER ALMOST ALL THE TIME AND VERY RARELY COME INTO CONFLICT.

It's as if they both register that the other is a lethal killer and have reached a truce, agreeing not to fight. However, sometimes this truce is broken, and then all hell breaks loose. It's often when a hippo calf wanders away from its mother and strays a little too close to a big croc. The instincts of the huge reptile take over and it just can't help itself. What happens next is key. Sometimes the mother realises too late and the croc can just escape with its oversized meal. However, there have been cases where the entire hippo pod decides to stick up for their own. In what must be one of the most brutal sights in nature, they go on the offensive and have been known to literally bite even giant Nile crocodiles clean in two.

**FOR A BIOLOGIST, DISPLAY IS ONE OF THE MOST IMPORTANT ELEMENTS OF AN ANIMAL'S BEHAVIOUR TO UNDERSTAND.**

Unless a creature is fast asleep or filling its face, it'll probably be putting on a display of some sort to someone! This can be a big showing off to a potential mate, letting them know that you have got some serious rizz going on. Or it could be a flex to a rival, advertising how hench you are, therefore not to be messed with. Animals are chatting to you, and to each other, all the time with their body language, and a big part of what I do for a living is learning to understand what they're saying!

Left: Illustration of Carnotarus with its tiny arms. It was the only meat-eating dinosaur known to have horns on its head.

Opposite: A male frill-necked lizard in full territorial display with neck flap extended and mouth open to make it look as big as possible.

## CARNOTAURUS

**ONE OF THE MOST ELEGANT IDEAS IN RECENT PALAEONTOLOGY AIMS TO EXPLAIN THE TEENY TINY ARMS OF THE 'CRETACEOUS BULL' CARNOTAURUS.**

This voracious and terrifying predator had the teeniest arms of any theropod, and they look... frankly a bit silly. Scientists noted, though, that Carnotaurus had especially mobile shoulder joints, and would have been able to spin those teeny arms around in circles. So the hypothesis is that maybe male Carnotaurus would have had bright colours on their arms, and would have danced for the females, spinning those flamboyant forearms about in a tantalising dance for her. What an image that is!

The frilly is all about display, shocking predators with its umbrella-like frill.

# FRILLED-NECK LIZARD

**AUSTRALIA'S FRILLY IS ONE OF THE MOST ICONIC ANIMALS OF THE OUTBACK, AND HAS ABOUT THE MOST DRAMATIC DISPLAY OF ANY REPTILE.**

We've filmed frillies hanging out around bushfires, snapping up bugs that are driven out of the flames. You'd barely know that there was anything special about them... until they have a point to prove. When showboating for rivals or mates, or when they feel threatened, the frilled-neck lizard lives up to its name. A great stretch of skin around the neck is expanded like someone opening a brolly. At the same time they gape their mouth open, with two pointy teeth on show, and stand up in a proud roaring-lion posture. The animal seems to double in size, and to go from a unimpressive critter to a dramatic dragon in seconds.

# PEACOCK SPIDER

## THIS MARVEL IN MINIATURE IS ONE OF MY ALL-TIME FAVOURITES. ONE OF THE SALTICIDS OR JUMPING SPIDERS, THEY ARE EXCEPTIONAL LEAPING PREDATORS OF VERY, VERY SMALL THINGS.

They have incredible eyesight, able to see a full 360°, with the two huge central eyes giving them advanced depth perception for pouncing on prey. They can see the full visual spectrum as well as ultraviolet light. However, their dancing display is as gorgeous as any bird of paradise. Erecting a flap on their abdomen and the third set of legs, the male peacock spider shimmers lurid, flamboyant colours towards his potential mate, while doing a funky little dance from side to side, advertising himself and his fitness.

Opposite: The male peacock spider has to impress a female with his dance and brightly coloured fan, or else he may end up as her next meal.

Below: Male Indian peafowl displaying to attract a female. He does this by vibrating the iridescent feathers and possibly also emitting deep rumbling mating calls.

Is this the world's most beautiful invertebrate? Or even most beautiful creature, full stop?

# Handicap principle

I was lucky enough to meet the scientist behind this elegant idea in Israel's Negev Desert early in my career. Amotz Zahavi proposed that some kinds of display – like the peacock or peacock spider's huge coloured tails – made life harder for them.

For the bird, it is much harder to escape from a leaping leopard with all that tail to drag around. For the spider, they're much more obvious to beady-eyed birds that may want to scoff them. Zahavi's proposal is that this is exactly the point. Animals that have these 'handicaps' are saying to a potential mate, 'Imagine how strong I must be to have survived despite carrying all these feathers around! I'm the man (inevitably these handicaps are carried by male animals) so be my girl!' Other scientists have suggested that many things human males do that involve risk might be a part of the same drive!

# STOTTING/PRONKING

**THE STOT IS ONE OF THE MOST OUT-THERE DISPLAYS IN NATURE. LET'S SAY YOU'RE STROLLING ACROSS THE AFRICAN SAVANNAH AND YOU SEE AN ANTELOPE LEAPING AS HIGH IN THE AIR AS IT CAN, OFTEN WITH STRAIGHT LEGS AND HEAD DOWN TOWARDS THE DIRT.**

It may seem that there is no point to this tiring and dangerous pursuit. In fact, surely this makes the animal more visible and uses up valuable energy that could be spent actually escaping or hiding. However, the antelope is showing the hunter that will inevitably be somewhere nearby that they have been spotted, and also that the predator has no chance of catching them. This particular display saves both parties a lot of effort. This is known as an 'honest signal', as it is one that the pronker (show-off) cannot fake. Almost as a trade-off for this, if big cats are wandering down to a watering hole and are not in a hunting mode, they exaggerate how obvious they are, walking in totally plain view, with excessive swagger. They appear to be deliberately nonchalant, as if saying through their own body language, 'Don't worry about me, you-all, my tummy is full already!' Yet again, this saves both parties a lot of effort!

Left: A springbok pronking or stotting over twice the height of an average man is a clear indication to all of physical ability and agility, Kalahari, Botswana.

Opposite: Great white shark and Cape fur seal trying to outmanoeuvre one another, South Africa.

The pronk or stot is a flex, a visible sign that you are too springy to chase.

# FUR SEAL AND GREAT WHITE SHARK

### ONE OF THE MOST DRAMATIC EXAMPLES I'VE SEEN OF THIS KIND OF DISPLAY WAS OFF THE COAST OF MEXICO WHILE DIVING WITH GREAT WHITE SHARKS.

Most of the endemic Guadalupe fur seals would stay close to the shore, and while in the water would have their heads facing straight down into the water to spot enemies coming from beneath. However, on one occasion we filmed a young fur seal that was out in blue water with the giant sharks. It would play right around the snout of the killer, twisting, turning and throwing somersaults right in front of those famous teeth. This was a clear message to the predator: 'I'm quicker and more manoeuvrable than you; you have zero chance of catching me!'

# LION

## THE LION'S MANE IS AN EXAMPLE OF WHAT IS KNOWN IN BIOLOGY AS A 'SECONDARY SEXUAL CHARACTERISTIC'.

This is something that one sex of a species has, and the other does not, but is not involved in reproduction. On the larger male lion, a great shaggy mane is a sign to other males that he's in charge, and to females that he is attractive and dominant. Darker manes seem to show that the male has more testosterone and therefore probably will be a better dad. However, the mane actually makes life harder for the guys. It snags and catches as they hunt, it makes them overheat on the hottest African middays... it's generally a pain. This may possibly be an example of the handicap principle at work!

Right: As a male African lion matures his mane gets darker. This can also be indicative of good health, high testosterone levels and dominance.

Opposite: Various species of animal display aposematic colours, to warn would-be predators that they are in fact poisonous. Mimics use similar colours even though they are non-venomous.

# APOSEMATIC COLOURS

## ONE OF THE FIRST THINGS WE ALL LEARN ABOUT WHEN WE STUDY NATURE IS THAT BRIGHT COLOURS ARE OFTEN A WARNING.

When colours warn other animals that the bearer is dangerous, we call them aposematic colours. The most obvious example of this would be the poison dart frogs of Central and South America. There appears to be a sort of collective learning process among other animals that would otherwise love a froggy meal, teaching them to leave colourful ones alone. This process has also led to lots of other animals, known as 'mimics', evolving to have the same warning colours without actually being dangerous. For example, coral snakes, members of the cobra family, have violent venoms and bright bands in red, yellow, black and white to warn other animals to leave them well alone. However, there are numerous 'mimics' pretending to be coral snakes that are actually non-venomous. These are known as Batesian mimics, after the famous biologist Henry Walter Bates, who discovered this sneaky process.

Was Spino's sail a billboard? A colourful advert to other Spinosaurus?

Left: Illustration of a Spinosaurus. Scientists are still pondering why this particular species alone had a distinctive sail on its back.

Opposite, top: The male mandrill in an excitable state, with bright red and blue nose to impress the females nearby.

Opposite, bottom: It may look beautiful but the flamboyant cuttlefish is the only known cuttlefish species that is venomous, so look but don't touch.

# SPINOSAURUS

## THE DISTINCTIVE SAIL ON THE BACK OF SPINOSAURUS IS A DINO-CONUNDRUM.

What was it for? Many scientists have looked at the pores in the skulls of Spino and suggested they may have been like modern crocodiles, catching sharks and sawfish in shallow waters. So what earthly purpose could that sail have? Some have suggested it could be about hydrodynamism or stabilising themselves in or under the water, but if that's the case, then why don't any other aquatic animals have permanent sails like this (sailfish and marlin can drop their sails when swimming at speed)? Others says it's about thermoregulation: losing or gaining precious heat. However, it is certainly possible that Spino had bright colours all over its famous sail, and it could have been a display, used to scare rivals or attract possible mates.

# MANDRILL

## THE MALE MANDRILL IS THE MOST COLOURFUL MAMMAL ON EARTH.

When they get excited, their nose takes on a vivid red splash, with bright blue flanges down its sides. To make them even more dramatic, their bottoms are naked, and bright red and blue. Females and youngsters are much more dowdy, making this a classic case of sexual selection, with the males having these colours to show off to and impress the ladies!

# FLAMBOYANT CUTTLEFISH

## ONE OF THE MOST REMARKABLE CREATURES I'VE EVER BEEN LUCKY ENOUGH TO FILM IS THIS GORGEOUS LITTLE CUTTLEFISH.

They are superlative predators, firing out their paired feeding tentacles to grab hold of teeny shrimp before mashing them in their tiny beak. The thing that sets them apart and gives them their name, though, is the dazzling light display that ripples across their bodies. These colours change in an instant, faster than any chameleon could dare dream of, and are matched with the ability to pucker up parts of the mantle and arms, to make the cuttlefish look totally different. What a beast!

DEADLY DEATH MATCH

Against a giant polar bear, a lone wolf would stand no chance.

WOLF VS POLAR BEAR

Facing down a pack of wolves, even the mighty white bear knows it's in trouble.

## WOLVES AND POLAR BEARS TEND TO AVOID EACH OTHER AT ALL COSTS.

Polar bears are far bigger than wolves, and one of the most powerful predators on the planet. As the ultimate pack predators, wolves have strength in numbers on their side. There is no way a tangle between these two will result in a clean kill, and inevitably the victorious animal is going to sustain an injury – something to be avoided at all costs in the treacherous, demanding world of an Arctic winter, where life and death are always in the balance. However, sometimes these fights are inevitable. Often it can be around prey: one has killed, and the other wants a piece of the action. Or if a polar bear is emerging from the winter den with a young cub, and the wolves threaten it. Often one wolf will distract the mother, while the others target the young bear. Should this titanic struggle occur, it'll be a numbers game. One filmed example of this showed seven adult wolves being given a sound thrashing by a single bear. However, there's little doubt that a big pack could certainly send a polar packing (sorry!).

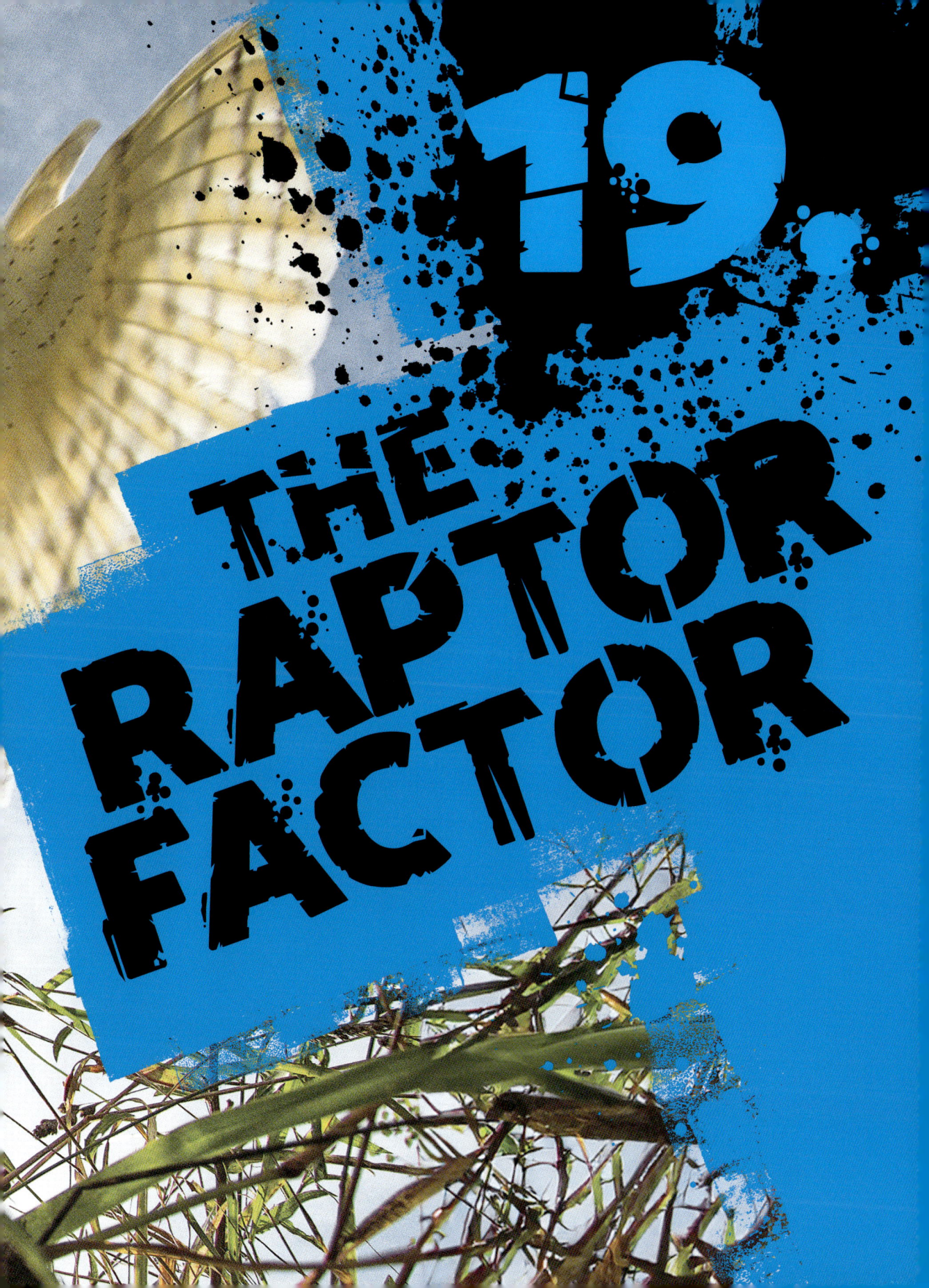

19.

# THE RAPTOR FACTOR

# HAWKS

## GENERALLY WITH ROUNDED WINGS AND A FAN-LIKE TAIL, THE HAWKS CONTAIN SOME OF THE MOST MANOEUVRABLE MID-AIR MASTERS.

The goshawk is a classic example, hunting inside dense woodland, ducking and weaving, with its broad tail being deployed as a rudder. Some, such as the sparrowhawk, may approach prey from behind natural cover, such as hedgerows or hills, appearing at the last second to kill with open talons. Prey is often dragged to cover and plucked before consumption. The sight of a furious-looking sparrowhawk gazing at you with malevolent eyes as it angrily rips the feathers out of a downed pigeon is something that will stay with you forever!

The sparrowhawk is one of my ultimate deadly raptors: fierce, fearless, brutal.

# Girls rule!

It's the norm among raptors for the female to be much bigger than the male. In some species she could be double the size of her partner. There are several reasons for this. The first is that she requires good reserves of fat and therefore energy for staying with, brooding and raising her chicks. The second is part of a natty bit of evolution called niche partitioning. The two birds can live in the same environment and focus on totally different prey. A female sparrowhawk may be feasting on pigeons, while the tiny male fills himself on… well, sparrows. With each sex having their own 'niche', it means their home patch will still have enough food to sustain them.

# FALCONS

**WITH CLASSICALLY MORE POINTED WINGS AND A NARROWER TAIL THAN THE HAWKS, THE FALCONS CONTAIN THE FASTEST BIRDS EVER KNOWN TO HAVE LIVED ON PLANET EARTH.**

And while the peregrine's speed may be the best known and most studied, it's likely that other falcon species can rival them for pace. Certainly the gyrfalcon – the largest species of falcon – takes prey on the wing using a stoop and gains prodigious speeds. Falcons have a notch on the upper beak called the tomial tooth or tomial notch. This can be used to sever the spine of smaller bird prey.

## Hunting on ice

The gyrfalcon is often considered to be the world's only marine bird of prey. This is down to the fact that many populations hunt out over Arctic pack ice. Although this provides a 'floor' of sorts, this is essentially soaring above frozen seas. Some natural populations of gyrfalcon (notably those from northern Greenland) are almost pure white, which gives them camouflage in an all-white world. It also makes them the most valued bird in falconry, particularly in the Middle East. A pair of pure white gyrfalcons can sell for hundreds of thousands of pounds, which has put huge pressure on the birds in the wild.

Opposite: Portrait of a gyrfalcon, the largest falcon in the world.

Right: With Nikita at Warwick Castle, where this female Steller's sea eagle is trained.

## EAGLES

### THE EAGLES ARE THE GIANT POWERHOUSES OF THE BIRD WORLD.

The heaviest is Latin America's harpy eagle, with the females weighing up to 9kg. That's roughly fifty times heavier than the smallest raptor, the Merlin! Africa's crowned eagle and the Philippine and New Guinea eagles are all very similar, also hunting within dense forests. With a hind claw or hallux that is as thick as a grizzly bear claw, they can stab right into a monkey, sloth or deer, killing instantly. Perhaps more impressive still, they can then fly away with that prey item dangling beneath them as they swoop it back to the nest. Despite their immense power, they have comparatively short wingspans. In contrast, the queen in this category is the Arctic Steller's sea eagle, my favourite bird in the world, with a wingspan that can near 3m.

# OWLS

## THE OWLS ARE VERY DIFFERENT FROM OTHER KINDS OF RAPTORS.

Classically they have a rounded facial disc with stiff feathers that works like a satellite dish to focus sound back to their exquisite ears. The eyes too are remarkable. Unlike our own spherical eyeballs, an owl has giant tubular eyes. These are superlative at dragging in light in murky twilight, but cannot swivel around like our own. Instead, an owl needs to move its whole head around. They have twice as many vertebrae in their spine as we humans, which enables them to look right around over their own shoulder. The biggest of the owls, like Blakiston's fish owl and the Eurasian eagle owl, are capable of taking surprisingly large prey, up to the size of foxes, hedgehogs and even small deer. Smaller prey is swallowed whole, which looks extremely uncomfortable!

## VULTURES

### THESE ARE THE MOST IMPORTANT, MOST UNDERRATED AND MOST THREATENED OF ALL RAPTOR GROUPS.

They're often maligned as living dustbins, undertakers of the natural world. However, this is a vital job, processing and cleaning carcasses that would otherwise spread disease. Their intense stomach acids can digest and destroy pathogens (illnesses, bacteria, viruses) that would kill other animals. Vultures are (often) huge flying birds, with good eyesight that enables them to spot carcasses from many miles away while soaring higher than any other bird (the record is over 10,000m from a Rüppell's vulture; that's higher than the summit of Everest). They can also be ingenious. Bearded vultures will carry tortoises up high and drop them onto rocks to break them open. The Greek philosopher Aeschylus was said to have been killed by being hit on the head by a tortoise dropped by a beardie! Then there are Egyptian vultures that will pick up stones and take them in their beaks to smash eggs open and get at the contents!

DEADLY 60

# LAPPET-FACED VULTURE

## IN AFRICA DEAD ANIMALS ARE NOT ALL CREATED (OR ENDED) EQUAL.

Big animals like elephants and rhinos die too, and when they do, most animals simply don't have the tools to get in through the hide. Without the massive meat cleaver beak of the lappet-faced vulture, things could never get started. I've sat for days near a carcass, with hundreds of white-backed and griffon vultures gathering in the trees nearby, waiting for a lappet-faced to turn up. Only then can the party begin! They are one of the biggest of all flying birds, and have to roost and nest on high cliff faces so they can just drop out of their nest, spread their shoulders and let the wind beneath their wings do the rest.

Opposite: Egyptian vulture using a stone in an attempt to break a (fake) egg, Spain.

Below: Lappet-faced vulture coming in to land by zebra carcass in Kenya.

Majestic in flight, controlled in landing, diabolical table manners!

RAPTOR

**VS**

PROTOCERATOPS

A titanic struggle frozen in time. Who would have emerged victorious? We'll never know.

**THIS DINOSAUR DEATH MATCH IS A REPRESENTATION OF THE EVENTS FROM ARGUABLY THE GREATEST FOSSIL IN HISTORY, WHICH DATES FROM 74 MILLION YEARS AGO AND SHOWS THE MOMENT WHEN A PROTOCERATOPS AND VELOCIRAPTOR ENGAGED IN MORTAL COMBAT, THEIR LIFE AND DEATH STRUGGLE FROZEN IN TIME.** The two fossilised skeletons are face to face; the Protoceratops seems to have its mouth open as if screaming in terror, but is locked onto the raptor's arm. The raptor appears to have delivered some near-mortal wounds to the throat of the pig-sized herbivore. I guess the big question is how they came to be captured in this death struggle. The major hypothesis states that a dune nearby had been weakened by rains and collapsed on top of them, burying them in an instant.

# INDEX

# PICTURE CREDITS

**FRONT COVER**

Steve Backshall © BBC; Sea eagle © Sergey Uryadnikov/Shutterstock; t-rex © Sport08/Shutterstock; cobra © Agus_Gatam/Shutterstock; wolf © Nynke van Holten/Shutterstock; Great white shark © Chase D'animulls/Shutterstock; Circle © babyuka/Shutterstock

**BACK COVER**

Steve Backshall © Seb Blach; Cheetah © Svetlana Foote/Shutterstock; Solifuge © MYN/Javier Aznar/NPL; Dunkleosteus © 3DMedisphere/Science Photo Library; Golden eagle © Staffan Widstrand/NPL

Front and back background images © Kuzminichna, Amovitania/Shutterstock

1 Gabriel Rojo/NPL; 2 Mark Sharman; 4 Nick Allinson; 6 Seb Blach; 7 Alex Hyde/NPL

**1 THE EVOLUTION OF DEADLY**

8–9 Jose Antonio Peñas/SPL; 10 Jordi Chias/NPL; 11t Phil Degginger/Carnegie Museum/SPL; 11b Ross Hoddinott/NPL; 12–13 Jose Antonio Peñas /SPL; 13t John Sibbick/SPL; 13b Anup Shah/NPL; 14 Christian Darkin/SPL; 15t BBC; 15b Hypersphere/SPL; 16 Solvin Zankl/NPL; 17t Stocktrek Images, Inc/Alamy; 17b Kirstine Davidson; 18–19 Mark Carwardine/NPL

**2 BIGGEST AND BADDEST**

20–1 Henley Spiers/NPL; 22 Ton Ponchai/Shutterstock; 23 Seb Blach; 24tl WaterFrame/Alamy; 24tr Franco Banfi/NPL; 24b Debbie Ryan/Cotswold Wildlife Park; 25 Jason Isley/Scubazoo; 26t Sergey Gorshkov/NPL; 26b Nikki Waldron; 27 Tony Heald/NPL; 28 Andy Rouse/NPL; 29l Joel Sartore/Photo Ark/NPL; 29t Piotr Naskrecki/Minden/NPL; 29b Kirstine Davidson; 30–1 Tony Wu/NPL; 30bl Joel Sartore/Photo Ark/NPL; 30br James Brickell; 31 Suzi Eszterhas/NPL; 32–3 Anup Shah/Minden/NPL

**3 COLD BLOODED KILLERS**

34–5 James Kuether/SPL; 36b Claudio Contreras/NPL; 36m Ann&Steve Toon/NPL; 37 Science Photo Library/Getty; 38 Warpaint/Shutterstock; 39t chrisbrignell/Shutterstock; 39m BBC; 40 Joel Sartore/Photo Ark/NPL; 41 Dante Fenolio/SPL; 42–3 Gudkov Andrey/Shutterstock

**4 BIOLOGICAL COMPETITION**

44–5 Ted Kinsman/SPL; 46–7 Wim van den Heever/NPL; 48 Svetlana Foote/Shutterstock; 49 Rowan Musgrave; 50t Emanuele Biggi/NPL; 50b Reinhard Dirschlerl/ullstein bild/Getty; 51t BBC; 51b Juergen Freund/NPL; 52t Edwin Giesbers/NPL; 52b James Brickell; 53 Michael D. Kern/NPL; 54t BBC; 54b Robin Chittenden/NPL; 55t MYN/Javier Aznar/NPL; 55b Charlie Bingham

**5 TOXIC TREATS**

56–9 Gary Bell/Oceanwide/NPL; 60t Joel Sartore/Photo Ark/NPL; 60b Jurgen Freund/NPL; 61 Gary Bell/Oceanwide/NPL; 62 MYN/Paul Marcellini/NPL; 63 BBC; 64 Peter Scoones/SPL; 65t David Gray/AFP/Getty; 65b Alex Mustard/NPL; 66b David Gray/AFP/Getty; 66m Mark Bowler/NPL; 66t blickwinkel/Alamy; 67bl Auscape/Getty; 67br Chris Troch/Shutterstock; 67 top Alex Mustard/NPL; 68b Graham MacFarlane; 68tl Nick Allinson; 68tr Science History Images/Alamy; 69t Andrew Yarme; 69b Keith Partridge; 70–1 Guy Edwardes/NPL; 70 Craig Adams; 72t Daniel Heuclin/NPL; 72m kristianbell/Getty; 72bl Robert Valentic/NPL; 72br Snake/Alamy; 73t Suzi Eszterhas/NPL; 73aml Paul Starosta/Getty; 73amr James Brickell; 73ml Vaclav Volrab/Alamy; 73mr Robert Valentic/NPL; 73b Ken Griffiths/Shutterstock; 74 CDC/James Gathany/Science Source/SPL; 75t Millard H. Sharp/SPL; 75b Louise Murray/SPL; 76t Ivan Kuzmin/Alamy; 76b Gerry Pearce/SPL; 77tl Nick Allinson; 77tr imageBROKER/Alamy; 77b Daniel Heuclin/NPL; 78t David Fleetham/NPL; 78b blickwinkel/Alamy; 79t MYN/Javier Aznar/NPL; 79m Fred McConnaughey/SPL; 79b Edwin Giesbers/NPL

**6 BEST BITE**

80–1 Nick Rains/Auscape/Getty; 82–3 Nick Allinson; 84 Michael Rosskothen/Shutterstock; 85 3DMEDISPHERE/SPL; 86 Theo Allofs/Minden/NPL; 87 Lou Coetzer/NPL; 88–9 Barry Mansell/NPL; 90t Nick Upton/NPL; 90m Noble Proctor/SPL; 90b Nicolas Primola/Shutterstock; 91 Giles Badger; 92–3 Pictorial Press Ltd/Alamy

**7 TEAM PLAYERS**

94–5 Brian Skerry/Minden/NPL; 96 Matt Heath/Alamy; 97 Bertie Gregory/NPL; 98t Jack Dykinga/NPL; 98b Laurent Geslin/NPL; 99t Steve Gettle/Minden/NPL; 99b Ann and Steve Toon/Alamy; 100 Paul D. Stewart/NPL; 101 James Brickell; 102–3 Christophe Courteau/NPL

**8 LETHAL LURES**

104–5 Dante Fenolio/SPL; 106t Louise Murray/SPL; 106b Doug Perrine/NPL; 107, 108t reptiles4all/Shutterstock; 108b Babsje; 109 David Shale/NPL; 110 Daniel Heuclin/NPL; 111 James Brickell

## 9 SUPER SENSES

112–13 Alex Hyde/NPL; 114–15 Claus Lunau/SPL; 115t Doug Gimesy/NPL; 115b Edward Kinsman/SPL; 116 Steve Gschmeissner/SPL; 116–17 Piotr Naskrecki/NPL; 118 Paulette Sinclair/Alamy; 119t Millard H. Sharp/ Science Source/SPL; 119b Stocktrek Images, Inc./ Alamy; 120 Staffan Widstrand/NPL; 121 David Tipling/ NPL; 122t Norm Heke 008/Te Papa (M.190318); 122–3 Dante Fenolio/SPL; 124 Tony Wu/NPL; 125 Nick Garbutt/ NPL; 126 Bruno D'Amicis/NPL; 127 Markus Varesvuo/ NPL; 128 Nick Garbutt/NPL; 129 Pascal Goetchelck/SPL; 130t Kyle McBurnie; 130b Alex Mustard/NPL; 131t Andrey Nekrasov/Alamy; 131b Deron Verbeck/iamaquatic; 132–3 Mark Rackley; 134t Brandon Cole/NPL; 134b Dominique Gorton; 135tl Blue Planet Archive LLC/Alamy; 135tr Alex Mustard/NPL; 135b Science History Images/Alamy; 136–7 Stefan Huwiler/NPL

## 10 DEADLY DEFENDERS

138–9 Nick Garbutt/NPL; 140 3DMEDISPHERE/SPL; 141 Sergey Gorshkov/NPL; 142 Lou Coetzer/NPL; 143 A.Madisetti; 144–5 Lou Coetzer/NPL

## 11 WEIRD WEAPONS

146–7 BIOSPHOTO/Alamy; 148 Stephen Dalton/NPL; 149t Nature Production/NPL; 149b Morley Read/NPL; 150t Bruno Manunza/Alamy; 150b Michael Richards/John Downer/NPL; 151 BBC; 152–3 Lou Coetzer/NPL

## 12 SUPER SKILLS

154–5 Stephen Dalton/NPL; 156 Pete Oxford/NPL; 157 Stephen Dalton/NPL; 158 Edwin Giesbers/NPL; 159t Digital Genetics/Shutterstock; 159b Solvin Zankl/NPL; 160–1 Paul Williams/NPL

## 13 SPINELESS WONDERS

162–3 Alex Hyde/NPL; 164t Wild Wonders of Europe/ Benvie/NPL; 164b John Serrao/SPL; 165 Edward Rowland/Alamy; 166t Paul Bertner/NPL; 166b Alex Treadway/Getty; 167 Alex Hyde/NPL; 168–9 Mark Moffett/Minden/NPL

## 14 TOUGH NUTS

170–1 Sergey Gorshkov/NPL; 172 Eye of Science/SPL; 173 Piotr Naskrecki/Minden/NPL; 174 Thomas Retterath/ Shutterstock; 175 Pete Oxford/NPL; 176 Klein & Hubert/ NPL; 177 Markus Varesvuo/NPL; 178 Sergey Gorshkov/ Minden/NPL; 179l MYN/Gil Wizen/NPL; 179r Kim Taylor/ NPL; 180–1 David Northall

## 15 PARASITES

182–3 Alex Hyde/NPL; 184t James Dunbar/NPL; 184b Kim Taylor/NPL; 185 Roman Willi/NPL; 186t Morley Read/ NPL; 186–7 Blue Planet Archive LLC/Alamy; 186 Doug Perrine/Alamy; 187 Henri Koskinen/Shutterstock; 188–9 Torontonian-New/Alamy; 190–1 Armida Madngisa; 191 Nigel Cattlin/NPL

## 16 STRENGTH

192–3 Ben Cranke/NPL; 194 Nikki Waldron; 194–5 Lucas Bustamante/NPL; 196 Ross Nussbaumer/NPL; 197 Isselee/ Dreamstime; 198 Donald M.Jones/Minden/NPL; 199 Scott Alexander; 200–1 Ann & Steve Toon/NPL; 201 James Brickell; 202 Stocktrek Images, Inc./Alamy; 203 Nick Garbutt/ NPL; 204–5 Eric Baccega/NPL; 205 BBC; 206–7 Sergey Uryadnikov/Shutterstock; 208 Jiri Lochman/NPL; 209t Piotr Naskrecki/Minden/NPL; 209b Hans Christoph Kappel/NPL; 210t Emanuele Biggi/NPL; 210b BBC; 211 imageBROKER/ Alamy; 212t Stephen Dalton/NPL; 212b Andy Newman's Tarantulas/Alamy; 213t MYN/Joao P. Burini/NPL; 213b John Serrao/SPL

## 17 BIG BRAINS

214–15 Anup Shah/NPL; 216 Chris & Monique Fallows/NPL; 217t Tony Wu/NPL; 217b Sylvain Cordier/NPL; 218 Hiroya Minakuchi/Minden/NPL; 219t ZSSD/NPL; 219bl, bm Michael Quinton/Minden/NPL; 219br Jeff Vanuga/NPL; 220 Andrey Nekrasov/Alamy; 221 Mike Veitch/Alamy; 222–3 Ken Haley/ Imago Images

## 18 DISPLAY

224–5 Will Burrard-Lucas/NPL; 226 3DMEDISPHERE/SPL; 227 Etienne Littlefair/NPL; 228 Michael Lun; 229 Theo Webb/NPL; 230 Media Drum World/Alamy; 231 Chris & Monique Fallows/NPL; 232 Ben Cranke/NPL; 233ml Piotr Naskrecki/Minden/NPL; 233tl,tm,mr Alex Hyde/NPL; 233m MYN/Dirk Funhoff/NPL; 233bl Alex Mustard/NP; 234 ANIMATE4.COM/SPL; 235t Mark MacEwen/NPL; 235b Alex Mustard/NPL; 236–7 Russell Millner/Alamy

## 19 THE RAPTOR FACTOR

238–9 John Walters/NPL; 240–1 Pal Hermansen/NPL; 242 Oscar Diez, BIA/Minden/NPL; 243–4 Phil Gould/Alamy; 243 Ellie Ryder; 244–5 Wild Wonders of Europe/Widstrand/NPL; 246 Angelo Gandolfi/NPL; 246–7 Eric Baccega/NPL; 248–9 Yuya Tami/Nagoya City Science Museum, Japan; 249 Jose Antonio Peñas/SPL

Images used for all interior graphics:
Itsmesimon/Shutterstock, Miloji/Shutterstock
NPL – Nature Picture Library; SPL – Science Photo Library

BBC BOOKS

UK | USA | Canada | Ireland | Australia
India | New Zealand | South Africa

BBC Books is part of the Penguin Random House group of companies whose addresses can be found at global.penguinrandomhouse.com

Penguin Random House UK
One Embassy Gardens, 8 Viaduct Gardens, London SW11 7BW

penguin.co.uk
global.penguinrandomhouse.com

First published by BBC Books in 2025
2

Publishing Director: Albert DePetrillo
Editors: Katie Fisher and Izzy Frost
Project Editor: Bethany Wright
Production Controller: Catherine Ngwong
Designer: Amazing15
Picture Researcher: Laura Barwick

Colour origination by Altaimage Ltd
Printed and bound in Germany by Mohn Media GmbH

The authorised representative in the EEA is Penguin Random House Ireland, Morrison Chambers, 32 Nassau Street, Dublin D02 YH68.

A CIP catalogue record for this book is available from the British Library

ISBN 9781785949739

Penguin Random House is committed to a sustainable future for our business, our readers and our planet. This book is made from Forest Stewardship Council® certified paper.